PREPARING THE 21ST CENTURY CHURCH

PREPARING THE 21ST CENTURY CHURCH

LESLIE H. BRICKMAN, D.MIN
Professor of Cell Church at Regent University

Copyright © 2002 by Leslie H. Brickman, D.Min.

Preparing the 21st Century Church
by Leslie H. Brickman, D.Min.

Printed in the United States of America

Library of Congress Control Number: 2002111323
ISBN 1-591601-67-3

All rights reserved. No part of this publication may be reproduced or transmitted in any form or by any means without written permission of the publisher.

Unless otherwise indicated, Bible quotations are taken from New American Standard Bible, The Open Bible Edition, Thomas Nelson, Publishers, © 1978, 1979 THE LOCKMAN FOUNDATION © 1960, 1962, 1963, 1971, 1972, 1973, 1975, 1977.

Xulon Press
11350 Random Hills Road
Suite 800
Fairfax, VA 22030
(703) 279-6511
XulonPress.com

To order additional copies, call 1-866-909-BOOK (2665).

Is. 40:3-8

A voice is calling in the wilderness,
"Prepare the way of the LORD;
Make smooth in the desert a highway for our God.

Let every valley be lifted up,
And every mountain and hill be made low;
And let the rough ground become a plain,
And the rugged terrain a broad valley;

Then the glory of the LORD will be revealed,
And all flesh will see it together;
For the mouth of the LORD has spoken."

A voice says, "Call out."
Then he answered, "What shall I call out?"
All flesh is grass, and all its loveliness is like the flower of the field.

The grass withers, the flower fades,
When the breath of the LORD blows upon it;
Surely the people are grass.

The grass withers, the flower fades,
But the word of our God stands forever.

Dedicated to my beloved wife, Twyla, without whose encouragement this book would not have found the light of day

Contents

Acknowledgements	13
Introduction	15
Chapter 1 - A People Unprepared	21
Ancient Israel – A Nation Unprepared	23
Modern America – A Nation Unprepared	25
A Church Unprepared	29
Reflections	33

UNDERGROUND REALITIES

Chapter 2 - Prepare the Ethical Base	37
I Will Build My Church	38
Design Criteria and Cell Church R&D	39
Christian Ethics and the 20th Century	42
Deontological versus Teleological Moral Theory	45
Old Testament Ethics - Clearly Deontological by Nature	46
New Testament Ethics are also Deontological	49
0-150,000 in Twenty-Five Years: A Deontological Approach	51
What in the World Have We Taught Them?	55
Who is Leading the Way?	64
Rangers Lead the Way!	66
The Church Must Lead the Way!	67
Reflections	68
Chapter 3 - Prepare the Value System	73
Introduction	74
What is a Value?	75
Are Values Really That Important?	82
Developing Your Values	93
Changing Values	95
Reflections	101
Chapter 4 - Prepare the Value System - EPBOM	103
Core Values - Overview	105
Challenging the American Cell Church	127
Reflections	128
Action Points	129
Chapter 5 - Prepare the Vision	131
The Necessity of Receiving God's Vision	132

Vision Component #1	133
The Church as the Family of God	
Vision Component #2	134
The Church as the Body of Christ	
Vision Component #3	137
The Church as the Army of God	
Vision Component #4	142
The Church Fulfilling the Strategy of God	
Vision Component #5	144
Discovering The Undiscovered Country	
For the Vision is Yet for the Appointed Time	149
Reflections	151
Action Points	152

Chapter 6 - Prepare the Value Discipline   155

Introduction	156
Outsiders - The Discipline of Market Leaders	156
Working Definitions	158
The Discipline of Operational Excellence - Overview	161
The Discipline of Entrepreneurial Leadership - Overview	161
The Discipline of Customer Intimacy - Overview	162
Why Choose?	163
The Discipline of Operational Excellence	164
Eglise Protestante Baptiste Oeuvres et Mission Internationale (EPBOM)	
The Discipline of Entrepreneurial Leadership	169
International Charismatic Mission (ICM)	
The Discipline of Customer Intimacy	172
Yoido Full Gospel Church (YFGC)	
Values-Driven Operating Models and	175
Natural Church Development	
What is a Pastor to Do?	180
Is All This Really Necessary?	183
Reflections	185
Action Points	186

ABOVE GROUND REALITIES

Chapter 7 - Prepare the Prototype	191
Introduction	192
Apples, Cokes, and the Cell Church	192
What is a Prototype?	194
Prototype Development - a Biblical Exercise?	195
How Can I Correctly Prepare a Prototype?	201
Not Yet Convinced?	214
Reflections	218
Action Points	219
Chapter 8 - Prepare the Program of God	221
Introduction	222
A Balancing Act	223
An Encounter with Christ	224
An Organism - Simple and Complex	224
A News Wineskin for New Wine	225
Implications	227
Chapter 9 - Prepare the Program of God - Equipping	231
A Current Generation with Few Disciples	232
Illustration - EPBOM's Model of Equipping	240
Challenging the Ineffectiveness of Our Own System	247
Chapter 10 - Prepare the Program of God - Evangelism	249
Evangelizing This Generation for Christ	250
Illustration - EPBOM's Model of Evangelism	256
Challenging the Ineffectiveness of Our Own System	270

Chapter 11 - Prepare the Program of God - Edification	273
Building Up the Body of Christ	274
Illustration - EPBOM's Model of Edification	277
Challenging the Ineffectiveness of Our Own System	286
Chapter 12 - Prepare the Program of God - Empowering	291
Empowering the Body of Christ	292
Illustration - EPBOM's Model of Empowering Leaders	293
Challenging the Ineffectiveness of Our Own System	297
Chapter 13 - Prepare the Program of God - Every Member Ministry	299
Releasing the Body of Christ	300
Illustration - EPBOM's Model of Mobilization	302
Challenging the Ineffectiveness of Our Own System	316
Chapter 14 - Prepare the Next Step	319
Works Cited	333

ACKNOWLEDGEMENTS

If it were not for certain people, this work would not have been possible. I especially want to thank my wonderful wife, Twyla Brickman, who provided unswerving support and encouragement throughout the long process of writing, editing, writing, ad infinitum. She was constantly there to lift me up, encourage me, and help me stay focused. Without her deep, personal sacrifice of time and her co-labor in the planting of Acts Alive! during this time, often bearing the full pastoral weight of the church plant, this project would not have seen the light of day.

I want to thank Dr. Ralph Neighbour, Jr., who has been a constant inspiration to me for almost 30 years of ministry. He has challenged me to do the seemingly impossible and has constantly been used by God to stretch me beyond my limitations. As iron sharpens iron, so Bill Beckham has sharpened my thinking over the years and challenged me to constantly think "outside the box". Sincere thanks go to these men for both their faith in me and their constant encouragement through the years.

Jim Lassiter was the first one who introduced me to the ministry of Dr. Yaye Dion Robert while I was still in seminary during the 1980's. Jim has been instrumental in helping to develop and maintain the personal relationship I have enjoyed with Pastor Dion over the years. Jim translated the initial sources used in this project from French into English.

Cindy Huling is deserving of special thanks. Cindy took two weeks, devoting herself tirelessly to the task of interpretation and translation for me while I was completing the research for this project in Abidjan, Cote d'Ivoire. Her insightful comments throughout the process were often like threads that wove together the immense tapestry of personal interviews.

I wish to thank Pastor Dion and the staff of *Eglise Protestante Baptiste Oeuvres et Mission Internationale* (EPBOM) for their graciousness and availability to me, especially in the midst of their final preparations before CIAMEL 2000. Pastor Dion lives more like the Lord Jesus than any man I have ever met.

Above all, I give tremendous thanks to the Lord. As a fellow Jew with a similar history, I echo the words of the Apostle Paul to Timothy (1 Timothy 1:12-14):

> **I thank Christ Jesus our Lord, who has strengthened me, because He considered me faithful, putting me into service, even though I was formerly a blasphemer and a persecutor and a violent aggressor. Yet I was shown mercy because I acted ignorantly in unbelief; and the grace of our Lord was more than abundant, with the faith and love which are found in Christ Jesus.**

INTRODUCTION

But beyond this, my son, be warned: the writing of many books is endless, and excessive devotion to books is wearying to the body.
> Ecclesiastes. 12:12

Introduction

When I began the transition of our church in 1989, the number of books on the subject of cell church could be counted on one hand. One need only scan church and ministry catalogs to be overwhelmed by the proliferation of related books today. So, you may wonder, why another book on cells and cell church? To play off of an old traditional Passover question, "Why is this book different from all other books?" Why, indeed!

I have spent the last thirty plus years as a pastor involved in developing some type of small group ministry. Since 1989 I have pursued vigorously the cell model. In those early years, when Ralph Neighbour in his now classic work *Where Do We Go From Here* warned against any attempt at transitioning an American church to a cell base church, the Lord said to transition. So, in obedience to His word, we embarked on the journey toward cell church. During those years I was blessed tremendously by my personal relationship to Bill Beckham and his early seminars. Bill was a wealth of knowledge and wisdom, as well as a source of great encouragement. TOUCH was for all practical purposes in its infancy, the Cell Magazine not even yet birthed.

In Joel Barker's terms, I am a paradigm pioneer. I am not a paradigm settler! Never have been, never will be. Settlers are important. One can not build a country on visionaries or pioneers. Settlers are vital, but I am a pioneer. Pioneers have no maps. They create the maps that others will someday use. They are cartographers, some better, some worse, yet cartographers just the same. The pioneers of Colorado discovered the un-fordable streams, the paths leading to steep precipices, the box canyons, and the impassible mountain passes. They discovered, too, the pleasant valleys, the cool rivers, and the open spaces upon which others would build towns. They made maps so those who would follow would not make the same mistakes. I am a map-maker. This book is my map. Yet, this book is not simply a map of my own journeys. It encompasses what others have experienced, yet never recorded. It is a map of their experiences also.

I have spent the last eight years as an investigator, a teacher and a consultant. From the frozen wasteland of Novosibirsk, Siberia in Russia to the green Shenandoah valley of Virginia, from the hustle and bustle of Houston, Washington DC, New York, Toronto, St. Petersburg, Russia and Abidjan, Cote d'Ivoire to the laid back solitude of rural North Dakota, I have observed and consulted with hundreds of cell churches and cell-church-wanna-be's.

I have watched many of these churches struggle and I have watched too many of them die. I still feel deeply the angst of fellow cell church planters, friends, who have pulled the plug on a cell plant already on life support and near death. Some have left the ministry. Some still wallow in the slough of despondency, self-condemnation, and self-recrimination. They had done the best they could. They did the best they knew. They had been faithful. What went wrong? What were they missing?

Then there are those men like Pastor Yaye Dion Robert and Vitaly Maximuk, men who have themselves pioneered. Pastor Dion has spent twenty five years quietly pioneering and developing a cell church whose local expressions number more than 680 and which are spread over 3 continents and nearly forty countries. Pastor Vitaly has, in my estimation, the most significant cell church in all Russia. An uncompromising man of character, his heart is to plant cell churches all over Russia.

While many ask only the more pragmatic *what* questions, as an investigator, an observer, a teacher, and a consultant, I have noted and asked the infrequently asked *why* questions and *how* questions. This book was born out of my original doctoral research asking how and why did a church of three grow into a church of more than one hundred fifty thousand in twenty five years. This book is far more than simply a map of my own journeys. It enfolds what others have experienced, yet never recorded, at least in English.

There is a map program and locator on the internet called Map Quest. Simply type in where you are and where you want to go and Map Quest will supply you with a map, of sorts. Now, I say a map of sorts, because the map can be quite general or quite specific. I used this program to navigate from Enterprise Car Rental at the O'Hare International Airport to the Best Western Hotel in Carol Stream, and from that hotel to my grandmother's apartment near downtown Chicago. The original map supplied sufficient detail for me to know the major highways. However, attempting to navigate downtown Chicago with simply that map would have proved disastrous. I needed finer detail. I needed their zoom feature. All this just to say that what you hold now in your hands is a general map. It will keep you going in the right direction, but you need finer detail to fully navigate. I have included reflection questions and action points at the close of each chapter to help you zoom in to a finer degree. Even so, the zoom feature is limited and still under development.

Twelve years ago when I began the cell church transition journey, I wish I had owned a book such as this. I was unprepared for the journey ahead. By God's grace we persevered and overcame. I understand today that I do not

Introduction

have time to make the same mistakes those who have gone before me have made. And why should I? Why should I have to re-invent the wheel? Why can I not learn from other's errors so as not to repeat them? Do I have to re-discover every blind canyon and impossible river? Why can I not receive from others what they have discovered? What time and effort it will save me! I then have the time to make new mistakes while building upon their progress.

Prepare well each of the six areas we will investigate. You may decide to skip, or quickly pass over, one or more of these areas as you walk out your journey. Do so at your own peril! Take short cuts today and you will rue that decision some future tomorrow. You will struggle with each chapter. You will struggle with the concepts and argue with yourself whether or not you have the time to do them. You will wrestle with God over their applications. That is ok. The purest water is that which has forced its way through solid rock to break forth.

In the end you will either choose to pay the price for what God has called and captured you to accomplish, or you will choose to build on an invalid ethical base, or you will settle for an inadequate value system, or you will proceed without a clear vision, or you will accept mediocrity, or you will re-work and re-work and re-work because you did not prototype, or you will build a program that has not the underground root system to support it. Choose wisely!

While the first seven chapters of *Preparing the 21st Century Church* will deal primarily with the underground realities vital for growing a healthy cell church or successfully transitioning to a cell based paradigm, the above ground reality of corporate life will also be addressed in the remaining six chapters. The book concludes with an exhortation to action.

Chapter 1 stands as an introduction to the need for preparation. It examines the state of unpreparedness the people of God have continually found themselves in, from wayward Israel of old to modern America and the church in America today. It is a call to leave behind the patterns of the past and prepare as a Bride anticipating the arrival of the soon coming Bridegroom.

Chapter 2 discusses the divorce of Christian ethics from biblical ethics in the 20th century, along with its ramifications for the church today in the 21st century. Deontological moral theory is contrasted with the more prevalent and pernicious teleological moral theory. The chapter closes with a challenge to lay a deontological ethical base in the church. The rapid growth of the *Eglise Protestante Baptiste Oeuvres et Mission Internationale (EPBOM)* in Abidjan, Cote d'Ivoire from 3 to 150,000 people in twenty five years is employed as an illustration of the results of a cell church building upon a deontological approach to moral theory.

Chapter 3 challenges the reader to clearly articulate the value system out of which the cell church is to function. Values are defined and their importance is stressed. The reader will discover how to both develop values and change values in the church. Practical reflection questions and action points help apply what the reader has discovered. Chapter 4 reflects upon the value system adopted by EPBOM and its impact upon the church.

Chapter 5 challenges the reader regarding the absolute necessity of receiving God's vision. Five vision components are looked at. The first three components, the church as the family of God, the Body of Christ, and the army of God, will be suggested as being foundational for all cell churches. The reader will be challenged to uniquely develop the final two components as the church fulfills the program of God and discovers the undiscovered country that lays ahead. Once again, reflection questions and action points are provided to help the reader assess his vision.

Chapter 6 will perhaps prove to be for the reader the most difficult underlying reality to grasp and implement, as value disciplines are examined. The reader will be introduced to a number of working definitions, followed by an overview of three value disciplines. Three world class cell churches will come under scrutiny as representative models of these three disciplines. The necessity of formulating an appropriate value proposition and building a values-driven operating model will next be addressed. The chapter will conclude with tips for establishing a value discipline agenda and, as in previous chapters, exercises designed to both stimulate and solidify thinking.

Chapter 7 will introduce the reader to the concept of prototype development and provide a practical tool for the initial development of cells. The what, when, and why of prototyping will be discussed. The answer to the question, "How can I correctly prepare a prototype?" will be supplied. The reader will be challenged to then take initial steps toward prototype development.

Chapter 8 is a transitional bridge between what has been developed underground and that which is about to burst forth above the surface for all to see. Chapters 9 through 13 examine what will be called the "Program of God". The development of the Program of God is the church's response to five questions:

1) How will the Body of Christ be built up (Edification)?

2) How will the Body of Christ be trained for service

Introduction

           (Equipping)?

   3) How will we raise up future leaders (Empowering)?

   4) How will we win this generation to Christ (Evangelism)?

   5) How will each Christian be released into action (Every Member Ministry)?

Chapter 9 is a challenge for the church to prepare a system to equip each member for ministry. EPBOM's model of equipping is employed as an illustration both to stimulate thinking and give encouragement. The chapter concludes with a challenge to the ineffectiveness of our present systems.

Chapter 10 is a challenge for the church to prepare a system to help each member effectively evangelize the lost. EPBOM's model of evangelism is again employed with a final challenge.

Chapters 11-13 follow the same outline as chapters 9 and 10. Preparing a system for edification, the empowerment of leaders, and the release of every member into corporate body ministry based on their spiritual giftedness is outlined in each of the respective chapters. Each chapter again includes an examination of the EPBOM model, both for encouragement and vision stimulation. Chapters 11-13 each conclude with a call to radically change our present ineffective systems.

Chapter 14 both summarizes what has gone on before and poises the reader for the next step in the journey.

1
A PEOPLE UNPREPARED

A VOICE IS CALLING, "CLEAR THE WAY FOR THE LORD IN THE WILDERNESS; MAKE SMOOTH IN THE DESERT A HIGHWAY FOR OUR GOD.   ISAIAH 40:3

Chapter 1   A People Unprepared

Is. 40:4 "Let every valley be lifted up,
   And every mountain and hill be made low;
   And let the rough ground become a plain,
   And the rugged terrain a broad valley;

Is. 40:5 Then the glory of the LORD will be revealed,
   And all flesh will see it together;
   For the mouth of the LORD has spoken."

Is. 40:6 A voice says, "Call out."
   Then he answered, "What shall I call out?"
   All flesh is grass, and all its loveliness is like the flower of the field.

Is. 40:7 The grass withers, the flower fades,
   When the breath of the LORD blows upon it;
   Surely the people are grass.

Is. 40:8 The grass withers, the flower fades,
   But the word of our God stands forever.

Is. 40:9 Get yourself up on a high mountain,
   O Zion, bearer of good news,
   Lift up your voice mightily,
   O Jerusalem, bearer of good news;
   Lift it up, do not fear.
   Say to the cities of Judah, "Here is your God!"

Is. 40:10 Behold, the Lord GOD will come with might,
   With His arm ruling for Him.
   Behold, His reward is with Him
   And His recompense before Him.

Is. 40:11 Like a shepherd He will tend His flock,
   In His arm He will gather the lambs
   And carry them in His bosom;
   He will gently lead the nursing ewes.

ANCIENT ISRAEL – A NATION UNPREPARED

The history of Israel is the history of a nation unprepared. The nation was unprepared for the coming of their King. When He came, only a few shepherds and foreign astrologers were prepared to visit him. Whether it was a matter of prejudice, prophetic viewpoint, worldview, or simply personal greed, they were all unprepared. John the Baptist was indeed the voice crying in the wilderness to prepare the way of the Lord, but few listened, and even fewer prepared (Luke 3:1-10).

> Now in the fifteenth year of the reign of Tiberius Caesar, when Pontius Pilate was governor of Judea, and Herod was tetrarch of Galilee,...the word of God came to John, the son of Zacharias, in the wilderness. And he came into all the district around the Jordan, preaching a baptism of repentance for the forgiveness of sins; as it is written in the book of the words of Isaiah the prophet,
>
> > The voice of one crying in the wilderness
> > 'Make ready the way of the Lord,
> > Make His paths straight.
> > Every ravine will be filled,
> > And every mountain and hill will be brought low;
> > The crooked will become straight,
> > And the rough roads smooth;
> > And all flesh will see the salvation of God.'
>
> So he began saying to the crowds who were going out to be baptized by him, "You brood of vipers, who warned you to flee from the wrath to come? "Therefore bear fruits in keeping with repentance, and do not begin to say to yourselves, 'We have Abraham for our father,' for I say to you that from these stones God is able to raise up children to Abraham. "Indeed the axe is already laid at the root of the trees; so every tree that does not bear good fruit is cut down and thrown into the fire."

Chapter 1 ☛ *A People Unprepared*

> And the crowds were questioning him, saying, "Then what shall we do?"

The common Israelite was unprepared!

> When He approached Jerusalem, He saw the city and wept over it, saying, "If you had known in this day, even you, the things which make for peace! But now they have been hidden from your eyes. "For the days will come upon you when your enemies will throw up a barricade against you, and surround you and hem you in on every side, and they will level you to the ground and your children within you, and they will not leave in you one stone upon another, because you did not recognize the time of your visitation." (Luke 19:41-44)

The Chief priests and the Sanhedrin were unprepared.

> Now the chief priests and the whole Council kept trying to obtain false testimony against Jesus, so that they might put Him to death. They did not find any, even though many false witnesses came forward. But later on two came forward, and said, "This man stated, 'I am able to destroy the temple of God and to rebuild it in three days.'" The high priest stood up and said to Him, "Do You not answer? What is it that these men are testifying against You?" But Jesus kept silent. And the high priest said to Him, "I adjure You by the living God, that You tell us whether You are the Christ, the Son of God." Jesus *said to him, "You have said it yourself; nevertheless I tell you, hereafter you will see the Son of Man sitting at the right hand of power, and coming on the clouds of heaven." Then the high priest tore his robes and said, "He has blasphemed! What further need do we have of witnesses? Behold, you have now heard the blasphemy; what do you think?" They answered, "He deserves death!" Then they spat in His face and beat Him with their fists; and others slapped Him, and said, "Prophesy to us, You Christ; who is the one who hit You?" (Matthew 26:59-68)

Preparing the 21st Century Church

They just did not "get it", they did not understand, or they would not have crucified their Messiah. They were unprepared.

> Yet we do speak wisdom among those who are mature; a wisdom, however, not of this age nor of the rulers of this age, who are passing away; but we speak God's wisdom in a mystery, the hidden wisdom which God predestined before the ages to our glory; the wisdom which none of the rulers of this age has understood; for if they had understood it they would not have crucified the Lord of glory (1 Corinthians 2:6-8).

MODERN AMERICA – A NATION UNPREPARED

As I sit and write, I find myself part of a nation caught unprepared in the past and unprepared to face the future. It has been just under two months ago that the World Trade Center in New York city was demolished by a terrorist act. Could we have been prepared for such a an unthinkable reality? Consider the following news item:

> Tuesday, Sept. 18, 2001 10:35 p.m. EDT
> Israel's Mossad Warned CIA of Attacks
>
> London's Telegraph reported that Mossad officials traveled to Washington last month to warn the CIA and the FBI that a cell of up to 200 terrorists was planning a major operation.
> The paper said the Israeli officials specifically warned their counterparts in Washington that "large-scale terrorist attacks on highly visible targets on the American mainland were imminent." They offered no specific information about targets, but they did link the plot to Afghanistan-based terrorist Osama bin Laden, and they told the Americans there were "strong grounds" for suspecting Iraqi involvement.
> A U.S. administration official told the paper that it was "quite credible" that the CIA did not heed the Mossad warning: "It has a history of being over-cautious about Israeli information." But the official noted that "if this is true, then the refusal

Chapter 1 ☛ A People Unprepared

to take it seriously will mean heads will roll."

The same week that twenty nine people tested positive for anthrax exposure in the Senate, the following item was reported by Fox News. Are we a nation prepared?

> Fox News Survey: Hospitals Not Ready for Large Bio Attack
> Tuesday, October 16, 2001
> CHICAGO — American hospitals are not prepared to handle a widespread biological disaster, researchers reported Monday. A survey of 30 hospitals in four states and Washington, D.C., found the institutions unequipped — disturbing news for a country gripped by fears of additional anthrax attacks.
> Just one of the hospitals in the study had medicine stockpiled to fight a bioterror attack, emergency-room workers said. Twenty-six hospitals reported they could handle only 10 to 15 victims simultaneously, and 22 said they were not ready for a chemical or nuclear attack at all.
> Staff at only seven hospitals had any training to care for casualties resulting from bioterrorism.

What will be the headlines tomorrow? Will there be more anthrax? Smallpox? Ebola? A nuclear briefcase explosion? We have had warnings in the past. We have had adequate time to prepare. We consistently choose not to prepare. As a consequence, we as a nation are presently unprepared to face the certainty of biological, chemical or nuclear terrorism. From the resources of WorldNetDaily comes the following headline and story.

> U.S. subject to 'weapons of mass destruction'
> CIA, experts say response capability to bio-chemical attacks lacking
> ---
> By Jon Dougherty
> © 2001 WorldNetDaily.com
> Wednesday October 3, 2001

Despite the CIA's dire predictions and Executive Branch directives to prepare the country for the possibility of terrorism via weapons of mass destruction, the U.S. remains woefully unprepared for such an attack. Worse, the infrastructure to confront a mass casualty incident caused by a WMD incident simply isn't in place.

On June 22-23, a senior-level war game called "Dark Winter" held at Andrews Air Force Base, which examined the national security, intergovernmental and information challenges of a biological attack on the American homeland, concluded that "an attack on the United States with biological weapons could threaten vital national security interests."

"Massive civilian casualties, breakdown in essential institutions, violation of democratic processes, civil disorder, loss of confidence in government and reduced U.S. strategic flexibility abroad are among the ways a biological attack might compromise U.S. security," said a summary of the exercise.

Also, officials found that "major 'fault lines'" existed between federal, state and local governmental agencies and the private sector, which would hamper any ability to manage a chemical- or bio-weapon release. "These 'disconnects' could impede situational awareness and compromise the ability to limit loss of life, suffering, and economic damage," the summary said.

Worse, "there is no surge capability in the U.S. health care and public health systems, or the pharmaceutical and vaccine industries," officials concluded, meaning that the "institutionally limited surge capacity could result in hospitals being overwhelmed and becoming inoperable." The limitations could also "impede public health agencies' analysis of the scope, source and progress of the epidemic, the ability to educate and reassure the public, and the capacity to limit casualties and the spread of disease.

"Should a contagious bioweapon pathogen be used, containing the spread of disease will present significant ethical, political, cultural, operational and legal challenges," the summary concluded.

Chapter 1 ☞ *A People Unprepared*

The theme of the game was the introduction of a smallpox outbreak in Oklahoma City, Okla., a year from now – the winter of 2002. "During the thirteen days of the game, the disease spread to 25 states and 15 other countries," according to the summary.

Sponsors of the game were The Center for Strategic and International Studies; the Johns Hopkins Center for Civilian Biodefense Studies; The ANSER Institute for Homeland Security; and The Oklahoma City National Memorial Institute for the Prevention of Terrorism.

"In terms of biological [attacks], there's a lot more we need to do to educate our doctors to recognize signs and symptoms of certain things," the government's expert said.

Also, officials say the U.S. medical capacity operates near full at all times, in an effort to trim costs by not having to maintain hospital rooms and staff that are not immediately needed. During a major catastrophe, that capacity would be taxed past its limit in a short period of time.

"In terms of the basic conclusions" of the Dark Winter exercise, "they have been attested to and elaborated on before Congress" by war-game participants and other experts, Reimer added.

"Most experts agree that the United States is vulnerable to terrorism," Brake concluded in his report. "While intelligence experts contend that the use of a WMD is less likely than the more conventional forms of terrorism, the consequences of a successful attack could be massive."

As a nation we have lived in a state of unpreparedness. We still make little preparation. When disaster once again strikes, I sincerely doubt we will have prepared adequately, if at all. Yet, is the church any different? Is the church in America at all prepared?

A Church Unprepared

How prepared is the church to face an uncertain future? How prepared is the church in America to face persecution, or peril, or famine, or the sword? How prepared are we for the return of the Lord? Will we be like the ten foolish virgins?

> Be dressed in readiness, and keep your lamps lit. Be like men who are waiting for their master when he returns from the wedding feast, so that they may immediately open the door to him when he comes and knocks. Blessed are those slaves whom the master will find on the alert when he comes; truly I say to you, that he will gird himself to serve, and have them recline at the table, and will come up and wait on them. Whether he comes in the second watch, or even in the third, and finds them so, blessed are those slaves. But be sure of this, that if the head of the house had known at what hour the thief was coming, he would not have allowed his house to be broken into. You too, be ready; for the Son of Man is coming at an hour that you do not expect. (Luke 12:35-40)

> Then the kingdom of heaven will be comparable to ten virgins, who took their lamps and went out to meet the bridegroom. Five of them were foolish, and five were prudent. For when the foolish took their lamps, they took no oil with them, but the prudent took oil in flasks along with their lamps. Now while the bridegroom was delaying, they all got drowsy and began to sleep. But at midnight there was a shout, 'Behold, the bridegroom! Come out to meet him.' Then all those virgins rose and trimmed their lamps. The foolish said to the prudent, 'Give us some of your oil, for our lamps are going out.' But the prudent answered, 'No, there will not be enough for us and you too; go instead to the dealers and buy some for yourselves.' And while they were going away to make the purchase, the bridegroom came, and those who were ready went in with him to the wedding feast; and the door was shut. (Matt. 25:1-10)

Chapter 1 ☞ *A People Unprepared*

How prepared are we to receive and process the harvest we so earnestly cry out for? There is a story tucked away in the pages of the Old Testament that speak to our situation today. It is the story of a prophet of God and a widow's preparation that allowed God to pour forth life instead of death.

> Now a certain woman of the wives of the sons of the prophets cried out to Elisha, 'Your servant my husband is dead, and you know that your servant feared the LORD; and the creditor has come to take my two children to be his slaves.' Elisha said to her, 'What shall I do for you? Tell me, what do you have in the house?' And she said, 'Your maidservant has nothing in the house except a jar of oil.' Then he said, 'Go, borrow vessels at large for yourself from all your neighbors, even empty vessels; do not get a few. And you shall go in and shut the door behind you and your sons, and pour out into all these vessels, and you shall set aside what is full.' So she went from him and shut the door behind her and her sons; they were bringing the vessels to her and she poured. When the vessels were full, she said to her son, 'Bring me another vessel.' And he said to her, 'There is not one vessel more.' And the oil stopped. Then she came and told the man of God. And he said, 'Go, sell the oil and pay your debt, and you and your sons can live on the rest.' (2 Kings 4:1-7)

The Lord is wanting to pour out the oil of His Presence in the church. We have no jars to hold the oil. We must prepare jars for the harvest. Jesus said we must prepare new wineskins for the new wine.

> No one puts new wine into old wineskins; otherwise the wine will burst the skins, and the wine is lost and the skins as well; but one puts new wine into fresh wineskins. (Mark 2:22)

Preparation usually begins in the overlooked or barely perceptible arenas of life. Who would have considered that one of the greatest prophets of God was being formed in the womb of Jeremiah's mother? Only years later was it revealed to Jeremiah his eternal appointment:

> Jer. 1:4 Now the word of the LORD came to me saying,
>
> Jer. 1:5 "Before I formed you in the womb I knew you,
> And before you were born I consecrated you;
> I have appointed you a prophet to the nations."

Consider this. Jeremiah the youth is about to be loosed upon the world to pluck up and to break down, to destroy and to overthrow, to build and to plant. How could that happen? God had fashioned Jeremiah during those early, quiet, unseen years. When the time of release arrived and Jeremiah balked at what lay ahead, the Lord was able to respond accordingly. Observe their conversation:

> Jer. 1:6 Then I said, "Alas, Lord GOD!
> Behold, I do not know how to speak,
> Because I am a youth."
>
> Jer. 1:7 But the LORD said to me,
> "Do not say, 'I am a youth,'
> Because everywhere I send you, you shall go,
> And all that I command you, you shall speak.
>
> Jer. 1:8 "Do not be afraid of them,
> For I am with you to deliver you," declares the LORD.
>
> Jer. 1:9 Then the LORD stretched out His hand and touched my mouth, and the LORD said to me, "Behold, I have put My words in your mouth.
>
> Jer. 1:10 "See, I have appointed you this day over the nations and over the kingdoms,
> To pluck up and to break down,
> To destroy and to overthrow,
> To build and to plant."

God prepares for growth first in the unseen realm. Initial development almost always occurs first where it is barely noticeable. Do you recall David's thanksgiving?

Chapter 1 ☞ *A People Unprepared*

> For You formed my inward parts; You wove me in my mother's womb. I will give thanks to You, for I am fearfully and wonderfully made; Wonderful are Your works, And my soul knows it very well. My frame was not hidden from You, When I was *made in secret* (italics mine), And skillfully *wrought in the depths of the earth* (italics mine); Your eyes have seen my unformed substance; And in Your book were all written The days that were ordained for me, When as yet there was not one of them. (Psalm 139:13-16)

This book is a call to prepare the way of the Lord. Prepare the wineskin critical for the church in the 21st century. Prepare the jars to receive the outpouring of God's oil. Prepare the oil today, for there will be no time to prepare once the trumpet has sounded and the Bridegroom has come. The mountains must be levelled and the ravines filled to prepare a highway for our God.

One final word of warning before we proceed. The development of the underground realities discussed in chapters three through five may be easily begun with the information supplied to the reader. However, when considering the creation of a prototype cell, I would suggest further study be undertaken before any final attempt is made. An excellent resource is my own work on prototype cell development. There the reader will find additional helps and even tested and proven templates for the five design criteria suggested in this work. As we approach the development of the Program of God in chapters eight through twelve, each chapter will introduce you to a perspective, expand your vision and understanding through the use of illustrative material, and conclude with a challenge to develop each aspect in an American context. What You will have to discover the details of your own "how-to" manual as you are on your knees before God.

You have before you a call to prepare first those unseen, underground dimensions before you embark on preparing a wineskin into which God can power His new wine. Prepare your ethical base! Prepare your values! Prepare your vision! Prepare your value discipline! Prepare your prototype cell! Prepare the program of Go!. Don't be like ancient Israel who failed to recognize her day of visitation, and perished. Prepare ye the way of the Lord!

REFLECTIONS

When embarking upon a journey, you must be sure to know from where you are starting out. In like manner, when embarking upon any change, an accurate assessment of your present reality must always precede your first steps, or effective change will be like the illusive butterfly.

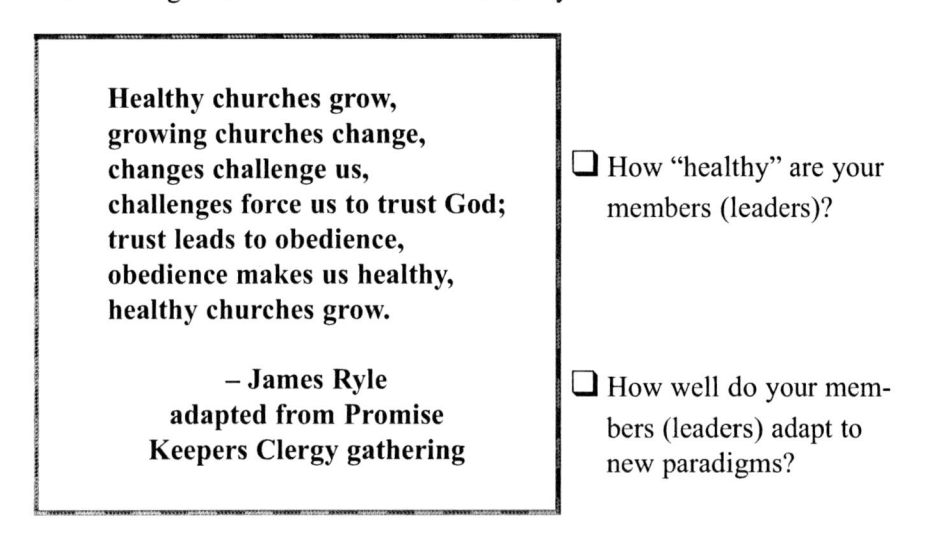

> **Healthy churches grow,
> growing churches change,
> changes challenge us,
> challenges force us to trust God;
> trust leads to obedience,
> obedience makes us healthy,
> healthy churches grow.**
>
> **– James Ryle
> adapted from Promise
> Keepers Clergy gathering**

❏ How "healthy" are your members (leaders)?

❏ How well do your members (leaders) adapt to new paradigms?

Preparing the way of the Lord will entail significant effort and change. Satisfaction with your present state will torpedo any plans to journey elsewhere, especially when the proposed journey is perilous or taxing. In other words, where complacency is high, change usually goes nowhere. Examine the following five sources of complacency. Which elements are present in your church?

❏ **Crises** - We have no major, visible crises. Finances are good. Membership has grown. Internal division is not a threat.

❏ **Resources** - We look around and see abundant resources. Our facilities scream "success". The subliminal message is clear: We are rich, and have become wealthy, and have need of nothing. We are winners. We must be doing something right or God would not be blessing us like He has been. Relax.

Chapter 1 ☛ *A People Unprepared*

- ❏ **Culture** - We have a kill-the-messenger-of-bad-news, low-confrontation culture. After all, bad news might reduce morale or lead to arguments (i.e. honest discussions).

- ❏ **Happy Talk** - We hear continuous happy talk and glowing reports from leadership. Sure we have challenges, but look at all we've accomplished!

- ❏ **Denial** - Life is more pleasurable without problems. We already have enough challenges and problems to keep us busy. When evidence of a problem appears, if we can get away with ignoring the evidence, we will.

Preparing the 21st Century Church

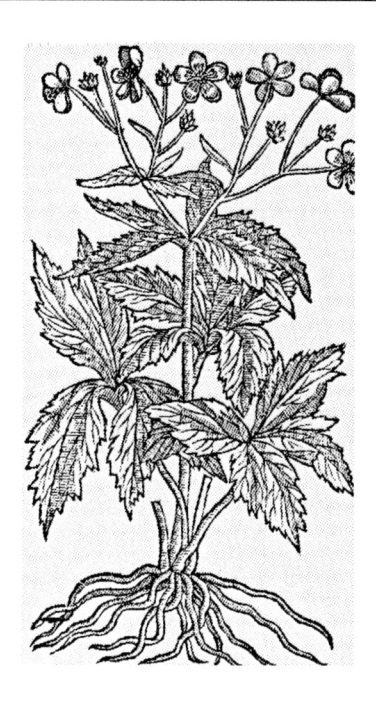

UNDERGROUND REALITIES

(ROOTS BEFORE FRUIT)

PHASE 1
PREPARE THE ETHICAL BASE

PREPARE YE THE WAY OF THE LORD

PREPARE THE ETHICAL BASE

I ALSO SAY TO YOU THAT YOU ARE PETER, AND UPON THIS ROCK I WILL BUILD MY CHURCH; AND THE GATES OF HADES WILL NOT OVERPOWER IT. MATTHEW 16:18

Chapter 2 ☛ *Prepare the Ethical Base*

I WILL BUILD MY CHURCH!

Jesus began and is still involved with the greatest building program of all eternity. He is building His church. When it is ultimately finished, it will be a holy temple, a dwelling of God in the Spirit.

> Eph. 2:19 So then you are no longer strangers and aliens, but you are fellow citizens with the saints, and are of God's household,
>
> Eph. 2:20 **having been built** on the foundation of the apostles and prophets, Christ Jesus Himself being the corner stone,
>
> Eph. 2:21 in whom **the whole building**, being fitted together, is growing into **a holy temple** in the Lord,
>
> Eph. 2:22 in whom you also are being **built together into a dwelling** of God in the Spirit.

Today it is continuing to be fitted together. It is in process of development. As unimaginable as it may seem, we have been invited to labor alongside with Him in this monumental building project.

> 1Cor. 3:9 For we are God's fellow workers; you are God's field, God's building.
>
> 1Cor. 3:10 According to the grace of God which was given to me, like a wise master builder I laid a foundation, and another is building on it. But each man must be careful how he builds on it.
>
> 1Cor. 3:11 For no man can lay a foundation other than the one which is laid, which is Jesus Christ.
>
> 1Cor. 3:12 Now if any man builds on the foundation with gold, silver, precious stones, wood, hay, straw,
>
> 1Cor. 3:13 each man's work will become evident; for the day will show it because it is to be revealed with fire, and the fire

itself will test the quality of each man's work.
1Cor. 3:14 If any man's work which he has built on it remains, he will receive a reward.

1Cor. 3:15 If any man's work is burned up, he will suffer loss; but he himself will be saved, yet so as through fire.

However, along with that invitation comes a sobering warning. Our work on the building will be evaluated, tested, even by the fire of God. The quality of our work will be made evident to all. We may find it being consumed in the fire of judgement, or remaining as an enduring testimony and witness to the quality with which we built. We may receive a reward, or suffer tremendous loss. As we build, we must be very sure that we do not either build with that which is flawed, or fail to build with that which is quality. Herein, far too often, lies our problem!

DESIGN CRITERIA AND CELL CHURCH R&D

In the early 1980's I worked bi-vocationally as an aerospace engineer for Pratt & Whitney Aircraft. I was assigned to the R&D department, research and development. My primary task was to identify performance flaws in existing systems prior to our developing prototypes of advanced systems. In order to identify existing flaws, it was necessary to scrutinize the system's design criteria, that is, the criteria by which the system had initially been designed. All systems have design criteria. Some system's criteria may be defined better than others, but the criteria are there nonetheless.

Whether a cell church has been planted from scratch or transitioned from an existing church, that cell church also has design criteria that define its nature and function.I have met and consulted with hundreds of pastors over the past years who were attempting to transition their church to a cell-based design and grow their church to a larger size. As a consultant, I find myself involved in somewhat the same process I was doing as an aerospace engineer, examining the cell church's design criteria and looking for flaws, those things that inhibit it from fully functioning as originally envisioned. Too often, there is a critical lack of defined design criteria and, therefore, inherent flaws in the very design

Chapter 2 ☛ Prepare the Ethical Base

of our churches. In other words, what I have observed in many cell churches is either a lack of those criteria which promote development, or a presence of those things which negatively affect the maturing of the church.

The various chapters of this book will address what I consider to be the basic design criteria needing to be addressed by a cell church plant or transition. This chapter begins to address the most basic criterion of all, that of a *deontological biblical ethical value system,* a value system that has linked and identified Christian ethics with biblical ethics and is based on a deontological approach to moral theory. If we are to be faithful to the whole counsel of God, then it is imperative that we set forth principles needed by the community of faith and the individual for ethical and moral living approved by God. Both ethics and the differing approaches to moral theory will be defined for the reader shortly.

The planting and development of a cell church must not be rooted in the shifting sand of human wisdom or human relativism. When all is said and done, we are not asking our people to exchange one theological and external structure for another. We are challenging our church members to first change their current value system, then adopt a biblical structure that will more readily permit them to live out that new value system in a manner consistent with a biblical ethic. Cell church structures then become simply expressions of value systems tied to an unchanging biblical ethical base.

Later on in this chapter I will direct the reader's attention to the cell church of which Dion Robert is the senior pastor in Abidjan, Cote d'Ivoire. At this point allow me to say simply that one need only briefly survey the history of *Eglise Protestante Baptiste Oeuvres et Mission Internationale* (EPBOM) to observe the aforementioned basic design criterion bred into the life of that church. Dion understands the Word of God and its function in his life, as well as the life of the church. Dion has chosen to live out of what we in the West would term, and what I have already mentioned, as a deontological biblical ethical value system. The church in turn has adopted the ethical system of its founder. Put simply, Christian ethics at EPBOM has been linked and identified with biblical ethics.

As we will observe, for the most part, what can been said to be true of EPBOM cannot be said to be true in the life and development of the average American cell church. In failing to prepare at this most basic level, whether transitioning or cell church planting, we have set the stage for slow and imperceptible growth in our cell churches, the exact opposite of what we long to see.

How could this have happened? The answer is quite simple. Unlike EPBOM, twentieth century American Christian ethicists have bequeathed to us a divided house as regards ethics and the Bible. Their influence has impacted every level within our churches, from pulpit to pew. To prepare the way of the Lord will necessitate an understanding of our present condition and thinking, repenting, and returning once again a biblical approach to ethics and morality.

CHRISTIAN ETHICS AND THE 20TH CENTURY

The word ethics is derived from the Greek εθος or ηθος (ethos or aythos). The former term occurs twelve times in the New Testament (Luke 1:9; 2:42; 22:39; John 19:40; Acts 6:14; 15:1; 16:21; 21:21; 25:16; 26:3; 28:17; Hebrews 10:25). The latter one appears only once, in the plural form in 1 Corinthians 15:33. Our corresponding English equivalent may mean "manner of life," "conduct," "custom," or "practice" as prescribed by some competent authority. The Old Testament has no abstract comprehensive term that parallels our modern term ethics. The closest that it came to ethics was the use of מוּסָר ("discipline" or "teaching") in latter Hebrew or ("way" or "path") in the canonical wisdom literature (Kaiser 2). Ethics can thus be thought of as the basis for the way we live our life.

Historically, Christian ethics and biblical ethics have enjoyed a successful marriage. The question arose in the 20th century whether or not Christian ethics should continue to be identified with biblical ethics. The traditional link and marriage between the Bible and Christian ethics was seriously challenged and flatly repudiated in the 20th century (Kaiser 39). Carl F. H. Henry quotes from several prominent ethicists that illustrate this rupture (236-237). Speaking of the 20th century, Walter C. Kaiser Jr. notes, "It is an agreed state of the discipline of Christian ethics in this century that the nature and content of morality is not to be equated with any formulation of the divine will supposedly found in biblical commandments, principles, precepts, or examples" (40). Christian ethicists in the last century have repudiated the marriage of Christian ethics and biblical ethics, to the detriment of the church, as we shall soon observe.

Hermeneutics Make Everything All Right!?

For most Christian ethicists, though, the Bible is still considered normative, that is, it supplies us with an accepted standard or a way of behaving or doing things that most Christians would agree with. In what way can Christian ethicists that reject any identification of Christian ethics with biblical ethics still consider the Bible to be normative? In their attempts to justify the divorce, they assume one or more of six hermeneutical stances.

Stance #1: General Orientation

Stance number one is to use the Bible as a general orientation to ethical issues. The emphasis here is on the community, especially the church, and the variety of biblical data. They suggest that Scripture alone is not enough. It can only supply a basic orientation towards particular decisions. James M. Gustafson is a representative of this model.

Stance #2: Multiple Variations

For others, stance number two, the Bible is used in multiple variations. The Bible can provide ethical insights, but we cannot move directly to Christian ethics from the Bible. Since there is no one right way regarding how to use the Bible, pluralism becomes the favored approach. Edward LeRoy Long, Jr. provides us with a representative model for this approach.

Stance #3: Source of Images

A third group contends that the Bible is to be used as a source of images. C. Freedman Sleeper explores the dynamic character of biblical language, including "images" and the relation between "images" of the Bible and "models" in the social sciences, drawing out the implications of biblical images for ethical theory and concluding, "We cannot expect to find biblical solutions to contemporary problems.... However, the exegesis [of the Bible] can clarify the way in which the biblical writers approached the problems of their own day" (443-60).

Stance #4: A Witness to God's Will

How does the Bible aid the Christian in making concrete ethical decisions? For Brevard S. Childs and the hermeneutical stance he represents, the Bible is to be used as a witness to God's will. Specifically, it may "sketch the full range of biblical witnesses" in the Bible on any given ethical issue or trace "the inner movement of the various witnesses along their characteristic axes" or "characteristic patterns" of thought relative to some of the Scripture's favorite themes (132-138). What is the bottom line for Childs? "It is of fundamental importance to recognize that at no point within the Bible is there ever spelled out a system or a technique by which one could move from the general imperatives of the law of God, such as [are] found in the Decalogue, to the specific application within the concrete situations" (129).

Stance #5: One Source Among Many

A fifth hermeneutical approach is to view the Bible not as the sole source of ethical wisdom, but as simply one source among many sources. Charles E. Curran is a representative of this camp. Curran has written, "…biblical ethics is not the same as Christian ethics…. The biblical renewal has emphasized the historical and cultural limitations of the Scriptures so that one cannot just apply the Scriptures in a somewhat timeless manner to problems existing in different historical circumstances. In addition the Scriptures were not really confronted with many of the moral problems we face today. What might be a valid and true norm in biblical times might not be adequate today" (32-37). His conclusion is, therefore, "…the Scriptures are not the sole source of ethical wisdom for the Christian, but…Christian ethics also derives wisdom and knowledge from other human sources. This generic approach will rely on human wisdom and reason as well as the Scriptures…" (53).

Stance #6: Character Formation

One final hermeneutical stance set forth by Birch and Rasmussen argues that the Bible's use in decision-making and action is not as significant or helpful as it is in character formation. It permits the Bible to function only as a source for establishing boundaries of moral behavior without allowing it to set a single biblical norm (53-54).

Summary

Each of these views in their own unique way serve to do their part in disconnecting the historical tie between Christian ethics and biblical ethics. Unfortunately, the average church member has embraced one or more of these ungodly ethical approaches to life.

Possibly the most prevalent approach adopted by the American church is the fifth stance, that the Bible is one source among many sources of wisdom, that as Christians we can derive our moral wisdom and knowledge from other human sources, including our own reason. When faced with unpleasant biblical injunctions, a common response is, "But I think...!" Another common response is to contend that times have changed and the Scriptures were not really confronted with the moral questions of today, questions such as those raised in the field of biomedics. After all, what does the Bible really have to say about stem cell research and cloning? A rather humorous yet sad cartoon found its way into the Friday, November 30th, 2001 edition of USA Today. Frame one depicts a large building with the sign over it reading "Biotechnology Company". A question is being asked, "During the cloning of a human embryo, is there anything discarded?" The answer back is, "Yes." The next frame shows the same company, this time with a hand protruding from the top window discarding "Ethics" into the trash can below.

All that I have said notwithstanding, like the average 20th century American Christian ethicist, we and our people have entered into the 21st century as "good" Charismatics and "good" Pentecostals and "good" Evangelicals, believing that the Bible is "normative" for our life. Yet, how can it be "normative" when we have anchored our life in anything other than or in addition to the written Word of God? I fear that while we may even fight for the adoption of inerrancy, we in fact have made the Bible of no account in our daily lives by our unconscious hermeneutical approach to the Scriptures. Can this be one reason why we do not experience a move of God in the church like we hear about elsewhere in the world? However, let us continue. The plot thickens, as they say.

DEONTOLOGICAL VERSUS TELEOLOGICAL MORAL THEORY

There exist two basic approaches to moral theory, two approaches determining how we make moral decisions. A *deontological* approach to moral theory (from the Greek word δεον, "ought" or "binding") maintains the position that the rightness or wrongness of an action or rule is not contingent on its results, but are directly related to specific commands that have been issued from God. By contrast, a *teleological* approach (from the Greek word τελειος, "having reached its end, finished") maintains the position that proposed actions are weighted by what brings the greatest good to the greatest number. In simplified terms, a deontological view approaches rightness and wrongness from the source, God's commands, while a teleological view approaches rightness and wrongness from the results, what brings the greatest good.

In light of the previous brief summary, it should be clear that most Christian ethicists today are moving away from a *deontological* moral position and moving toward a *teleological* position. From the previous examples, it should also be becoming clearer that Scripture is no longer viewed by most Christian ethicists today as supplying the content for ethical character or decision making, whether that content is defined as propositional or conceptual. Instead, the more popular approach today is to view Scripture as presenting either a set of witnesses to the mighty acts of God and/or the person of Christ, or to a set of images.

Kaiser well sums up the ramifications of continuing with the current trend. "There just are no two ways about it; the church, if she is to continue to be Christ's church, must come to terms with the Scriptures to which he pointed and affirmed 'these are the Scriptures that testify about me' (John 5:39), 'Scripture cannot be broken' (John 10:35), and not the smallest letter, nor the least stroke of the pen, will by any means disappear from the Law until everything is accomplished' (Matthew 5:18). To reject them or the sense in which they were intended is ultimately to reject him as Lord of his church" (57).

I fear that the average Christian church member is approaching his or her life today teleologically, rather than deontologically. We have taught them to continually ask the question, "What will be the result of my actions?" Rarely, if ever, have we taught them to simply ask the question, "Is what I am about to do intrinsically right or wrong?" The most common response to that question would be, "There is no way to know for sure!" Yet, the basic characteristics of both Old and New Testament ethics demand the church take a deontological approach to ethics today.

OLD TESTAMENT ETHICS ARE CLEARLY DEONTOLOGICAL

As we briefly survey the nature of Old Testament ethics before turning to the New Testament account, we will find Old Testament ethics to be grounded in the Person of God, to be theistic, internal, and universal in nature.

Old Testament Ethics are Grounded in a Person

Ethics are grounded in the express commands of the absolutely holy person, God, made known by historical acts of revelation. Ethics are grounded on the definitely expressed will of the divine Person. Fallen man was unable to discover for himself what was good and right and ethical. The appeal was always "to the law and to the testimony" (Isaiah 8:20). The appeal was also grounded in the character and the revealed will of the One who commanded: "Be holy because I, the Lord your God, am holy" (Leviticus 19:2).

Old Testament Ethics are Theistic

In contradistinction to our society, the Scriptures know nothing about an autonomous ethic. It is intimately joined to a personal knowledge of God. "Trust in the LORD with all your heart and do not lean on your own understanding. In all your ways acknowledge Him, and He will make your paths straight. Do not be wise in your own eyes; Fear the LORD and turn away from evil." As Proverbs 3:5-7 assesses it, man is to lean on God in order to understand the path his life is to take. He is not to lean on his own understanding of life. To know the God of Israel was to both know and practice righteousness and justice (Jeremiah 22:15-16). This can be seen in the biblical call to holiness, often repeated in the Old Testament. The standard for the good, the right, the just, and the acceptable is nothing less than the person of the Living God. "Be holy because I the Lord your God am holy". While the gods of surrounding nations supposedly indulged in many of the vices of their worshippers, the character of the God of Israel is seen in the prayer of Habakkuk, "Your eyes are too pure to look on evil; you cannot tolerate wrong" (Habakkuk 1:13).

Old Testament Ethics are Internal

They are concerned as much with the internal response as with the outward act. David understood what God wanted even before He would accept any outward sacrifice for David's sin with Bathsheba – "a broken spirit; a broken and contrite heart" (Psalm 51:17; cf. vv. 16 and 18). Repeatedly the prophets lament the fact that Israel tried to substitute outward acts of piety for the necessary inward prerequisite for offering these gifts (Isaiah 1:11-18; Jeremiah 7:21-23; Hosea 6:6; Micah 6:6-8).

Old Testament Ethics are Universal

Old Testament ethics embrace the same standard of righteousness for all the nations of the earth as it did for Israel. "Indeed, long sections and even books of the Old Testament are specifically addressed to the nations at large such as Isaiah 13-23, Jeremiah 45-51, Ezekiel 25-32, Daniel 2 and 7, Amos 1-2, Obadiah, Jonah, and Nahum. At the heart of those messages, often sent by messengers and ambassadors to the foreign nations (e.g., Jeremiah 27:3; 51:61), was God's standard of righteousness. Accordingly, any narrow, chauvinistic, or parochial interpretation of Old Testament ethics that limits its application to a single people in a particular socio-economic setting stands in opposition to the claims of the text" (Kaiser, 11).

Summary

In summary then, Old Testament ethics are concerned with the manner of life that the older covenant prescribes and approves. The ethical contents of the older covenant are not offered in isolation, but are viewed as demands, actions and character that God expects from men and women. This close connection between ethics and theology constitutes one of the distinctive features of the Bible's own set of ethics. Accordingly, what God is in His character, and what He wills in His revelation, defines what is right; conversely it is right, good and acceptable, and satisfying to all because of His own character and will. In contrast to philosophical ethics, which tend to be more abstract and anthropocentric (man-centered), biblical ethics was never considered apart from the religion or theology with which it was connected. It should also be noted, parenthetically, that this manner of life was never intended to be salvific. Romans 4:3 is clear on the matter:

> For what does the Scripture say? "Abraham believed God and it was credited to him as righteousness."

To contend that Old Testament ethics are grounded in a Person is to contend that they are not grounded in our situation. If they are grounded in a Person, if that Person has revealed Himself and His heart to us, then it is indeed possible to know for a fact whether or not a given proposed activity is "right" or "wrong". If they are theistic and indeed joined to a personal knowledge of God, then we are to trust in the Lord and not lean on our own understanding. Our understanding is not to become a source of wisdom. In adopting a teleological approach to the things of God I fear we have become like the Pharisees of old who Jesus chided:

> Mark 7:6 And He said to them, "Rightly did Isaiah prophesy of you hypocrites, as it is written:
> 'This people honors Me with their mouth,
> But their heart is far from Me.
>
> Mark 7:7 'But in vain do they worship Me,
> Teaching as doctrine the precepts of men.'
>
> Mark 7:8 "Neglecting the commandment of God, you hold to the tradition of men."
>
> Mark 7:9 He was also saying to them, "You are experts at set-

ting aside the commandment of God in order to keep your tradition.

NEW TESTAMENT ETHICS ARE ALSO DEONTOLOGICAL

Turning from the Old Testament records to the New Testament, can we rightly assert that the New Testament is just as deontological as the Old Testament in its approach to ethical questions? Again, a brief survey of both Paul's and Jesus' position will confirm the deontological nature of New Testament ethics.

The Apostle Paul

Most of Paul's major epistles first lay down a theological or doctrinal base followed by a hortatory section of moral exhortations. Usually, the more practical section of the epistle is introduced with a favorite word of Paul, "therefore". Of all his epistles, Beach and Niebuhr claim that "next to the Sermon on the Mount no other biblical document has had greater influence on the ethical reflection of the Christian Church than the letter to the Romans" (Maston, 185).

Upon examining the structure of Romans, we discover that chapters 1-11 provide Paul's readers with a doctrinal and theological base for what follows. The hortatory section of the epistle begins with the twelfth chapter. In characteristic form, Paul begins this section with "I appeal to you therefore, brethren, by the mercies of God, to present your bodies as a living sacrifice, holy and acceptable to God, which is your spiritual worship" (Romans 12:1). Four chapters containing one exhortation after another then follow. What is the background of the "therefore"? The background is the previous eleven chapters. What are "the mercies of God" found in those chapters? The first chapters of Romans are without doubt one of the best sources for the underlying and unifying ethical concepts of Paul's thoughts. They read as a listing of the moral qualities of God. He is revealed as righteous (1:17; 3:21, 22, 25), kind, forbearing, and patient (2:4), impartial (2:11), faithful (3:3), truthful (3:7), loving (5:5,8; 8:39), generous (5:15), and merciful (9:15-16; 12:1). Paul was in fact pleading with his readers to present their bodies on the basis of the kind of God they served. Paul's approach is definitely deontological and not teleological.

The Lord Jesus Christ

There is definitely a deontological approach in the teachings of Jesus. Just before His crucifixion, Jesus said to His disciples, "I am the way . . . no one comes to the Father, but by me" (John 14:6). What was He saying? He is neither simply pointing out the way, nor is He the guide to or along the way. To the contrary, He is the way. "This means, among other things, that Christian morality is the natural expression or outgrowth of one's relation to the One, who is the way. This outgrowth is so natural that it becomes a proof of the relationship." (Maston, 233-234)

Closely related and supplementary to the above quote by Jesus is John's exhortation found in I John: 'He who says He abides in Him ought to walk in the same way in which He walked' (I John 2:6). Christ is not only the way to the Father; He is also the way of the Father for those who are His. His disciples ought to walk in that way. "Ought" becomes the key word of John's ethics. It carries the idea of an obligation or a debt. To walk in the way of the Lord means to walk in fellowship with Him, which in turn means to walk in the light, in righteousness, and in love. One of John's three tests for genuine faith (1 John) is whether or not the believer exhibits in his life these and other qualities that belong to the character of God as revealed in His Son. In similar fashion to the Old Testament, the standard of conduct for the child of God in I John is not in a code, but in a Person. That Person has given commandments, and to know Him and to walk in His way entails obedience to those commandments.

Summary Thoughts

I have gone to great lengths to demonstrate the biblical basis for a deontological approach to moral theory today. Some of you, though, may still be asking, "So what? Does it really matter? Why should I embrace it? Why should I or my church worry about thinking either teleologically or deontologically?"

As cell churches, we assert that what we are believing and doing is rooted and grounded in the Scriptures. I question the reality of that assertion at its most basic level. I think too many of our people really feel like my former church member who finally blurted out to me one day, "I don't care if it is in the Bible! Its not Baptist!" I could paraphrase that thinking a hundred different ways. "I don't care if it is in the Bible! Its not our tradition! Its not what our denomination holds to! Its not what I think! Its not what I'm feeling! Its not what I want!" The most common assertion is this one, "Its not what works!" Its not what works? How teleological can we get? No matter that God said it. No matter that it is clear in the Scriptures. Its not what works! After all, aren't we after what will work, what will grow the church large, what will bring us success? How many pastors and churches in America over the last ten years have embarked upon the cell church journey, only to turn back along the way because it did not yield the immediate results they thought would quickly come? Now the cry is heard, "We tried it and it didn't work!", which translated is, "We began the journey, it was hard, we did not have immediate results, so we quit!" Why do we do what we do? Why do we not do what we don't do? The answer should start with something like , "Because the Bible says...", or "Because God's Word teaches...", etc. "Impossible!", you say? "Unrealistic!", you say? Our African brothers and sisters have learned to live that way.

0-150,000 IN TWENTY-FIVE YEARS: A DEONTOLOGICAL APPROACH

In September of 1975, in an area called Sogefiha in the neighborhood of Yopougon-Gare, a suburb of Abidjan, Cote d'Ivoire, the work we today recognize as *Eglise Protestante Baptiste Oeuvres et Mission Internationale* was begun as a prayer cell in the living room of Dion Robert. That first prayer cell consisted of just three people: Dion, his wife Helene and their daughter Sympathie. On Sunday the 9th of November in two apartments that were put together at No. 2925 and 2926, Dion had his first service. From that rather inauspicious beginning in September of 1975, the church today numbers over 150,000 members, comprising over 18,000 house churches worldwide (14,000 adult and 4,000 children), and organized into 685 local churches (52 in the city of Abidjan alone), served by 293 full time missionaries.

Dion Robert and the leadership of EPBOM have clearly operated from and communicated a deontological biblical ethic. They consider the Bible as normative for life and practice. Recall once again Kaiser's assertion that "It is an agreed state of the discipline of Christian ethics in this century that the nature and content of morality is not to be equated with any formulation of the divine will supposedly found in biblical commandments, principles, precepts, or examples" (40). In contradistinction, EPBOM has equated the divine will with

Chapter 2 ☞ *Prepare the Ethical Base*

those biblical commandments, principles and precepts found in the Bible.

Rather than moving away from a deontological type of moral theory toward a teleological theory, the leadership of EPBOM has chosen to accept and teach that the rightness or wrongness of an action or rule is not contingent on its results, but is instead directly related to specific commands that have been issued by God. God is seen as setting forth certain demands, actions and character that He expects from men and women who accept Christ. For EPBOM's leadership, what God is in His character and what He wills in His revelation defines what is right.

This is then communicated to converts won to Christ. The leadership teaches new converts to move directly toward Christian ethics from the laws and principles of the Bible. Their members are expected to make concrete ethical decisions by moving from the general imperatives of the law of God to specific application within their own personal situations. For new converts, the Bible early on becomes the sole source of ethical wisdom.

Contrary to the majority of Christian ethicists today, scripture is viewed at EPBOM as the only source supplying the content for both ethical character and decision making. Consider the personal testimony of Boka Faustin. When he first came to EPBOM, he was surprised that a Christian could have a Bible. Having been given a Bible, he was told that it was the Word of God contained in a book. Regarding the Bible, Boka states unequivocally, "If we believe that God wrote it, then it is God who speaks to us. He didn't speak to us through an audible voice, but He speaks to us through the Word of God. I understand the value of the Word of God. I understand through the Word of God that God can speak to me. So, if there is a decision to make, it is through what I have read."

When Boka reads, for example, that if someone confesses his sin, then he will have mercy, he accepts that and believes that in confessing and leaving his sin he will have mercy. Today, Boka overseas the development of the House Church Department. Everyone he trains he brings to understand the value of the Word of God. When Dr. Dion is teaching them in the Spirit, Boka does not see him as a man speaking, but as God speaking through His Word. That, Boka contends, is what has made the church strong. When Dion teaches, they know that it comes from the Bible and so they practice it.

Upon receiving Christ, the new believer receives six months of intensive instruction prior to being baptized. Following baptism, this instruction continues for an additional six months prior to being released into corporate body ministry. Weekly instruction during these first six months of pre-baptismal instruction includes a study of Dion's book, *So You're Born Again*, subtitled, "Base Bible Studies for a Normal Christian Life"! The candidate is straightway instructed as to the place the Bible must hold in his life:

> The goal of this study is to help the new Christian to understand that regardless of his life there are regulations by teachings contained in the book in which is entitled "The BIBLE". Outside of God, man walks and is led according to his vanity and his thoughts because his intelligence is obscure. While being a stranger to the life of God and hardening his heart and largely his spirit, he wastes his life by sin. Through this study on the Bible, the candidate for baptism discovers that only obedience and the putting in practice the biblical teaching makes him a new creature, a mature man and a boiling Christian. It tries to help the new convert to understand that regardless for him, it not profitable to live contrary to the teaching of the Bible. He must make the Bible, at the end of the course, the ideal guide for the rest of his life. (8)

This initial instruction is then followed by an explanation as to what the Bible really is:

> The Bible is the Word of God written down into a 'book'. It is the only infallible guide for man. It is the only book of the world that instructs in a very certain manner, honestly and worthily on the will and the plan of God for each human being. The Bible contains the message of God for all times. (8)

Neither is the authorship of this book left to doubt or question. Who is the author of the Bible?

> The Lord, the Living God, Creator of the heavens and the earth is the author of this precious book. God exposed to man His will and the way he must follow to be happy. God proposes the true way which is led by His full Knowledge: what God wants, what He hates; what He loves and what He loathes; what to do for Him to be agreeable, comes from His grace and His bless-

> ings. All of this was revealed to man by our Father and was conserved in this book we call the Bible. (9)

The authoritative nature of the Bible and the consequences of obedience to it are driven home to the baptismal candidate from the very start of his study. "The authority of the Bible is made by the Word of God, the Almighty, the Creator. It is the Word and the Will of Him who give us movement and being, and even respiration. It emanates God entirely and expresses His thoughts." (Born Again, 10)

Since God is the authoritative author, no one else has the authority to alter the Bible. The Word of God has authority over all the angels. No angel, with whatever power it has, can change any of the teachings of the Bible. "But even if we or an angel from heaven should preach a gospel other than the one we preached to you, let him be eternally condemned!" (Galatians 1:8) As the angels are limited in power, so man has absolutely no power to modify the Word of God. Those that do will bring as curse upon themselves. (Rev. 22:18-19)

EPBOM teaches that "many men pretend to be Christians but their behavior demonstrates the contrary. Their testimony of living is opposed to true faith and the Word of God. Those kinds of people can not experience the transformation and the newness of life that is produced profoundly by the Word of God in all obedient believers." (Born Again, 11)

During their second period of instruction, newly baptized believers are collectively taught, among other things, the manual, *Working According to the Model*. Dion spends considerable time in the manual calling for a reformation and restoration by the church in her way of teaching and proclaiming Christ. Six-to nine-month-old new believers are taught regarding the Word of God and its place and authority in their life and that:

> The biggest obstacle that faces the Church of Jesus Christ in our day is the alteration or the falsification of the Word of God. Instead of placing themselves under the influence and authority of the Bible, to listen to it, to receive and practice it, the people in the church adopt the dangerous and demonic attitude of arranging, correcting and adapting the message of God to this present century. This embezzlement has led to many so-called "reviewed or revised versions" as if God who talked through the prophets had been mistaken somewhere in His message or

even more it is as if the prophets and the apostles had been mistaken in the transcription of the divine message. Those false doctors forget that theology, a philosophical science on God and on their gods, cannot supplant God Himself or His Word. (Working, 32)

New believers are additionally instructed how "men have used their own feelings, their own personal experiences, judgement and reasoning, the opportunity and culture as norms of interpretation of the divine message. Men also placed themselves above the authority of the Bible, pretending to be 'masters' of the Word witnessing to the revelation of God. The state of the Church, which is more and more apostate in our day, is the consequence of this situation." It is out of this deontological biblical ethic that the seven core values of *Eglise Protestante Baptiste Oeuvres et Mission Internationale* arise.

WHAT IN THE WORLD HAVE WE TAUGHT THEM?

In preparing the way of the Lord, a cell church's ethical system must be linked and identified with a biblical ethic that is deontological. We have seen how EPBOM functions out of a deontological ethical base. Earlier I alleged that, for the most part, American cell churches do not operate from a deontological approach to ethics. Is it fair to state that the majority of American Christians are not deontological in their understanding and practice of moral theory? In framing your own answer, consider the following statistics researched by the Barna Research Group and available on their web site at http://www.barna.org.

- 69% of Baptists, 63% of non-mainline attendees, 36% of mainline attendees, and 19% of Catholics believe strongly that the Bible is totally accurate. (1999)

- 13% of born again Christians disagree that "the Bible is totally accurate in all of its teachings." (2000)

- A majority of all born again Christians reject the existence of the Holy Spirit (55%). (1997)

Chapter 2 ☛ *Prepare the Ethical Base*

- 45% of born again Christians deny Satan's existence. (1999)

- 7 out of 10 Catholics (70%) say the devil is non-existent. 62% of Protestant mainline church attendees, 49% of Protestant non-mainline church attendees, and 43% of Baptists also agree that Satan is only a symbol of evil. (1999)

- 39% of Americans say that Jesus Christ was crucified, but He never had a physical resurrection. Nearly the same proportion of born again Christians (35%) embrace this thinking. (1997)

- One out of every five adults (18%) contend that one of the renowned portions of the Bible - the Ten Commandments - is not relevant for people living today. (1992)

What in the world have we been teaching the people in our churches? Is the following news report really surprising?

> James Vicini WASHINGTON (Reuters) - The U.S. Supreme Court on Tuesday allowed the removal of a granite monument of the Ten Commandments from the front of an Indiana city hall. This happened on Tuesday, May 29, 2001, which happens to be Sivan 7, or the second day of Shavuot on the modern Jewish calendar. Ironically, Shavuot celebrates the GIVING of the Ten Commandments by God to Moses, "the ministration of death, written and engraven in stones" (2 Corinthians 3:7), when 3,000 died (Exodus 32:28). It is also the same as the Day of Pentecost, when 3,000 people were given life (Acts 2:41). On Shavout, God giveth, and on the same day, the U.S. Supreme Court taketh away.

I believe you will agree that I am not overstating the case when I contend that the majority of American Christians are not deontological in their understanding and practice of moral theory. How did this travesty come about? How did our thinking change? What thinking changed? What in the world have we been teaching the average person in the pew? Perhaps more appropriately we may need to rephrase the question, "What has the world been teaching the average person in the pew?" Alas, the average person in the pew in America has opted out of a theistic worldview. If we do not address their forsaking of that theistic world view, we have little to no hope of bringing them back to a deontological biblical ethical approach to life. Furthermore, if our view of life is not anchored in the Word of God, what point is there in attempting to change the structure of our churches to cells?

Worldviews in Conflict

What do I mean when I speak of a "worldview"? A worldview can be thought of as the key to unlocking the universe. In a sense, it is the lens of our glasses through which we see the world. A credible worldview will provide answers for life's ultimate questions of purpose, design, relationship and the future. In other words, they seek to answer the following:

1. Is there purpose to life? If so, what is the purpose? (This corresponds to the philosophical question of *ontology*.)

2. What is the design of the universe? If there is design, how do I come to understand it? (This corresponds to the philosophical question of *epistemology*.)

3. How does my life relate to other people, history, and to the universe?(This corresponds to the philosophical question of *axiology*.)

4. Where is history going? Is there a goal? Is there an end? (This corresponds to the philosophical question of *teleology*.)

Howard Snyder (EarthCurrents, 153) notes "...a half-dozen emerging worldviews are changing the way we see the world. Earth is now a marketplace of competing worldviews. The global shopping mall offers not only goods and services but also quite different views of reality." If our people are to adopt a biblical ethical system, their worldview and concept of reality must also be biblical. Unfortunately, as American Christians, we are affected by conflicting worldviews more than we realize. The result is inner turmoil and inconsistent living. I would like to briefly survey two of the conflicting worldviews that constantly tear at the fabric of our being and adversely affect our life for Christ.

Global Economics: Pragmatic Worldview

Much of America lives out of a global economic pragmatic worldview. It has come to shape our thinking. It has become the lenses through which we look at life. It has sought to provide answers to the fundamental questions of life that each of us struggle to discover. Briefly examine with me what this worldview teaches, then let us examine its affect upon the church.

Question #1: Is there Purpose to Life?

We all struggle with the meaning of life. Does life really have a purpose? The economic worldview views the purpose of life as providing a prosperous existence for all people and nations. Good economics will make art and ethics possible. Only as the economic problems of humanity are solved can people reach their full potential. What is "good" is economic well-being.

To what degree have we been affected by this thought pattern? Allow me to ask this question. What is the goal of the average American Christian man? Is it not to provide economically and financially for his family? Is not the spiritual responsibility too often relegated to the woman because the man is "too busy"? Busy, I ask, doing what? Why, making a living, of course! Do not men strive to reach their full potential in their professions? Rarely is a man's profession in any way sacrificed for his spiritual growth. Have we not also defined the "good" life as being economically well off? We may argue that our job or profession is not the ultimate goal, but what we seek betrays our argument. How often do we lower our standard of living so as to have more time for Kingdom living? How often now do we contend that a married couple must both work "just to survive" economically?

What has happened to the words of Jesus recorded by Matthew in chapter six of his "Good News"? Perhaps they just supply a source of images (hermeneutical stance #3). Perhaps they simply provide us with a general orientation towards economic decisions (hermeneutical stance #1). Perhaps we simply cannot move from that Scripture to a specific application within our present economic situation (hermeneutical stance #4). Too bad they no longer apply!

> Matt. 6:24 "No one can serve two masters; for either he will hate the one and love the other, or he will be devoted to one and despise the other. You cannot serve God and wealth.
>
> Matt. 6:25 "For this reason I say to you, do not be worried about your life, as to what you will eat or what you will drink; nor for your body, as to what you will put on. Is not life more than food, and the body more than clothing?
>
> Matt. 6:26 "Look at the birds of the air, that they do not sow, nor reap nor gather into barns, and yet your heavenly Father feeds them. Are you not worth much more than they?
>
> Matt. 6:27 "And who of you by being worried can add a single hour to his life?
>
> Matt. 6:28 "And why are you worried about clothing? Observe how the lilies of the field grow; they do not toil nor do they spin,
>
> Matt. 6:29 yet I say to you that not even Solomon in all his glory clothed himself like one of these.
>
> Matt. 6:30 "But if God so clothes the grass of the field, which is alive today and tomorrow is thrown into the furnace, will He not much more clothe you? You of little faith!
>
> Matt. 6:31 "Do not worry then, saying, 'What will we eat?' or 'What will we drink?' or 'What will we wear for clothing?'
>
> Matt. 6:32 "For the Gentiles eagerly seek all these things; for your heavenly Father knows that you need all these things.

Chapter 2 ☛ *Prepare the Ethical Base*

Matt. 6:33 "But seek first His kingdom and His righteousness, and all these things will be added to you.

Matt. 6:34 "So do not worry about tomorrow; for tomorrow will care for itself. Each day has enough trouble of its own.

Question #2: What is the Design of the Universe?

A worldview also provides an interpretation for the design of the universe. Is there a design, a master plan? How can I come to know it? The global economic pragmatic worldview would contend that the design of the universe is not a given. It must be built or discovered. When that design is ultimately discovered, it will prove to be fundamentally economic. The destiny of nations and individuals is largely economically determined. Economic structures must be developed to lift the impoverished out of their misery to well-being. Ultimately, since no man is an island, much less a nation being an island unto itself, economics means global economics. The prosperity of any one sector depends upon the prosperity of the whole.

Are we immune from this infectious thinking? The church today engages in massive social programs, but few genuine man-to-man evangelistic endeavors. Our destiny and service in church is often economically determined. We move from community to community for better employment and a higher standard of living. Rarely is the church and ministry we leave a factor in our decision. After all, there are other churches "out there" that we can join. How many have been about to enter into service or about to be set apart as an elder when economic opportunity calls and we answer, "Here am I. Send me!"

Question #3: How does My Life Relate to Others?

Worldviews attempt to show us how our lives relate to others, to the universe, and even to history. The particular worldview under discussion here would have us believe that human relationships are at base, economic. In fact, all history is economic history. All life is related economically. Marriage, family, the city, the nation, all is economically interdependent.

What of the church in America? Have we bought into that understanding of life and history? Well, I am afraid that economics too often drive the Christian family. We noted earlier that we live in a society where two incomes are considered "essential". Our work and careers are often discovered to interfere with the healthy development of parent-child relationships. Yet, too frequently, we continue to work anyway. We do not stop to consider that we are sacrificing relationship with our children on the altar of economic desire. We continue to relate to one another based upon economic levels of achievement, job titles, and neighborhoods. "White collar or blue collar?" "Upper, middle, or lower class?" "Yuppie neighborhood or slum?" "Do you own your own home or rent?" "What do you do for a living?" What of the poor that God finds so important? They are the socially and economically disadvantaged. Our goal too often is to raise their standard of living and education, not their relationship with Christ.

Question #4: Where is History Going?

Where is history going? Is there a goal, an end? Worldviews answer this final question also. The global economic pragmatic worldview would have us believe it is an economic matter. The agenda must be to build a global order that allows for the hopes and dreams of people to find fulfillment in the present. Questions of an afterlife are relegated to the fields of religion and philosophy. The goal of history is material well-being and global prosperity.

What of the church in America? What does the future hold for the American Christian? "Material well being", you say? How many of our most spiritual saints are on an economic quest for the holy grail of secure retirement, sufficient IRAs, Social Security benefits and the "good life"? Those who do not prepare for their economic future are thought "foolish". Don't tell me the goal of the majority of American Christians is not economic well being and prosperity.

Worldviews in Conflict

Can we really expect the church to adopt a deontological ethical system while it views life through the portal of a global economic pragmatic worldview? I think not. Consider the rich ruler's inner struggle. Following Jesus conflicted with his economic worldview!

> Luke 18:19 And Jesus said to him, "Why do you call Me good? No one is good except God alone.

Chapter 2 ☛ *Prepare the Ethical Base*

> Luke 18:20 "You know the commandments, 'Do not commit adultery, do not murder, do not steal, do not bear false witness, honor your father and mother.'"
>
> Luke 18:21 And he said, "All these things I have kept from my youth."
>
> Luke 18:22 When Jesus heard this, He said to him, "One thing you still lack; sell all that you possess and distribute it to the poor, and you shall have treasure in heaven; and come, follow Me."
>
> Luke 18:23 But when he had heard these things, he became very sad, for he was extremely rich.
>
> Luke 18:24 And Jesus looked at him and said, "How hard it is for those who are wealthy to enter the kingdom of God!
>
> Luke 18:25 "For it is easier for a camel to go through the eye of a needle than for a rich man to enter the kingdom of God."

Postmodern Worldview

To understand the postmodern worldview, it we would be well advised to look at the transition from premodern to postmodern thinking. Then we will more adequately be able to identify inroads into the church's thinking. I would like to quote at this point again from Howard Snyder (217-218):

> The premodern worldview affirmed a fixed, unchanging, eternal order that was reflected in all human life, including the structures of society. Life had meaning precisely as a reflection of this unchanging order, however that order was specifically conceived. Fundamental truth was real and unquestioned. History reflected the verities of the eternal.
>
> The modern worldview was grounded in Renaissance, Reformation, and Enlightenment. It rejected much of the premodern perspective, but not all. Modernity was full of ideas of

progress, fresh discoveries, and the making of a new world based in large measure on human achievement...Modernity included such diverse and conflicting movements as rationalism, romanticism, and surrealism.

The postmodern worldview represents the triumph of the subjective, the ephemeral, and the fragmentary over the unchanging and the universal. It rejects the tension inherent in modernism as both impossible and destructive. Postmodernity signals the triumph of the contingent, the transitory, and the ironic.

As a worldview, postmodernism exhibits a number of characteristics, many of which can be easily observed in the thinking of the 21st century American church.

First, postmodernism "is a rejection of universal or totalizing perspectives, of theories or viewpoints that claim to put everything together in a coherent whole" (Snyder, 221). Recall for a moment once again the hermeneutical stances presented earlier. Each of them in their own way reject the unifying nature of the Scriptures in favor of a relativistic fragmentary understanding of biblical ethics. Together they proclaim that there is not a possibility of a coherent biblical system of ethics. They vie for a separate and limited understanding. This is an outgrowth of a postmodern world view.

Second, postmodernism's focus is on the individual and the particular. Rejecting a holistic view, it considers the individual person, motif, artifact, or subculture as the proper focus of attention. "The idea that all groups have a right to speak for themselves, in their own voice, and have that voice accepted as authentic and legitimate is essential to the pluralistic stance of postmodernism," notes Harvey (48). Has the church evidenced this second characteristic of a postmodern worldview? Judging by the wire services, the church applauded the memorial service in Washington DC following the September 11, 2001 destruction of the World Trade Center, a service which gave equal voice to Jew, Muslim, and Christian. Pluralism ruled the day! Each conflicting voice must now be accepted as authentic and legitimate. Gone is the call to repentance and faith in the Lord Jesus Christ. Others must not be offended. How narrow to believe there is only one way to God!" How deceived we have become!

Third, reality for the postmodern is what they experience and feel, particularly at this moment. Everything else is secondary. "Disney World and Elvisland become prime icons of postmodernity. The artifact is created to pro-

Chapter 2 ☛ Prepare the Ethical Base

vide private thrills to the consumers and hard cash to the investors (Snyder, 221). Snyder concludes that:

> Postmodernism is partly a response to globalization and the sense of living in a world of great diversity and pluralism. When Rome, London, Washington, or Moscow and Beijing are no longer the center of the world–when the world is centerless, with diverse points of action, initiative, and influence–the inevitable result seems to be pluralism, relativism, and the collapse of totalizing ideologies and empires. (230)

What can be said of our local churches? Is there a unifying vision that integrates all that is done together into a comprehensive whole? Or, has the church become a collage of programs giving expression to individual voices and designs, each valuable in and of itself? Are our services designed to affect life, or make people feel good? How many Christians move from church to church because "they just don't feel good any more when they leave the services"? How many have made music and worship and the attending feelings the goal, rather than the medium through which they encounter Christ? Christian hedonism becomes pervasive when what we feel is determined to be reality. Paul warned Timothy that in the last days men would become lovers of pleasure (hedonism) rather than lovers of God. Isn't that what we are seeing in too many of our churches across America?

WHO IS LEADING THE WAY?

The world in which we find ourselves living is clearly a teleological world. The ends, we are informed, actually do justify the means. I noted earlier the current stem cell research debate. What is important are the results. "Be realistic," we are told, "Such research may cure what are now incurable diseases, or at least greatly advance our understanding toward such cures!" So, the ends make it permissible to use the unborn for scientific research, if such study will yield highly profitable results. In the area of economics, everyone knows you should not live beyond your income level. It is financial suicide. So, I inquire, why are the vast majority of Americans so highly leveraged? The explanation is easy. What we want today but cannot afford justifies indebtedness far into tomorrow in order to obtain it. Where have we learned such a teleological approach to life? From our uncle, of course. Uncle Sam has lived this way for the better part of a century.

"This may be the situation in the world, but not the church!" you argue. Isn't it now? Is it only non-Christian America that is in bondage to debt? Did not the Apostle Paul write (Romans 13:8), "Owe nothing to anyone except to love one another; for he who loves his neighbor has fulfilled the law". Can we deny our guilt of giving assent with our understanding to a deontological approach to debt (Romans 13:8) while at the same time living teleologically (But I really need that, now!)? Or, consider this. How many church planters are given one, two, maybe three years to "demonstrate results", or their funding is pulled? That is not a teleological approach? Whatever happened to the issue of the will of God? How many churches, even cell churches, still evaluate their health by the unholy trinity of buildings, budgets, and baptisms? Admittedly, in our case as cell churches, the buildings have often been redefined as homes and cell groups. Make no mistake, healthy churches do grow, but growing churches may or may not be healthy! Author and reader alike know of many unhealthy churches that have grown through charismatic leadership, massive programmatic offerings, or even downright manipulation.

As church leaders in America, are we not guilty of evaluating success and failure by the results of one's ministry? Jeremiah's success was minimal at best. Ezekiel was told he was being sent to a rebellious people (Ezekiel 2:1-7), "to them who should listen to you; yet the house of Israel will not be willing to listen to you, since they are not willing to listen to Me. Surely the whole house of Israel is stubborn and obstinate (Ezekiel 3:6-7). Using the same standards of measurement we use today, we would have to conclude that Jesus' three and a half years of ministry was a failure, that He was "out of the will of God!" After all, "the proof is in the pudding". Look at His results prior to the resurrection and coming of the Spirit.

Does the church actually have a worldview that can successfully compete in the present marketplace of competing worldviews? With so many views of reality hawking their wares, does the church really have THE ANSWER? if so, then why are we so apologetic in our proclamation and bend over backwards to be "fair" to alternate view and answers? What has happened that we avoid proclaiming throughout our country today, "Thus saith the Lord!"?

Chapter 2 ☛ *Prepare the Ethical Base*

RANGERS LEAD THE WAY

"Rangers lead the way" is the cry of the U.S. Army Rangers. Read carefully below their creed:

> Recognizing that I volunteered as a Ranger, fully knowing the hazards of my chosen profession, I will always endeavor to uphold the prestige, honor, and high esprit de corps of my Ranger Regiment.
>
> Acknowledging the fact that a Ranger is a more elite soldier who arrives at the cutting edge of battle by land, sea, or air, I accept the fact that as a Ranger my country expects me to move farther, faster and fight harder than any other soldier.
>
> Never shall I fail my comrades. I will always keep myself mentally alert, physically strong and morally straight and I will shoulder more than my share of the task whatever it may be. One-hundred-percent and then some.
>
> Gallantly will I show the world that I am a specially selected and well-trained soldier. My courtesy to superior officers, neatness of dress and care of equipment shall set the example for others to follow.
>
> Energetically will I meet the enemies of my country. I shall defeat them on the field of battle for I am better trained and will fight with all my might. Surrender is not a Ranger word. I will never leave a fallen comrade to fall into the hands of the enemy and under no circumstances will I ever embarrass my country.
>
> Readily will I display the intestinal fortitude required to fight on to the Ranger objective and complete the mission though I be the lone survivor.

The Ranger creed is deontological. One example should demonstrate that fact. "I will never leave a fallen comrade to fall into the hands of the enemy". Why did nineteen Rangers and Special Forces die in Somalia in 1993? During an insertion into enemy territory in Mogadishu, Somalia, a Blackhawk helicopter went down. "I will never leave a fallen comrade to fall into the hands of the enemy". Our teleological approach to life would say that the needs of the many out weigh the needs of the few. To sacrifice more men to retrieve the bodies of fallen comrades would be pointless. The potential results do not justify the risk in sending additional Rangers to the crash scene. So, why was it done? Why would Rangers go back in? "I will never leave a fallen comrade to fall into the hands of the enemy". It was, simply speaking, the right thing to do! Doing what is right for a fallen comrade, even one already dead, outweighs the potential loss of my own life! Rangers lead the way!

THE CHURCH MUST LEAD THE WAY!

It is time for the Church to assume her rightful position and to lead the way!

Is it possible for American cell churches to experience the move of God similar to that which EPBOM has experienced over the last twenty-five years? The answer is a resounding, but qualified, "Yes!" Yes, but only if we purge out of our thinking the economic and postmodern worldviews that have crippled us. Yes, if we embrace once more a biblical theistic worldview. Yes, if we once more link Christian ethics with biblical ethics. Yes, if we return to a deontological moral theory and practice of life and forsake the teleological ethical approach we have embraced whereby the results determine our course of action. Kaiser's words bare repeating at this point. "There just are no two ways about it; the church, if she is to continue to be Christ's church, must come to terms with the Scriptures to which he pointed and affirmed 'these are the Scriptures that testify about me' (John 5:39), 'Scripture cannot be broken' (John 10:35), and not the smallest letter, nor the least stroke of the pen, will by any means disappear from the Law until everything is accomplished' (Matthew 5:18). To reject them or the sense in which they were intended is ultimately to reject him as Lord of His church" (57). We will never grow as long as we "reject him as Lord of His church".

The Church's ethical system must be prepared if the Lord Jesus Christ is to reign as the Lord of the Church in the 21st century! The Lord is returning for His Bride! The Lord is returning to judge this world! It is imperative to prepare the way of the Lord. Church, prepare the way! Church, lead the way!

Chapter 2 ☞ *Prepare the Ethical Base*

REFLECTIONS

> **Lev. 19:2 "Speak to all the congregation of the sons of Israel and say to them, 'You shall be holy, for I the LORD your God am holy.**

1. Should Christian Ethics be identified with Biblical Ethics? Why or why not?

2. How is the Bible "normative" for you? What hermeneutical approach do you take?

3. Has your approach to life been more Deontological or Teleological? Site examples.

        a). _____

        b). _____

        c). _____

4. As you re-examine the four questions noted on page 57, site at least three ways your own thinking has been colored by what has been described as the Global Economic Pragmatic Worldview.

   a). _____

   b). _____

   c). _____

List at least three ways you see the thinking of your church members (leaders) infected by the Global Economic Pragmatic Worldview.

   a). _____

   b). _____

   c). _____

5. As you re-examine the four questions noted on page 57, site at least three ways your own thinking been colored by what has been described as the Postmodern Worldview?

   a). _____

   b). _____

   c). _____

Chapter 2 ☞ Prepare the Ethical Base

List at least three ways you see the thinking of your church members (leaders) infected by the Postmodern Worldview.

a). _____

b). _____

c). _____

6. Is it truly possible to change the worldview of your members (leaders)? How can such a monumental undertaking be accomplished? (Hint: The answers lie in the next chapter!)

PHASE 1

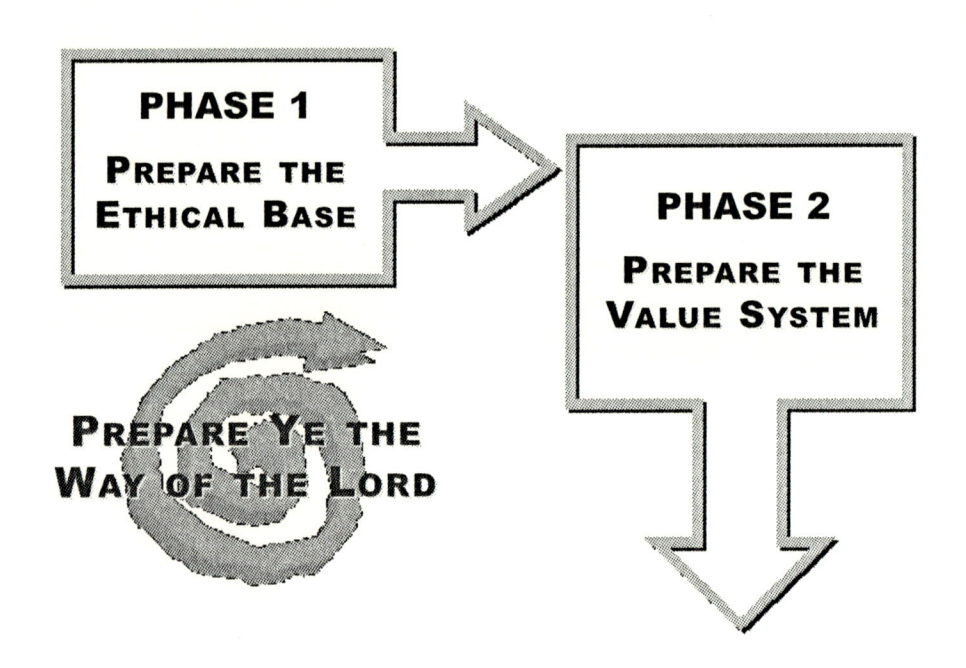

PREPARE THE ETHICAL BASE

PHASE 2

PREPARE THE VALUE SYSTEM

PREPARE YE THE WAY OF THE LORD

3
PREPARE THE VALUE SYSTEM

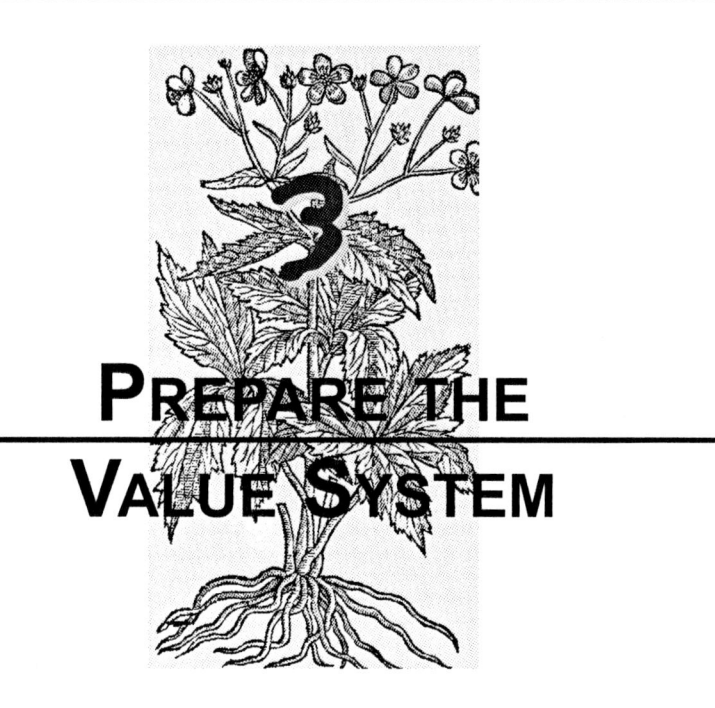

OBSERVE HOW THE LILIES OF THE FIELD GROW; THEY DO NOT TOIL NOR DO THEY SPIN. MATTHEW 6:28

Chapter 3 ☞ *Prepare the Value System*

INTRODUCTION

Observe how the lilies of the field grow. Most of us read that Scripture as an instruction to look at the lilies of the field and notice how beautiful they are. That is not the command. We are to observe *how* they *grow*. We are to examine (κρινα) growth factors, developmental factors, and understand the *how* of that development. How do lilies grow? There are two dimensions to a lilly's growth. There is that dimension which is above ground that we see. However, that dimension of growth, the dimension we see, only comes later. The growth of a lily does not begin aboveground. It begins in the heart of the earth. Then there is that dimension of reality that is underground that we do not see. What causes the lilies to grow? It is the underground dimension that initiates growth. Before the lilies break forth into sight, God has accomplished His design in the unseen realm. The seed germinates. Life springs forth. Root systems are developed. The lily grows strong until it breaks forth from its underground incubator into the light of day. Then, the beauty of the lily is seen above ground. However, the source of that beauty remains underground.

We look around and see the beauty of a cell church like *Eglise Protestante Baptiste Oeuvres et Mission Internationale* in Abidjan, Cote d'Ivoire, or like that of *International Charismatic Mission* in Bogota, Columbia, or of *Yoido Full Gospel Church* in Seoul, Korea. What we fail to observe are the underground realities that germinate in the beauty we so admire and wish to emulate. In our enthusiasm and zeal to achieve a similar beauty, we fail to observe, to discern, to correctly judge their underground realities. The lily develops underground step by step, stage by stage. The cell church, too, develops step by step, stage by stage. God's ethical base must be first established, or development will go awry. From out of the ethical base must be developed that set of core values that will drive the cell-church-to-be. In the final analysis, a cell church is a values-driven church. For this to occur, cell church leadership must be values-driven leadership.

So, we turn our attention now to the development of core values and what it means to become a values-driven cell church. The following chapter will provide the reader an actual illustration from the life of *Eglise Protestante Baptiste Oeuvres et Mission Internationale*.

WHAT IS A VALUE?

When I say the word *value*, what comes to mind? The very word brings to our mind various images. Each of us carry with us our own definitions. We need, however, to all be playing on the same field and off of the same page. So then, let's begin our discussion of values by agreeing as to what we mean. Before attempting to define what a value is, it would be exceedingly helpful to first define what a value is not. Unfortunately, there are a number of terms that are bantered about as being almost synonymous with the meaning of *value*, such terms as vision, principles, strategies, and doctrinal statements.

Values are Not the Same as Vision

As a professor, an early assignment requires the student to clearly articulating his or her personal set of core values. Over the years the students have found this to be a challenging experience. In their responses, I am constantly receiving from them "values statements" that are in reality "vision statements". A few examples will illustrate the problem and help clarify the difference. Although originally submitted as value statements, both statements below are in reality vision statements.

- **All Members Ministering**—Everyone faithfully serving the Lord according to the way each is uniquely shaped for ministry by the Lord and uniquely equipped for service by the leadership.

- **Disciplines for Spiritual Growth**—Growing in our relationship with Jesus and developing Godly character through practicing personal Bible Study, prayer, repentance and other spiritual disciplines.

The first statement paints a mental picture of what a perceived tomorrow will look like, while the second statement is focused on where the church is heading in the future and the vehicles it will use to arrive at its destination.

A vision statement is a directional statement. Vision always clarifies the destination. It is much like a telescope that brings the destination, still yet on the distant horizon, into clearer view. A vision statement will focus the church's direction. Vision statements announce to all who are around where we are going. Because vision is bound up with questions of destination, vision is a focus on the future. It is a mental picture of what tomorrow looks like, of what the church prefers the future to be like.

Core values, on the other hand, are what propel the church toward its destination. Values drive the ministry of the church. Values supply the reasons behind the vision, behind the destination. Why are we going there? They supply reasons for why we do what we do; why we are going where we are going. All churches will have core values, but not all churches will have a vision. Values come before and actually determine our actions. To understand the "why" of a church's actions, we uncover its values. Values do not focus on the future, but they look to the present or the past. A church's present values may or not be its present values. For one reason or another, a core value may have been lost or replaced. The church must be built on the values that people already embrace. It is not feasible to build a church on values you hope may be embraced in the future. This is a critical point for both church planters and transitioning pastors.

Too many transitioning pastors hope to institute the cell structure and bring the church along to adopt it. Structures are altered before values are changed, often with catastrophic results. On the other hand, when values are altered first, structures and lifestyle follow with minimal resistance. We'll talk later about how to change the values of those in transition. Church planters have the unique opportunity to establish from the outset the values upon which the future church will be built. If this is done, values being clearly stated, then those joining the movement will then be those who have experienced a values paradigm shift. EPBOM in Abidjan has done a masterful job at this and as a direct result the church has experienced exceptionally rapid and continual growth.

Values are Not the Same as Principles

The following statement was submitted by one of my students as a values statement. It is in reality a principle.

- **Education**: I have devoted a lot of time and energy into learning, having never stopped going to school since I was five years old. I view it as essential for shaping and mold-ing my ability to think and solve problems. I view it as the Scriptural fulfillment of Prov. 2:2 in my life as directed by God to gain knowledge, wisdom, and understanding.

You may have noted that education in this context is the means to an end, the enhanced ability to think and solve problems. Education is not the end in itself. It can be reduced to a more basic value. Additionally, education as articulated here may also be thought of as a strategy answering the question "How are we going to shape and mold my ability to think and solve problems?".

By way of contrast, principles are fundamental truths. Principles are obtained by abstraction and serve as general guidelines for human conduct, becoming individualized in the concrete situations of our life. Principles often serve as the means to an end. If perseverance in our children is the end we desire, then a biblical principle that can serve as a general guideline for helping us rear our son to that end might be Proverbs 22:6: "Train up a child in the way he should go, Even when he is old he will not depart from it." In contrast to principles, values will provide the foundation on which the principles are based. In the case above, the core value is perseverance.

Values are Not the Same as Strategies

While vision sets the direction for the future and answers the questions, "What are we doing?" and "Where are we going?", strategies answer the question, "How are we going to do it?" A strategy will articulate the plan by which we will attempt to accomplish our vision.

Again, by contrast, values answer the question, "Why?" Values ask of vision, "Why are we heading there?" Values ask of strategies, "Why are we doing what we are doing?" "Why are we choosing this road toward that destination and not another road?" "Why are we implementing this plan, and not another plan?"

Below is one more submission of a value that in actuality is not a value, but a strategy.

- **Equipping**: I place a high value on equipping others to find their own spiritual gift-mix and helping them develop it and deploying them to serve God with it (Eph. 4:11).

This value is at the core of my ministry as pastor-teacher. It also drives my mentoring relationships and life focus.

If the destination is finding the gift-mix, equipping then becomes the strategy, the how-are-we-going-to-do-it by which this is accomplished. If deployment is the destination, then equipping becomes the strategy to help them reach that destination. I will speculate that spiritual gifts may very well be the underlying value here, or perhaps mobilization.

Values are Not the Same as Doctrinal Statements

The most frequent confusion encountered is the confusion between doctrinal statements and values. Doctrinal statements are the church's theological beliefs based on the Bible. Inspiration is an example of a church's doctrinal position regarding the Word of God.

- **Inspiration of the Bible** - This is in contrast to humanistic liberalism. I believe that the Bible is accurate and contains words that were given by God to inform, inspire, and instruct people for his or her practical and spiritual development.

Now that we have seen what a value is not, it is time to discover what a value is.

So How Do We Define a Value?

Values are core beliefs that drive our life and ministry. In the life of a Christian, those core beliefs are rooted in the Scriptures and sourced in God. As we have seen previously, they should be grounded in and flow out of a deontological biblical ethical system. They are at the core, the heart of all that we are and do. They are like the driver behind the wheel of both our life and ministry. We know their presence by the influence they exert.

1. Values Drive How We Make Decisions

We make hundreds of decisions every day. Why do we decide to go one way and not another? How do we determine what decisions are correct, and which are incorrect? Nearly all of our decisions are rooted in and flow out of our value system. Some of our core values have been clearly articulated, others have not. They affect us just the same. That is why it is so vital to both define and articulate our values. In this way our living and profession will be one.

The Twelve Apostles had a set of shared values. When faced with the situation involving distribution to the widows, their decision was driven by their core set of values. They were to give themselves to the Word and to prayer. Others were to take care of the needs of the widows. Thus they did not wait on tables. Relationship is a core value of God. Based upon His value for relationship, He made the decision to extend grace to Israel (Ezekiel 16:6-14). We learn from Isaiah 41:8-18 that it was that same value that led Him to extend protection to Israel.

2. Values Drive How We Determine Risk Level

Each of us individually and each of our churches take risks every day. Every time a decision is made, a risk is taken. How much risk will we take? How much is acceptable? These are questions best answered by our values.

Paul and Barnabas were "men who have risked their lives for the name of our Lord Jesus Christ" (Acts 15:26). What leads men to take such risks? Paul had made a decision. "More than that, I count all things to be loss in view of the surpassing value of knowing Christ Jesus my Lord, for whom I have suffered the loss of all things, and count them but rubbish so that I may gain Christ" (Philippians 3:8). He had exchanged one set of values for another. The value of knowing Christ Jesus was enough for Paul to lay aside all other things, to count them as dung, and to risk even life and limb. Jesus' value for relationship led Him to take the ultimate risk of investing the remaining years of His life in training twelve disciples. Think of the risk the Father took in sending His Son, simply so we could enter into relationship and have fellowship with Him!

3. Values Drive How We Resolve Conflict

The Church is not immune to conflict. In fact, conflict characterized

Chapter 3 ☛ *Prepare the Value System*

both the church at Corinth (1 Corinthians 1:10-18) and Philippi (Philippians 4:2). James also had to address the problem of conflict. He writes,

> What is the source of quarrels and conflicts among you? Is not the source your pleasures (ηδονων) that wage war in your members? You lust and do not have; so you commit murder. You are envious and cannot obtain; so you fight and quarrel. You do not have because you do not ask. You ask and do not receive, because you ask with wrong motives, so that you may spend it on your pleasures (ταις ηδοναις). You adulteresses, do you not know that friendship with the world is hostility toward God? Therefore whoever wishes to be a friend of the world makes himself an enemy of God. (James 4:1-4)

The underlying source of conflict in the people to whom James wrote was their ethical system and value base. Hedonism can be thought of as the philosophy that pleasure, and only pleasure, is intrinsically good. Thus, the goal of moral endeavor is the increase of pleasurable experience and decrease of painful and unpleasant experience. A hedonist may attach value to things other than pleasure, for example, knowledge, freedom, justice; but only in so far as they are instrumental to pleasure. In the Scripture before us, the source of their inner conflict and outward quarrels identified by James is what he calls "their pleasures" (ηδονων), their hedonism. Their external behavior which led to conflict was driven by their internal value set.

Only by addressing conflicting values can the conflict be resolved. James surfaced and clarified the values in conflict, friendship with the world or friendship with God, the adultery of hedonism or faithfulness and relationship to God. James did not address the fruit of their conflict, but their root.

Ephesians 2:11-19 presents another example of conflict resolution. God's value for relationship with us led to His doing what was necessary to bring us, who were formerly far off, near to Himself. He brought the conflict to resolution through the blood of Christ.

4. Values Drive How We Solve Our Problems

When we discover we are in the midst of problems, we must address the solution to our problems within the context of our values. How would our core values lead us to solve the conflict? In the case of Adam's loneliness (Genesis 2:18,22-25) God created a woman. In the case of man's nature as a sinner and God's nature as righteous (Romans 5:6:-9), God resolved our need to be reconciled in such a way that not only maintained His value of holiness but expressed His value for relationship with us.

In our church plant we faced a crises as to how to care for the children during our corporate gathering. Initially they were cared for by a paid worker. When the paid worker could no longer care for the children, the church was faced with the problem of what to do. Should we simply hire another worker, or was there another solution? Was God using this crisis to speak to us? It was at this point that the church's values of children, relationship, and spiritual gifts came to bear upon the problem. The church was led to recognize its corporate responsibility for the discipleship of the children in its midst. Until God raised up an anointed, called, and gifted individual within the body to work with the children, the church family would consider it an opportunity for the adults to develop a more intimate relationship with the children. This was especially important as these particular children came from single parent families where a male presence was absent or the father figure was spiritually uninvolved. Thus, actualizing the value system determined how the church solved two problems. First, the adults took on a greater awareness of the children's needs during worship and interacted with them as needed. Second, each adult on a weekly rotational basis began to take the children out of the service during the preaching time in order to lead a study for them on their own level.

5. Values Drive How We Establish Our Priorities

What is important to you? If I asked you to list everything that is important to you on a piece of paper, the list would be nearly endless. What is most important to you? Now the list shrinks, considerably. While many things are important to us, to what is most important we will devote our time, our energy, and our resources. These most important items have become our priorities. If you are unsure what really matters to you, or want validation for what you think matters, I suggest you examine closely your daytimer, your checkbook, and, if married, ask your spouse. These three sources will reveal clearly toward what you devote your time, energy, and resources. I'll warn you in advance, though. What you say you value and what your lifestyle reveals may not be the same!

We can readily identify our priorities once we have identified our val-

Chapter 3 Prepare the Value System

ues. Our core values signal to us what is most important and where we are to focus our energies. The term *most* is a superlative term. When something is *most*, we cannot speak of something "moster" or "mostest". Most is the most. Why then do I speak of items, plural, that we consider most important, singular. Think of your priorities no longer in a hierarchical manner: first, second, third, etc. Think of them in an integrative manner, say for example, like the pieces of a pie. All the pieces are now "most" important. Each is vital to the whole. The whole would no longer be the whole if any piece was missing. In like manner, your core values lead to the development of your most important priorities. The whole becomes greater than the sum of the individual parts.

God has a number of important priorities flowing from His core value of relationship. One of these values we discover in the Song of Solomon 2:10,13-14.

> Song 2:10 "My beloved responded and said to me,
> 'Arise, my darling, my beautiful one,
> And come along.
>
> Song 2:13 'The fig tree has ripened its figs,
> And the vines in blossom have given forth their fragrance.
> Arise, my darling, my beautiful one,
> And come along!'"
>
> Song 2:14 "O my dove, in the clefts of the rock,
> In the secret place of the steep pathway,
> Let me see your form,
> Let me hear your voice;
> For your voice is sweet, And your form is lovely.

What is God's priority? Here is an invitation to fellowship. Arise and come along. Let me see your form! Let me hear your voice! His priority is fellowship with that one He calls darling and beautiful one.

ARE VALUES REALLY THAT IMPORTANT?

We have considered what values are as well as what values are not. But, does it really matter in the long run? Are values a vital root of a cell church?

Preparing the 21st Century Church

Someone once said about women, "You can't live without them and you can't live with them." Values, in that respect, are much like women. You and I cannot live without them. However, we often find it very difficult to live with them. In the large picture, values are a vital part of every culture. They can be thought of as the treads that comprise the very fabric of society. Yet in the small everyday picture, they can be the key between success and failure. Many businesses fail without even trying. In like manner, too many churches also fail without even trying. The difference between success and failure is tied to the issue of values.

How to Fail as a Business Without Really Trying

How would you answer the following questions posed in the national bestseller, *The Discipline of Market Leaders* (3)?

- Why is it that Casio can sell a calculator more cheaply than Kellogg's can sell a box of cornflakes? Does corn cost that much more than silicon?

- Why is it that it takes only a few minutes and no paperwork to pick up or drop off a rental car at Hertz's #1 Club Gold, but twice that time and an annoying name/address form to check into a Hilton hotel? Are they afraid you'll steal the room?

- Why is it that you can get patient help from a Home depot clerk when selecting a $2.70 package of screws, but you can't get any advice when purchasing a $2,700 personal computer from IBM's direct ordering service? Doesn't IBM think customer service is worth its time?

The managers at Kellogg, Hilton and IBM do not get up every morning and tell themselves, "Another day to fail!" Yet, for all practical purposes, they are choosing failure. The issue is that of value.

Customers today want more of those things they value. If they

Chapter 3 ☛ *Prepare the Value System*

value low cost, they want it lower. If they value convenience or speed when they buy, they want it easier and faster. If they look for state-of-the-art design, they want to see the art pushed forward. If they need expert advice, they want companies to give them more depth, more time, and more of a feeling that they're the only customer. (Discipline, 4)

Why pick on Kellogg, Hilton or IBM? Today each of those companies is on a slippery slope. "One or more companies in their markets have increased the value offered to customers by improving products, cutting prices, or enhancing service. By raising the level of value that customers expect from everyone, leading companies are driving the market, and driving competitors downhill (Discipline, 4). Obviously they can't excel in each of the three dimensions of value noted above. However, those that are market leaders have chosen to hone at least one component of value to a level of excellence that puts their competitors to shame.

From what I have said, it should be obvious that in the business world the key values are price, time, service, and quality. How a business addresses or fails to address those values will be the deciding factor in success or failure. To fail to address these issues at all is to fail without even trying. I can hear your self talk right now, "That may be true for the business world, but I don't know that it is true for the church. The church is different!"

How to Fail as a Church Without Really Trying

Lyle Schaller once noted that the most important single element of any corporate, congregational, or denominational culture, however, was the value system. As in the business world, so any church that ignores the importance of core values will do so to its own detriment. That church will fail without even trying!

Years ago I watched as the John Hancock Center was being built in Chicago. What amazed me the most was the tremendous foundation that was laid. The architects had laid out in precise detail the floor plan for each floor. Electrical was laid out in detail. Plumbing was organized. The location of staircases and elevators was not in doubt. However, all these components had to rest upon a foundation. Had the foundation not been laid properly, the beautiful structure with all its various components would not have lasted. The foundation, though never seen by the observer who would gape in awe at the finished skyscraper, was the most critical part of this grand structure. In similar fashion, core values are essential, critical, to the structural integrity of your church. Without an articulated values base, what ever grand design you use to build your church will be, in the immortal words of William Shakespeare, "full of sound and fury, signifying nothing."

Aubrey Malphurs (Values-Driven, 29) notes 10 reasons why values are so critical to the building of the church. Journey with me as we explore each reason in greater detail.

1. Values Determine Ministry Distinctives

The church you pastor is not the same as the church I pastor. True, there are tremendous similarities. However, we are different. The social context in which we minister are different. The economics of our churches are distinct. The people we are reaching with the gospel are probably different people groups. How we worship differs. In other words, the very culture of each church varies. Further, the things we stand for are rather unique to us. Each of us has like Luther, in a sense, nailed our thesis to the door and proclaimed, "Here is where I stand. I can stand nowhere else! This is what this church is all about. This is who we are. This is what we can do for you."

To change metaphors for a moment, each church is like a bus, heading to a similar destination, but by a unique route. "This is our route. This is our bus." What defines the nature of our bus and makes us distinct from every other bus? Is it not our values?

We can see this in the first century. All may have sprung from the mother church in Jerusalem and then Antioch, but they were unique. What made the churches in Galatia different from the churches throughout the rest of Asia Minor? Their highest value was their observance to the Mosaic Law. What of the church in Corinth? Was not their distinction their emphasis on spiritual gifts? Look at the churches the Lord speaks to in Revelation.

Each church in our community is distinct, standing for something. Perhaps what sets each apart is a contemporary worship style, or a traditional approach. Perhaps the distinction is evangelism to the inner city poor. Perhaps what is unique is involvement with social issues. What is responsible for such diversity within the Body of Christ? Is it not differing core values which bring about such ministry distinctives?

2. Values Dictate Personal Involvement

It is a rare person who will commit his time, energy, and resources to a cause he does not value! Why get involved if we do not share the core values of those we are asked to be involved with? How can we be passionate about something that is low on our list of values? On the other hand, when we walk through the front door of the church clearly understanding that we share the core values of this church, we will not be so prone to walk out the back door!

Allow me a word to pastors who are in transition. Transition is first about changing values, then changing structures. Why is there so much resistance? We have done a poor job at articulating the new values affecting change at the values level in our members' lives. Why the apathy and refusal to get involved? Our members have little or no value for what we are asking them to commit to. Sure, they may be committed in their thinking. But being conceptually committed will never enable them to live out new values with passion. How to change values will be covered in a later section. That values need to be changed must first be established. If you too often feel like a clown attempting to keep all the ministry plates constantly spinning, you have encountered a significant values issue.

What about church planters? We can spare ourselves and our members untold grief if we will communicate our values up front to all who would become members of our church plant. Let's encourage those with similar values to join our work, and stop seeking for crowds that do not share our values.

3. Values Communicate What is Important

If I want the best athletic shoe, I will purchase a Nike. Why? Nike's bottom line value is quality. Ditto for a Sony Walkman. If I want to establish a long term relationship with those from whom I purchase my clothes, I will shop at Nordstrums, not Target. Why? Nordstrum's bottom line value is customer intimacy. They want a relationship with me! If I want to eat a hamburger quickly and without a hassle, I will go to McDonalds. However, McDonalds does not want to create a relationship with me! Neither will McDonalds give me the finest hamburger money can buy. Yet, their hamburgers will be medium priced. I can purchase one quickly and be on my way. If I have a problem, they will give me hassle free service. By the way, that is true at a McDonalds anywhere in the world. Besides in the USA, I've eaten at McDonalds in Canada,

Singapore, and Russia. Why is this true? Their bottom line value is to deliver a reproducible hassle free hamburger. Values communicate what is important!

Values signal the bottom line. What in the final analysis is most important, what is worthwhile, what is most desirous? What truly matters. Your core values are what answer these questions. Think for a moment with me again of the Twelve Apostles in Acts 6:1-7. What was their bottom line? What mattered most? Was it serving tables or being in prayer and the Word? Now, I didn't say what mattered, but what mattered *most*! Their core values drew a line in the sand over which they would not step. We spend our time and focus our energy toward that which is in line with our values. Had they themselves ministered to the widows in question, what would that have communicated to the rest of the church about the Twelve's core values of prayer and the Word?

How often do we as pastors and staff find ourselves involved in ministries that, in reality, we should be delegating to others, so we can give ourselves to those dictated by our values? Too often we do not, and the reason is guilt. Yet, the outcome is a waste of time, inner dissatisfaction and frustration that we need not experience.

4. Values Provide an Anchor in the Midst of Change

Everything today is in a state of flux a state of change. The economy is undergoing massive changes due to a recessionary spiral. The terrorist attack of September 11, 2001 has forever changed the way we ride an airplane. Constant terrorist updates keep us in a heightened state of anxiety. Anthrax scares have caused significant changes in postal regulations and mail handling. The government continues to move the location of the Vice-President. The law of the land is in a state of fluctuation. Liberties we have enjoyed without question for years are suddenly being adjusted. Against this changing and fluctuating landscape stands the church, constant and eternal. Or, is it?

The church herself is undergoing rapid change. Our programs are changing. The forms of worship and outreach have changed. Sacred cows are continually being slaughtered in the name of progress. And let's be honest, nobody likes change, not really. We all resist change, even good and beneficial change. So, in the midst of all that is in flux around us, where is our anchor in the midst of change? Our ethical system and our core values are the only anchor points in a culture that is constantly in a state of ever accelerating change. Especially in a transitioning church where even sacred structures will be

Chapter 3 ☛ *Prepare the Value System*

altered, only core values will serve as the glue holding the vision and church together and providing a consistent sense of direction in the midst of transition. Programs may come and go. Practices may be redefined. Personnel will not be here forever. Forms will change. In the midst, Scripture does not change, our ethical base is sure, and our core values provide a necessary and useful anchor.

5. Values Influence Overall Behavior

In the real estate industry, they say the key is "location, location, location". The key to behavior is "value, value, value". Values define our behavior. If our behavior is what we do and do not do, then values are the basis for all our behavior. Values form the bottom line for what we will and will not do. Why did Joseph choose not to sleep with Potiphar's wife? Why did Moses forsake the riches of Egypt and choose rather to identify with the people of God? Why did Paul vehemently persecute the church of Jesus? Why did John Mark forsake Paul and Barnabas on their missionary journey? Why did Barnabas give him another chance while Paul refused?

Why do many churches find themselves in conflict between their stated policies, practices or goals and their actual behavior? Why the inner turmoil? Our external behavior either gives expression to our inner values, or our external behavior results in internal conflict. I remember clearly a church service in San Antonio, Texas, in November 1972. The speaker was Miss Bertha Smith, an elderly former missionary to China and participant in the Shantung Revival. Miss Bertha explained that the Chinese word picture for a nervous breakdown was a heart and mind that were not in agreement. When planting or transitioning, how vital it is to get in touch with our core values before we attempt to establish our external behavior! Yet, that is exactly the opposite of what is usually done.

6. Values Inspire People to Action

What is it that can transform Passive Pew-warming Peter and make him Persistent Participating Peter? What will stimulate him? What will sustain him? Will rewards move him? Will perks increase his commitment? Will promises motivate him? If we could discover an elixir and bottle it, we would be rich beyond measure!

In reality, the answer is quite simple. Dion Robert has discovered the answer. Yonggi Cho has discovered the answer. Cesar Castellanos has discovered the answer. They have touched their people at a level that gives their lives greater meaning and significance. They have provided them something that the people feel is worthy of their best efforts. Their followers have committed to something truly worthwhile and larger than themselves, something eternal, something that has given meaning to their life. These leaders have discovered the secret of infusing their followers' lives with meaning, meaning that has in turn inspired them and moved them into action.

You will discover in each case above that an articulated value system is being shared by pulpit and pew, leader and non-leader alike. The common member has found common cause with their church. Their energies have been captured and their gifts released. It could be argued that each church has answered the age old philosophical question of teleology. "What is my destiny?" "What has meaning in my life?"

7. Values Enhance Credible Leadership

Leadership has been loosely defined as as the influence we exercise over others. Leadership itself is an amoral process. Moses and Abraham were each great leaders. Yet, we would have to say that Adolph Hitler was also a great leader. Those who are "evil" wield tremendous influence even as do those who are "good". We may not agree with Hitler's values as a leader, but they established the parameters for everything he would do as well as for everything Germany would do. Whether good or evil, it is the leader's core values that provide credible leadership.

Hitler had core values. He valued the reunification of Germany. He valued the Aryan race. He valued economic prosperity. He modeled a lifestyle consistent with those values. This was the key to the credibility of his leadership. Even in prison, he was consistent. He instilled those values in others through what he said, but they found lasting root because of how he lived. Because his behavior was consistent with his inner values, large doses of credibility infused his leadership.

Watchman Nee possessed core values also. He valued leadership development, especially in light of what he perceived coming to China. He too modeled a lifestyle consistent with those inner values. Even in prison, he was consistent. Nee, like Adolph Hitler, instilled those values in others through what he said, but achieved lasting impact because of how he lived. Because his behavior was consistent with his inner values, his life profoundly impacted those

Chapter 3 ☛ *Prepare the Value System*

around him. His leadership. His impact is still being felt today.

8. Values Shape Ministry Character

How we live life is a direct outgrowth of our character. In turn, our character is shaped by our inner values. Our character rests upon the foundation of our values and is the foundation for life. The same is true for the churches we pastor. Each church has a character reputation. It is known for something. It may be known for excellence. It may be known for mediocrity. It may be known for the release of its members into ministry. It may be known for the bondage and control its membership is under. It may be known for its concern for those around it. It may be known as an elite social club. Its reputation is how others see it express its life and character. Dig below that life and character, that reputation, and you will discover the values to which the church *really* holds.

9. Values Contribute to Ministry Success

How do we define success? Malphurs defines success as "...the accomplishment of the ministry's vision without compromising its vital, bottom-line values" (26). How then do values lead to our success? What is the incentive for people to serve longer, work harder, and sacrifice more? In some cases it may seem to be recognition. In other cases it may seem to be financial reward. Yet, beneath the surface, the real incentive has to do with their values. People will not work aggressively for what they do not care for. Enthusiasm and excitement cannot be maintained if values are not touched. Look again at the early church.

> They were continually devoting themselves to the apostles' teaching and to fellowship, to the breaking of bread and to prayer. Everyone kept feeling a sense of awe; and many wonders and signs were taking place through the apostles. And all those who had believed were together and had all things in common; and they began selling their property and possessions and were sharing them with all, as anyone might have need. Day by day continuing with one mind in the temple, and breaking bread from house to house, they were taking their meals together with gladness and sincerity of heart, praising God and having favor with all the people. And the Lord was adding to their

> number day by day those who were being saved. (Acts 2:42-47)

Note how they were of "one mind". Out of this oneness sprang forth continual devotion, a sense of awe, personal sacrifice of possessions and time, and praise. The leaders had no need to prop up the people and keep the ministry plates spinning. Inner motivation did the trick. Look again at the following Scripture.

> And the congregation of those who believed were of one heart and soul; and not one of them claimed that anything belonging to him was his own, but all things were common property to them. And with great power the apostles were giving testimony to the resurrection of the Lord Jesus, and abundant grace was upon them all. For there was not a needy person among them, for all who were owners of land or houses would sell them and bring the proceeds of the sales and lay them at the apostles' feet, and they would be distributed to each as any had need. Now Joseph, a Levite of Cyprian birth, who was also called Barnabas by the apostles (which translated means Son of Encouragement), and who owned a tract of land, sold it and brought the money and laid it at the apostles' feet. (Acts 4:32-37)

Again we see the congregation of one heart and soul. The result was a freewill offering of possessions as any had need. There was submission to leadership. There was the experience of abundant grace. Shared values ruled the day. The result was a commitment to minister to the real physical and spiritual needs of another.

> Now at this time while the disciples were increasing in number, a complaint arose on the part of the Hellenistic Jews against the native Hebrews, because their widows were being overlooked in the daily serving of food. So the twelve summoned the congregation of the disciples and said, "It is not desirable for us to neglect the word of God in order to serve tables. Therefore, brethren, select from among you seven men of good reputation, full of the Spirit and of wisdom, whom we may put in charge of this task. But we will devote ourselves to prayer and to the ministry of the word." The statement found approval with the

whole congregation; and they chose Stephen, a man full of faith and of the Holy Spirit, and Philip, Prochorus, Nicanor, Timon, Parmenas and Nicolas, a proselyte from Antioch. And these they brought before the apostles; and after praying, they laid their hands on them.

In most churches today, 20 percent of the people are doing 80 percent of the work. The church of today is not mobilized, Yet, as we examine the early church, we discover a church highly mobilized. Why? Because of shared values. People will commit to meaningful purpose, a purpose expressing their core values.

10. Values Determine the Ministry Vision

Our core values will guide the development of our ministry vision in a number of significant ways. Recall that we have said vision has to do with the direction a ministry takes, with the destination ahead. It answers the question, "Where are we going?" That which we value will determine what we give our time, energy, and resources for. Where there is no vision, there will be no clear allocation of our three most precious commodities. Where there is a multiple vision, our time, energy, and resources will be diffused. They will prove insufficient to arrive at any destination. A multiple vision is often evidence of competing values among those who are the vision casters.

Our values will guide how we employ information critical to our vision selection. For example, a core value of the poor will affect our outreach, the people group targeted, possibly the geographic location in which we minister, and certainly the development of programs expressing our "values proposition" (defined further in chapter 4). A core value of integrity will affect the very way in which we advertise our presence. Is marketing a legitimate exercise? When does marketing cross the line of integrity and is no longer legitimate?

Especially critical for church planters, our core values will determine which possible visions will be adopted. While in Florida, part of our team strongly desired to establish a "deliverance ministry". Deliverance was crucial to the healing of those saved and joining the church. However, it was not to serve as either the sole or major component of the vision of the church. It was simply one of a number of sub-components of the vision to release the captives. Those church planting must develop their vision from their articulated core values.

Both church planters and transitioning pastors are faced with the problem whether or not those who follow have really accepted and bought into their vision. The question behind that question is really whether or not their followers share their core values. Where core values are not shared, those involved will move in separate directions to reach separate visions. Where core values are shared, a team can pull together.

DEVELOPING YOUR VALUES

Convinced that values are important, even vital? Good. We can proceed.

Concerning the development of our value system, Ralph Neighbour Jr. once remarked, "We pick up our values like germs off the street." His statement may be closer to the truth than you realize. I remember growing up in the Synagogue in Tucson, Arizona in the 1960s. Every Saturday during Sabbath School I was given an hour instruction in ethics and values. Most people never have a clear explanation of ethics and/or values until college! That is not to say that they have not developed a system anyway. They have. We all have. The problem is that we do often pick up our values like germs off the street. Worse still, by the time we are birthed into the Kingdom of God, we already have a well defined, though unarticulated, value system that we are living by, but one that has been thoroughly indoctrinated and fashioned by this world and the kingdom of our previous father, the devil.

Somehow we are now suppose to walk in newness of life as Christians and walk as citizens of our new Kingdom and subjects of our new King. This makes great theory, but lousy practice. Our old man is thoroughly imbued with the world system and our new man is ignorant of God's ways. Is it any wonder that we cry out even as did the Apostle Paul:

> For we know that the Law is spiritual, but I am of flesh, sold into bondage to sin. For what I am doing, I do not understand; for I am not practicing what I would like to do, but I am doing the very thing I hate. But if I do the very thing I do not want to do, I agree with the Law, confessing that the Law is good. So now, no longer am I the one doing it, but sin which dwells in me. For I know that nothing good dwells in me, that is, in my flesh; for the willing is present in me, but the doing of the good

Chapter 3 Prepare the Value System

> is not. For the good that I want, I do not do, but I practice the very evil that I do not want. But if I am doing the very thing I do not want, I am no longer the one doing it, but sin which dwells in me. I find then the principle that evil is present in me, the one who wants to do good. For I joyfully concur with the law of God in the inner man, but I see a different law in the members of my body, waging war against the law of my mind and making me a prisoner of the law of sin which is in my members. Wretched man that I am! Who will set me free from the body of this death? Thanks be to God through Jesus Christ our Lord! So then, on the one hand I myself with my mind am serving the law of God, but on the other, with my flesh the law of sin. (Romans 7:14-25)

How do we move into a position to serve the law of God with both our mind and our flesh? Obviously by putting on the Lord Jesus Christ and making no provision for the flesh. Practically speaking, Paul put it this way:

> Therefore I urge you, brethren, by the mercies of God, to present your bodies a living and holy sacrifice, acceptable to God, which is your spiritual service of worship. And do not be conformed to this world, but be transformed by the renewing of your mind, so that you may prove what the will of God is, that which is good and acceptable and perfect. (Romans 12:1-2)

Simply put, our minds must be renewed. They must be renewed with the Truth if we are to be set free. Thus, we must develop afresh our value systems. It is only of little benefit to discover the value system we currently hold so dear. If we speak of discovering our heart-value set, then as we have already seen, that value system has already been thoroughly polluted by the worldviews we have grown up with. If we are speaking of discovering our head-value set, we are not living out of those values anyway.

It is time to have our minds renewed by the Truth. It is time to embrace a biblical moral theory of ethics. It is time to discover that which God values and embrace that as our own. It is time to embrace the value system of the Kingdom of God. This is preparing the way of the Lord!

Our ethical base is usually covered over by layers of practices, priorities and unbiblical values. Periodically in history, God breaks through and moves His church layer by layer back to the bedrock from which values are lived out. The bedrock is God Himself. It is hard, but necessary work to dig down through our comfortable practices we have developed. It takes sweat to penetrate the old priorities toward which we have for years focused our actions. We must redouble our efforts if we are to break through those things we have valued and for which we have given our time, energy and resources. Once through these values, we arrive at the base that is the foundation for our actions. We must dig through to the very heart and Presence of God Himself. When we have broken through to the Presence of God we are then ready to develop a new life in God, a new worldview, new values, new priorities and new practices for our life. This is when permanent change occurs.

Most of our lives we have lived out of our practices and priorities. We then justify our values as being valid. Some develop an ethical base, but one not rooted and grounded in the nature of God. We must reverse the process and understand our ethics from the Presence of God, formulate our values out of these God-based ethics, set our priorities according to the ethically based values and reshape our practices so the priority of the very life of God is manifested through all that we do. Ethics, values, priorities and practices that do not grow out of the heart of God, over time, become religious law, programs and traditions. We must never be satisfied until we can live out of the Presence, power and purpose of God Himself.

CHANGING VALUES

Changing values happens neither automatically nor easily. Value change carries with it the inherent likelihood of conflict, resistance and confrontation. Why? Value change usually means you have one party who has internalized a new value. That person is a Change Agent. On the other hand, not everyone embraces the same new value at the same time. These are Change Resisters. They resist change because they do not know about it, understand it or like it. When Mr. Change Agent decides to teach Mr. Change Resister about his new value, old and new values come into conflict. The Change Agent must understand the process of change that is necessary before someone else embraces a new value.

The chart which follows, developed by Dr. Ralph Neighbour, Jr., helps

Chapter 3 ☞ *Prepare the Value System*

us to see the relationship between the Change Agent, the Change Context and the Change Resister. The perspective of the Change Agent is different than the perspective of the Change Resister who may very well be a Potential Follower who just has not experienced the process of change. Let's examine each piece of the problem before us. In so doing, we will be more adept at helping our people undergo a values transformation.

The Potential Follower will likely be at one of five positions along the change continuum. It is of the utmost importance that you first correctly identify the stage each of your leaders and people are at. Only then can you provide what is necessary to move them along the continuum.

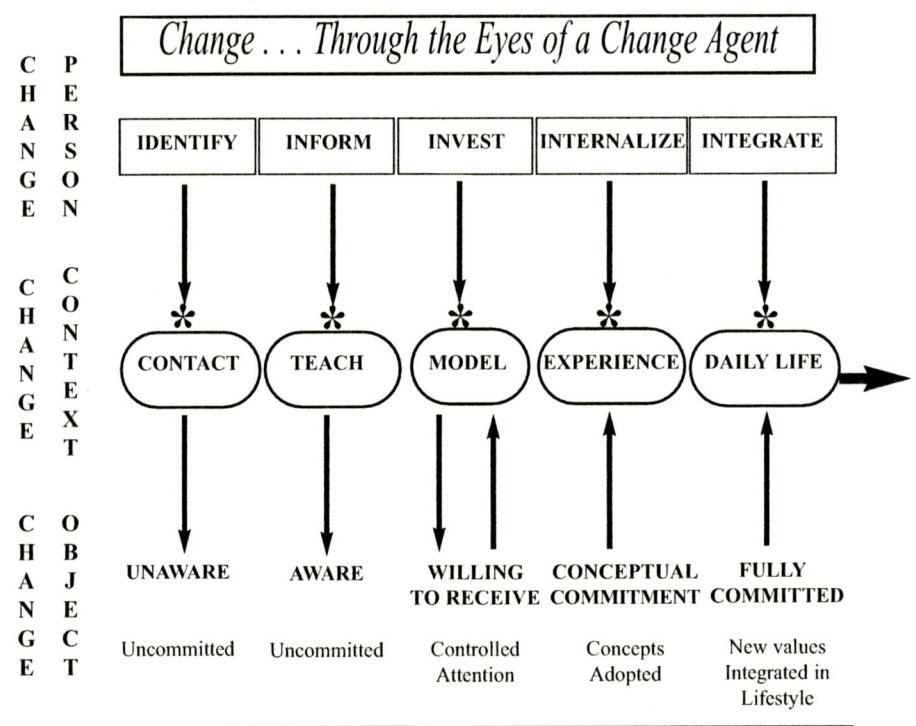

CHANGE	PERSON	**Change... Through the Eyes of a Change Agent**				
		IDENTIFY	INFORM	INVEST	INTERNALIZE	INTEGRATE
CHANGE	CONTEXT	↓	↓	↓	↓	↓
		CONTACT	TEACH	MODEL	EXPERIENCE	DAILY LIFE →
		↑	↑	↑	↑	↑
CHANGE	OBJECT	UNAWARE	AWARE	WILLING TO RECEIVE	CONCEPTUAL COMMITMENT	FULLY COMMITTED
		Uncommitted	Uncommitted	Controlled Attention	Concepts Adopted	New values Integrated in Lifestyle

Change... from the Perspective of a Potential Follower

Let's begin with Unaware Alfred. To begin with, Unaware Alfred may simply be unaware of the change you are desiring to implement, be it a change in his values or change in the structure of the church. You may have preached your vision a number of times. Alfred, however, was sick, on vacation, or simply distracted the moment you emphasized that all important point from the pulpit. Alfred does not read your flyers or your bulletins. You cannot imagine how a member of your church sitting under your teaching can simply and honestly be unaware, yet Unaware Alfred is actually unaware! So then, how in the world can you expect Unaware Alfred to be committed to that of which he is unaware and ignorant?

Then we have among us people like Fully Aware Florence. Florence has read your flyers. She reads your bulletins and hangs on every word of your message. Her predicament is not ignorance. She is aware, much aware, painfully aware. However, she is still uncommitted. Now, at this point we would like to charge Fully Aware Florence with being just downright rebellious. Not so fast, though! She is not necessarily rebellious. You may just have not yet convinced her. It is clear to you, but not to her. Also, she may be dealing with other issues that impact her willingness to commit

Then we have Willing to Receive Randolph. You have Randolph's undivided attention. He is thinking things through. The jury is still in deliberation. The final verdict is not yet in. He continually comes back with more questions, wanting to examine more evidence. Willing to Receive Randolph is often one of your *early majority* who is wanting and needing to see a workable model of what you are saying. Show me a working cell! Demonstrate what this new value will look like in your life! You have his attention.

Generally the pastor's favorite person on the change continuum is Conceptually Committed Casper. Finally, someone who has caught the vision! Someone who is wanting to follow. You have convinced Conceptually Committed Casper beyond any shadow of doubt. He is with you. In fact, he is excited. Your new "thing" is the best thing since sliced bread and apple pie! "Why have we not been living like this for years? Relationship? Yes, this is the most vital of all core values! Spiritual Gifts? Of course I believe they must be used in the church and cell! Evangelism? The world is going to hell. We must win the lost at any cost! Pastor, you lead and I will follow!"

Critical and fatal errors are made at this juncture. Pastors surround themselves with Conceptually Committed Caspers, amassing an army. However, they have amassed an army of ghosts. Pastors charge forward only to find that the army is not following. Why? "You're asking me to spend how much time each week building relationships with my cell members? Don't you

Chapter 3 ☛ *Prepare the Value System*

know the schedule I have to keep as a busy professional? Of course I believe in spiritual gifts, but that young man who had a word of knowledge and asked to pray for me in cell is a baby Christian. I can't receive from him! Of course I believe in evangelism, but I can't take time away from my family or sports teams to build relationship with the lost. I am too pressed."

What is the problem? Why has Conceptually Committed Casper suddenly vanished like the ghost for which he was so appropriately named? He liked the idea. He believed it to be biblical. His mind was impacted truly enough, but his heart was not quite ready to follow and commit to a new lifestyle. Be warned, many of our best innovators and early adopters are Conceptually Committed Caspers. Rejoice they are with you, but if you leave them at that stage on the change continuum, it will be to your own peril and destruction!

Finally we have Fully Committed Coleen. She is with you. She may not live everything out perfectly, but she is on her way. While she talks the talk, more importantly, she is walking the walk. Cell churches can only be successfully built with Fully Committed Coleens.

Having identified the continuum level an individual is at, what is the next step in attempting to transform their values? Next you must identify what it is they need. Obviously, Unaware Alfred needs to be made aware of what you are asking him to become committed to in his life. Contact him and help make him aware. Fully Aware Florence is possibly the hardest nut to crack. Her problem may be lack of sufficient cognitive information. Then again, her problem may be more at a non-cognitive level. You may be dealing with fears of the unknown, hurtful past experiences, or even present fears of rejection by her peer group should she embrace what they have not yet embraced.. There are many dynamics in Florence's life. The core blockage needs to be revealed by the Holy Spirit and addressed through appropriate teaching. Willing to Receive Randolph is in need of an actual model. Thinking about what it will look like is not sufficient. Randolph wants to see a *working* model. He may need to be part of a model, or at least receive the tangible benefits of a real model. Conceptually Committed Casper needs experiences to help him move what is in his head the eighteen inches down into his heart. Fully Committed Coleen needs her new values fully integrated into a new lifestyle. She needs daily life experiences. Review the chart on the previous page once again. What is the context that each change resistor needs to help them change and move to the next level? Contact? Teaching? Modeling? Deliberate Experiences? Daily Life?

Understanding where each individual is located along the continuum and the context you must supply to help move them further along is only half the battle. The difficult part yet remains. What will be your God-given strategy to help them move along the continuum? Allow me a few illustrations from my own life and ministry at this point.

Fully Aware Florence: Fully Aware Florence understood the nature of cell groups and the inherent values so vital to their success. Florence listened for a number of years. Why did she not move forward and become willing to receive? Why did she continue to stand aloof? Florence was deathly afraid of people. She needed teaching coupled with a safe environment before she would be willing to enter into close interpersonal relationships.

Willing to Receive Randolph: Willing to Receive Randolph had been hurt in small groups, yet the promise of genuine relationships touched him deeply. It was in reality an integrity issue. I said that relationship was the basic core value from which all other values in the church emanated. I was committing to relationship with Randolph. Our relationship became the model and my integrity became the issue. To what degree would I commit? At what point would I bail out and give up on Randolph? How long would I persevere? Through what kinds of interpersonal trials and conflicts would I walk with him? Over an eight year period I watched as Randolph moved from willingness to conceptual commitment to becoming fully committed. Eventually, his basic lifestyle and values forever changed.

Conceptually Committed Casper: Conceptually Committed Casper had been a Christian for years. He understood the values. He understood the structure. He understood the lifestyle. Over a period of a year I was able to provide experience after experience for Casper that challenged his lifestyle as a pastor of cell pastors. Late night visits. Prayer together. Drives together. Debriefings with cell leaders. Daily personal interaction with cell leaders. Lunches, lunches and more lunches. Coffee, coffee and more coffee. Time, time, and more time. Then one night it happened. Sitting in cell he said it was as if his eyes were opened for the first time. Church was about relationships, not meetings at the church building. He was suddenly free.

Will values change if you as a leader are not proactive in assisting them to change? Possibly, given enough time. After all, the Holy Spirit is committed to changing all of us into the full image of Christ. That we will be changed is not the issue. How we come to be changed is the issue. I recall a saying by Jack Taylor, a renown pastor and teacher. He use to say, "You can come easy, or you can come hard. But you will come!" I for one would rather come "easy". If I am proactive with my people in assisting them to change, I believe they may well come along a lot "easier", too.

Now is the time to have our minds renewed by the Truth. Now is the time to embrace a biblical moral theory of ethics. Now is the time to discover that which God values and embrace that as our own. Now is the time to embrace the value system of the Kingdom of God. Now is the time to prepare the way of the Lord! We must become proactive, now!

The *Eglise Protestante Baptiste Oeuvres et Mission Internationale* in Abidjan, Cote d'Ivoire, provides one example of a church that has taken seriously the mandate to prepare the way of the Lord. Before we examine the core values of that church, I have provided an exercise on the following page. On the left column are ethical demands derived for the most part out of the Decalogue. See if you can develop a set of corresponding biblical values of your own.

Reflections - Ethically Centered Values

MY VALUE

INTERNAL WORSHIP (EX 20:3)	
EXTERNAL WORSHIP (EX 20:4-6)	
VERBAL WORSHIP (EX 20:7)	
RIGHT RELATIONS WITH WORK (EX 20:8-11)	
SANCTITY OF THE FAMILY (EX 20:12)	
SANCTITY OF LIFE (EX 20:13)	
SANCTITY OF MARRIAGE (EX 20:14)	
SANCTITY OF PROPERTY (EX 20:15)	
SANCTITY OF TRUTH (EX 20:16)	
SANCTITY OF MOTIVES (EX 20:7)	
THE HOLINESS OF GOD (Rev. 4:8-9)	
THE LOVE OF GOD (I John 4:7-11)	

PHASE 1

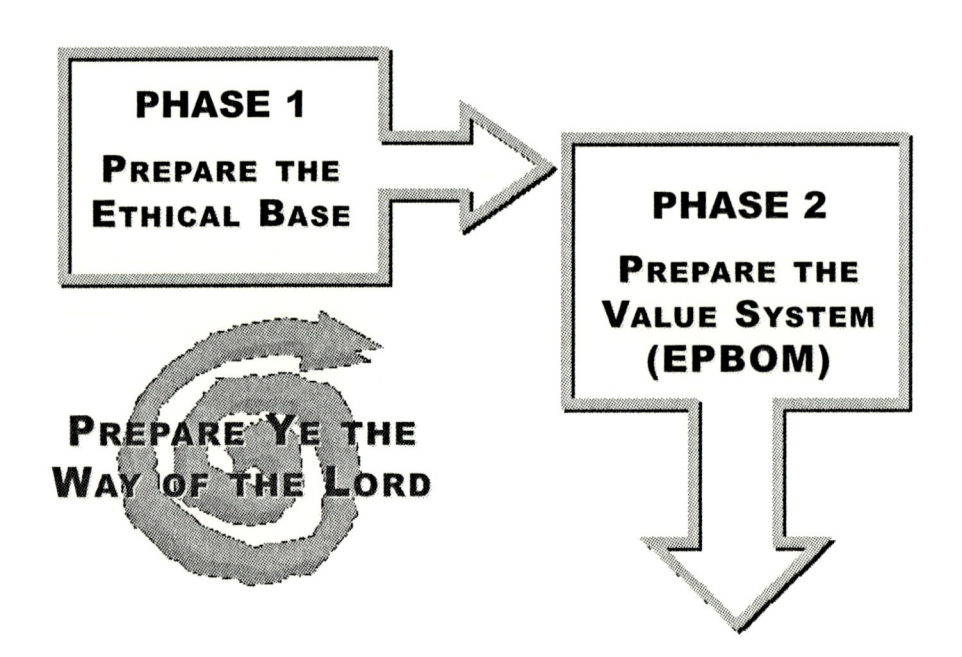

PREPARE THE
ETHICAL BASE

PHASE 2

PREPARE THE
VALUE SYSTEM
(EPBOM)

PREPARE YE THE
WAY OF THE LORD

4

Prepare the Value System - EPBOM

> **B**LESSED ARE THE PURE IN HEART, FOR THEY SHALL SEE GOD. MATTHEW 5:8
>
> **B**UT THE THINGS THAT PROCEED OUT OF THE MOUTH COME FROM THE HEART, AND THOSE DEFILE THE MAN. FOR OUT OF THE HEART COME EVIL THOUGHTS, MURDERS, ADULTERIES, FORNICATIONS, THEFTS, FALSE WITNESS, SLANDERS. MATTHEW 15:18-19

Chapter 4 ☞ *Prepare the Value System- EPBOM*

CORE VALUES OF
EGLISE PROTESTANTE BAPTISTE OEUVRES ET MISSION INTERNATIONALE,
ABIDJAN, COTE D'IVOIRE

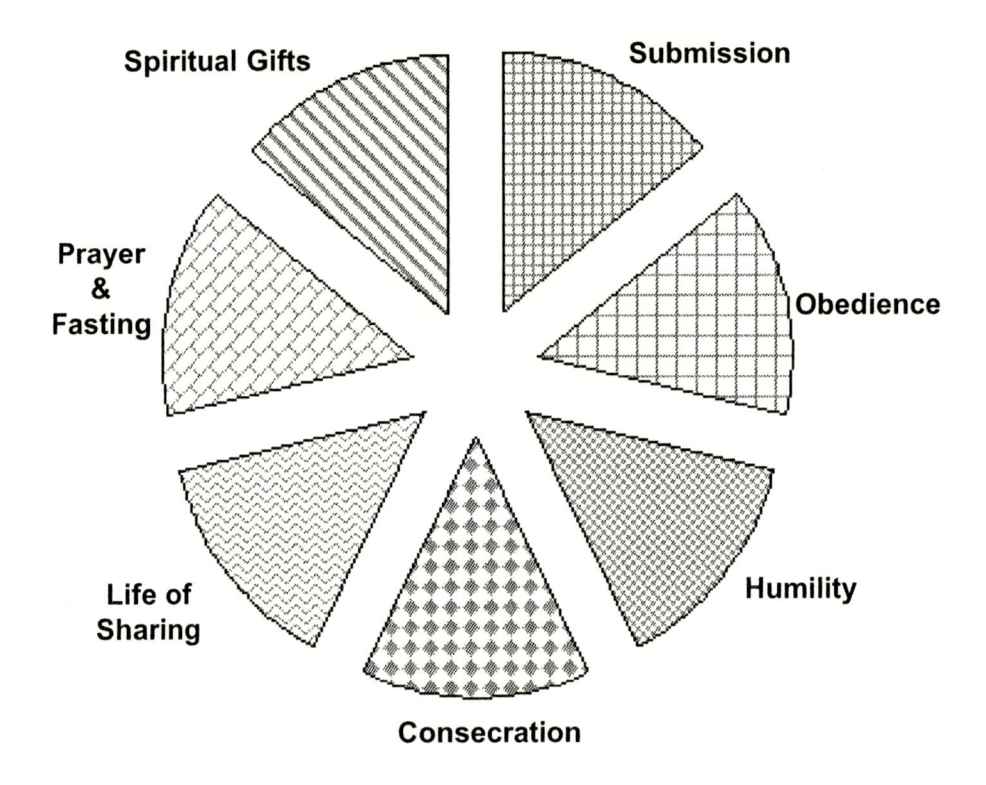

- Spiritual Gifts
- Submission
- Obedience
- Humility
- Consecration
- Life of Sharing
- Prayer & Fasting

CORE VALUES - OVERVIEW

I suggested earlier that we think of core values as pieces of a pie rather than as a numbered list. The leadership at EPBOM does just that, thinking in an integrative rather than hierarchical manner. Consequently, it is necessary to think of their values in terms of a completely integrated system where the sum is greater than the individual pieces, rather than as a hierarchy of independent factors. For this reason, EPBOM's value system is illustrated by use of a pie chart. There are seven core values articulated throughout the writings at EPBOM.

An aspirational value is a value that may have been articulated, but has not been actualized in the lifestyle of the church. In other words, one would be hard pressed to cite examples where the value in question is being lived out. One may aspire to the value, but it has not yet been incorporated into the lifestyle. On the other hand, an actual value can be clearly seen as both present and integral to the lifestyle and activity of the one(s) who would claim it.

In the remainder of this chapter, we will examine each of these core values and seek to establish 1) whether they have been clearly articulated by the church, and 2) whether they are in fact actual or merely aspirational values.

Value #1: SUBMISSION

Submission - An Articulated Value

One of the first things taught to a new believer is the value of submission. When an unbeliever comes to Christ, he is immediately placed as part of a cell in his neighborhood. Though he weekly attends pre-baptismal classes for six months at the local church headquarters, the cell worker (cell leader) will make sixteen home visits to the new believer using the manual written by Pastor Boka Faustin. "This manual, *The Follow-up of the New Christian At Home*, has been developed to bring every new born in Christ to understand, to love, to know Jesus Christ his savior, to be like Him and to rely on Him alone. *The Follow-up of the New Christian At Home* is a precious tool for the following up of all Christians" (3). The study is designed to help the cell worker lead the new Christian in the first steps in following Christ.

It is instructive that the theme of the first home visit is to make sure that

Chapter 4 — *Prepare the Value System- EPBOM*

Christ is the center of the new Christian's life. From the very first visit, the new Christian is presented with the necessity of a life of total submission to Christ. Visit three explains to the new believer what he is in Christ and how he no longer belongs to himself, but to Christ. This is followed up in visit five with the teaching that he has been crucified with Christ. At the end of the fifth home visit his book concludes with the quote from Colossians 3:1: "In Christ you can't do what ever you want because you are crucified with him, for the crucified one seeks the things above" (12).

The value of submission is again reinforced during his pre-baptismal training. Here, submission to Christ is extended to include those whom Christ places in authority in His church. "The secret to spiritual stability remains in entire submission to leaders that Christ established over us and to Himself, who is Christ the Lord, the head of the Church." (Robert, Born Again 98)

Submission - An Actual Value

In too many American cell churches we would (and have!) preached the same value from the pulpit. In this sense we may have articulated submission as one of our values. The real question, however, is whether or not submission has germinated, bloomed, and produced the harvest of visible fruit in the day-to-day lives of our people. Are our people more like Conceptually Committed Casper or Fully Committed Coleen? The answer cannot be validated by what we say or believe. The evidence is in how we live!

Turning from us to EPBOM, is submission at EPBOM an actual value or merely a stated aspirational value? Asked another way, is there an evident impact on the lives of the people made by that value? In August of 2000, I spent three weeks living on the central church's compound in Abidjan, while researching my dissertation. As the official language of Cote d'Ivoire is French, Cindy Huling, an American serving now as a missionary *for* EPBOM, provided her services as my interpreter during that time. I would say that during the three short weeks I was there, I continually saw evidence of this value in the lives of the people.

Fixing Cindy's clutch on her car was one such experience. She was having severe problems driving and we were hoping simply to make it back to the church after lunch. The clutch finally went out in an area without a gas station. We had three Ivorian women in the car with us. One of the women, Pastor Delphine, was in charge of the Women's Department and needed to see a lady in an apartment building, which is why we were where we were, and not back at the church when the clutch went out. Pastor Delphine went off and came back with a fellow that was going to fix the clutch. She then left to find the woman she needed to visit while the man worked on the car. We were there about an hour on the side of a busy road in some sort of business area, without phone capabilities. When the pastor returned, she and the other two women took a cab back to the church. Pastor Delphine said to wait, she would return. That statement proved to be key. The "mechanic" finished the clutch very soon after Pastor Delphine and the other women departed. We waited and waited for the Pastor to return. We waited nearly two hours. Cindy discussed with herself whether to leave or not. I offered no counsel. Bottom line, Cindy would not leave because Pastor Delphine said she would return. Though herself a missionary, Cindy was also a part of the Women's Department and under the authority of Pastor Delphine. Cindy is an expatriate who has been living in Cote d'Ivoire and serving the church there for over six years. To tell you the truth, I would have had a hard time in the US waiting two hours for any pastor to come back! The inner struggle I observed within Cindy was at heart an issue of submissiveness to authority. She had learned the value of submission. We waited until Pastor Delphine returned.

While attending CIAMEL 2000 (CIAMEL is a French acronym), a gathering of over 40,000 meeting each morning and evening for a week at stadium Champroux of Marcory, I was amazed at the crowds' submissive response to the ushers. From my personal journal dated 08/21/00 comes the following observation:

> The crowds were intensely worshipping. Tens of thousands clapping, yelling, dancing men, women and children! At one point they began to dance on the track outside the field and move down field. They were soon stopped and pushed back by red shirted ushers, "God's Policemen" they call them. (A number of years ago the police were asked to keep order at the stadium. When they arrived, they observed the ushers at work, turned and left saying that they (the ushers) were doing better than they themselves could to control the crowd and they (the police) were not needed.) The ushers worked in coordination like a well disciplined army. Parenthetically, when I arrived early one morning, I saw a squad of red shirted ushers in two

Chapter 4 ☛ *Prepare the Value System- EPBOM*

lines jogging as in formation. When they paused because our car was turning in front of them, they jogged in place. As they continued to sing while jogging in place waiting for us to move on, they reminded me of Marines on a march, drilling. This night the ushers pushed the crowds back to where they had begun.

Most amazing to me, though, was the response of the people when the worship time was over. I have been in numerous large conferences and churches across the United States and Canada and have noticed how difficult it is and time consuming to have people return to their seats after worship. They continue to linger and seem to ignore instructions. One night during CIAMEL I timed how long it took to clear a football field of 10,000 to 15,000 worshippers who had been there nearly half an hour. It took 90 seconds to clear most of the field! In less than two minutes, the crowd was completely dispersed and the people back in the bleachers.

Is this just "African culture"? I do not believe so. Cindy is an American. The struggle in her was at a level of value transformation. Listen to the words of Pastor Boka when challenged with the accusation that submission is just African culture:

Those who say this are those who don't know us, who don't know Africans, who can say for example an African can have two wives. It is not true. It doesn't exist. Those who do it sin. Even in the pagan villages they don't do it. It is adultery. They don't have the Spirit. That is why they do it. So, when you come to the Lord, they submit and they put things in order.

Here is an example. When your father is a fetisher, he has power and wants to delegate his power to the children. He wants you to be a fetisher along with him. There are those who accept the delegation of power and receive it. However, among his children you also have those who say, "No!". They do not want that way. The father could curse them, but his curse will not have touched them.

I knew a young man who is not Christian. The parents

wanted him to worship a river. He did not worship the river. They wanted to kill him with sorcery and they tried everything, but it didn't work. The day he gave himself to the Lord, he understood that even in error, even in paganism, when we do not do the bad, God is with us. The submission in Africa is not blind. It depends on those who want to obey, and those who don't want to obey. It is not a culture. It is not a custom. However, it is what we teach. If you are going to greet someone who is important, then there are attitudes that you must show to demonstrate respect. You give them everything that is demonstrating respect and blessing. You cannot say that the Africans just submit stupidly or haphazardly. (Interview)

Value #2: OBEDIENCE

Obedience - An Articulated Value

Obedience is a second articulated value at EPBOM. While submission is willingness to place ourselves under the authority of another, obedience may be viewed as the demonstration of that submission through carrying out the commands of those in authority.

It was noted earlier that, through the bible study book, *So You're Born Again!*, the candidate for baptism soon after conversion discovers that "only obedience and the putting in practice the biblical teaching makes him a new creature, a mature man and a boiling Christian" (Robert 8). "Grace does not authorize us to live in licentiousness, but it favors even more a life of holiness, of purity and of obedience to God" (Robert 48). What is the reason for obedience? Again, allow Pastor Dion Robert answer that question:

> Before, we were in the darkness, but the day that we accepted to obey God a new life, a new beginning started. God gave us His power to accomplish what we have become: His children. He is in us, and He leads us as a Father forever (Ephesians 4:8). This is why the Christian must watch out and not sadden the Holy Spirit by a disorderly life, a lack of meditation, disobedience, unfaithfulness, etc. (Ephesians 4:30). (Robert, Born Again 25)

At EPBOM, the cross of Christ and obedience are synonymous:

> The cross of Jesus is obedience. It produces life. It is something other than the Roman cross (pieces of crossed wood) which is the product of the curse and death. The cross of Jesus is obedience and it produces resurrection and life. A Church that preaches the cross (obedience) brings the listeners to life, to the fullness of God, to victory over curse and death, to authority over Satan and his demons, to the power of God over the world and its system. (Robert, Born Again 38)

Chapter six of EPOBM's instructional manual for newly baptized believers is devoted to the practical aspects of obedience. The chapter is entitled, "Bringing the Sheep to Crucifixion". It was written so that those who joined themselves to the church could be further instructed and would continue with one heart and mind in following the Lord. The following quotations are taken from section one, "How to Bring Them to Crucifixion":

> There is a need to understand that life before the cross is not true life, but life after the cross is eternal life; a life of power and of joy.
> A Christian who is not crucified is a carnal Christian without experience, and can easily fall. A church, which is not crucified, is a worldly church without real power or without real faith - the key to life and reign with Christ, the Living God.
> It is by teaching the Word that we apply the life of God to men. It is from being taught that they pass from death to life. It is by teaching that we crucify humanity so that it may resemble Christ and so that it be reconciled with God by Christ (Jn.1:12-13). It is by teaching that we bring humanity to do the will of God in order to be saved (Matthew 7:21). It is by teaching that we bring humanity to eat Christ to be filled with Him and to live by Him (John 6:57) It is by teaching that we bring humanity to be consecrated to God (John 4:34).
> Through evangelization, we draw in souls for Christ to introduce them into His House (the Church) and fulfill God's purpose in their lives in making them disciples of Christ

(Matthew 28:19). After the step of evangelization, we must absolutely bring the men thus won by evangelism to be crucified, so to make them disciples. This means we must make each one of these people Christians submitted to the discipline of Jesus Christ, for them to live the principles of the Kingdom of God (Isaiah 54:13).

The teaching is very precious for it is written: "My people are destroyed from lack of knowledge. Because you have rejected knowledge, I also reject you as my priests; because you have ignored the law of your God, I also will ignore your children (Hosea 4:6)." By teaching, we open the eyes of the spiritually blind and they walk in the light, in the knowledge of the true God. To do this, the teaching cannot be just anything, but it must be a systematic teaching that talks to men. To reach the goal of God, the teaching must directly address man. It must not be complacent or general. That is the message of the cross of Jesus.

To preach the cross is to preach the message of the truth, Jesus is the truth. To preach the cross is to teach sanctification without which no one can see the Lord. Many of those who are called Christians are kept in ignorance for want of direct teaching. Therefore the church cannot live a life of power, authority and of sanctification. Some pastors deceive by their religious philosophy and are complacent. They look for revival, but harvest emotion; they look for the presence and power of God, but they harvest apostasy and luke warmness of the members. In our day, true teaching based on the Truth, or on Christ, is accused of being legalistic. People prefer the theology of the 'new morals' which advocates a freethinking and freedom of action in the church and in the world. The teaching that should be the Sword of the Spirit to cut the ties of iniquity and curse or to destroy the works of the devil is corrupted by human feelings, adapted to the course of the world and its culture, and that is apostasy. (Robert, Working 37-38)

Chapter 4 ☛ *Prepare the Value System- EPBOM*

Obedience - An Actual Value

If the new Christian accepts the supreme authority of the Bible, then he is called upon to demonstrate that acceptance "by obedience to the Word of God (Luke 6:46)" (Robert, Born Again 10). The new believer is instructed that "the Christian must manifest his Christian life by a total obedience that reflects itself by an internal and external testimony, as we have already studied. He must glorify God in his spirit and his body, which belongs to God. His life is a letter read by the whole world, as we are telling the world: 'here is the true life, come and live, this is how you must live'" (Robert, Born Again 62). The following story Dion tells will amply illustrate this value:

> One day, a young Christian man came to me for spiritual help. Since the time he accepted Jesus Christ, feelings of guilt still gnawed at his spirit. He was in the church, sang like all the others, but sadness always filled his heart when he returned home. He wanted to be helped. I asked him to tell me openly what was making him sad. This is what he confided in me:
> "Since the time I came to town to look for work, I have been living with an uncle. I wasn't yet a Christian. This uncle loved me a lot and, as a way of honoring him, I became the intermediary between him and a young woman from the area where we lived. My uncle gave me the responsibility of delivering messages to his beloved. The things that torments me, pastor, is to see my hypocrisy and my wickedness with my uncle and his mistress. How could I help my uncle by betraying him with this extra marital relationship? I never feel at ease or at peace in the presence of this woman. I feel a continuous sense of guilt. What do I need to do to be free?"
> I told him to go and confess to the woman the implications of their union. Not doing so would permit Satan to continue his accusation. He needed to go to his uncle and testify to him of his new life in Christ, of the love, which the Holy Spirit had given him for his uncle and for his Aunt. This love from God pushed him to confess his sins to both his Uncle and the mistress. This is what God now asked him to do.
> He followed my advice and went and told his uncle that all

> the things between him and this mistress was an abomination and wickedness in the eyes of God. He asked his uncle to forgive him for sinning against the home over which God had made him the head.
>
> The young man came to me later, joyfully testifying to the greatness of God. He no longer had the burdens or the accusations that he'd been carrying. His uncle had become interested in the Word of God after what his nephew had done, which had given him the desire to set his life in order. (Soul Therapy 27-28)

What about the Christian who merely gives lip service to obedience, but whose life has not changed? For Dion, the case is pretty cut and dried. "Spiritual growth, the Christian walk, obedience to the Word of God are current events in the life of all serious children of God. He who does not obey God, nor honor Him, is dead spiritually" (Born Again 96).

It is this value of obedience, possibly more than any other, that both channels the tremendous energy resident within the church, propelling it forward in ministry, and which causes the church, like a team of horses, to pull in the same direction.

Value #3: HUMILITY

Humility - An Articulated Value

Dion continually articulates the need for humility among his people.

> Humility is like the sea, primordial. To bring the people to the cross, to teach them in such a way so that they are broken and they no longer exist, so that the will of God exists, so that they are consecrated and obedient, can't be done without humility. God Himself is humble. He created everything there is, but we don't see Him. He is, however, manifested through His works. So that Christians will be instruments of victory to the glory of God, we must bring the church to embrace that they themselves must be erased. They must be humble in everything. (Interview)

Chapter 4 ☞ *Prepare the Value System- EPBOM*

God began His work of humility first with Dion. He worked first in Dion's life so that he would experience first hand what it is to be "erased". Only then could God's works be seen in his life. Dion asserts, "I am nothing, really. It is God who is something. We bring the church to that dimension, so that the power of God will always rest among us." Since God is opposed to the proud, but He gives grace to the humble, Dion attributes their long lasting revival to this work of humility.

Humility is one of EPBOM's articulated core values. I would suggest this is one reason why God has so graced and exalted that church. In their humility they have received greater grace to care for a greater number of new souls. Humility underscores all their work. Quoting Dion once again, "We bring the church to that dimension, so that the power of God will always rest among us."

Humility - An Actual Value

I have spent time with Dion in various places and under various circumstances during the last decade. He has stayed for a week in my home. I have visited him in Africa. We have ministered together in North Dakota and St. Petersburg, Russia. I had meetings with him in Houston over the years. Whether he was speaking, meeting people, eating, praying for someone, or relaxing after a service, I have never seen even a hint of pride. He has been gracious, gently, thoughtful of others, and humble. Dion is somewhat short in physical stature, standing about 5'2". He is so self-effacing that if you were to pass him on the street, you would pay him little notice.

I served as lead presenter for *The Year of Training* seminar in St. Petersburg, Russia during 1997-1998. I had secured an invitation for Pastor Dion and Pastor Boka (Boka gives oversight to EPBOM's cells) to be with us for a week of training during the fall module in 1997. While there, Pastor Boka demonstrated a degree of humility I still vividly remember.

It occurred our first Saturday evening in St. Petersburg. Chuck Squeri, the entrepreneur who had financed the training and brought us together, had slipped that morning while stepping out of a Russian bathtub and badly sprained his ankle. The team had spent the day and early evening at the publishing house, finalizing details for Monday's training launch. By late evening, Chuck was unable to walk or even place any weight on his ankle. At so late an hour, there was no possibility of either getting him to a doctor or obtaining a crutch for him. We were in an office building a number of floors up without an elevator.

I watched as Pastor Boka lifted Chuck on his back, carried him down the faintly lit flights of stairs, out into the rain and over the mud soaked ground to a waiting van at the opposite end of the alley. He repeated this again when we arrived at the hotel. It was a sincere act of service, humbly doing whatever was deemed necessary to meet the need of a brother. I have rarely seen that type of spirit in another Christian. Even rarer have I seen it in a pastor of Boka's stature and position. Bear in mind that Pastor Boka at the time oversaw more than 14,000 cells encompassing over 100,000 people. Dion's words ring true. Boka was erased so that God's works could be seen through him.

Value #4: CONSECRATION

Consecration - An Articulated Value

Like submission, obedience and humility, consecration is also articulated as a core value. Pastor Dion's constant concern is to see the entire Christian world consecrated to Christ without reservation (Soul Therapy 1). "To be sanctified is to be consecrated or dedicated to God to do His will (Romans 12:1-2)" (Working 42).

For Pastor Dion, consecration is simply a part of working according to God's model for life. "The Bible declares that the Church is the Body of Christ, we are the limbs and Christ is our Head: He is the Head of the Body of the Church; He is the beginning, The first born from the dead, so as to be is in all things the beginning. In our days, the conception that Christians have of God, Christ and His Church does not allow them to have a true consecration." (Working 31)

What are some of the attitudes preventing "true consecration"? Pastor Dion notes a number of them. First, distractions often destroy our motivation for consecrated living. We live in a materialistic century. He sees many that live in "developed" countries as preoccupied to the point of living for nothing but the love of material things and pleasures. In other words, they are so occupied that they don't have time to consecrate themselves to the things of God. If they go to church, it is with a divided heart tied to the clock and their personal interests. (Working 31)

What else prevents genuine consecration? People no longer like the teaching of the cross. Churches have replaced it with a general living guideline,

Chapter 4 ☛ Prepare the Value System- EPBOM

a teaching that is complacent and maintains the people in their comfort. (Working 31)

Third, lack of consecration today is the result of the "spiritual death in many churches where the people live in total independence from God. They can love God outside of the Church and be separated from Christ. Owing to wrong teachings, they are ignorant of the fact that Christ is the Head of His Church which is His body and that the Lord God is in Christ, thus in His Church. To live independent from God, from Christ and from His Church, to love God away from Christ or His Church, not to devote oneself totally to the Church and to her work, is to deny God, Christ and the Church (the brothers)." (Working 31)

Those who are members of EPBOM are taught that if they are to live a victorious life, then consecration to the Lord and a spirit of worldliness must be seen as mutually exclusive. "To bring a Christian to a victorious life and to maintain his spiritual growth, the Christian must be free of worldliness, that is, the taste he had for the pleasures and distractions of the fashionable society. He no longer belongs to the world, to this society founded on sexual relationships, entertainment, pleasures and luxury." (Robert, Born Again 54)

Consecration - An Actual Value

One example of how consecration is lived out can be seen in the life of Pastor Amoa Paul. Pastor Paul, head of the Social Works Department, was converted to Christ in 1986. He accepted the Lord through an evangelistic campaign at Abobo, a neighborhood of Abidjan. At the time he was working as a building technician.

In 1988 while the church was building their headquarters in Yopougon, a pastor from another church said to him, "They are constructing their temple (their church building), have you seen it?" He came here to see what was going on. He saw that those building the church building were doing the same kind of work that he was doing in his secular job. He asked his employer for a leave of absence so he might help EPBOM build their facilities. When he was refused his request, he quit his job. In 1988, leaving his secular employment, he consecrated his life to the service of God, helping to physically construct what would become EPBOM's future headquarters. For two years he worked without a salary, until the inauguration of the headquarters in 1990.

Following the inauguration of EPBOM's headquarters, Amoa Paul received two job offers. At the same time, the Lord called him to serve Him in full-time service. He had to choose which fork in the road to travel. So, in November 1991 he chose to serve God full time and has continued doing so up to the present.

What is it like for a man to quit his secular job to work without salary in the service of God? Amoa Paul's family intensely persecuted him because of his decision. Everyone rejected him. Yet even intense family persecution did not deter his selfless consecration to the work of God. He knew God had a reason even for the persecution. Today, Amoa Paul and his family have been reconciled. His family has even come to understand and agree that he made the right choice at that crucial fork in the road he faced.

In 1992 he oversaw the construction of a medical center at Attecoube. Today he is a full time Pastor leading the Department of Social Works. Amoa Paul's department is in charge of the construction of all of the church's physical projects.

Another example is that of Jonas Kouassi. What is it that leads a career diplomat to view himself first as an ambassador for Christ, and second as an ambassador for his country? Why would a career diplomat spend time praying "like a pastor"? How is it that a senior counselor in the embassy can live so different a life that it results in the salvation of his Ambassador? What drives a diplomat, posted in a foreign country, to spend every moment outside of work planting a cell and growing it up into a local church? It is his spiritual act of worship. It is a life lived in total consecration to God. This is the secret behind the life of Jonas Kouassi.

Jonas Kouassi is a career diplomat, currently a senior counselor in the Embassy of Cote d'Ivoire in Denmark. He has had a long career with the diplomatic corps in Cote d'Ivoire, serving first in Canada and then at the headquarters of the Minister in Abidjan before being posted to Denmark in 1994.

Before Jonas left for Canada, he considered himself simply a religious man. He was a member of the Methodist church. Though his father was one of the deacons of the Methodist church, Jonas was just, in his terms, religious.

Returning from Canada, he met Pastor Dion through a conference. Dion spoke with authority, inner conviction and power, talking about the power a man can have in Jesus Christ. He spoke about how once really converted to a disciple of Jesus, how as a son of God, a child of God, a Christian was protected against the darkness. Jonas was shocked. Jesus said in the Bible that He and the Father were one, that whoever believed in Jesus, Jesus would live in him and he would live in Jesus. Jonas was amazed to hear that the one who lives in

Chapter 4 ☞ *Prepare the Value System- EPBOM*

Jesus also lives in the Father. That night he came to understand that someone who is really converted and committed to Jesus Christ, who is living in Jesus Christ, is living in the Father. Although the power of darkness likes to attack his life, there is no one stronger than Jesus, or stronger than the Heavenly Father. He saw that, in a certain way, if you are hidden in Jesus Christ, in God through Jesus Christ, you will never be destroyed by the power of darkness.

He was so convinced about that point that after the conference he went rapidly onto the podium to speak to Pastor Dion. His discourse with Pastor Dion following that conference remains vividly in Jonas' memory.

JONAS: Pastor Dion, I am troubled by the conference. I am a Christian (Because no one wants to say he is not a Christian. That was in 1988 when I was exactly 40 years old.) Having heard the conference, I would like you to tell me about the difference. What is your secret? Do you have something special that the other pastors don't have, because I have never heard a man of God or a pastor telling about the devil or the power of darkness in this convicted way.

DION: I have no secret. (He was holding his Bible) This is my secret.

JONAS: Yes, pastor Dion, but I have my Bible, too.

DION: Oh, you have a Bible, that is very good. Praise the Lord. But may I ask you a question?

JONAS: Yes, pastor.

DION: Are you reading your Bible on a regular basis?

JONAS: No.

DION: This is the difference. If you don't read your Bible and if you don't eat the word that is in your Bible, you will not experience the power of God. You must read it and live a life that is according to the will of God as He expressed in the Bible.

JONAS: Where can I go to read my Bible or have the opportunity to be trained in it?

DION: I give every Wednesday free Bible studies in my church. So, if you want, you can come.

This is how Jonas began to come. Once at EPBOM, he discovered that Dion wasn't just a simple pastor who was delivering a message Jonas could go back home and ignore. Dion was standing in the fire of God and talking to his audience on behalf of God with 100% conviction about the Word of God. He was living daily in the Word of God.

After the first meeting at church Jonas joined Dion again on the podium and asked, "Pastor Dion could you pray for me?" Dion prayed, and Jonas afterwards asked him if he had time for a meeting. He related his life story and how he needed Dion to help him cope with the power of darkness and be strong and really live the life God wanted him to live.

Dion's response was quite simple. "This is not a problem. You only need to come regularly and to submit yourself to the Word of God. Do what the Word of God asks you to do. Then you will see how God will appreciate your life and He will dwell in you. Once He dwells in you, you will live a powerful life, a marvelous life, you will get set free, and your life will totally change." So that is exactly what Jonas did.

In joining the church Jonas laid aside all his accomplishments in the world and came into the church like a child beginning kindergarten. Having been saved and now meeting with the church two months, Pastor Dion asked Pastor Boka to invite Jonas to the baptism ceremony that they were doing in the river. Pastor Boka asked Jonas to get baptized. As Jonas recalls, "Once baptized, I was committed, highly committed in the church!"

For eight years in the church every Friday, every Sunday, every Wednesday, Jonas would take notes like a student. He kept all the books that helped him take these notes. He continued to come like a child who was very thirsty and hungry to get more and stronger food to eat.

Chapter 4   Prepare the Value System- EPBOM

He started by being a member of a cell. In time, Jonas dedicated his home to the church as a permanent place for the cell to meet. The Holy Spirit asked Jonas one day to open a prayer meeting service in his office and the ministry and to use his office for a new cell. He knew nothing about how to start. He came and talked to pastor Dion about it. He asked Dion to send him a pastor to lead it. He was told he was the pastor. How was he to lead it? He had a personal experience with the Lord when was saved. He was to begin by telling them of his experience, how God touched his heart. He was to speak of his consecration and commitment to Christ. Jonas began to come every Saturday to the home cell pastor training class held weekly in the church. In this way he received training as a home cell group pastor. He continued his home cell group in his home and remained as a member. Every Sunday from 4:00-5:00 p.m. he was a member participating in a cell group. Tuesday in his office he was the pastor of a cell group. He was a trained as a worker every Saturday. This was how Jonas became firmly rooted in the Word of God and rooted in the spiritual aspect of the church. That training continued until he was posted to Denmark in 1994.

He recalls, "When I left, I was like a pastor who was leaving Abidjan to Denmark. I was feeling like a man of God who was going on mission, not only the governmental mission, but as a man of God who was going to reach out to people in Denmark." Once in Denmark, Jonas started praying every morning and noon. Saturday was spent ministering with his wife and children. He started to invite people. "Can you come? We have a prayer meeting. Can you join us?"

Soon everybody in his office in the embassy was calling him "pastor", even his boss. Very soon his boss, the Ambassador, a general in the army, became converted to Christ. How did that happen? The Ambassador would say to him, "Since you are here something new has come into our mission. When I talk to you, you respond differently. You have never lost your temper. When we have a problem you are always saying, 'It will be better.' Every time you simply say, 'Yes it will be better, it will be better, it will be better.' You calm me down."

One day the Ambassador decided that a spirit haunted his residence. He and his children felt it. He was trying to get a priest who would go and exorcise the residence. The First Counsel told him, "Jonas is the pastor in the mission and I think he can do this work." He called Jonas into the office and asked him, "Are you a pastor?" Jonas acknowledged he was, but not an ordained pastor and asked the Ambassador to explain why he had asked. The Ambassador shared what was going on and asked Jonas for help.

Jonas agreed to pray for the house because "Jesus is with us". He told the Ambassador, "If you wish, we can fast. If you permit me to do so, we can ask Jesus to clean the house and He will do it because we are always with Him." The Ambassador, a Catholic Christian, was surprised that Jonas didn't intend to burn a candle or use incense. There was no blessed water or cross. He agreed. Jonas, along with some others, fasted and prayed three days. The last day they came into the house, laid hands on the walls and cast the demons out. The Ambassador could see immediate results.

Soon after that episode, the Ambassador came to say, "I have never known that Jesus was that strong. I want to give Him my life." Jonas started to minister to his Ambassador every night. He would meet him and the Ambassador would say, "Ah, pastor, you have come. Come and we will go into my upper room." Once he discovered in Jonas someone who had the Spirit of God and was anointed, they became close friends. Even today they remain close friends.

As the small church started praying, people began to come by ones and twos. They have continued to pray since 1995. They are now about 40 persons. In 1999 they baptized five persons, followed by six more during the first part of 2000. In June of 2000 they experienced an outpouring similar to that which Dion experienced during his first watch night. The church today is on fire.

Value #5: LIFE OF SHARING

Life of Sharing - An Articulated Value

In an interview with Pastor Boka Faustin, we catch a glimpse of the church's value for a shared lifestyle.

> We see the church as a family. When a man comes to the church, he is a brother. Automatically he is a brother. We give him what we have, as they did in the primitive church. It is a life of sharing, giving his life for his brother. In Cote d'Ivoire we have 67 ethnic groups. We do not view a man him as Yakouba, or as Beti. That is what we did when we were not Christians. In Christ that distinction disappears. We see the other one as a brother or sister. So, the life of sharing that con-

Chapter 4 ☛ *Prepare the Value System- EPBOM*

sists of exchanging words, prayer one for another, visiting one another, this is the second value that I see.

Is there a theological basis behind EPBOM's adoption of a life of sharing as a core value? Though he does not develop the theme further, Pastor Boka put his finger on the heart of it when he defined the church as the family of God.

Life of Sharing - An Actual Value

If the church genuinely views itself as a family, we would expect a life of sharing to be a normal part of their lifestyle. Are there evidences of this? Pastor Boka supplies us with a number of such evidences:

> This first case involves the sharing of money. There was a brother who invited a thief to church. He didn't know that the visitor was a thief. He only knew that he had come to Christ. At the end of the week the police came to look for that man. The brother who brought him was obliged to accompany him to the police station. The police accused the man of stealing 250,000 cephas. They alleged he stole it from a white man. If he didn't reimburse this money, they were going to take him to prison. So, the brother came back and visited with a few other brothers in the church. He collected the 250,000 cephas and repaid the former thief's debt. Why? He did it because the thief, having come to Christ, was now a brother in the Lord. It is this value that they seek to develop.
>
> This second example involves the sharing of time. A Christian who works a secular job is kept busy by that job. But, even in his lack of time he makes time to be at church Wednesday afternoons for the Bible studies, Fridays for prayer, on Sunday mornings for the service, on Sunday afternoon for cell, and even to be present at other programs throughout the week. Their people are absorbed in the work of God. However, they understand that in committing to the Lord's Body, their time no longer belongs to them.
>
> Also, because they work, each man understands they must also honor God with their goods. When there are missionary

trips to take, information is given to the people regarding the cost of the necessary plane tickets for the missionaries. Automatically the people will start giving money. Their goods are to serve the Lord.

Once there was a pastor who was supposed to go to France. The people were praying for the ticket, that the money would come in to pay for it. There was an individual who heard God say, "Do not pray!" He heard again, "Do not pray. Close your mouth. If you do not pray, I am going to show you that I am God." He stopped praying while the rest of the people assembled continued to pray. Before they finished, though, the man lifted his hand. Boka called him forward. He related how God told him to stop praying because those who are in the family of God were praying because they did not have money to send out a missionary. God told him, however, "You have money. It is in the account and your checkbook is in your sack. Write a check. Those who pray don't have money. You, you can't pray because you do have money. All you have to do is write a check. Through you, if you will write a check, I will be exalted." He wrote the check and everyone applauded the Lord. He came to understand that he was in the family, and that, in the family, the father was going somewhere and was needing money, yet the provision was already there. The man acted upon what he had been taught about the value of sharing. This is not to say that each church member cannot have their own goods or their own house. But whatever they have, they give to the Lord. If they don't have, then they are taught not to complain and they don't give. If they do not have, they pray that God will raise up someone else who can provide for the need. If they can contribute, then they contribute. That is the basis of sharing in the work at EPBOM.

One last illustration will further evidence this life of sharing among the people. Often there are Christians who are won to Christ from certain sects and then persecuted by their families. These new believers are entrusted to those who are employed so they can house them. The church also assumes the responsibility for paying for their schooling if they are in school and providing them with a scholarship and aid. The same work is done with students. Wherever they are, that is their place of evangelization to win their fellow students and their friends. Great emphasis is also placed on follow-up through those who are married. Those who are married understand their responsibility to prove to be a good couple and provide a good home for others in need. If the home is healthy, the church will be healthy also. The church places emphasis upon couples watching over those that are single. Those who are employed seek to meet the needs of those who are unemployed. The church cannot help everyone, but EPBOM encourages every member to actively share in the ministry of helping those in need.

Value #6: PRAYER AND FASTING

Prayer and Fasting - An Articulated Value

Prayer is an integral value at EPBOM. The sixth home visit made by a cell worker to a new believer instructs the new believer as to the proper place of prayer in the new Christian's life. This is followed up in week seven with a study regarding obstacles to prayer (Faustin, Follow-up 16).

This is reinforced by an entire chapter devoted to the life of prayer in the manual of instruction for the baptismal candidate. Prayer is presented as "an effective element to dialogue between the creator and man. Even if God knows in advance our needs, it is acceptable to Him if we pray. This proves our dependence and our acknowledgment to His paternal and divine authority" (Robert, Born Again 48). The victorious Christian life is presented as having its roots in prayer. "It is by prayer, one of the arms of all Christians (Ephesians 6:10-20) that makes us strong. Numerous blessing await each one of us, if we will make prayer one of our principle priorities" (Robert, Born Again 52).

Prayer & Fasting - An Actual Value

Prayer is practiced continually and openly at every level of the church's life. Prayer and intercession for the lost is an integral part weekly of each cell meeting. The Division of Intercession within the Demonology Department works day and night (Robert, Working 49).

While visiting the church in Abidjan, I had a room for nearly three weeks on the third floor of a building located next to the main sanctuary and one story above it. Each night without fail there was a gathering in the sanctuary that prayed from 12:00 midnight to 4:00 a.m. each morning. The intensity of their prayers and intercession was unmistakable, even though offered up in French. During CIAMEL 2000, a group of intercessors gathered directly under the platform used by the worship team and speakers to pray. Next to the deliverance area was another area dedicated to intercession. Both areas were in constant use during the services. Intercessors also pray regularly during each normally scheduled Sunday morning service.

When Dion was with our team in Russia in October of 1997, he had over 500 members back home praying and fasting for us during the week he was with us. Prayer at EPBOM reminds me of breathing. It is so constant as to be almost unnoticeable by the one doing it.

Value #7: SPIRITUAL GIFTS

Spiritual Gifts - An Articulated Value

The absolute necessity of spiritual gifts is taught early on in the Christian walk, even to the candidates for baptism. "By the spiritual gifts, God equips the Church to better aid His people to keep healthy and to live easily the Christian life in His power. The manifestation of the kingdom of heaven are the activities of God through the Church" (Matthew 12:28; 1 Cor. 12:4-11)" (Robert, Born Again 24). Chapter four of *So You Are Born Again!* is dedicated to teaching the new convert about the person, work, and ministry of the Holy Spirit in his life.

One of the twelve stated requirements of every cell is "to permit faithful members to learn to manifest grace and spiritual gifts" (Robert, Working 57). That is first taught in the disciples' classes after baptism, and then reinforced in the experience of the cell. As an additional part of their training through the discipleship classes, every newly baptized believer is further taught that all the different church departments he will ultimately work as part of actually "constitute the different gifts of the Holy Spirit" (Robert, Working 58).

Chapter 4 ☛ *Prepare the Value System- EPBOM*

Spiritual Gifts - An Actual Value

Many churches talk about the gifts of the Holy Spirit, but few provide an opportunity for their people to utilize them. Christian Schwarz discovered through his research regarding Natural Church Development that "no factor influences the contentedness of Christians more than whether they are utilizing their gifts or not" (24). He went on to write that, "None of the eight quality characteristics showed nearly as much influence on both personal and church life as 'gift-oriented ministry'" (24). He additionally noted that, "Of all the variables associated with this quality characteristic, the question on 'lay training' has the greatest correlation with church growth" (25).

The role of the cell leader is to help his member to identify his gift and to then integrate him into the appropriate ministry department. "The training program of the cell includes the practice of spiritual gifts, prayer for the sick, healing wounded hearts, delivering captives from the influence of evil spirits, spiritual help for the weak and material assistance to the needy" (Robert, Cell Group 26). The cell strategy and structure allows each member to become "more dedicated to the cause of the Lord as they allow the Holy Spirit to manifest Himself powerfully through them by the spiritual gifts and fruit" (Robert, Cell Group 7).

The departments of the local church "incarnate" the different ministries through which the Holy Spirit manifests powerfully for the success of the church (Robert, Working 47). Once discovered through the cell ministry, every member of the church is then established in a department commensurate with the gifting discovered. In the context of that department, they become active channels of the Holy Spirit's activities and "incarnation."

We can see, then, that EPBOM provides initial teaching on the gifts, opportunities in the cell for a proving ground, a means of employing the gifts in the corporate body, and the equipping required to continue to function.

LIVING KINGDOM VALUES
CHALLENGING THE AMERICAN CELL CHURCH

Few pastors in America have taken the time and effort to develop, define, and articulate their own set of core values. Even fewer churches have been guided down that highway. As a result, the outward beauty of our churches often withers quickly in the intense heat generated by the conflicting values of pastor, boards, denominations and people. We are driven by our denominational priorities, our programs, material, or even our lofty purposes. We are not values-driven churches with values-driven leadership. As a consequence, our ministry distinctives are blurred. Personal involvement is minimal. That which is deemed most important languishes. We have no sure anchor in the midst of change. We experience disconnect between our goals and our behavior. Our people remain uninspired, and therefore unmotivated. Our credibility as leaders is questioned. Ministry vision becomes nearsighted. We take little risk, fail for the most part at resolving conflicts and lack clues how to solve our problems. And we wonder why we experience so little success! All this, because the underground reality of an articulated and actualized value system grounded in a deontological ethical moral system does not exist. Insanity is continuing to do the same thing day after day, week after week, month after month, and year after year, all the while expecting the outcome to be different. It is time to move from insanity to sanity. It is time to develop what we have hitherto either been ignorant of or disobedient toward and become values-driven. It is time to Prepare the Way of the Lord!

Chapter 4 ☛ *Prepare the Value System- EPBOM*

REFLECTIONS

1. As a leader, can you articulate your core values? If yes, what are they? Identify your top 7-9 personal life core values. To whom are you accountable for living out your core values?

2. Can you articulate the values that undergird your church? If yes, what are they? Does your church have a single, dominant value? If so, what is it? How do you know it is dominant?

3. What core values does your church hold on a conscious level? Can you identify any core values that it holds on an unconscious level? How have the conscious and unconscious values affected the church's ministry?

4. What core values do you share with your church? What values are not shared. How has this affected your attitude toward and involvement in your church?

ACTION POINTS

1. Take your list of personal core values. How have you seen these values demonstrated through your behavior? For each one you articulated, provide substantive illustrations to demonstrate that they are actual values and not simply aspirational values.

2. Take the list you compiled of your church's core values. For each one you identified, provide substantive illustrations from the life of your church to demonstrate that they are actual values and not simply aspirational values.

3. Refer to the graphic on page 96 entitled *Change...Through the Eyes of a Change Agent* and complete the following exercise:

    ❑ Select a core value from your earlier reflections.

    ❑ In a single column, list your staff, elders and other key leaders that must embrace that core value before any significant change can be affected in your church.

    ❑ Beside each name, write where they currently are along the change continuum.

    ❑ Next, record what context you as a change person must provide for them in order to move them toward a full embracing of that value. What is their need? Teaching? Modeling? Experience?

    ❑ Finally, record your specific plan to help them as you interact with them day by day.

PHASE 1

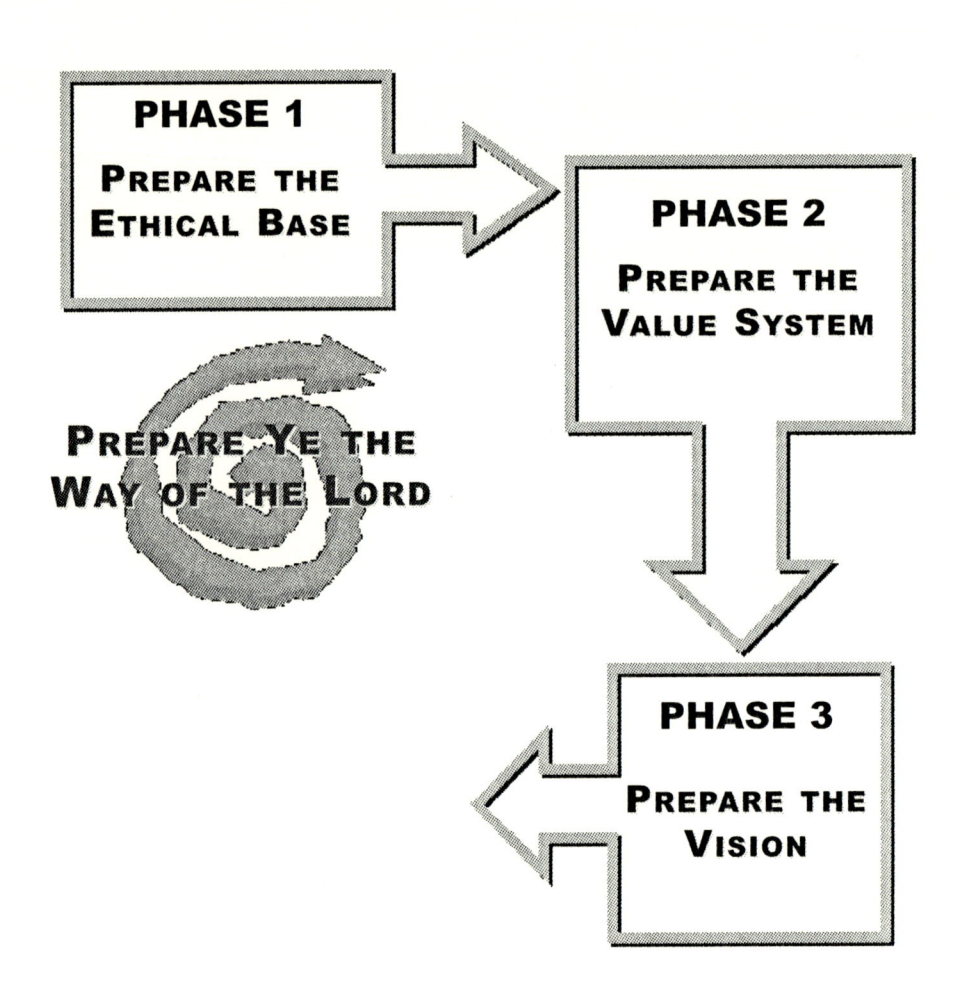

PREPARE THE ETHICAL BASE

PHASE 2

PREPARE THE VALUE SYSTEM

PREPARE YE THE WAY OF THE LORD

PHASE 3

PREPARE THE VISION

5
PREPARE THE VISION

Then the Lord answered me and said, "Record the vision and inscribe it on tablets, that the one who reads it may run. For the vision is yet for the appointed time; it hastens toward the goal and it will not fail. Though it tarries, wait for it; for it will certainly come, it will not delay.

Habukkak 2:2-3

Chapter 5 ☞ *Prepare the Vision*

THE NECESSITY OF RECEIVING GOD'S VISION

For the church to grow you must have a vision. What you don't see you cannot have. What we see is what we take. The quality of the work depends on the quality of the vision. If the vision is good, the work is good. If the vision is mediocre, then the work will be mediocre. So, the first thing that is needed is the vision that God gives. When you start, it is because you have a vision, a good vision. Know God in all the areas and avoid thinking you are wise in your own eyes without Jesus. Once we have these two things, we must agree with God regarding what He says. That is to say, we cannot communicate the Word of God from what people think or what people say. You can only communicate what He says, regardless of what it does. That way, He is with you. (Robert, Interview)

In Numbers 27:15-23 we discover Moses, the leader of Israel, asking that God would "set a man" over the congregation of Israel. In this way they would no longer be sheep without a shepherd. Moses became that "set man". There must be that "set man" appointed by God, that man carrying the mantle of leadership and direction, that man receiving the vision from the Lord for His people. I suggest that any vision the set man receives will encompass at least five basic components. Three of these I believe are general and universal. Through the years I have observed that where any of these first three components are absent or deficient, growth becomes retarded, we are inhibited from developing the lifestyle we say we desire, and we fall short in significantly impacting those around us. The remaining two components will be unique and rather specific to the vision given.

VISION COMPONENT #1
THE CHURCH AS THE FAMILY OF GOD

It is my observation that many cell churches, regardless of the motif presented, create cells out of a business or sports paradigm, rather than out of a family paradigm. Leadership serve as "facilitators," "leaders," "coaches," "apprentices," "supervisors," and "managers." One need only examine the extant cell literature detailing leadership development and cell structure to verify this contention. While we talk about a cell being a family with fathers, young men and children, this nomenclature is usually reserved for a description of a cell member's relative Christian maturity, not a model for relationships among and between cell members themselves. Father-son and mother-daughter relationships are given lip service, but are too often non-existent. Cell leaders and interns do not look at their responsibilities as fathering, mothering, or even being big brothers and sisters. Yet, as we shall see, the family paradigm is the one God has chosen to reveal in Scripture as one of three primary images of the church. A vision lacking this essential component is simply deficient.

From the beginning, it has been God's intention that His people exist as a community. This reflects the very nature of the triune God as Father, Son and Holy Spirit. God, though one, is an expression of community. Our lives are lived out in community as families, tribes and nations. Only within the context of a living dynamic community can we understand our responsibility and accountability one to another. The church as community originated in the mind of God. His activity brought it into being. He has given it its structure, its ministry as well as its mission. The Christian's life style described by the Apostle Paul throughout the letter to the Ephesian church is only possible if the Christian is living within community with other believers.

From Old Testament Israel we understand that relationship both to others and to God is the essence of community. We find that God was vitally interested in how His people were organized for living out these relationships. While the first four of the Ten Commandments detailed their relationship to God, the remaining six outlined how they were to live in relationship with one another.

These relationships are lived out in the context of the family. The whole community was divided into the basic family, the extended family, units of hundreds and units of thousands. The head of the family was accountable to the leader of the extended family. In turn this leader was accountable to the leader of hundreds and he in turn was accountable to the leader of thousands. Ultimately, every leader was accountable to the tribal leader and then to the nation's leader, who himself was accountable to God (Exodus 18). It is in the family gatherings that we find the family celebrating the immanence of God, the God Most Nigh. This is particularly revealed in the Passover meal. It is in this meal that we see the God that comes close. It was in the small group gathering of the family and extended family that they remembered and passed on to their children that their God had specifically concerned Himself with their well being.

In the New Testament church, relationship both to others and to Christ is also the essence of community. These relationships are also lived out in the context of the family. In Ephesians 2:19 the apostle Paul calls the church "God's household," God's oikos. The relationships that exist between believers are those of brothers and sisters through their common adoption into the family of God (Ephesians 1:5; John 1:12). Paul constantly describes his relationship with those he led in family terms, especially as a father-son relationship. In I Corinthians 4:14-17, Timothy is referred to as a son. Paul speaks of his relationship to the Corinthian church as a father (I Corinthians 4:14-17) The heart of cell life must be that of a redeemed family!

VISION COMPONENT #2
THE CHURCH AS THE BODY OF CHRIST

Second, I have come to observe that many cell churches employ a business organizational paradigm to understand and define their structure at the corporate level. I know of pastors who call themselves the CEO of the church and relate to those around them as any corporate CEO would relate. I know of far too many church boards made up of elders and/or deacons who make decisions like any corporate board and run the church like a business. Yet, the paradigm of the church as a body, as a living organism and not as an organization, is the paradigm God has chosen to build upon in Scripture. So, alongside the component of family, the vision must incorporate a second component, that of the church as the Body of Christ.

The term *Body of Christ* is used in Scripture to partially define the essence of the church. This New Testament image is highly significant in setting forth the nature of the Church. As the Body of Christ, the Church is in a vital and dynamic relationship with Christ as the Head. Additionally, membership in the Body results in body parts being mutually interdependent and assuming mutual responsibility for one another. As Body members, individual members of the church then learn how to conduct themselves in an orderly fashion as part of the church. As the Body of Christ, the church has a vital relationship with Christ, having no life outside of Jesus Christ, the head. This vital relationship can be seen through her incorporation into Christ, through her total dependence upon Christ and her complete subjection to Christ.

As the body, which belongs to Christ, the individual members of the church are to conduct themselves in an orderly fashion as "body members" set by the Holy Spirit. In Romans 12:3ff., believers are admonished to know their own place in the church as a whole. This is elucidated by Paul's use of imagery of the body in which the body is seen as comprised of many members, but in which every member does not have the same function. In like manner, the church, too, is to know itself: "we as many are one body in Christ, but individually members one of another" (v. 5).

Without a doubt, the mutual unity and diversity of the church is illustrated and commended under the figure of the human body. The designation of the church as the Body of Christ is not intended primarily to qualify its mutual unity and diversity, but to denote its unity in and with Christ. The distinguishing feature of the idea of the church as the Body of Christ is that the many, by virtue of their common belonging to Christ, now form in Him a new unity with each other. They are altogether in Him, not each one individually, but as a corporate unity. With all the diversity of gifts, one is always to keep in view the unity of the Spirit. This now brings a corporate consciousness to the church, rather than fostering an individualistic consciousness. Each member thus has a consciousness of being part of a greater whole while at the same time understanding how to conduct himself as part of that greater whole.

How is this worked out in practice in a growing cell church? As an illustration, turn your attention with me again to Pastor Boka Faustin and *Eglise Protestante Baptiste Oeuvres et Mission Internationale*. In his interview, Boka paints a detailed picture of the interdependence between the individual members and the various organizational departments:

> We know that the eye sees, but the eye doesn't walk. The feet walk, but can't take things with their hand or help a man eat. So is the local body. We start from the head, that is the

Council of the Church. It has ears to hear and eyes to see and a nose to smell and a mouth to give counsel. So the four senses are the leaders who are above. We have the organs of touch. These are the different departments that receive the counsel. They receive the word of the council and then they execute it. So that the core will be constituted, we talk about discipleship. We train each person. When we understand what he can do, if he is an arm we put him as an arm. He works as an arm. If he is a leg, he is a leg so he can work. We see the body as the different functionings of the church.

We don't use the expression, "This is my gifting." We say that we are polyvalent, multipurpose. It is true that God places us in a ministry from a gifting that has been discovered. However, we must be able to do everything. We have never asked and we will never ask, "Who can do this?" No. We know who can do it because, starting from baptism, we give six months of training. During those six months, before baptizing them, we see who can do what. Then for another six months they do through the discipleship cycle. We discover what he can do. So we do not say, "Who can chase this demon? Who can file papers with the government?" No, All the ministries are already there. We don't say that we have a gifting. God is a Spirit and God can use each person as He needs. All we do is put them into the interior of those ministries and say, "Ok you do this and you do that." If we don't follow this step, then we can have false prophets in the church. Or they could have this prophecy and make it a ministry. It can destroy the pastor or even destroy the vision of our church. Because the pastor is the head, would it not be God to speak to him? But if God did not speak to him, but spoke to a prophet who was under him, that would not be normal.

We were in Tennessee. There was a woman who said to Dion, "The pastor doesn't listen to me. I am the prophetess. When I say this, he does the contrary. And because of that, I took a certain number of people and went out and we want to make our own work. Was this alright?" We said, "No, this is not alright. It is not you who God established." The same example was with Moses and those who followed him. They said all of us have the spirit of God. But God said no, Moses is not like you. I chose Moses and you must listen to him. We know how Miriam was struck and Aaron bowed before Moses. It is true that God can raise up prophets, but that one which God has placed to manage and lead the church must manage all of this. For us, it starts at the training session for discipleship.

Pastor Dion cannot come to me and say, "Can you do this?" He knows what I must do. He knows what pastor Julien must do. He knows what pastor "X" must do. He knows those things. It is not to say, though, that we are canonized there. No. There are people, however, who are specialized in certain areas and they manage that ministry. (Interview)

In view of Pastor Boka's response likening Dion to Moses, the reader may wonder regarding pastoral accountability. Is Pastor Dion accountable to anyone else? There is accountability by all the pastoral staff. Pastor Dion has established both a General Council and Department of Coordination of Ministries. His formal accountability is maintained at that level, though informally he has those who speak into his life also from among the pastors.

VISION COMPONENT #3
THE CHURCH AS THE ARMY OF GOD

Third, I have come to observe that most cell churches in America continue to look at themselves as non-militant, even pacifistic when it comes to the Kingdom of God. Yet, the military paradigm is the one God has chosen to stress. I have even been told by leaders within the cell movement in America that the mindset such as found in the church in Abidjan is to militaristic and would never fly in America. Perhaps Paul's words to Timothy were for another place and another time, and not relevant for 21st century America! Perhaps we are not called to suffer hardship as a good soldier. Perhaps we are no longer to consider ourselves in active service. Perhaps it is now fine to become entangled in the affairs of everyday life and live unprepared as a soldier of Christ! Or, perhaps we should read closely when Paul exhorts:

Chapter 5 — Prepare the Vision

> 2Tim. 2:3 Suffer hardship with me, as a good soldier of Christ Jesus.
>
> 2Tim. 2:4 No soldier in active service entangles himself in the affairs of everyday life, so that he may please the one who enlisted him as a soldier.

The third vision component is the vision of the church as the army of God. The church is an army, make no mistake about it! EPBOM's vision has settled that question for them.

> The church is also an army. As an army, we act to extend the Kingdom, to conquer the earth, to conquer the kingdoms. When we save a soul for example, that kingdom was conquered. We free that person. God takes possession of that person. The church is an army that must conquer to win, to win the world. So it is a family. When we win someone, we introduce him into the family. But it is also an army. It is organized as a family, but it is also organized as an army. She plays the two roles.
>
> For example, in an army, we have the general. We have the colonels. We have the lieutenants. We have sergeants and all the others. We have the recruits. They are the newcomers. Maybe the sergeants and the corporals are already being trained as a worker. But the commander is seen as a cell group worker who leads others. Above them you have pastors of pastors. Then you have the head. Then you have Jesus Christ. Then you have God Himself. That is how the church is organized. (Dion, Interview.)

As we seek to embrace the paradigm of the church as the army of God, we must first come to understand that the church is involved in a cosmic war between God's Kingdom and Satan's kingdom. Jesus has won the decisive battle. He has broken the power of the enemy. However, the battle rages on. Jesus calls His followers to wage war against the kingdom of darkness just as He did. He has given His followers power and authority to wage effective warfare. A cell church's life must flow out of this military paradigm, viewing herself as the army of God, if she is to do the work of the Kingdom.

Jesus proclaimed war when He stated that the Kingdom of God was near (Mark 1:14-15). Jesus came to destroy the works of the devil (1 John 3:8). Note His decisive declaration: "The Spirit of the Lord is upon me because he anointed me to preach the gospel to the poor. He has sent me to proclaim release to the captives, and recovery of sight to the blind, to set free those who are downtrodden, to proclaim the favorable year of the Lord" (Luke 4:18-19).

In the Gospels Satan is pictured as a strong man. "His palace or house is 'this present evil age' (Gal. 1:4), and his 'goods' are men and women under his evil influence. However, he has not been left in peace to manage his affairs. A stronger, Jesus, has assailed and overcome him. The victory over Satan is the same whether it is described as a binding of the strong man (Matthew 12:29) or stripping him of his armor (Luke 11:22). In metaphorical language Jesus interprets his own mission among men as an invasion of Satan's kingdom (Matt. 12:26) for the purpose of assaulting the Evil One, overcoming him, and despoiling him of his goods" (Ladd, 151).

Through His life, death and resurrection, Jesus won the decisive battle against Satan and his kingdom. In His life Jesus bound Satan (Mark 3:23-27). In His ministry, healing the sick, cleansing the lepers, raising the dead, rebuking and expelling demons, Jesus began to plunder Satan's kingdom. On the cross He broke the power of Satan (Hebrews 2:14). In His resurrection He disarmed Satan (Colossians 2:15). At His return He will completely destroy Satan and his kingdom (Revelation 20:10).

Jesus recruited and trained His followers to do exactly what He did. He gave them power and authority to do the work of His Kingdom. To the Twelve He gave power and authority (Matthew 10:1, 7-8; Luke 9:1-2). He likewise empowered the seventy (Luke 10:1-20). That they engaged in the warfare at hand and the church experienced tremendous growth is obvious from the record of the book of Acts. Wagner and Pennoyer write that, "At least 10 kinds of sign phenomena in the book of Acts produced evangelistic growth in the church. Specifically called 'signs and wonders' nine times, they include healing, expelling demons, resuscitation of the dead, sounds 'like the blowing of a violent wind' from heaven, fire over the heads of people, tongues and being transported from one place to another.... In the book of Acts there are 14 instances where both apostles and non-apostles, for example, preached, performed works of power, and saw significant church growth" (25-26). The table below summarizes their findings (26).

Chapter 5 ☛ *Prepare the Vision*

Correlation of Works of Power, Preaching, and Church Growth in the N.T.

WORKS OF POWER	PREACHING	CHURCH GROWTH
Pentecost (Acts 2:4)	Peter (Acts 2:14)	3,000 added (Acts 2:41)
Cripple Healed (3:1)	Peter (3:12)	5,000 believed (4:4)
Miraculous Signs (8:6)	Philip (8:6)	Men/Women Believe (8:12)
Philip Appears (8:26)	Philip Teaches (8:35)	Eunuch Baptized (8:38)
Angel Appears, Vision Falls (10:3,12,44)	Peter (10:34)	Gentiles Baptized (10:47)
Lord's Hand with them (11:20-21)	Men from Cyprus (11:20)	Many Believe (11:21)
Evidence of God's Grace (11:23-24)	Barnabas (11:23)	Multitudes Believe (11:24)
Holy Spirit Falls (13:1-3)	Barnabas, Saul (13:1)	Churches in Asia (14:23) and in Europe (17:11)
Miraculous signs and wonders (14:1-7)	Paul and Barnabas (14:3)	People Divided (14:4,21,22)
Cripple Healed (14:8-18)	Paul & Barnabas (14:15)	Disciples Gather (14:21)
Cast out Demon (16:16)	Paul & Silas (16:14)	Believers Gather (16:40)
Earthquake, Prison Opens (16:25, 26)	Paul & Silas (16:31-32)	Jailer & Household (16:34)
God's Power (18:1; cf. 1 Cor. 2;1, 4, 5)	Paul (18:5)	Many Believed (18:8)
Extraordinary miracles (19:11-12)	Paul (19:10)	Churches in Asia (19:26)

We too have been commissioned to enter the strong man's house and plunder his goods. The war is not over. Jesus commissioned His disciples to continue His work until He returned (Matthew 28:18-20). Paul's exhortation and reminder to Timothy (2 Timothy 2:3-4) is as applicable for us today as it was when originally given for Timothy. We are to join together and partner with those who are soldiers for the Lord, facing the vile, ugly, horrible and foul crcumstances all around us and if we must, then suffer to get the job done!

Paul continues to employ this figure frequently of the church. Epaphroditus is referred to as "my brother and fellow worker and fellow soldier" (Philippians 2:25). Archippus is noted as "our fellow soldier" (Philemon 1:2). The Apostle speaks of giving the devil a bivouacking place, *topon*, another military image in Ephesians 4:27.Each soldier must have a consciousness of being part of a greater whole, the army of God, while at the same time understanding how to conduct themselves as part of that greater whole.

Turning once again to **Eglise Protestante Baptiste Oeuvres et Mission Internationale** as an illustration, we discover that the vision of the church being the family of God, the Body of Christ, and the army of God has been effectively transferred from Dion to his leadership team. The symbiotic relationship of these three concepts is easily identifiable in the thinking of Boka Faustin, the pastor responsible for the church's over 14,000 cells:

Because He is called the God of Heavenly Hosts, automatically we are soldiers, which makes us an army. (In French, the native language in Cote d'Ivoire, actually the head of the army is the word for the Lord of hosts!)

In the army, it is not always a pleasant word the head speaks. They may give an order, "go and do this. Just go. When you are finished, if you want an explanation, then we will give it to you." Christians understand this in the church. They see the pastors as generals and the workers that are really well trained as colonels and captains. The others are the corporals. So, all of us work according to what the head says. Everyday that is what I live here. Dr. Dion comes, and says, "Go and pay a plane ticket for that person." Sometimes we do not have money. We go look for it. We don't say we don't want to. We live the cross. When we went to South Africa, there was a pastor that said, "come down a little from the cross and walk around a little." We said, "No, for us the cross is obedience to authority. And if it comes from God we cannot go against it." So it is like the work of the army.

You know that every military person is equipped. We train the Christians to play the role of a true military person through watch-nights, through fasting, through conferences and seminars, through everything that we can do so they can understand their role.

[Between the family and the army] the family is the priority, because everything depends upon the explanation that is given to the Christian family. If they didn't understand that the family, *Eglise Protestante Baptiste Oeuvres et Mission Internationale*, is led by pastor Dion Robert, they couldn't submit to me, because the orders come from him. I take them and communicate them to them. Look at Joshua 11:15. It is written that God ordered Moses and Moses ordered Joshua. Joshua accomplished everything without forgetting anything. So, if you did not understand that within this family that pastor Dion is the first, or the head, and we are behind him and they are with us, then no one would accomplish what he said, and no one would be a soldier. (Interview)

While maintaining corporate consciousness as a family, and a body and an army, individual members are able to function out of their giftedness and fight out of their authority. A functional family does not consist of independent members. Rather, each family member is in an interdependent relationship with every other member and integrated into the whole. In like manner, the army and the body, to function properly, is integrated and also interdependent. While these three components are essential for a balanced vision, there is a fourth component that ties them all together.

VISION COMPONENT #4
THE CHURCH FULFILLING THE STRATEGY OF GOD

The three vision components previously discussed are universal and fundamental. They must be incorporated within the overall vision of every local church. To not do so is to cripple the work of the church. Beyond these three, however, the pastor must also have God's specific wisdom for the advancement of the work in the local church for which he is responsible. It is only through God's revelation of this specific wisdom that the pastor can discern the unique strategies God would employ to further His Kingdom.

Without a doubt, *Eglise Protestante Baptiste Oeuvres et Mission Internationale* would never have experienced the rapid growth it has without the initial vision of the senior pastor, Dion Robert. In the early days, Dion lacked neither zeal nor a love to see souls saved. He burned to see multitudes saved. Yet, all his labor bore little fruit until the Holy Spirit, the Living God, created in him His Vision. In this divine vision he saw in the spirit multitudes of men, women and children converted, healed, delivered and restored. It was at that point that God's word became more and more clear to him. Hearing God's voice was no longer a problem or a mystery. His voice became familiar to Dion with the result that His wisdom and His guidance led the work. Dion saw the vision of God. He heard and knew how to transmit that vision to others. He continues to receive fresh vision and to organize even the structure of the church according to the vision and wisdom he receives.

According to Pastor Dion, the work of God must not be improvised. The work must be done according to the model and strategy that is received from the Lord. A senior pastor must both obtain the vision from God and be able to transmit that vision to his people. As Dion makes clear, the work of the Kingdom depends upon this:

> Nothing is improvised in the Kingdom of God. The servant of God who lives by the Spirit will make exploits with God. God uses him to bring about great things, to accomplish His design. This is why it is absolutely necessary to have the vision of God. It is written: 'Whoever has will be given more, and he will have an abundance. Whoever does not have, even what he has will be taken from him' (Matthew 13:12). In the framework of the minister of God, we generally give but what we have received from Him. To receive from Him takes a disposition of spirit or heart for God, in view of a clear vision. We understand why there are some that are more successful than others are. We must know how to listen to God, how to receive from Him, and above all, know Him. Thus I started to learn to live by the Spirit and by faith. The result was not long to come. The Lord opened my spirit and my eyes. He communicated His wisdom, which sustains everything living. I started to organize the church according to the model that He showed me, little by little. You must see the vision of God. You must know how to hear and transmit His message. The success of a ministry depends on that. (Working 44-45)
>
> It is imperative to work according to the model in view of Christ. "A divine work, such as the church of Jesus Christ is not led with eyes closed" (Interview).

Once again Pastor Dion forcibly drives this point home:

> After these fundamental elements, you must look next to God for the wisdom to advance the work step by step. That is what God gives in Ezekiel 47. He gave that to me as well. He gave me where and how we were to go, step by step. The water, the water comes from heaven. We are in it to our ankles, to our knees, to our waist and after that we swim in it. Within it you have the fish. You have trees. You have the workers that must

bring forth fruit. You have the strategies, a lot of nets, so that the work will not be dead. You must have many strategies because men which we save do not resemble one another. They are all men, but they are different psychologically. You must know them, how to bring them in. That is why you need nets. It is all this that you must do. You must follow the program of the Lord. When the church follows the program of God, the revival is there, the fruit is there. But, if we leave the program of the Lord and establish our own program, it will not work. That is why a lot of churches do not go very far.

Jesus came. He founded His Kingdom and said these are the principles of My Kingdom. These are the activities of My Kingdom. Now we lay them aside and put in our own principles, and it doesn't work. Even a newcomer must understand that the church, the structure of the church, must be based on the program of the Lord. Then the Lord Himself works. Use His program and the Lord will be with you. (Interview)

VISION COMPONENT #5
DISCOVERING THE UNDISCOVERED COUNTRY - THE FUTURE

Introduction

Although the words were first penned by William Shakespeare, Star Trek popularized the phrase *The Undiscovered Country* in its movie by that same name. What was this undiscovered country? It was, and is still, the future. Leaders, especially senior leaders, are not called upon to invent the future, but to discover how God is already working, join Him, and paint a picture for others that will motivate them also to join the work of God.

Underlying all is the assumption that God is already at work. Hear the words of Jesus in John 5:17-20.

> But He answered them, "My Father is working until now, and I Myself am working." For this reason therefore the Jews were seeking all the more to kill Him, because He not only was

breaking the Sabbath, but also was calling God His own Father, making Himself equal with God. Therefore Jesus answered and was saying to them, "Truly, truly, I say to you, the Son can do nothing of Himself, unless it is something He sees the Father doing; for whatever the Father does, these things the Son also does in like manner. For the Father loves the Son, and shows Him all things that He Himself is doing; and the Father will show Him greater works than these, so that you will marvel."

The ministry of Jesus was based upon seeing what the Father was doing, and joining HIm. The Father, for His part, was freely showing His Son what He was doing. Jesus' vision for His own ministry flowed out of a heart that reflected God's heart.

In the final analysis, people are motivated not by the needs they see, but by the vision set before them. Needs, especially great needs, can often be overwhelming and lead only to depression and frustration. Vision, on the other hand, can help people focus their energies so that they can actually meet the real needs that would otherwise be so overwhelming. Case in point is the situation in Jerusalem during the time of Nehemiah.

Nehemiah the Visionary Leader

The situation that came to the attention of Nehemiah was so overwhelming that for days he could only weep, mourn, and pray (Nehemiah 1:1-4). Jerusalem, ransacked years earlier, was still in dire straits. Her walls had not been rebuilt. Her torched gates were still unrepaired. As a result, the city was open and defenseless. The people were a reproach and lived in distressing circumstances.

Having arrived on the scene in Jerusalem, he surveyed the situation first hand. What prevented Nehemiah from becoming completely overwhelmed? The answer is found in verse twelve. God was putting into Nehemiah's mind what he was to do. Nehemiah was inspecting more than destruction, God was taking him on a tour of the undiscovered country.

Neh. 2:11 So I came to Jerusalem and was there three days.

Chapter 5 ☛ *Prepare the Vision*

> Neh. 2:12 And I arose in the night, I and a few men with me. I did not tell anyone what my God was putting into my mind to do for Jerusalem and there was no animal with me except the animal on which I was riding.
>
> Neh. 2:13 So I went out at night by the Valley Gate in the direction of the Dragon's Well and on to the Refuse Gate, inspecting the walls of Jerusalem which were broken down and its gates which were consumed by fire.
>
> Neh. 2:14 Then I passed on to the Fountain Gate and the King's Pool, but there was no place for my mount to pass.
>
> Neh. 2:15 So I went up at night by the ravine and inspected the wall. Then I entered the Valley Gate again and returned.
>
> Neh. 2:16 The officials did not know where I had gone or what I had done; nor had I as yet told the Jews, the priests, the nobles, the officials or the rest who did the work.

Now came the somewhat difficult part. How was he to harness the energies of the people and motivate them toward rebuilding. How could he effectively communicate the vision God was placing in his heart and mind? He was going to personally live out his vision. Notice his communication to the leaders and the people. He used "we" and "us" consistently in his communication. His communication was unwavering, it was with conviction.

> Neh. 2:17 Then I said to them, "You see the bad situation **we are in**, that Jerusalem is desolate and its gates burned by fire. Come, **let us** rebuild the wall of Jerusalem **so that we** will no longer be a reproach."

He told stories and used images and examples.

> Neh. 2:18 I told them how the hand of my God had been favorable to me and also about the king's words which he had spo-

146

ken to me. Then they said, "Let us arise and build." So they put their hands to the good work.

Nehemiah appealed to common values and beliefs to continue to motivate the people. When those around threatened their work and incited fear among the people, Nehemiah responded in great faith:

> Neh. 4:14 When I saw their fear, I rose and spoke to the nobles, the officials and the rest of the people: "Do not be afraid of them; remember the Lord who is great and awesome, and fight for your brothers, your sons, your daughters, your wives and your houses."

When specific goals are set, feet are put to the vision. People can then be invited to begin walking out the vision. Goals should be attainable, measurable, specific, and significant. In the end, they must stretch our faith without being presumptuous. Read Nehemiah chapter 3 in its entirety. Don't either skim this chapter or pass it by completely, thinking it non-relevant. On the contrary, it illustrates the specific goals set forth by Nehemiah and the degree of ownership embraced on the part of the people. A vision is only strong when it is shared by others. Note also as you read the chapter how each of the goals encompassed several objectives. Under the leadership of Nehemiah, the remnant in Jerusalem discovered and entered the Undiscovered Country of God's future.

> Neh. 6:15-16 So the wall was completed on the twenty-fifth of the month Elul, in fifty-two days. When all our enemies heard of it, and all the nations surrounding us saw it, they lost their confidence; for they recognized that this work had been accomplished with the help of our God.

Discovering the Undiscovered Question - Visionary Leadership Questions

The visionary leader must receive God's mind and heart regarding the five basic questions facing each church (future chapters will address each one):

1. How will the church be built up?   (Edification)

Chapter 5 → *Prepare the Vision*

2. How will the church be trained for ministry? (Equipping)

3. How will future leaders be raised up? (Empowering)

4. How will we reach this generation for Christ? (Evangelism)

5. How will the church be mobilized for ministry? (Every Member Ministry)

The visionary leader must answer the fundamental question, "How is God moving to strengthen and buildup the church? What is the Undiscovered Country of Edification?" Specific questions must be addressed. What principles of edification will be embraced? What model of edification will be developed? What structures on both the cell and corporate level will be set in place to facilitate edification?

The visionary leader must answer a second fundamental question, "How is God moving to train and equip the church? What is the Undiscovered Country of Equipping?" This aspect of the vision must also be fleshed out. What are our equipping objectives? What is our venue? Will it be classroom based, resource based, or perhaps a combination of both. Will training be synchronous? What training will be facilitated through the cell structures and what training must be accomplished on the corporate level?

The visionary leader must also answer a third fundamental question, "How is God moving to mature and release leaders within the church? What is the Undiscovered Country of Empowerment?" Certainly empowerment can happen through vision-casting. However, how will this be done? Will empowering be accomplished through modeling? If so, how can this be systematically done in a reproducible manner? Will empowering be accomplished through a coaching system? What will that system look like?

The visionary leader must answer a fourth fundamental question, "How is God moving to increase and multiply the church? What is the Undiscovered Country of Evangelism?" Who is God's target group for this particular church? How will evangelism be done on the personal level, oikos level, and corporate level. What system will be developed for follow-up?

The visionary leader must answer a fifth and final fundamental question, "How is God moving to mobilize and release each member in the church? What is the Undiscovered Country of Every Member Ministry?" Will our paradigm be gift-based? Where and how will members discover and be released to experiment with their spiritual gifts? What system will be utilized to mobilize members into service based upon their gifts? What on-going training will be created to further develop their giftings in each area of service?

FOR THE VISION IS YET FOR THE APPOINTED TIME

> Hab. 2:1　I will stand on my guard post
> And station myself on the rampart;
> And I will keep watch to see what He will speak to me,
> And how I may reply when I am reproved.
>
> Hab. 2:2　Then the LORD answered me and said,
> "Record the vision
> And inscribe it on tablets,
> That the one who reads it may run.
>
> Hab. 2:3　"For the vision is yet for the appointed time;
> It hastens toward the goal and it will not fail.
> Though it tarries, wait for it;
> For it will certainly come, it will not delay.

Where there is no vision, people are unrestrained. If the churches we serve are not gripped by a vision of themselves as the family of God, we will live like Israel of whom God inquired during the days of Haggai, "Is it time for you yourselves to dwell in your paneled houses while this house lies desolate? (1:4)" They were busy going about their own individual lives. God's rebuke was that, "Each of you runs to his own house" (1:9). They lacked a greater sense of community. When the heart of cell life once more becomes that of a redeemed family, the church will truly live as "God's household", God's oikos.

If our churches are not gripped by a vision of themselves as the Family of God, then our cell structures, and especially our oversight mechanisms, will continue a deficit of relational intimacy. We will continue to view supervision from a management perspective, not a familial perspective. Oversight will continue to be thought of in terms of paper forms and exercise of authority, rather than in terms of father-son and father-daughter relationships. We will continue to be impersonal facilitators, rather than spiritual fathers and mothers and older brothers and sisters.

If our churches are not gripped by a vision of themselves as the Body of Christ, then our leaders will continue to experience burn out. We will continue to function as a volunteer organization where 20% of the people do 80% of the work, rather than as a dynamic organism where each part is vital and every member, "fitted and held together by what every joint supplies, according to the proper working of each individual part, causes the growth of the body for the building up of itself in love."

If our churches are not gripped by a vision of themselves as the army of God, we will remain AWOL or imprisoned POW's. Without such vision, we will be ineffective in proclaiming release to the captives, recovery of sight to the blind, and setting free those who are oppressed. Sacrifice is expected in war. Sacrifice is shunned during peace. If we are not gripped by such vision, we will never pay the price necessary for spiritual victory, personally or corporately, "enduring hardship as a good soldier of Jesus Christ".

If we do not set before our people a vision of their specific role in the fulfillment of the greater program of God, then the service they render will seem to them as inconsequential, as unimportant, and lacking eternal value or meaning. If we do not set before them a canvas upon which God is painting a picture of the future, if we do not lead them to see a God who is already at work, if there is no undiscovered country to discover, then their energies and attention will be focused on the things of this world.

Laying the correct ethical foundation is critical. Being transformed into a values-driven church is essential. But, if we are going nowhere, all our work becomes rather self-serving. We must prepare the way of the Lord, the Lord's vision! Only then will the church be able to enter into the purposes of God, laboring and fighting in partnership with Jesus as He builds His Body and extends the rule of His kingdom throughout this world.

REFLECTION QUESTION

1. How does your vision reflect each of your core values?

2. Identify the key elements of your vision. As an example, the key elements listed in this chapter include the church as the Family of God, the church as the Army of God and the church as the Body of Christ. Additional vision elements may include equipping, edifying, empowering, and mobilizing every member, as well as evangelizing the lost.

Chapter 5 ☛ *Prepare the Vision*

ACTION POINTS

1. Having identified the key elements of your vision, use the APA (Achieve-Preserve-Avoid) Analysis on the following page to sharpen your vision. This exercise may be done alone and then re-done in conjunction with a team. For each element of your vision:

    a). Record what you sense God is calling you to **Achieve**. This will be the very heart of your vision.

    b). Reflect on your past experience and record what it is that you would like to **Preserve** from the past.

    c). Record what you would like to **Avoid** as you carry out God's vision.

Achieve	Preserve	Avoid

PHASE 1

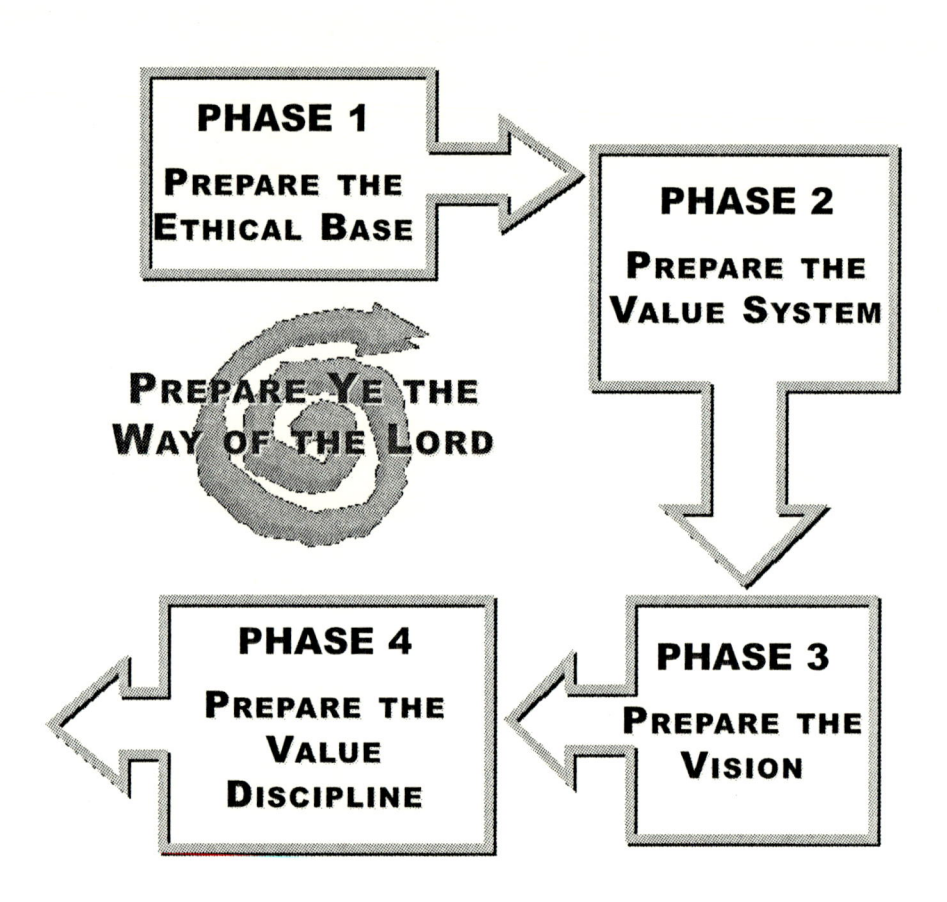

Prepare the Ethical Base

PHASE 2

Prepare the Value System

Prepare Ye the Way of the Lord

PHASE 4

Prepare the Value Discipline

PHASE 3

Prepare the Vision

Prepare the Value Discipline

Again, the kingdom of heaven is like a merchant seeking fine pearls, and upon finding one pearl of great value, he went and sold all that he had and bought it.   Matthew 13:45-46

For where your treasure is, there your heart will be also.
                    Matthew 6:21

Chapter 6 ☞ *Prepare the Value Discipline*

INTRODUCTION

We have seen how the development of a cell church must be grounded in a deontological biblical ethical system. Having prepared the ethical base, we can then turn our attention to the articulation of those core values out of which God has called us to live our lives. Articulating these values is only the beginning. They must then move from being aspirational values to actual values, from being in the head to being in the heart, from being on our wish list to being lived out. This is often a painfully slow process that is worked out in the midst of co-laboring with Him in building His church. Without vision, though, we will remain static, or worse, adrift in life without direction. Vision shows us the future, and our place in it. Vision gives us direction. Vision gives us focus. Knowing what God requires of our future and arriving at that future destination are not the same thing. We face three rather daunting questions. First, how can we challenge and motivate others to embrace our God-given vision so they come with us? Second, as we develop an operating model that will move us toward our vision, how will that model operate? What will it look like? Third, how can we move into that future with excellence?

In his video, *The Paradigm Pioneer*, Joel Barker states, "By consulting or listening to others outside your traditional boundaries, you challenge your paradigms and move further along on your own paradigm curve. The pathway of the paradigm pioneer is opening for you!" Prepare yourself to journey with me in this chapter outside your traditional boundaries, and to think outside your current paradigm as we seek answers to the questions above.

OUTSIDERS - THE DISCIPLINE OF MARKET LEADERS

In their groundbreaking book, *The Discipline of Market Leaders*, Michael Treacy and Fred Wiersema provide a revolutionary way for the business world to think about their customers, competition, markets, and the fundamental structure of business organization. As the cover flap to their book states:

> The author's thesis is deceptively simple: that successful organizations–the market leaders–excel at delivering one type of value to their chosen customers. The key is focus. Market leaders chose a single "value discipline"–best total cost, best

product, or best total solution–and then build their organization around it. They sustain their leadership position not by resting on their laurels, but by offering better value year after year. Choosing one discipline to master does not mean abandoning the other two, only that a company must stake its reputation–and focus its energy and assets–on a single one to achieve success over the long term. No company can reliably succeed today by trying to be all things to all customers.

Their closing words are strangely familiar when compared to those written by George Barna in *User Friendly Churches*:

In speaking of declining churches, a common thread was their desire to do something for everybody. They had fallen into the strategic blackhole of creating a ministry that looked great on paper, but had not ability to perform up to standards. Despite their worthy intentions, they tried to be so helpful to everyone that they wound up being helpful to no one.

Is it possible that the Lord of Creation has revealed to two perhaps unbelieving business people principles and truth applicable to His Church in the 21st century? Is it possible that leading cell churches of the 20th century have actually, unwittingly, yet even sovereignly, been led to deliver one type of value to those they are reaching, that they have chosen a single value discipline to master, and then have built their organization around it?

I strongly contend this is just the case. In this chapter, I will attempt to describe how the three value disciplines of Operational Excellence, Product Leadership, and Customer Intimacy, may be applied to the cell church movement. For purposes of this study I will henceforth refer to Product Leadership as Entrepreneurial Leadership. In addition, I will attempt to illustrate how *Eglise Protestante Baptiste Oeuvres et Mission Internationale* (EPBOM) in Cote d'Ivoire, *International Charismatic Mission* (ICM) in Bogota, Columbia, and *Yoido Full Gospel Church* (YFGC) in Seoul, Korea, epitomize these three different disciplines in the cell church world.

But first, let us proceed and seek to define and understand some basic concepts.

Chapter 6 ☛ *Prepare the Value Discipline*

WORKING DEFINITIONS
(ADAPTED FROM TREACY & WIERSEMA)

1. Value Proposition

> The implicit promise a church makes to both its members and target community to deliver a particular combination of values.

> In the case of a church, as opposed to that of a business, the "customers" who were originally identified as the target community may eventually become members of the church itself. Additionally, the "customers" who in fact are the church members, are not really "customers" at all, but instead part of the very "business". This understanding will prove helpful when examining the value discipline of Customer Intimacy.

2. Value Components
   Time:

> Speed of response is a key value dimension. The implication for the church is clear: Continuously shrink the interval between the people's need and when you meet it.

Premium Service:

> Not long ago in the marketplace, only special customers felt entitled to special service. Today, what was once extraordinary is now becoming ordinary. So too in the church. Churches must now go beyond the expected and provide the unexpected.

Quality:

> Churches can no longer compromise quality in any area. Churches must provide quality training, quality care, quality worship, etc. Good is no longer good enough.

3. Values-Driven Operating Model

Operating models are made up of operating processes, church structure, management systems, and culture, all of which are synchronized to create a certain superior value and give a church the capacity to create unsurpassed value and to deliver on its value proposition. If the value proposition is the end, the value-driven operating model is the means to the end. Different value disciplines demand different operating models.

4. Value Disciplines

The three desirable ways in which churches can combine operating models and value propositions so as to excel. Each discipline hones at least one component of value to a level of excellence that puts other churches to shame.

Choosing to pursue a value discipline is not like choosing to pursue a strategic goal. One cannot simply graft a value discipline on to or integrate it into a church's normal existing philosophy.

The selection of a value discipline is a central act that shapes every subsequent plan and decision a church makes, coloring the entire church organization/organism, from its competencies to its culture. The choice of a value discipline defines what a church does and, to some degree, what a church is.

5. The Four Rule Assumption Regarding a Church's Activity

Rule 1: Provide the best offering by excelling in a specific dimension of value.

Rule 2: Maintain threshold standards on other dimensions of value.

You must not allow performance in other dimensions to slide so much that it impairs your own unmatched value. Yet, you do not have to strive to be the best in each of these other dimensions. Focus your energy on what separates you from the rest of the pack and perform at a predetermined acceptable level in the other areas.

Rule 3: Improve value year after year.

Life is never static. Follow the Japanese's principle of *kaizen*. *Kaizen* is continuously improving every aspect of the product or process by some small increment every day. Every day you must find some small way to improve an aspect of your ministry or service and the process by which it is created and delivered. A change as small as 1/10th of one percent will yield significant results. When an organization or church practices *kaizen*, it moves up the paradigm curve much faster than without it. It becomes very difficult to catch a paradigm pioneering church that practices continuous improvement.

Rule 4: Build a well-tuned values-driven operating model dedicated to delivering unmatched value.

Producing unsurpassed, ever improving value requires a superior, dedicated operating model. The operating model is the key.

What is needed on the part of the Senior Elder today is to discern his or her Values Discipline, define an unmatched Value Proposition, build a Values-driven Operating Model, and sustain it through constant transformation and improvement in time, service, and quality.

Having defined the rules common to all three disciplines, let us move forward with a more unique overview of each of the value disciplines.

THE DISCIPLINE OF OPERATIONAL EXCELLENCE - OVERVIEW

Operationally excellent churches deliver a combination of consistency and quality that no one else can match. They execute extraordinarily well, and their value proposition may be encapsulated as the promise to fully disciple and release you as a minister of the Lord Jesus Christ.

They have built an operating model based on four distinct features:

- *Processes* for discipling that are optimized and streamlined to minimize energy costs and hassle

- *Operations and structures* that are standardized, simplified, tightly controlled, and centrally planned, leaving few decisions to the discretion of the member at large

- *Management systems* that focus on integrated, reliable, high-speed care and compliance to established norms

- A *culture* that abhors waste and rewards efficiency

THE DISCIPLINE OF ENTREPRENEURIAL LEADERSHIP - OVERVIEW

A church pursuing Entrepreneurial Leadership continually pushes what they offer into the realm of the unknown, the untried, or the highly desirable. Their proposition to their target customer is the best product, period. What that product actually is can translate into a number of things in the church. The end product could be a leader, as we will see with ICM. To ensure that they are constantly reaching their goal, they challenge themselves in three ways.

First, they must be creative. This means they must recognize and embrace ideas that originate anywhere–inside their own local church or out. They have a vested interest in protecting the entrepreneurial environment they have created.

Second, they must implement their ideas quickly. Product Leaders

Chapter 6 Prepare the Value Discipline

avoid bureaucracy at all costs because it slows down the implementation of their ideas. It is often better to make a wrong decision and correct it than to make a decision too late or not at all. They decide today and implement tomorrow. Their internal processes are geared for speed. Their strength lies in reacting to situations as they occur. They do not plan for every possible contingency, nor do they spend much time on up front detailed analysis.

Third, they must relentlessly pursue ways to leapfrog their own service.

The operating model of the church that has adopted a Entrepreneurial Leadership value discipline is very different from the Operationally Excellent church. They also have built an operating model based on four distinct features:

- A focus on the *core process* of invention

- S*tructure* that is loosely knit, ad hoc, and ever changing to adjust to the entrepreneurial initiatives and re-directions that characterize working in uncharted territory

- *Management systems* that are results-driven, that measure and reward product success, and that don't punish the experimentation needed to get there

- A *culture* that encourages individual imagination, accomplishment, out-of-the-box thinking, and a mind-set driven by the desire to create the future

THE DISCIPLINE OF CUSTOMER INTIMACY - OVERVIEW

A church that delivers value via customer intimacy builds bonds with those it is targeting to reach, like those between good neighbors. The Customer Intimate church makes it a priority of knowing the people it is attempting to reach and the services they need. Its proposition is: "We take care of you and all your needs," or "We have the best total solution for you." The Customer Intimate church's greatest asset is, not surprisingly, its members' loyalty.

Customer Intimate churches cultivate relational connections. They are adept at giving their people more than he or she expects. By continually upgrading what they give, they constantly stay ahead of their people's rising expectations, expectations they themselves create. They have designed operating models that allow them to produce and deliver a much broader and deeper level of individual support.

The operating model of the Customer Intimate church is again very different from that of either the Operationally Excellent church or the Entrepreneurial Leader. They have built an operating model based on four distinct features:

- An almost obsession with *core process* of solution development (i.e. helping their people understand exactly what they personally need), results management (i.e. ensuring the solution gets implemented properly), and relationship management

- A *structure* that delegates decision-making to those closest to the individual member

- *Management systems* that are geared toward creating results for carefully selected and nurtured clients

- A *culture* that embraces specific rather than general solutions and thrives on deep and lasting contacts

WHY CHOOSE?

Choosing a value discipline both commits a church to a single path to achieve its goals and purposely destines the church to choose a secondary role in the other disciplines. This is because each discipline requires a church to emphasize different process, to create different church structures, and to gear management systems differently. As can be observed from the following chart, when thinking of the structure, the Customer Intimate church moves more of the decision-making responsibility out to the boundaries of the church organization, closer to the average member. Operationally Excellent churches do best with the major leadership at a central location where standard operating procedures get refined and decisions are made. The entrepreneurial church thrives on ad hoc and fluid structure to foster invention. Not choosing means ending up in a muddle. It means hybrid operating models. To paraphrase Barna again, it means trying to be so helpful to everyone that you wind up being helpful to no one.

Chapter 6 ☛ *Prepare the Value Discipline*

Operational Excellence	*Entrepreneurial Leadership*	*Customer Intimacy*
• **Core Processes** for discipling that are optimized and streamlined to minimize energy costs and hassle • **Operations and Structures** that are standardized, simplified, tightly controlled, and centrally planned, leaving few decisions to the discretion of the member at large • **Management Systems** that focus on integrated, reliable, high-speed care and compliance to established norms • **Culture** that abhors waste and rewards efficiency	• A focus on the **Core Process** of invention • **Structure** that is loosely knit, ad hoc, and ever changing to adjust to the entrepreneurial initiatives and re-directions that characterize working in uncharted territory • **Management Systems** that are results-driven, that measure and reward product success, and that don't punish the experimentation needed to get there • **Culture** that encourages individual imagination, accomplishment, out-of-the-box thinking, and a mind-set driven by the desire to create the future	• An almost obsession with **Core Process** of solution development, results management, and relationship management • **Structure** that delegates decision-making to those closest to the individual member • **Management Systems** that are geared toward creating results for carefully selected and nurtured clients • **Culture** that embraces specific rather than general solutions and thrives on deep and lasting contacts

THE DISCIPLINE OF OPERATIONAL EXCELLENCE
EGLISE PROTESTANTE BAPTISTE OEUVRES ET MISSION INTERNATIONALE

    Let's examine closer some of the characteristics that help define the unique nature of an Operationally Excellent Church. Sprinkled among the characteristics will be illustrations from *Eglise Protestante Baptiste Oeuvres et Mission Internationale*.

    According to Treacy and Wiersema, operationally excellent companies, for our purposes I would also add operationally excellent churches, deploy an operating model based on a set of design principles handed down from Henry Ford. "Ford's business was highly regimented, proceduralized, rule driven. There was only one way–the efficient way–to do everything. Complex work was divided into similar repetitive tasks and combined, via the assembly line, into an integrated process. The result: efficiency of effort *and* efficiency of coordination" (49).

In writing my Doctoral dissertation, *Rapid Cell Church Growth And Reproduction:Case Study of Eglise Protestante Baptiste Oeuvres et Mission Internationale, Abidjan, Cote d'Ivoire,* I was able to spend a number of weeks on site interviewing and observing both the leadership and average member of the central church in Abidjan. What I observed could easily be described as highly regimented, proceduralized, and rule driven. There was only one way–the efficient way–to do everything. There certainly was efficiency of effort and efficiency of coordination.

"Operationally excellent companies run themselves like the Marine Corps: The team is what counts, not the individual. Everybody knows the battle plan and the rule book, and when the buzzer sounds, everyone knows exactly what he or she has to do" (50). This again describes EPBOM.

Recall that CIAMEL is the church's yearly gathering where pastors and missionaries and leaders are gathered from all over for training and exhortation and encouragement at stadium Champroux of Marcory. The daytime attendance in 2000 was in excess of 30,000. A crusade was held each evening and the crowd swelled to over 40,000. I remind the reader of my personal journal entry dated 08/21/00 which I included as part of chapter four. The way the ushers functioned, the way they jogged, the way they handled the crowds, all was done like a well disciplined military machine.

The heroes in this kind of culture are the people who fit in, who have worked their way up through the ranks. They are dependable. They have a proven track record. They are trainable. In the business world we could say they would be taught the Wal-Mart–or UPS, or Southwest–way of business. In the church world, they will be taught that particular church's way of doing things. What is important is not who you are but what the church will make out of you.

The heroes of EPBOM are men like Jonas Kouassi. You were introduced to Jonas earlier. A product of EPBOM's discipleship, Jonas progressed through the normal discipleship process at EPBOM. When it came time to serve in a department, because he was a diplomat he was asked to serve in the Public Relations Department. At one of the church's large conferences, he was asked

Chapter 6 ☛ *Prepare the Value Discipline*

to take care of the foreign delegation and to use his English background to translate, interpret and help the delegates if they would like to go to the market or buy something. His service was related to his language background. Later, when the church was involved in building their medical center, or there arose any kind of question between the church and the government, Jonas served as a liaison. Whenever there was a problem and the church needed outside experience, Jonas was often the person who could help. Jonas did not stay in the Public Relations Department. As God moved on his life, he served according to the gifts that God manifested. This eventually led him to the Cell Department to be trained as a cell leader. As a cell leader he eventually reached out with a professional in his office. Having been sent by the government to Denmark, he began to simply do there what he had done in Abidjan. In Denmark he soon led the Ambassador to the Lord. Under Jonas' leadership the cell grew. He and the church experienced a significant breakthrough in January of 2000.

Hosting a cell in his home, starting a professional cell in his office, winning an Ambassador to the Lord, planting a church in a foreign country among those who are different in language, culture, and color, casting out demons in his parlor, taking care of the souls of men and women, all while holding down a professional job – this is the story of Jonas. However, it is not a unique story. It is just one of hundreds of similar stories. These are the heroes of EPBOM.

The desire of Operationally Excellent churches is to make sure their ministry and service is effortless, flawless, and instantaneous. One of the main keys to achieving operational excellence in service is: Do it one and only one way. Variety kills efficiency.

This is beautifully illustrated by EPBOM's Department of Demonology. While taking nothing away from the absolute necessity of discernment and empowerment by the Holy Spirit, those ministering as part of the Department of Demonology all follow the same model. This was observable as I watched one hundred teams of four demonologists minister at the conclusion of each night's crusade during CIAMEL. Even the manner by which they physically restrained the demonized individuals was similar. This is further illustrated as one examines their training manuals. Those within the Department of Demonology will, as part of their training, receive instruction through the following manuals:

1. The Department of Demonology
2. Characteristics of an Approved Demonologist
3. The Demonologist According to the Model of Jesus

4. How to Succeed with the Demonology Ministry in the Local Church
5. The Principles of Healing According to Jesus
6. How to Break the Bondage of Masturbation
7. The Demonologist Facing the Spirit of the 3rd Millennium
8. The Devil in Rosecrucianism
9. How to Vanquish and Cast Out the Siren Spirit

Their ministry is extremely efficient and effective. Again, though, lest the reader think the power is in the system or the model, let me again emphasize their total reliance on the power and presence of the Lord. Their model is simply what they have discovered and discerned to be the most effective and efficient delivery system for their ministry and service to the demonized.

Why are Operationally Excellent churches uniquely qualified to deliver superior ministry? The first reason is focus. Ministry is a key part of their unmatched value proposition.

> Nothing is improvised in the Kingdom of God. The servant of God who lives by the Spirit will make exploits with God. God uses him to bring about great things, to accomplish his design. This is why it is absolutely necessary to have the vision of God. It is written: 'Whoever has will be given more, and he will have and abundance. Whoever does not have, even what he has will be taken from him' (Matthew 13:12). In the framework of the minister of God, we generally give but what we have received from Him. And to receive from Him, it takes a disposition of spirit or heart for God, in view of a clear vision. We understand why there are some that are more successful than others are. We must know how to listen to God, how to receive from Him and above all, know Him. Thus I started to learn to live by the Spirit and by faith. The result was not long to come. The Lord opened my spirit and my eyes. He communicated His wisdom, which sustains everything living. *I started to organize the church according to the model that He showed me, little by little. You must see the vision of God. You must know how to hear and transmit His message. The success of a ministry depends on that (emphasis mine).* (Working 44-45)

Chapter 6 ☞ *Prepare the Value Discipline*

Second, their operating models support efficient, zero-defect service. The practices of Operationally Excellent churches are part of the rule book for zero-defect service. In other words, it is imperative to work according to the model in view of Christ.

> The structure of a church must conform to the model described in the book of the Lord and it must also be made up of the elements of the program considered by the Lord for salvation and victory through the Church. When God appointed Moses to the priests, He first showed him how the Tabernacle was to be constructed and what it was to be made up of. "See to the pattern shown you on the mountain (Hebrews 8:5b)." Thus, every minister of the worship services of Jesus Christ must organize and make the Church function according to the model of the program communicated by the Lord. This is all the more important since no part of it must be neglected if you want to do a work that is productive, victorious, and a work that is of good quality and considerable quantity. Nothing is improvised in the Kingdom of God. *Everything must function following the Plan of God, His vision and His design (emphasis mine)*. (Robert, Working 35)

What is in it for the church? Growth! Operationally Excellent churches are able to replicate their process anywhere. They are able to transport an efficient, standardized ministry to a new location. Once the formula has been defined and perfected, the church can fire up its cloning machine. When the mother church plants other churches, it simply replicates the processes it already performs. They transfer their methods and even management style virtually anywhere in the world.

EPBOM's system has been effectively transplanted across the world. In EPBOM's system, each cell has the desire to grow and multiply into a local church. When the cell has multiplied several times and has reached 50 people, it becomes an annex church and a part-time pastor is usually assigned to it. When it reaches 150 adults, it is considered to be a local church and a full time pastor is assigned to it. Local churches are further organized on a regional level, then a national level, etc. Eglise Protestante Baptiste Oeuvres et Mission Internationale has planted upward of 52 churches in the city of Abidjan. It has planted churches additionally in over twelve regions of Cote d'Ivoire. Churches have also been planted in more than 16 African nations. Oversight within Africa has been delegated on a northern, southern, eastern, and western regional basis. Within Europe churches have been planted in France, England, Sweden, Denmark and Italy. Churches have even been planted in Canada and America on the North American continent. Wherever churches have been planted, they follow the same model. All roads lead no longer back to Rome, as the saying goes, but to Abidjan, and in particular to the central church in the suburb of Yopougon. There is one model, one system, one process. EPBOM reminds me of a massive octopus with hundreds and hundreds of tentacles reaching out to spread the gospel of the Lord Jesus Christ and establish the Kingdom of God.

The secret of succeeding with this value discipline is summed up in one word: formula. Formula often has a rather negative connotation, but for Operationally Excellent churches like EPBOM, formula has contributed to a highly successful ministry.

THE DISCIPLINE OF ENTREPRENEURIAL LEADERSHIP
INTERNATIONAL CHARISMATIC MISSION

A number of years ago, I was fortunate enough to accompany my Senior pastor to a small gathering of then cutting-edge and rather select pastors from around the United States. We met for two days. The topic: How to increase the results of evangelism in the church. Sadly, what came out of that meeting was nothing more than a refinement, repackaging, and reformulation of old ideas. How to squeeze the last drop of wine out of an old and no longer flexible wineskin paradigm. Too many churches are caught up in the same quagmire. They simply recycle old worn out ideas that once worked well, but have now plateaued on the paradigm curve and are being supplanted by new paradigms.

Remember how Nabisco expanded its Oreo cookie line? It stocked store shelves with mini Oreos, Double Stuff Oreos, larger packs of Oreos, smaller packs of Oreos, and seasonal packs of Oreos. The consumer yawned and Nabisco experienced negligible growth. A one time innovation with countless "improvements" did not impress the cookie buyers of America. Where is the cookie that incites a passionate customer response? Where is the church, by the way, that incites a passionate response from its membership?

We would do well here to learn from Thomas Edison. "Edison began by

Chapter 6 ☞ *Prepare the Value Discipline*

creating an inspiring vision of each new product before development work ever started. He believed he needed to fuel his organization with the dream of improbable achievements" (86). Unlike those within the organizationally excellent discipline who are driven by procedure, those within this discipline are driven by the vision and giftings of key individuals whose every step along the way is focused on realizing the vision.

Like Edison, Entrepreneurial Leadership has learned how to harness the motivating power of ambitious targets. "Edison's target wasn't a light bulb; it was the ability to light a building or even a town. That lofty target channeled his creativity. He then worked backwards from the goal to figure out the steps required to achieve it" (87). This is known as working right-to-left, and is a pervasive characteristic of this discipline.

The beginnings of *International Christian Mission* (ICM) in Bogota follow this pattern. "what kind of church would you like to pastor?" God asked Cesar Castellanos, the Senior Pastor, in 1983. He pictured a church of 120, the size of the largest church. Castellanos explains:

> I was striving to expand that number in my mind, but I couldn't. So I began to look at the sand of the seashore. As I looked at it, each grain of sand became a person, and I began to see hundreds of thousands of people. Then the Lord said: "That and much more I will give you, if you are perfect in my will." (Comiskey, Groups of 12, 21)

Encouraged by the vision, Castellanos began ICM. His first goal was to reach 200 people in six months. In just three months ICM had grown to 200 people. In 1991 he cried out,

> "Lord, I need something that will help me accelerate the growth." God showed him the missing link, revealing the concepts that have become known as the G-12 model. This revelation, according to Castellanos, was like Newton discovering the law of gravity. (Comiskey, Groups of 12, 22)

Generic operating procedures and structured processes are not the goal of the entrepreneurial leader. Instead, entrepreneurial leaders create flexible organizational wineskins and robust processes that enable the people to flex both their minds and muscles without creating disruption. They provide sufficient, efficient coordination, while still permitting inventiveness and discipline. To help accomplish this they keep people on track by organizing what is to be done in a series of well-paced challenges, each with a clearly defined outcome and tight deadline.

At ICM, this is evidenced as every new convert is prepared quickly (within six months or less) to become a cell leader. However, training is not optional. There are eight pre-defined steps toward leading a cell group (Groups of 12, 66-73).

Entrepreneurial churches stretch member's potential by throwing tough challenges at them and by inciting a collegial "rivalry." Great colleagues bring out the best in each other. People ratchet up one another's standards and performance levels. Entrepreneurial leaders impose few constraints upon people beyond the massive goals set before them.

The heroes of the faith at ICM are men like Luis Salas and Freddy Rodriguez. In January 1994 Luis Salas began his first cell group. By February 1995 he was overseeing 14 groups. In October 1995 he left his groups under the care of others and began from scratch under the direction of Cesar Castellanos. By August 1996 his original cell had grown to 46 cells. By November of that year he had 86 cell groups. In December he had 144 cells. In June 1997 he was overseeing 250 cells. Three years after he had started over, he had more than 600 cells. (Home Cell, 40) From 1990 when he began to 1999 Freddy multiplied to over 1500 cells (Groups of 12, 87).

We noted previously that the structure of the operating model is loosely knit, ad hoc, and ever changing to adjust to the entrepreneurial initiatives and re-directions that characterize working in uncharted territory. Joel Comiskey notes:

> ICM doesn't hold tightly to methods, since it is following the leading of the Spirit of God and creating its structures as they move ahead...ICM is a moving target rather than a fixed one. The church is willing to change in order to fine-tune and develop its cell experiment. Each time I've visited ICM, I've noticed major changes. (Groups of 12, 31)

In addition, the management systems of the Entrepreneurial Leadership operating model are results-driven, measure and reward product success, and don't punish the experimentation needed to get there. Once again this describes ICM.

> ICM believes in adapting its methodology to more effectively reap the harvest. They're pragmatic. They're willing to test and experiment for the purpose of saving and discipling more souls for Christ's glory. Because the old cell system wasn't producing the desired results, they created the G-12 system. Even after developing the G-12 strategy, ICM continues to adapt its methods. This attitude resembles the life and ministry of John Wesley. (Groups of 12, 40)

Here, the highest form of recognition–the award that these talented people most treasure–is selection for the next, even more challenging mission. Successful leadership is clearly measured at ICM and new challenges embraced, as the following illustrates.

> Successful leaders are those who have planted a number of new groups, have raised up new leaders to lead other groups and are now leaders of leaders. If someone has been successful in doing this and is now training leaders, that person receives a promotion in the church. To qualify for a part-time staff position at ICM, a leader must multiply his or her cell group 250 times. A full-time position is reserved for those who have multiplied their cell group 500 times. (Groups of 12, 80-81)

THE DISCIPLINE OF CUSTOMER INTIMACY
YOIDO FULL GOSPEL CHURCH

Customer Intimate churches are unmatched at addressing the totality of their members' and target groups' unique needs and supplying for them an unmatched total solution by customizing the services and ministry they offer. Such a church is proactive and change-oriented. In suggesting that *Yoido Full Gospel Church* (YFGC) exemplifies the Customer Intimate church model, I am indebted to Karen Hurston for her insights into the working of the church, as set forth in her book, *Growing the World's Largest Church*. In her research, Hurston gives insight into the development of this Korean church from its humble beginnings to its present position as the largest church in the world today. Her father served on staff in the early years with Pastor Cho.

More than Operationally Excellent churches or Entrepreneurial Leadership churches, Customer Intimate churches can tell you the unique needs of those they serve. Karen's work provides three examples that illustrate this characteristic.

> Okja found something else that happened in bringing people to the Savior: "When I talked with these people we had targeted to evangelize," she said, "I discovered one thing. If a person ever told me of a need or problem, it let me know that person was receptive. It never failed that I could then lead that person to faith in Jesus Christ" (Hurston, Growing 104).

> The ultimate aim of evangelistic visitation is to find people with needs and problems and then lead them to the Problem Solver, Jesus Christ. A sub-district leader, Leebu Pak, tells her cell leaders, "Look for problems. When you find someone with a problem, you are almost guaranteed that person will come to Jesus" (Hurston, Growing 104).

> A frequent practice of female cell and section leaders is called "holy eavesdropping." The leader keeps her ears open, especially in places where her neighbors shop or congregate. If she overhears a conversation mentioning a need or difficulty, she makes a mental note and begins to pray for that person and that concern. After prayer, she might then visit that women with fruit or flowers, plus that week's copy of the church newspaper. In response to the gift, the woman often invites the leader inside for tea or coffee. In the process of the conversation, trust is developed and the warm, caring attitude of the leader puts the woman at ease. When the woman expresses a need or difficulty, the cell leader shares her testimony of how Jesus met her own needs and how He is concerned with people's daily problems (Hurston, Growing 104-105).

Customer Intimate churches often then mold themselves to fit the needs of others through an extraordinary variety of activity. YFGC has more than

Chapter 6 ☛ *Prepare the Value Discipline*

twenty outreach fellowships, each targeting a different segment of society, offering a wide range of activities.

> Domestic outreach fellowships now target diverse occupations and segments of society, including military personnel, entertainers, medical personnel, athletes, lawyers, transportation personnel, university and college professors, police personnel, prison inmates, industrial workers, churches in farming and fishing communities, beauty operators, and those socially ignored and derelict, such as prostitutes and the institutionalized insane. (Hurston, 126)

The central management challenge in Customer Intimate churches is to assemble, integrate, and retain talented people who can stay at the forefront of that which affects their peoples' lives. Leaders at YFGC share five common characteristics: contagious enthusiasm, clear testimony, dedication, access to time and money, Spirit-led life. Regarding contagious enthusiasm, Hurston notes, "Staff pastors first look for believers who are enthusiastic in witnessing and in their Christian walk and have a positive attitude about divine intervention in human problems. One staff pastor told me, "When a person has a problem, he does not need human sympathy. He does need someone to join with him in faith-filled prayer and point him to Jesus Christ, the Master Problem Solver" (73). Deeply rooted in the culture of the relationally intimate church is the sense that if the member/pre-Christian does well, I've done well and we've done well.

Customer Intimate churches take the long view, desiring long term relationship. The stronger the relationship, the better the opportunity for a total solution. Toward this end, the system of home visitation is a key to establishing those long term relationships. "In 1990, nearly all of the over six hundred pastoral staff pastors were involved daily in visitation. That year, staff pastors made a recorded total of over six hundred thousand home ministry visits" (Hurston, Growing 111).

Customer Intimate churches create an unmatched value proposition of best total solution, best pastoral care. For a church to become truly Customer Intimate, it must decide–and throw its full weight behind that decision–to offer those to whom it ministers: a willingness to share in their risks and real, meaningful tailoring and customization of ministry and services. YFGC has done just that.

Most churches and pastors in Korea practice home visitation. It is a way of life in that country's continuing revival. But few staff pastors in Korea practice ministry visits as frequently or as systematically as those at YFGC. And no church is larger.

YFGC considers ministry visitation a top priority for its pastoral staff and lay leaders. They integrate ministry visitation into every part of church life. Nearly all the pastoral staff of more than seven hundred spend the bulk of their days in ministry visitation. An unpublished YFGC report reveals that the average staff pastor spends sixteen days monthly in visitation, making a total of ninety-one visits each month and more than a thousand ministry visits a year. Seeing the example of their staff pastors, the typical home group leader makes three to five home visits a week. Other lay leaders make one home ministry visit weekly. In addition, each of the church's outreach fellowships has its own cadre of lay leaders to make ministry visits. Doesn't so much visitation become overkill? What makes it meaningful is genuine concern for the welfare of each person visited. (Hurston, Growing 113)

Dr. Cho asserts, "Ministry visitation is essential. When a person belongs to our congregation, he should be regularly visited by pastors and lay leaders. Visitation is a key to a strong sense of unity and belonging within any church" (Hurston, 114).

VALUES-DRIVEN OPERATING MODELS AND NATURAL CHURCH DEVELOPMENT

The North American Church is not growing significantly. Charles Arn (Journal, 73-78) provides the following statistics for us.

- Every year 3,750 churches close their doors for the last time.

- The Church failed to gain an additional 2% of the American population in the last 50 years. No county in

America has a greater churched population today than ten years ago.

- During the last ten years, the combined communicant membership of all protestant denominations has declined 9.5% (4,498,242), while the national population has increased 11.4% (24,153,000).

We have seen that each of the three value disciplines necessitate a unique operating model. Will developing a superior operating model to deliver on our value proposition significantly alter these statistics in the future? Am I suggesting that the operating model is that critical? The answer is at the same time both no, and yes. As I have so far described the operating model, the answer is, "No!". The principles alone may be sufficient to work in the field of business. However, taken by themselves, they are insufficient to see significant growth in the church.

It is an unfortunate state of affairs, but too often true, that literature written for the American cell church movement has given the impression that just "going to cells" will somehow make your church grow. Too many American churches have sought to utilize the cell paradigm as a church growth principle, to no avail I might be quick to add. Churches that were unhealthy with a traditional structure were somehow going to become healthy by changing to a cell structure. The truth of the matter is that unhealthy traditional churches become unhealthy cell churches when the sources of sickness in the church are not dealt with and only the structure is altered.

God causes the Church to grow. One need only examine in some detail Mark 4:26-29 to become persuaded of this. What a man can do is sow and harvest, sleep and rise. What a man cannot do is to bring forth the fruit. "The soil produces crops by itself" (Mark 4:28 αυτοματη γαρ η γη καρποφορει). The Greek αυτοματη, *by itself,* is the derivation of our word *automate.* Unlike our current thinking, the underlying thought in Hebraic thinking is that what is observed to be automatic is in fact being performed by God. Thus, fruit or crops that develop seemingly automatically by themselves are in reality a work of God.

The church must be thought of as an organism. All living things grow. God has placed within each living thing a growth dynamic. Yet, we must not relegate that growth dynamic to an impersonal growth principle, a rather Deistic approach. No, we must see that growth as being performed by God. Growth is in reality a work of God. The question then becomes how to release the very life God has placed within the church so that it can grow "all by itself".

The development of an operating model that does not address this vital question is to take a very technocratic approach to church growth and merely look at the church as an organization to which apply only organizational principles. Automatic then degenerates to, "Insert the correct amount of coins and the Coke will drop down automatically!", or, "Develop the right operating model and the church will grow automatically!".

The church must be thought of as both an organization and an organism. These two understandings must be held in tension. A superior operating model with distinctive core processes, structures, management systems and culture must be developed. At the same time, the growth principles by which God has implanted life in the church must be released, regardless of the value discipline chosen, the value proposition set forth, or the corresponding operating model developed. As we develop our operating model, how can this also be accomplished?

I would suggest a missing critical element in the development of healthy cell churches has been the findings of Christian Schwartz and the Institute of Natural Church Development. I refer the reader to http://www.churchsmart.com or http://www.naturalchurchdevelopment.com and the resources listed there for greater development of the NCD themes I will but briefly touch upon below.

The basic research question investigated can be stated as, "What church growth principles are true, regardless of culture and theological persuasion?" The research process included an extensive survey done among 1,000 churches in 32 countries employing eighteen languages on 5 continents. A total of 4.2 million pieces of date were collected and thoroughly analyzed using the approved methods from social science. The research followed stringent scientific procedures to assure the accuracy of the results as touching both reliability and the validity of the questionnaire. The empirical research method first identified eight essential quality characteristics and then developed a method to quantitatively measure the characteristics and norm them to a median quality index of 50 for the average church.

What the research learned was that growing churches clearly scored above the median in all eight categories, while declining churches were below the median. It was further discovered that no single factor led to church growth; rather the interplay of all eight elements. While churches which grow numerically may have a below-average quality index (quantitative growth is attainable by methods other than the development of the eight quality characteristics, such as effective marketing, contextual factors, etc.), there was one rule for which the research did not find one exception. Every church in which a quality index of 65 or more was reached for each of the eight characteristics was a growing church. In fact, whenever all eight values climbed to 65, the statistical probability that the church is growing is 99.4 percent.

I am indebted to Robert Logan (<u>Releasing</u>, 1.8-1.10) for the following definitions of the eight quality characteristics.

Empowering Leadership

Effective leadership begins with an intimate relationship with God, resulting in Christ-like character and a clear sense of God's calling for leaders' lives. As this base of spiritual maturity increases, effective pastors and leaders multiply, guide, empower and equip disciples to realize their full potential in Christ and work together to accomplish God's vision.

Gift-Oriented Ministry

The Holy Spirit sovereignly gives to every Christian spiritual gift(s) for the building of God's kingdom. Church leaders have the responsibility to help believers discover, develop and exercise their gifts in appropriate ministries so that the Body of Christ "grows and builds itself up in love."

Passionate Spirituality

Effective ministry flows out of a passionate spirituality. Spiritual intimacy leads to a strong conviction that God will act in powerful ways. A godly vision can only be accomplished through an optimistic faith that views obstacles as opportunities and turns defeats into victories.

Functional Structures

The Church is the living Body of Christ. Like all healthy organisms, it requires numerous systems that work together to fulfill its intended purpose. Each must be evaluated regularly to determine if it is still the best way to accomplish the intended purpose.

Inspiring Worship

Inspiring Worship is a personal and corporate encounter with the living God. Both personal and corporate worship be infused with the presence of God resulting in times of joyous exultation and times of quiet reverence. Inspiring worship is not driven by a particular style or ministry focus group – but rather the shared experience of God's awesome presence.

Holistic Small Groups

Holistic small groups are disciple-making communities which endeavor to reach the unchurched, meet individual needs, develop each person according to their God-given gifts and raise leaders to sustain the growth of the church. Like healthy body cells, holistic small groups are designed to grow and multiply.

Need-Oriented Evangelism

Need-oriented evangelism intentionally cultivates relationships with pre-Christian people so they can become fully-devoted followers of Jesus Christ who are actively participating within the life of the church and community. Using appropriate ministries and authentic relationships, believers can guide others into the family of God.

Loving Relationships

Loving relationships are the heart of a healthy, growing church. Jesus said people will know we are His disciples by our love. Practical demonstration of love builds authentic Christian community and brings others into God's kingdom.

These eight quality characteristics must be built into the very core process, structure, management system, and culture of the operating model we create for the value discipline we have chosen. Improving quality in the church's "minimum factors" often result in quantitative growth. In light of this, the principle of *kaisen* takes on new importance as the church's "minimum factor" is systematically and continuously improved in every area of the operating model. The results may very well be explosive.

WHAT IS A PASTOR TO DO?
SETTING YOUR VALUE DISCIPLINE AGENDA

How can a pastor begin to excel in that which God has called him to accomplish? The best answer will be one that defines precisely the exceptional value the church is prepared to offer, and that describes an operating model capable of delivering this value. To accomplish this will require three rounds of deliberation and disciplined assessment on part of the pastor and his leadership team.

Round One: Understand Your Current Situation

Those in decision making must see the current situation the same way. All concerned must occupy common ground. How can this be accomplished? The way to achieve this will be to find fact-based answers to five very fundamental questions:

- What dimensions of value do our members and target group care about?

- For each dimension of value, what proportion of our members and target group focus on that dimension of value as their primary or dominant decision criterion?

- What other churches provide the best value in each of these value dimensions?

- How do we measure up against those other churches on each dimension of value?

- Why do we fall short of the value leaders in each dimension of value?

Facing up to reality often takes guts. Self-assessment is taxing work. Working through disagreements is emotionally draining. If we have not developed a team spirit, or if decision makers are representing his or her own self interest, the process can be exceedingly painful. Yet, in the end, it must be done.

Round Two: Develop Realistic Alternative Value Propositions & Operating Models

For each dimension of value we have determined important to our members and target group, we now must ask these follow-up questions:

- What are the benchmark standards of value performance that will affect both our members and target groups expectations?

- For those we have determined to be value leaders, what will their standards or performance be three years from now?

- How must the operating models of these value leaders be designed to attain those levels of performance?

The bottom line is this. Life is never static, except sometimes in the church! When building an operating model, we must build with a view to the future, not just an understanding of the present. Changes we make or systems we begin to develop will not be completed until sometime in the future. How sad to arrive at our destination only to be outdated and no longer relevant because we built simply with a view to what was then the present situation, and not with a view to a possible future scenario. Ever know of a church that built a worship center that was to small and outdated by the time construction was completed? At the end of this phase you should have a small set of options.

Each incorporates a clearly defined value proposition and a sketch of the operating model needed to attain it.

This phase will require creative thinking and a setting a guard against squashing innovative ideas too quickly. Those involved in this process, especially the senior leader, must understand that they must be disentangled from the bonds and binders of expertise. Although they may be "experts", they in reality have a detailed knowledge of yesterday's operating models, not tomorrow's.

Round Three: Commit to One Value Discipline

Realistic options must now be turned into practical solutions. How does a church choose a discipline from among the options developed during phase two? Each of the viable options from phase two must finally be run through the filter of these last series of questions.

- What would the required operating model look like? What would be the design specifications for the core processes, management systems, structure, etc.?

- How would the model produce superior value?

- What levels of threshold value will be required in the other dimensions of value. How will these be attained?

- How large will the "market" be for this value proposition?

- What are the critical success factors that can make or break this solution?

- How will the church make the transition from its current state to this new operating model or if a church plant, develop this operating model over a two-to three-year period?

Senior leadership ultimately comes down to making the hard choice of a value discipline. What will the church stand for and how will it operate to back up its promise? As previously discussed, the value discipline may come out of a revelation from God to the Senior Pastor and be largely based upon his own personal style and God-designed make-up. For example, an entrepreneur will more likely go with an entrepreneurial Leadership value discipline than either of the other two options. That decision will commit the church to a path that it will remain on for years, if not permanently. Selecting a value discipline is not merely a choice about what to do, it is also a choice about what not to do. What are we going to leave behind? What will we not provide? What will we not be the best at? Churches typically do not like to narrow their focus.

IS ALL THIS REALLY NECESSARY?

This chapter has probably been very taxing for many of you. It is, bottom line, a call to put feet to our vision. How we move toward our God-given vision must be consistent with our values, our ethics, and how God has created us. We must move into tomorrow with understanding. We must move forward with excellence.

If we are indeed a values-driven people, we are promising to deliver a particular combination of values to our target people groups. Integrity demands we build a values-driven operating model that will enable us to deliver on that promise. So, the processes we develop, the church structure we build, the management/leadership systems we utilize, the very culture we create, all must work together to give us the capacity to create and deliver that unsurpassed value. The discipline we choose will influence our entire organization for years to come.

We can choose not to expend the time, the energy, the prayer, and endure the struggle of preparing our value discipline. We can choose to live in mediocrity. We can continue to judge ourselves by how we stack up against others and come away pretty satisfied. To paraphrase George Barna, we can continue to try to do something for everybody and remain in the strategic blackhole of creating a ministry that looks great on paper but is unable to perform up to standards. If we choose this route, we must be prepared to accept that the fact that in the end, we will be helpful to no one.

On the other hand, we can bite the bullet, struggle with the issues of life, take the time, expend the effort and prepare our value discipline. We can choose to excel in the calling of God on our life and ministry. We can choose to walk out our vision with understanding, diligence, and excellence, and enter into our God-ordained future hearing the commendation of the Lord, "Well done, good and faithful slave. You were faithful with a few things, I will put you in charge of many things; enter into the joy of your master" (Matthew 25:21). We can choose the path of least resistance, or we can chose to prepare the way of the Lord. Which will you choose?

REFLECTIONS

1. Reflect what might serve as a possible **Value Proposition** for you? Write down two or three options.

    a). For each possible proposition noted above, what might be the implicit promise your church would be making both to its membership and your target population to deliver a particular combination of values? Write these down.

    b). What might be those specific values that would combine to create your implicit promise?

2. Which **Value Discipline** do you lean toward mastering? Upon what dimension of value would you stake your reputation and the reputation of the church? Why do you lean toward that value discipline?

    a). How would the selection of that particular value discipline color the culture of your church?

    b). How would the selection of that particular value discipline affect plans currently being implemented? How might it affect subsequent planning and decision making?

Chapter 6 ☞ *Prepare the Value Discipline*

ACTION POINTS

1. Review the section entitled *What is a Pastor to Do? - Setting Your Value Discipline Agenda.* Begin to work through each of the three phases answering their corresponding questions.

   Phase One: **Understand Your Current Situation**

   - What dimensions of value do our members and target group care about?

   - For each dimension of value, what proportion of our members and target group focus on that dimension of value as their primary or dominant decision criterion?

   - What other churches provide the best value in each of these value dimensions?

- How do we measure up against those other churches on each dimension of value?

- Why do we fall short of the value leaders in each dimension of value?

Phase Two: Develop Realistic Alternative Value Propositions & Operating Models

- What are the benchmark standards of value performance that will affect both our members and target groups expectations?

- For those we have determined to be value leaders, what will their standards or performance be three years from now?

- How must the operating models of these value leaders be designed to attain those levels of performance?

Chapter 6 — *Prepare the Value Discipline*

Phase Three: Commit to One Value Discipline

- What would the required operating model look like? What would be the design specifications for the core processes, management systems, structure, etc.?

- How would the model produce superior value?

- What levels of threshold value will be required in the other dimensions. How will these be attained?

- How large will the "market" be for this value proposition?

- What are the critical success factors that can make or break this solution?

- How will the church make the transition from its current state to this new operating model or if a church plant, develop this operating model over a two-to three-year period?

Preparing the 21st Century Church

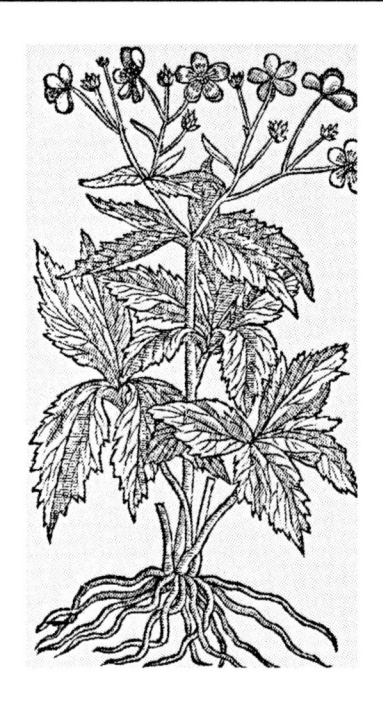

ABOVE GROUND REALITIES

(FRUIT AFTER ROOTS)

PHASE 1 — Prepare the Ethical Base

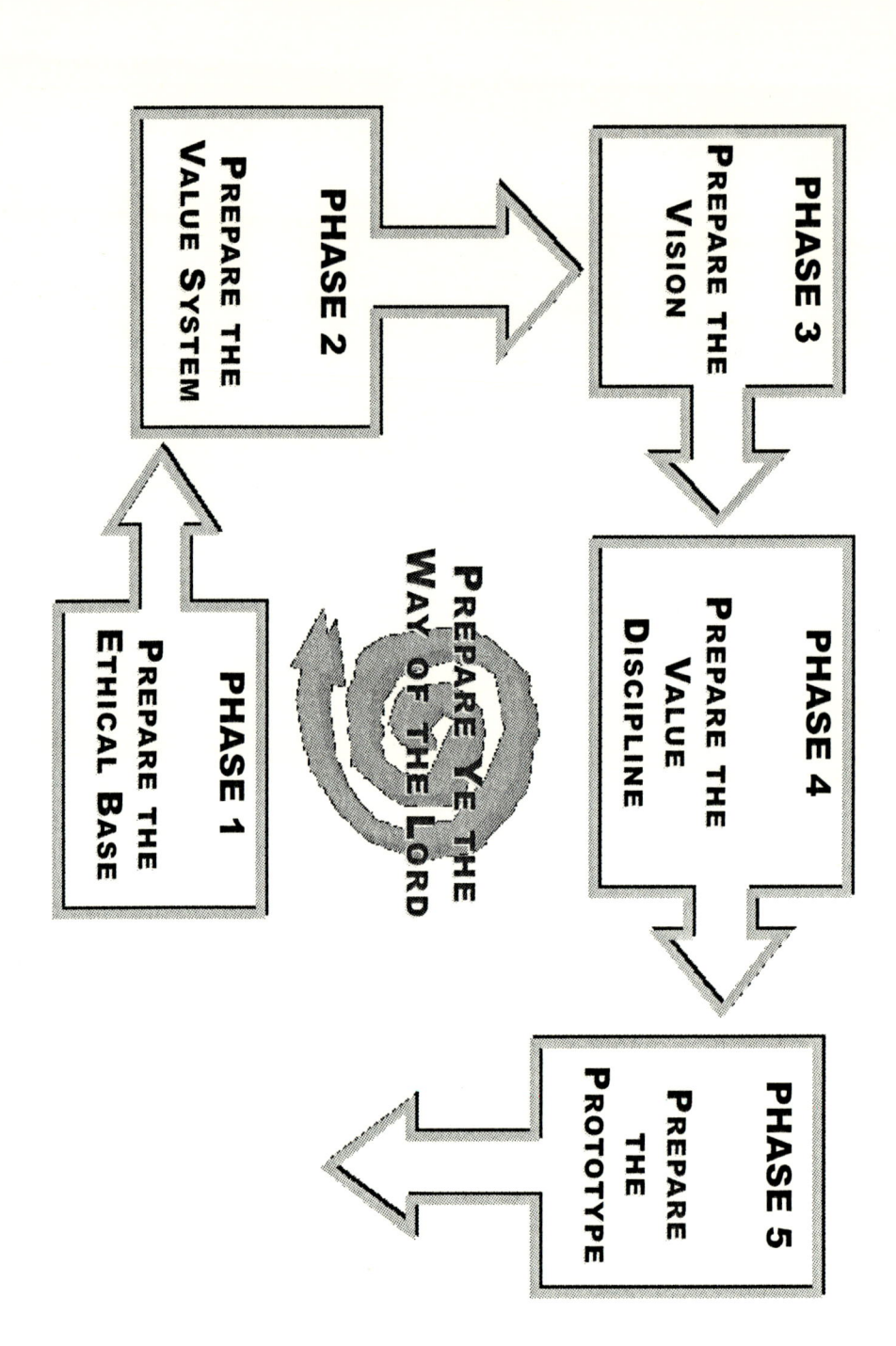

PHASE 2 — Prepare the Value System

PHASE 3 — Prepare the Vision

PHASE 4 — Prepare the Value Discipline

PHASE 5 — Prepare the Prototype

Prepare Ye the Way of the Lord

ABOVE GROUND REALITIES
PREPARE THE PROTOTYPE

FOR YOU YOURSELVES KNOW HOW YOU OUGHT TO *FOLLOW OUR EXAMPLE*...WITH LABOR AND HARDSHIP WE KEPT WORKING NIGHT AND DAY SO THAT WE WOULD NOT BE A BURDEN TO ANY OF YOU...IN ORDER TO OFFER OURSELVES *AS A MODEL FOR YOU*, SO THAT YOU WOULD *FOLLOW OUR EXAMPLE.*

2 THESSALONIANS 3:7-9

Chapter 7 ☛ *Prepare the Prototype*

INTRODUCTION

Now that you are, hopefully, committed to doing what is biblical, regardless of the consequences good or bad, now that you have begun to wrestle with your real values, now that you are before the Lord receiving greater clarification of your vision, now that you are more aware of who exactly you are in terms of your value discipline, you are finally ready to start with a cell group! Having laid a foundation, you can now begin to build upon it. However, before you leap into mass production of your cells, you would be well advised to make sure you are going to multiply exactly what you both really desire and envision. Toward this end, you are now ready to prepare the Prototype.

APPLES, COKES, AND THE CELL CHURCH

Apple Computer sold over 400,000 of the original Powerbook notebook computers in the first year following their product launch, making the Powerbook the most successful new product in Apple's history. However, the subsequent model of Powerbook, the Duo, had to be even smaller, lighter, and more powerful in order to remain competitive. One major obstacle to reducing the thickness of the original Powerbook was the thickness of the trackball mechanism. Consequently, a new trackball became one of the key elements of the Duo development effort. Though now replaced by touchpads, trackballs were commonly used in early portable computers as a substitute for the computer mouse. The ball, recessed in a housing, was manipulated by the user in order to control the position of the cursor on the computer screen. In addition to the dominant goal of reducing the size of the trackball, the development team at Apple hoped to decrease its cost while simultaneously increasing its quality. Throughout the development of the trackball, the team used a variety of prototypes.

When the Coca Cola Company ran early prototype tests of its New Coke with customers, the results suggested strong support for the new product. But the tests only focused on taste. The testers never asked: "How would you feel about this new product if it were to replace Coke?" The remarkable protests that took Coca Cola by surprise when it replaced Old Coke with New Coke and swiftly led to the reintroduction of "Classic" Coke suggests the dangers of ill-conceived early customer involvement in development and prototyping of a new product.

You may be wondering at this point, "What does all this have to do with the cell church?" Remember (p. 19-20) that every church, cell church or otherwise, is faced with five basic questions. How do we build up Christ's people (Edification)? How do we reach unbelievers in this generation for Christ (Evangelism)? How can spiritual children be brought to the maturity of spiritual fatherhood (Equipping)? Where will our future leaders come from (Empowering)? How can we mobilize the members of the Body of Christ into active service (Every Member Ministry)? The cell church maintains the answers to these fundamental questions are most effectively accomplished in the context of the small group functioning as the Basic Christian Community.

This is both a radical departure from 20th century small group design and a grand boast. Leader, if you intend to deliver the goods, so to speak, if you intend for your small groups to be the hotbed for Edification, Evangelism, Equipping, Empowering Leaders, and Every Member Ministry, you had better do everything in your power to make certain that your groups succeed! That, in a nutshell, is one of the motivations for first developing a fully functional prototype cell before you mess around changing your entire church structure. Let's develop a working model, and you won't have the outcry of "Coke" customers, "I liked the old groups better! Why did you change them?"

Prototype development is not an insurmountable task. Neither is it beyond the ability of the average cell church pastor. Though it may seem daunting at first, remember how you learned to drive. You climbed into the driver's seat. First there was the seat belt to fasten. Then the rear view mirror needed adjusting, as well as perhaps the outside mirror. Brake, clutch, ignition. Though not difficult, their order of execution was vital. Then there was the development of the skill of releasing the brake while giving the car gas. Not too fast. Not too much. Right proportions were critical. Passengers did not like to feel "jerked" around, neither was it healthy for the car. Then came the hard part, backing out into the street. Checking for stray pets and wandering children was a must. A glance over the shoulder was insufficient. You must be seeing where you are going. Then came the sidewalk. Why in the world did the law say that you must stop before crossing the sidewalk on your own property? Little things to remember. Then came the street. Decision time arrived! Is it safe to back out into traffic? Is there enough time before that car down the street arrives? What about cross traffic? On top of all this, you had to concentrate while passengers talked away and requested a different radio station. Talk about being unnerved! Finally, there was the ever watchful and critical eye of the unseen nervous par-

Chapter 7 — Prepare the Prototype

ent watching you take their pride and joy out for a spin, more fearful with each lurch of the car. Today, driving is a snap. What once was cause for agonized thought now comes second nature. Multiple things are done simultaneously. You can't even imagine why it seemed so hard when you began! Trust me. Prototype development is like learning to drive.

As we journey through this chapter I will attempt to answer a number of questions. What is a prototype? Is preparing a prototyping simply an engineering principle, or is it a biblical principle? What are some of the short-term and long-term benefits of preparing a prototype? How do I actually prepare a prototype?

WHAT IS A PROTOTYPE?

Our word *prototype* is derived from the combination of two Greek words. *Proto* means *first*. *Tupos* is the Greek word for *model*. A prototype is thus a *first model*. It is our first attempt to model, or approximate a concept or "product" in which we are interested. In general, a prototype is an approximation of this concept or product along one or more dimensions of interest. These dimensions of interest are those particular or special characteristics that we want to produce and then faithfully replicate as the original model is mass produced. In particular, for our purposes in the creation of a cell church, we are defining a prototype cell as the approximation of a Basic Christian Community along one or more dimensions of interest by which Basic Christian Community has been defined.

For the purposes of our immediate study, these dimensions of interest will encompass the aforementioned elements of Edification, Equipping, Empowering, Evangelism, and Every Member Ministry. However, realize that your own distinctive prototype may not be limited to these five elements and may encompass other elements as well. As an example, your desire to have intergenerational cells as opposed to gender specific adult cells will necessitate an additional element to prototype, i.e., children in the cell.

Prototyping is therefore the process of developing such an approximation of our understanding of Basic Christian Community. It is the process of developing a cell which will approximate each of the dimensions with which we are interested.

Most modern products are carefully prototyped before they are mass produced and distributed to the consume. Cars undergo three to five years of design and prototype development before mass production. Electronic components pass through rigorous product and consumer testing. Computer software goes through Alpha and often Beta testing before final versions are released.

Adjacent is a picture of Sky Venture, along with its creator and designer, Mike Palmer. Sky Venture provides an exciting, realistic, yet safe indoor sky diving experience. I remember the model construction that Mike was involved in prior to actual creation of the finished product. In visiting in his home one day during its early development, Mike showed me a scale model of Sky Venture. The detail was precise. Why did he not simply build the final product? Why spend the time modeling? The time and cost necessary to build was considerable. Failure was not an option. A test model was built in Virginia to better ensure success in Orlando and beyond!

PROTOTYPE DEVELOPMENT - A BIBLICAL EXERCISE?

While prototype development is continually engaged in by the secular world, can we legitimately contend that preparing a prototype is also biblically grounded? God the Father created the first prototype. His Son engaged in prototype development. The Apostle Paul both learned this lesson well and passed it on to those who followed.

The Father's Work of Creation - Preparing the Prototypes of Life

Creation was the the most mammoth prototype enterprise in all of history. Read the Genesis creation account (Genesis 1:1-31) again through new lenses, the lenses of prototype development. God the Father created one original model for everything in the world. He looked it over, decided it was exactly as His thought, and so declared it "good"! With that single utterance He announced that every model was ready to multiply. There would be no recalls. They all met His specifications. The necks of the giraffes were not too long, their legs not too short. No need to speak again! Every tree was unique; its fruit

Chapter 7 ☛ *Prepare the Prototype*

as it should be. They were ready to bear much more. The swarming things, the flying things, all were just as He had determined. With each creative act, God brought into being His thought and pronounced it "good". He did not have to re-do anything. His creation was ready to be multiplied.

Imagine with me a moment the unthinkable scenario. God creates, and yet there exists a flaw, the model does not quite match His expectations. However, He decides to multiply the model and fix the flaw later. What a mess! No, His ways are perfect. The model is perfect. Each element of approximation for each and every model is perfect – legs, necks, gills, fins, roots, blossoms. "God saw all that He had made, and behold, it was very good."

The Lord Jesus Christ - Preparing the Prototype Cell and Disciple

Jesus continually modeled the very skills, passion and values that his followers themselves would later need in ministry. Note for example Mark's account of His servanthood.

> Mark 10:42 Calling them to Himself, Jesus *said to them, "You know that those who are recognized as rulers of the Gentiles lord it over them; and their great men exercise authority over them.
> Mark 10:43 "But it is not this way among you, but whoever wishes to become great among you shall be your servant;
> Mark 10:44 and whoever wishes to be first among you shall be slave of all.
> Mark 10:45 "For even the Son of Man did not come to be served, but to serve, and to give His life a ransom for many."

By putting these before them and then involving and supervising them in actual ministry, His disciples learned the very things they would carry forward and pass on in their own ministries. In this way, what they needed to learn for ministry and what they were actually taught were one and the same.

Is the development of a prototype cell with all of the time, energy and resources it demands, really vital? Can't we just "wing it", or "fly by the seat of our pants"? Can't we just leave it up to God to just naturally develop? Won't time take care of it all, anyway? The answer must be a resounding, NO!

Jesus spent years developing His prototype. The cost was high and the risk was great. However, Jesus did what was necessary. He paid the price. He would not take shortcuts. He could not afford failure. His cell must function properly. His followers must succeed. There was to be no second opportunity, no opportunity to rework the model.

The selection by Jesus of the twelve from the band of disciples who had gathered around Him is an important landmark in the gospel history. It divides the ministry of our Lord into two portions. In the earlier period Jesus labored single-handed, His miraculous deeds were confined, for the most part, to a limited area, and His teaching was, in the main, of an elementary character. By the time the twelve were chosen, the work of the Kingdom had assumed such dimensions as to require organization and division of labor. The selection of a limited number to be His close and constant companions had become a necessity. It was His wish that certain selected men should be with Him at all times and in all places. He was entering into a special community relationship with them. These twelve were to be fellow laborers in the work of the Kingdom, and eventually Christ's chosen trained agents for propagating the faith. From the time of their choosing, the twelve entered upon a regular apprenticeship. In the course of that apprenticeship they were to learn what they should be, do, believe, and teach as His witnesses.

The Senior Pastor's selection of an initial prototype cell parallels Jesus' selection of the twelve. The Senior Pastor must choose those into whom he will pour his life like no others. These are special relationships, more intense than that which he will have with the other sheep in his flock. The Senior Pastor has reached the place where he is no longer laboring single handed. The work has become too great. Those included in this prototype cell will become co-laborers with him. They will be entering upon a regular apprenticeship under his personal tutelage.

What shall we say then about those initially chosen to become part of the prototype? Notice I use the word chosen. These members are not volunteers. The call to belong to the prototype is not, "whosoever will may come". The prototype cell members are hand picked, chosen. They are de facto neither the deacons nor the elders of the church. Remember the change continuum in chapter three? These initial cell members are those individuals who are conceptually committed. They are not those whose attention you may have and are now scrutinizing your every move. These are your innovators and early adopters. They are not part of your early majority who need a working model before they buy in. These are the ones who will become your first cell leaders and apprentices. They will be the ones who in

Chapter 7 ☛ Prepare the Prototype

two or three multiplications will begin to father and pastor your cell leaders. In a church transition, the Senior Pastor will choose the few from among the many. However, in a church plant, you may not have that luxury, and very well may need to start with those the Lord has originally brought to you.

In the early period of the discipleship of the twelve, hearing and seeing seem to have been the main occupation. It was only later that He brought them into the actual doing of His works with His Spirit. Jesus taught His disciples to pray. He showed them how to live. He did not teach merely cognitively. He modeled and lived before them. He included instructions in the practice of fasting and Sabbath observance. He trained them in humility, self-sacrifice, service, and the meaning of the cross in daily life.

It is imperative the Senior Pastor follow the model of Jesus. Transparency does not come easy for those of us in ministry. Seminary teaches us not to get close to any church member. Our culture mitigates against honesty and transparency. Our upbringing as men have ingrained within us a pattern of non-communication. We find it difficult even to develop close relationships with our wives. WYSIWYG (what-you-see-is-what-you-get) may be a value for computer software development, but it is not a value senior church leadership has bought into. However, it was true of Jesus. Humility, self-sacrifice, self-disclosure, service, daily death of the old man in interpersonal relationships, these we must live and model before our future leaders. To not do so will be to cripple the development of our prototype.

There were regular periods of evaluation in the original prototype model. Jesus sends forth the seventy and then evaluates their work in evangelism (Luke 11). Correction is often necessary. Peter is corrected (Matthew 16:13-20), the sons of thunder are corrected (Luke 9:51-56), as well as the two sons of Zebedee (Luke 18:31-34). Jesus spent the time necessary with His disciples to prepare them. They were not thrust out prematurely. They eventually had their season when they experienced His "benign neglect".

Even from a cursory reading of the gospel records, one cannot but come away with the impression that Jesus' training of the twelve was very focused and deliberate. His prototype had a definite beginning, a focused purpose, a limited time frame and included regular times of evaluation. It could be argued that Jesus even did Alpha, Beta and Pre-production development before He initiated assembly line production on the day of Pentecost. I refer the reader to the classic work by F. F. Bruce, "The Training of the Twelve" for a clearer understanding of the "dimensions of interest" Jesus prototyped.

Man did not initiate the concept of prototype development – God practiced it first. I have provided some seed thoughts for you. However, I encourage you to re-think your paradigm and take the time to re-examine the ministry of Jesus and the training of the twelve in the context of a prototype development process. You and your prototype cell will be greatly enriched by such an examination!

The Apostle Paul - Preparing the Early Church Prototype

In the final analysis, a prototype is a model in which the bugs have been worked out and which is now reproducible *en mass*. The concept of modeling with a view toward mass reproduction is very biblical. Not only Jesus, but the Apostle Paul also frequently set forth this concept of modeling as an essential element of the Christian life. In *Alternative Models of Mennonite Pastoral Formation*, Jim Egli noted the following:

> Paul writes to the Galatians, "I plead with you, brothers, become like me, for I became like you" (Galatians 4:12). Paul held up his life as a model for his converts (2 Thessalonians 3:7ff), for local leaders (Acts 20:31), and for his younger partners (2 Timothy 3:10). It is obvious from the epistles that lifestyle modeling was a very deliberate part of Paul's strategy. He encourages the Christians at Thessalonica to "imitate" (Greek mimeomai) the example he has set (2 Thessalonians 3:7,9). In the same way he exhorts the Corinthians to become his "imitators" (1 Corinthians 4:16). Then he again tells them, "Become imitators of me, just as I am of Christ (own translation of 1 Corinthians 11:1). In the same way, he asks those at Philippi to become "co-imitators" in following his example (Philippians 3:17). Paul realized that people need more than to be taught how to live, they need to be shown.
>
> Just as Paul held out his life as a "model" (Greek tupos), so he expected his converts and assistants to become models to others. As the Christians at Thessalonica became imitators of Paul, his co-workers and the Lord, they themselves "became a model to all the believers in Macedonia and Achaia" (1

Chapter 7 ☞ *Prepare the Prototype*

Thessalonians 1:6,7). Paul also commanded Timothy and Titus each to be a "model" to those they served (1 Timothy 4:12, Titus 2:4f).

The principle of modeling is repeated in leadership training throughout the New Testament: Jesus modeling attitudes and skills for his disciples (e.g., Mark 10:42ff); Barnabas serving as an example for Paul; Paul acting as a model for still other leaders.

Modeling far surpasses simple informational learning as a primary basis of training. It assumes the reality of close, caring relationships where ministry can be demonstrated and taught through actions and attitudes as well as information. Perhaps the clearest and most powerful principle for us to realize from the New Testament is modeling. When we do leadership training we must realize that we are continually modeling. The question is not, "Are we modeling?" We are modeling whether we realize it or not! The question is, "What are we modeling?" Those who watch what we model will consciously and unconsciously repeat in their own ministries the patterns we put before them in our ministry.

I remember the anti-smoking commercial of a few years back. A small boy is walking beside his father, imitating his every move as they together walk along. The father bends down, picks up a rock, and skips it across the water. The little son, like father, picks up a stone and attempts to skip it across the water. Dad sits down beneath a tree, legs outstretched. Both are sitting backs against the tree when dad reaches for a smoke and tosses the cigarette package on the grass. The little boy reaches for the smokes. Like father like son. We are modeling whether we realize it or not!

Years ago while a pastor in North Dakota, I had a young man approach me after a Sunday evening service. He had been faithfully attending our services in the evening, though he was not a member and attended elsewhere in the morning. He approached me with these words, "I have been watching you and your wife for the last two years. I would like you to marry me and my fiancee." His words bowled me over. He had been watching me, watching my relationship with my wife, evaluating my life for over two years. I had not realized the power of a model. What if I had provided a defective model of marriage and ministry?

We have seen how important right modeling was for Paul. What if he had provided a defective model for the Thessalonians, who in turn would have provided a defective model "to all the believers in Macedonia and Achaia"? What would have been the damage to the work of God's Kingdom?

We might envision Paul's concept of modeling like a stone dropped in a pond which sets in motion ever-widening ripples. Christ's supreme example dropped into the reality of human history was transforming Paul's life whose own example was impacting others and then extending to still others. This expansion of Christ's life in Paul's mind and practice involved modeling – living out the message and example of Christ. If we as leaders cannot live out Basic Christian Community in all its facets, we have no right to tell our people to do so. We must do it. And we must do it correctly! Having come to understand what a prototype is and its biblical nature, the question looming before us remains, "How in the world can I correctly prepare one?" To this we now turn.

HOW CAN I CORRECTLY PREPARE A PROTOTYPE?

As we attempt to chew on this question, let's first break the answer down into three manageable bites. Preparing a successful prototype demands we first select the appropriate type of prototype. We must learn to distinguish between differing types and select the type most appropriate for our needs. Second, we must select the appropriate application. For what purpose will we be preparing our prototype? Third, we must prepare the planning process. The planning process will birth our concepts into reality.

Distinguishing Differing Types

When considering the selection of an appropriate type of prototype cell, we are faced with the issue of selecting either a physical or analytical prototype, and selecting either a focused or comprehensive prototype. This results in the possibility of four differing options, as noted in the chart below. A physical prototype is a tangible prototype. It is a tangible artifact created to approximate the product that is to ultimately be produced. Physical prototypes are models which look and feel like the product. They are experimental models used to validate the functionality of the product. In the cell church context, a prototype cell would be a 21st century model which would look and feel like the biblical model of community; a fully functional experimental model that would validate

Chapter 7 ☞ Prepare the Prototype

the contention that cells can genuinely "function" in an urban center like Houston, Texas, or a rural setting like Grand Forks, ND, or some setting in between.

> **Differing Types**
>
> **Focused-Analytical**
>
> **Focused-Physical**
>
> **Comprehensive-Physical**
>
> **Comprehensive-Analytical**

Analytical prototypes represent the same product in a non-tangible, usually mathematical manner. In this case, aspects of the product are analyzed rather than built. While employed as an engineer at Pratt & Whitney Aircraft, I was tasked with the development of prototypes that were never physically built. Rather, what were developed were mathematical models used to determine the feasibility of the concept. These were mathematical laser simulations prior to the development of the actual physical prototype hardware.

Physical and analytical prototypes may be either comprehensive or focused. The differences are easily understood.

Comprehensive prototypes implement most if not all of the attributes of the final product by development of a full-scale, fully operational version of the product. For example, when Ford Motor Company develops a comprehensive prototype, what is created is a full-scale, fully operational automobile. For our purposes, a comprehensive prototype cell would be a cell group fully operational in the areas of Edification, Equipping, Evangelism, Empowering and Every Member Ministry. Of course, the criteria by which we determine our cell to be "fully operational" will need to be specifically defined for each area of interest.

Focused prototypes implement only one, or a few, of the attributes of the final product. A common practice is to use two or more focused prototypes together to investigate the overall performance of a product. One often will be a "looks like" prototype, while the other will be a "works like" prototype. By building two separate focused prototypes, a leadership design team may be able

202

to answer its questions much earlier than if it had attempted to create one comprehensive prototype. As an example, we might consider the development of a prototype cell testing only evangelism criteria. This may be helpful in a transitioning cell church where the other design specifications (Edification, Equipping, etc.) have already been implemented and are functional in the cells, but where oikos evangelism has not been implemented as a value or functional in lifestyle.

The great danger at this stage is for the Senior Pastor to inadvertently attempt to establish cell groups out of a comprehensive analytical prototype. Here is the typical scenario. The Senior Pastor either reads cell literature or goes to a cell conference where he gains cognitive information. This information is next processed through his paradigm of New Testament ecclesiology. Light bulbs explode in "Aha" moments of insight and revelation. The Senior Pastor continues to process his thinking, refining it more and more until he "sees" the whole of it. In his excitement and enthusiasm, he gathers his leaders and shares his insights. He paints what he believes to be vivid pictures. His leaders become enthused. They are then charged with going out and starting cell groups that will bring this vision to pass. In the course of time the pastor visits their cells. What he experiences is neither what he "saw", nor what he thought he had communicated! He takes the cell leaders aside and corrects and instructs them afresh. They are then sent out to "do it again". The vision, however, never really comes to pass. He has created an analytical prototype - a prototype in his mind. Yet his leadership are not mind readers. They need to experience what he "sees". They need something tangible, something real. They cannot pass on what they have themselves never experienced. They need a physical prototype, not merely an analytical prototype. They further need a comprehensive prototype if they are to ever replicate all that the Senior Pastor "sees".

I have seen this scenario played out time and time again in churches moving to a cell paradigm. The result is disappointment, disillusionment, discouragement and ultimately delay. Vision, as we have seen, is critical. However, preparing the prototype correctly will help ensure the vision can come to pass in a timely manner. Haste makes waste!

Selecting the Proper Application

Let's re-examine our previous chart, this time filling in some of the blanks. We discover that prototypes may have one of four primary applications:

Chapter 7 ☛ Prepare the Prototype

Learning, Communication, Integration, Milestone. Let's turn our attention toward each application in some detail.

Differing Types	Learning	Communication	Integration	Milestone
Focused-Analytical	MA	LA	LA	LA
Focused-Physical	MA	MA	LA	LA
Comprehensive-Physical	MA ⟵	MA	MA	MA ⟶
Comprehensive-Analytical		RARELY POSSIBLE		

Appropriateness of different types of prototypes for different purposes (**MA** = More Appropriate, **LA** = Less Appropriate). Note that comprehensive-analytical prototypes are rarely possible.

Prototypes may often be employed as a **Learning Tool**. As a learning tool, prototypes are used to answer two questions: "Will it work?" and "How well does it meet the "customer's" needs?" When speaking to Russian pastors, I contended that the biblical model of cells functioning as Basic Christian Communities would work in a Russian context and meet the pastoral care needs of church members better than the current model they were using, while at the same time providing more effective evangelism than currently experienced by the average Russian church. The average Russian pastor agreed that cells worked in Singapore and in Korea. However, they did not know whether or not cells would work in Russia. A prototype cell would help them learn how well cells would work in their localized context. Will cells work in an urban setting? Will they work in a rural setting? Will they work in differing cultural contexts? A prototype cell will both answer the questions and help identify how to contextualize and indigenize the cell for various locales. In this way, church leaders will gain valuable insights and learn important lessons regarding cell development.

A second application of a prototype is as a **Communication Tool**. Prototypes enrich communication with leaders, partners and those who will ultimately benefit from the product. This is particularly true of physical prototypes. A visual, functional representation of a product is much easier to understand than a verbal description or even a sketch or diagram. "Look and Feel" prototypes allow for potential "customers" to give feedback about the features being designed. Innovators and early adopters in our church normally will quickly embrace the new paradigm. They, however, comprise but a small population in most of our churches. The majority of our members desire a physical, visual and functional representation of a cell before they will embrace it. The prototype ensures they will have that desire met. Even those who readily embrace the new paradigm will find it much easier to understand and communicate that vision if they have a visual and functional representation. The prototype becomes the tangible demonstration and picture of what we have otherwise only verbally described.

Prototypes also serve as **Integration Tools**. Prototypes can be used to ensure that components and subsystems of a product work together as expected. Comprehensive physical prototypes are most effective as integration tools in development because they require the assembly and physical interconnection of all the parts and subassemblies that take up the product. In doing so, the prototype forces coordination between different members of the development team. If the combination of any of the components of the product interferes with the overall function of the product, the problem may be detected through physical integration in a comprehensive prototype. Common names for these physical prototypes are experimental, beta, alpha, preproduction prototypes.

Most small groups on the American scene today focus on the edification aspect of cell life. Some have added evangelism. Few, though, have added an established equipping system or look to the cell for the development of leaders or provide opportunity for every member interfacing on a corporate level in ministry. When we begin to combine all five aspects together in a prototype, we discover in what ways our combining of these different components interfere with the desired overall function of the cell itself. Through our physical integration of all of these aspects into a comprehensive prototype, we discover problems and are able to correct them prior to rapid multiplication.

One additional illustration may further clarify the importance of employing a prototype as an integration tool. Consider this scenario. Your church's cell groups are functioning well on every level. However, you have chosen to use only gender specific cells, i.e. men's cells and women's cells. You are now impacting a segment of the community where your strategy may need to change to the use of intergenerational cells. The questions facing you are clear. How will the introduction of intergenerational cell elements affect the current level of evangelism? Will evangelism be greater or slack off? How will the present level of edification be affected? The introduction of intergenerational cell elements into a "prototype cell", a current cell presently functioning well, will impact the overall function of that cell. Evaluation of each cell component within the new prototype and correction of detected problems prior to the establishment of additional intergenerational cells and/or the transition of current cells to the intergenerational paradigm will ensure greater success for the launch of the intergenerational cell model.

Finally, prototypes may also serve as **Milestones**. In the later stages of development, prototypes are used to demonstrate that the product has reached the desired level of functionality. Milestone prototypes provide tangible goals, demonstrate progress, and serve to enforce the schedule. Senior pastors, elders, and/or denominational authorities often require a prototype to demonstrate certain functions before they will allow the transition of a church to proceed.

Of perhaps particular importance is the unfortunate fact that many Senior Elders have veto-power people to whom they have to answer. These veto-power people make the ultimate decisions regarding whether transition will proceed or be terminated, whether the church plant is cell/celebration based or not. The prototype thus comes to serve as a Milestone. The prototype will demonstrate that the anticipated level of functionality has been successfully reached. The prototype provides for these veto-power people a demonstration of tangible progress and the attainment of tangible goals. A green light can then be given to continue the transition and/or plant along a cell-based design. The prototype in this case is your final exam for a pass/fail grade!

While all types of prototypes are used for all four of these purposes, some types of prototypes are more appropriate than others for some purposes, as can be seen in the chart above. In addition, though there is often overlap in purpose, there should be one primary purpose defined for the prototype.

Developing the Planning Process: A Five Step Process

A potential pitfall in product development is what is called the "hardware swamp". The swamp is caused by misguided prototyping efforts, that is, the building and debugging of prototypes that do not really contribute to the goals of the overall product development. One way to avoid this swamp is to define carefully each prototype before embarking on an effort to build and test it. What follows is a five-step methodology for planning a prototype. I have included an abbreviated sample template for recording the information generated from this methodology. The sample template will address only one of our design elements, evangelism

Step 1: Define the Purpose of the Prototype

```
SAMPLE CELL PROTOTYPE
DEVELOPMENT TEMPLATE


PURPOSE

(Communication, Learning, Integration, Milestones)
Integration - Oikos Evangelism becomes an integral part of
cell lifestyle
```

Recall the four possible purposes of prototypes: learning, communication, integration, and milestones. In defining the purpose of the prototype, the Senior Pastor and his team must identify his specific learning and communication needs. Next, he must list any integration needs and whether or not the prototype is intended to be one of the major milestones of the overall transition to a cell church or the planting of a cell church. In many cases, the cell prototype will very likely be a milestone prototype vital for the transition or plant to successfully take place. For our purposes here, though, because I am illustrating only one criterion, the prototype must be thought of as a focused prototype with integration serving as the primary purpose. In a real life church plant or transition situation, the prototype would more likely be comprehensive rather than focused.

Chapter 7 ☞ *Prepare the Prototype*

Step 2: Establish the Level of Approximation

> # SAMPLE CELL PROTOTYPE DEVELOPMENT TEMPLATE
>
> PURPOSE
>
> (Communication, Learning, Integration, Milestones) Integration - Oikos Evangelism becomes an integral part of cell lifestyle
>
> LEVEL OF APPROXIMATION
>
> 90% Of Cell Members Have Developed Ongoing Relationships With Two Unbelievers From Among Collective Cell Oikos List. That means nine out of ten Cell Members have added two unbelievers to their oikos (relating to them a minimum of one hour per week over the initial nine month life cycle of the prototype.

Planning a prototype requires that the degree to which the final product is approximated be defined. Usually, the best prototype is the simplest prototype that will serve the purpose established in step one. Each attribute of the product that is being prototyped needs to have a level of approximation, some quantifiable standard against which we evaluate "success".

I have identified five major attributes that need to be realized in a successful cell. Each attribute would need a defined level of approximation. In other words, how will we know that each attribute is actually "operating successfully" in our prototype? The only way we will know is to first define some measurable level of operation which we define as "success", and then periodically evaluate each attribute in light of that level. So we ask and answer the following questions. What will be the level of approximation for edification? How will we measure evangelism? How will we define "successful" equipping? At what quantifiable level will we declare leadership empowerment and every member ministry has been achieved?

As an example, let's consider just the attribute of evangelism. The final cell we desire to reproduce we envision to be a cell which lives out a "fishing net" evangelism paradigm. This evangelism paradigm views effective evangelism, i.e. fishing, as being accomplished by cell members working together to cast a relational net, even as the disciples worked together to cast a large physical net for the fish (Matthew 4:19). This evangelistic paradigm can be contrasted with "fishing pole" evangelism, an evangelism paradigm that encourages primarily each individual to reach out to those individuals they are attempting to reach with the gospel.

Therefore, a level of approximation must be established for the cell prototype relative to "fishing net" evangelism". This means that in the prototype, the evangelism paradigm of the members must be shifted from "fishing pole" to "fishing net". A primary evidence that this has happened will be by cell members developing relationships outside of the weekly cell gathering with the lost oikos members of other cell members and together with that cell member reaching out to their lost oikos member. Building upon our previous sample template, we now derive the following.

Step 3: Outline an Experimental Plan

Usually, the use of a prototype in development can be thought of as an experiment. Good experimental practice helps to ensure the extraction of maximum value from the prototyping activity. When many variables must be explored efficient experimental design greatly facilitates the process. A good experimental plan should include the following elements:

- The identification of the variables of the experiment
- A test protocol
- An indication of what measurements will be performed
- A plan for analyzing the resulting data

What are some of the variables in our test case? Both the idea of oikos and oikos evangelism need to be defined for our cell members. A personal oikos list (those each individual is focused on reaching for Christ) must be defined, as well as a cell oikos list (those the cell will focus on reaching with the gospel).

SAMPLE CELL PROTOTYPE DEVELOPMENT TEMPLATE

PURPOSE

(Communication, Learning, Integration, Milestones) Integration - Oikos Evangelism becomes an integral part of cell lifestyle

LEVEL OF APPROXIMATION

90% Of Cell Members Have Developed Ongoing Relationships With Two Unbelievers From Among Collective Cell Oikos List. That means nine out of ten Cell Members have added two unbelievers to their oikos (relating to them a minimum of one hour per week over the initial nine month life cycle of the prototype.

OUTLINE OF TEST PLAN

1. EXPLAIN Oikos Evangelism, Oikos Contact List, and Cell Goal
2. CREATE Cell Oikos Contact List
3. BEGIN to pray Over Oikos Contact List
4. CONTACT 1st New Unbeliever
5. DEVELOP Relationship (Sports, Dinner, Hobby, Interest, Work)
6. CONTACT 2nd New Unbeliever
7. DEVELOP Relationship (Sports, Dinner, Hobby, Interest, Work)

The "different tomorrow" that we envision includes our cell members having developed relationships with two unbelievers. Our protocol must somehow systematically move our cell members from identifying their own oikos to developing a relationship with another cell member's oikos member. What will quantitatively and qualitatively indicate that our vision of tomorrow has been reached? Our answers to these questions will move us forward in the development of our experimental plan. I am well aware that this kind of step by step planning drives some of you crazy! However, it is this kind of systematic thinking and planning that separates many pie-in-the-sky cells that fail from those that ultimately work and reproduce successfully.

Step 4: Create a Schedule for Procurement, Construction, & Test

Three dates are particularly important in defining a prototype effort.

First, the team must identify when the parts will be ready to assemble. This is sometimes called the "bucket of parts" date. For example, if your prototype is to include written material such as an inductive Bible study to be used with unbelievers your members will be building relationships with, then the material should be available and on hand prior to the launch of the prototype.

Second, the team must identify the date when the prototype will first be tested. There must be established a schedule for the initial and on-going testing and evaluation of each design attribute defined. Too many times I have heard the mournful refrain from pastors and cell leaders, "We don't know why it didn't work." Too often those involved have no clue as to the reason for their failure, and worse still, they were not even aware of the signs of failure staring them in the face all along the way. Constant evaluation must be done. It will do us no good to finish nine months of our prototype, scratch our heads wondering why no one was saved, and suddenly discover that our members had little to no contact with either their own lost friends or the friends of their fellow cell members. That lack of contact would have been noted and corrected had periodic evaluation been done.

Third, the team must identify the date when it expects to have completed testing and produced the final results. The prototype cell should not go on indefinitely. Establish a multiplication date from the start. After all, each succeeding generation will have a start and multiplication date. If you are expecting future cells to multiply every six months, the prototype should generally multiply within six months.

SAMPLE CELL PROTOTYPE DEVELOPMENT TEMPLATE

PURPOSE

LEVEL OF APPROXIMATION

OUTLINE OF TEST PLAN

PROPOSED SCHEDULE

Week #1	EXPLAIN	Done by Senior Pastor
Week #2	CREATE	Done as Cell, Pastor Oversees
Week #2	BEGIN	Weekly in various ways i.e. in Cell, as AP's, etc.
Week #4	CONTACT	New Unbeliever
Week #4-#13	DEVELOP	On-Going Relationships
Week #13	**1ST MAJOR EVALUATION**	
	True for 30% of Cell Members	
Week #14	CONTACT	New Unbeliever
Week #14-#26	DEVELOP	On-Going Relationships
Week #26	**2ND MAJOR EVALUATION**	
	True for 60% of Cell Members	
Week #27	CONTACT	New Unbeliever
Week #27-#39	DEVELOP	On-Going Relationships
Week #39	**3RD MAJOR EVALUATION**	
	True for 90% of Cell Members	

Step 5: Planning Your Milestone Prototypes and Developing Your Timelines

Comprehensive prototypes used as development milestones benefit from additional planning. Milestone prototypes are defined during the project planning phase of development. In theory, a team would prefer to build as few milestone prototypes as possible because designing, building and testing prototypes consumes a great deal of time and resources. However, in reality, few highly engineered products are developed with fewer than two milestone prototypes, and many efforts require four or more. As a base case, a team should consider using *alpha*, *beta* and *preproduction* prototypes as milestones. The team should then consider whether any of these milestones can be eliminated or whether in fact additional prototypes are necessary.

Alpha prototypes are typically used to asses whether the product works as intended. It is the first generation prototype. Before we alter the very structure of the church and loudly proclaim how much better our cells will now engage in evangelism, or edification, or equipping, or empowering, or releasing members into body ministry, it would be wise to have a workable model to point to as evidence.

Beta prototypes are typically used to asses reliability and to identify remaining "bugs" in the product. These are often given to customers for test in the intended use environment. Upon multiplication of our initial prototype into two cells, any remaining "bugs" in the system can be worked out. While your initial prototype will consist of the creme de la creme of your church's membership, your second generation prototype will have a relatively more "common" membership. For this reason alone, problems should be anticipated in your second generation. If any of your attributes fell short of their approximated level, now is the time to raise their quality level up to standard.

Preproduction prototypes are the first products produced by the production process. The production process is not yet operating at full capacity but is making limited quantities of the product. Keep this in mind when we talk about the prototype multiplication cycle. These prototypes are used to asses production process capability, are subjected to further testing. *Preproduction* prototypes are sometimes called *pilot production* prototypes.

The temptation for transitioning churches is to forego building a milestone prototype because of the required time and resources. If our emphasis was on structural change, this might be ok. However, we are actually involved in transitioning paradigms and transforming value systems. Values are not changed through cognitive understanding. They are refashioned in the crucible of life experience. To forego the development of a milestone prototype is, as the saying goes, to "shoot yourself in the foot." Often, there is considerable need also for the development of a second generation prototype (the two cells birthed from the original prototype cell), and even possibly a third generation prototype (your first three cells).

Are deviations from the standard prototyping plan possible? You may choose to eliminate one of the standard prototypes, usually the Alpha Prototype. In theory this may be possible if the product being developed is very similar to other products already developed or if the product is very simple. However, in the case of cells, the cell life being developed is radically different from our current experience. That being the case, it would be best not to eliminate an Alpha prototype.

Once preliminary decisions have been made (number of prototypes, characteristics, time required to assemble and test them), the team can place these milestones on the overall time line of the project. A timeline will also illustrate how the cell prototype development fits into the overall church transition process in terms of time. Again, planning out a realistic timeline will be critical before agreeing to a church board's or denomination's time frame for "success". Remember, typical transitions take between three and seven years!

NOT YET CONVINCED?

"Developing prototypes take time! Building a prototype requires too much effort and work! Creating a prototype cell will significantly reduce the speed with which we I transition or plant this church! I'm just not wired to do prototypes. I think I can develop cells just from what you called an analytical prototype without actually first building one myself. My leaders are godly men; they will catch what cell is all about and be able to pass it on without first having to be in a prototype led by me."

Weighed in the Balances

You must weigh the cost to prototype against the cost of failing to prototype. You must weigh the time and resources necessary to build and evaluate a prototype against the anticipated benefits of reducing risk and failure. There is a high price to pay to prototype correctly. There is also a high cost to pay when prototype development is not pursued, or implemented poorly. Prototype development is critical when one or more of the following is true.

- What we are doing is High in Risk

- There exists a High Cost of Failure

- What we are doing is Revolutionary in Nature

The paradigm shift necessary to understand cells as the Basic Christian Community is revolutionary. You are introducing a revolutionary new way of living as the church. Cells are not only high risk, demanding of cell members significant lifestyle changes, but also carry with them a high cost to pay for failure. Consider the following two benefits as you weigh your options. To prototype or not to prototype, that is the question!

Chapter 7 ☛ *Prepare the Prototype*

Benefit #1: A Prototype Will Detect Unanticipated Detrimental Phenomena

Physical prototypes are required to discover unexpected elements. A physical prototype often exhibits unanticipated phenomena completely unrelated to the original objective of the prototype. Some of these surprises may manifest themselves in the final product. In this case, a physical prototype can serve as a tool for detecting unanticipated detrimental occurrences that may arise in the final product. Analytical prototypes, in contrast, can never reveal phenomena that are not part of the underlying analytical model on which the prototype is based. For this reason, at least one physical prototype is almost always built in a product development effort.

The implication for the development of cells is crucial. As previously noted, many pastors move into cell development from a strictly analytical model, i.e. the biblical principles and theory of how to do it, without taking the time to actually develop a physical model. The results are almost invariably catastrophic. Unanticipated detrimental phenomena invariably show up in the final product, often destroying cell development or necessitating major changes that could have been detected and corrected "up front".

What types of "detrimental phenomena" often show up? One such "detrimental phenomena" may be resistance to time commitments necessary for cell life to be actualized as a lifestyle. Cell members often give verbal commitments to the necessity of adopting a cell lifestyle. They are conceptually committed. However, when the time comes to actually allocate their time and make necessary adjustments, they are often reticent. Or, maybe there is an initial agreement in theory to the necessity of an equipping track by which to train. However, resistance to personally embracing that particular material selected by the church raises its ugly head when an equipping track is presented to them that differs from what they personally think is needed. At other times there may be agreement in principle to the value that every member is a minister. Yet, often that same individual will resist receiving ministry except by a "spiritual few", especially in the cell group. Only the leader seems to be able to minister to them. Others agree in principle to self disclosure and transparency as vital to cell life, but resist personally walking that principle out. They rarely self-disclose when the cell is sharing. As one final example, though certainly not the final phenomena, there is often agreement to the necessity of mutual accountability. Yet, as the cell leader checks upon accountability partners, he finds there is continued failure to meet with an accountability partner week by week.

Why are we surprised when these show up? Often the reason lies in our misjudgment as to where our leaders and people are on the change continuum (see chapter three). Pastors invariably have to be optimistic. Pessimistic pastors do not last long in ministry. As optimists, we continually give people the benefit of the doubt and too often pass over significant signs of resistance to change. The result? We determine our leaders are fully committed when the fact of the matter is that, at best, they are only conceptually committed. If we evaluated them correctly, we would understand that as change agents, what we need to provide for them is a mechanism to move them into full commitment and an integrated lifestyle. We need a prototype cell!

Benefit #2: A Prototype Reduces the Risk of Costly Iterations

Since taking the time necessary to build and test a prototype will allow the pastoral team to detect a problem that would otherwise not have been detected until after a costly launch, the prototype will thus reduce the risk of having to experience multiple "do-overs", a process taxing and often destructive for a transitioning church. Multiple "do-overs" can prove more than taxing for cell church plants – they can prove fatal. Most church leadership will not tolerate several false-starts before the church has cells that "work". The time, energy, credibility and resources expended in multiple starts is too great. The creation of cells is high risk and carries with it a high cost for failure – "we've tried cells before and they don't work!"

Do not pass over the prototyping phase in your rush to see the church quickly develop. The nature and quality of what you build will be tested by fire. Build to last, not to impress. Take time to build with gold, silver, and precious stones. Resist the temptation to build your first cell quickly with wood, hay, and straw. Remember, what you build is what you will multiply and reproduce. When tested by fire, you want it to remain. Prepare the prototype, wisely!

Chapter 7 • *Prepare the Prototype*

REFLECTIONS

1. What do you see as the advantages and benefits of prototyping an initial cell? Disadvantages?

2. Have you been guilty of attempting to develop an analytical cell prototype? How? What can be done now to correct this situation?

3. What do you consider to be the essential rock bottom elements of cell life? Why?

4. Would a comprehensive or focused prototype be more beneficial to your situation right now? Why? If a focused prototype would be more beneficial, what element would you focus on? What present cell would you use as a test cell?

ACTION POINTS

☐ Define the primary purpose of your cell prototype. Explain why you selected that particular primary purpose as opposed to either of the other three options.

☐ Identify and define each element of your prototype cell.

☐ Establish a level of approximation for each element of your prototype cell. Be specific. Remember that this is what you will be evaluating throughout your development phase.

☐ Outline an experimental plan.

☐ Create a schedule for procurement, construction and test. What should happen in cell and out of cell for each week of your cell life cycle should be detailed

☐ Create a project time line.

Assume either a six-month or nine-month prototype cell cycle.

PREPARE YE THE WAY OF THE LORD

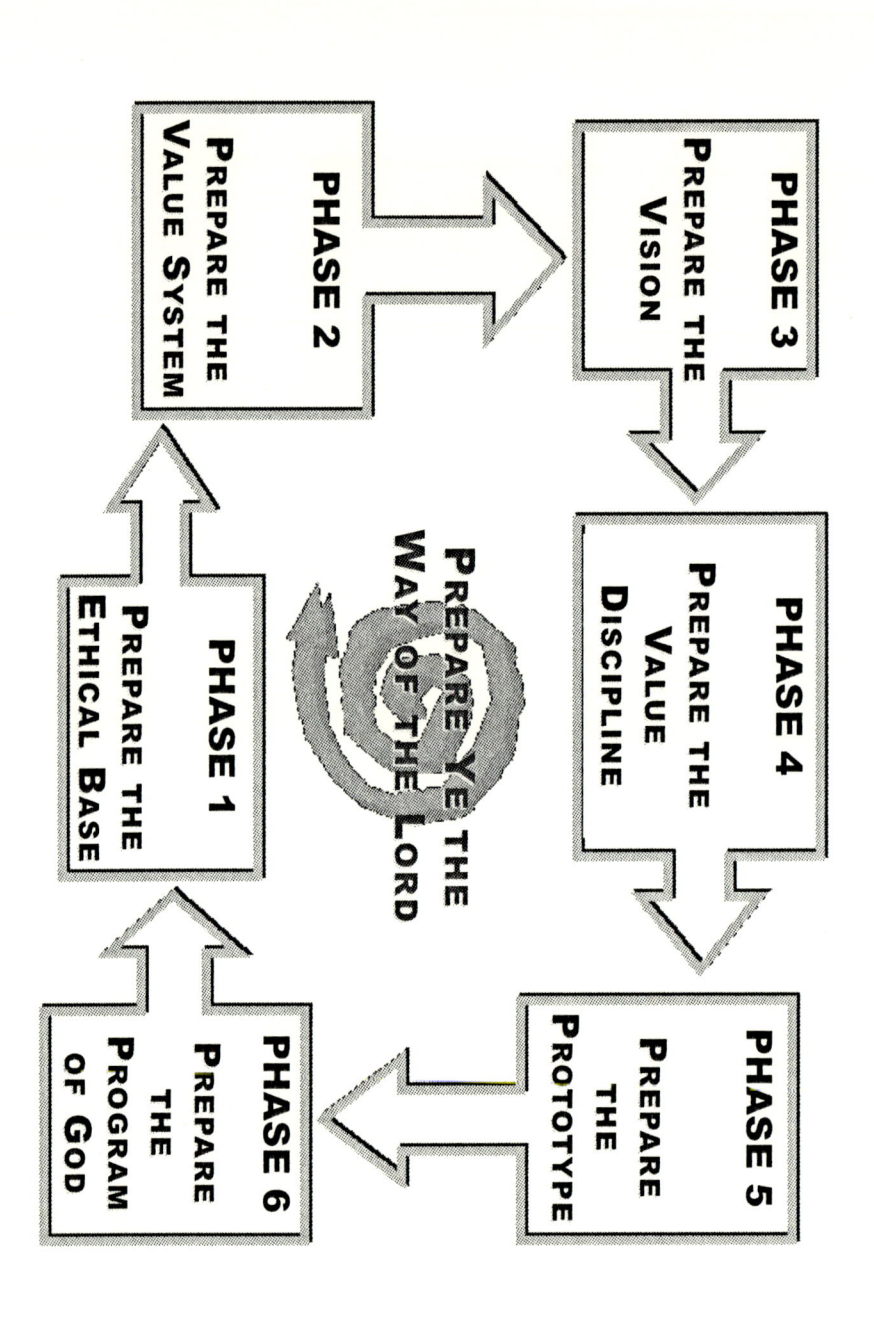

PHASE 1 — Prepare the Ethical Base

PHASE 2 — Prepare the Value System

PHASE 3 — Prepare the Vision

PHASE 4 — Prepare the Value Discipline

PHASE 5 — Prepare the Prototype

PHASE 6 — Prepare the Program of God

ABOVE GROUND REALITIES
PREPARE THE PROGRAM OF GOD

Our fathers had the tabernacle of testimony in the wilderness, just as He who spoke to Moses directed him to make it according to the pattern which he had seen. ACTS 7:44

Chapter 8 ☛ *Prepare the Program of God*

Introduction

Large redwoods have a tap root downward almost the size of the giant tree that towers upward. Before God grows a large tree, He takes the time to develop a strong root system. We have spent considerable time, five chapters, examining the unseen realities of this cell church root system–the ethical base, the value system, the vision, and the value discipline. Weak root systems impact both the health and growth of any plant. A weak cell church root system will greatly and negatively impact the ability of the church to both grow and prosper in health. Ethics, values, vision and value disciplines must be at the core, the center, of all that we develop. They comprise the root system that receives its sustenance from the Person of Christ. When, in the last chapter, we turned our attention to the prototype cell, we began, in effect, to observe the first stem breaking above ground. The prototype cell is the first observable reality that the cell church is developing. In a church planting scenario, as the prototype breaks forth upon the surface of the earth, it becomes the first fruit of what will later become known as the corporate congregation. In a transitional church, the prototype will begin to function like leaven, growing and permeating the entire church, until all aspects of the church are transformed. What will this transformed cell church look like?

Let me digress for a moment before proceeding to answer that vital question. The American cell church has embraced a new paradigm regarding cells as the basic Christian community. In like manner, it must now embrace a new paradigm which will transform its corporate existence and operation from an organization to an organism. Pastors of cell churches are faced with two temptations. Temptation number one is to impose the current structure of the existing church back upon the cells. When this happens, existing programs and activities continue un-altered, existing values and lifestyles remain unchanged, and old games are simply assigned new names. We all know of "cell churches" that have baptized their current programs in the name of the cell. Now, the bus ministry has "bus cells". Now that every ministry is a "cell ministry", the number of cells in the church has grown astronomically!? Have values changed? Have lifestyles been brought in line with the Kingdom? No, but, at least now we have a lot of "cells" to report! Temptation number two is for leadership to decree which new structures and activities will develop, then seek to man them with cell members. Now we have a cell church with all our cell members involved. Right? Wrong! What we have is a traditional church that remains the same but has grafted cell members into its traditional structure. The alternative is to allow the cells to grow and multiply until they ultimately replace the old traditional corporate structure with a new gifted-based church structure created as cell members are empowered and released to serve out of their gifts and callings.

To return to the question at hand (What will this cell church look like?), permit me four illustrative parallels to help us move into this new paradigm of the corporate cell church. First, consider cell church as being neither *Cell* church nor cell *Church*, but *Cell Church*, a balancing act between cell community and corporate community. Second, cell church is an encounter with Christ. Third, cell church can be likened to a simple and complex organism. Fourth, think of cell church as a new wineskin for new wine. Let's examine these illustrations one by one in greater detail.

A Balancing Act Between Cell & Corporate Community

First, cell church is a balancing act. Cell churches walk a tightrope balancing the cell community and the corporate community. Cell church is neither overbalanced in its emphasis to the small group side (house church) nor to the large group side (traditional church). The Christian life is lived out both in the context of a small group experience as well as a large group experience. The cell emphasis is on the individual part; the corporate emphasis is on the whole. The cells are not optional parts or appendages of the the whole; the whole provides cohesion and purpose for the individual cells. The individual cells together form the whole; the whole has no existence apart from the individual cells. Yet, while the whole has no separate existence from the parts, the whole is greater than the sum of the parts! God has provided the human body to help illustrate these dynamics. Within the cell community, each individual is a family member learning about family relationships. In the corporate community, we all are members of the Family of God, fulfilling our familial responsibilities to the larger family. Within the cell community, each cell member is discovering their spiritual gifts. As part of the corporate community, we are members of the Body of Christ, serving the Body out of our spiritual gifts. As members of a cell, each one serves as a squad member, preparing for war. As members in the corporate community, each squad member sees himself as a soldier in the Army of God, establishing the Kingdom of God.

Chapter 8 — *Prepare the Program of God*

An Encounter with Christ

Second, cell church is an encounter with Christ. While in the cell we encounter the living Presence of Christ, it is as part of the corporate community that we powerfully manifest His living Presence before the world. While as members of the cell community we encounter Christ's edifying power through ministry, it is as members of the corporate community that we are released fully to minister His edifying power to those around us, both in and outside the community of faith. As part of the cell community we encounter Christ's ministering purpose for those in the world. As members of the corporate community we are fulfilling His ministering purpose toward those in the world.

An Organism - Simple and Complex

Third, cell church can be likened to a simple and complex organism. The single cell is like a simple organism. In the natural world, cells form the basis of all life. In the spiritual, cells form the basic unit of community. While in the natural we understand that DNA contains the instructions for life and development, so in the spiritual we understand that Christ is the DNA of all cell life. The corporate community can be likened to a complex organism. In the natural scheme of things, God has created cells as the basic unit of life, formed tissues of similar cells performing the same work, created organs from differing tissues working together, created body systems from organs working together to accomplish the same function, and finally formed a complex organism from these body systems. In the spiritual, interconnected cells are to be in vital relationship with one another. Cells are to depend upon one another to carry out their appropriate functions within the larger Body of Christ. Body systems are created to work in concert for the release into service of those equipped. The corporate expression of the church is composed not of disjointed isolated cells, but interconnected, interdependent cells. On the one hand, one large gathering without cells is simply a massive amoebae. On the other hand, multitudes of unconnected cells are simply blobs of unrelated protoplasm. Cells that are vitally connected to one another and the head form the Body of Christ. Paul brings out this simple and complex organism dynamic when he writes in Ephesians 4:16, "...the whole body, being fitted and held together by what every joint supplies, according to the proper working of each individual part, causes the growth of the body for the building up of itself in love."

A New Wineskin for New Wine

Fourth, cell church is a new wineskin for new wine. As such, it is neither a gathering of independent or interconnected house churches, nor is it a mass of disconnected cells, but an administrative and relational structure for life. Some have erroneously assumed that cell churches do not have any programs. In fact, the very word has taken on very negative connotations within the cell church movement. That assumption is completely invalid. One need only study *Eglise Protestante Baptiste Oeuvres et Mission Internationale* in Cote d'Ivoire, or *Yoido Full Gospel Church* in Seoul, or *Faith Community Church* in Singapore to see how invalid that thinking really is. These large and significant cell churches have a plethora of programs, possibly even more than a large traditional American church! As a new wineskin, cell church is not a denial of the need of programs, but a revealed Program of God based upon Kingdom values. This program of God is the focus of the remaining chapters of this book. It is the program of God that we actually see. The program of God is what grows above ground. This new wineskin is not an absence of departments, but a structure for coordinating gift-based ministries. This too will come under our scrutiny in the chapters to follow. As we seek to understand what it is I am calling the *Program of God*, I will rely heavily once again upon *Eglise Protestante Baptiste Oeuvres et Mission Internationale* for illustrations and examples.

As we move forward to examine this above ground reality, the *Program of God*, along with its attendant structures, we will begin with the diagram on the following page. The reader will immediately notice that the five factors already considered when planning the prototype cell are repeated here. Why is that?

The issues represented by these five elements must be addressed whether we speak of life on a cellular level or life on a corporate level. In fact, these issues have greater need of attention on the corporate level than even on the cell level. While it is certainly true that each cell member must experience edification, how much more true is it that the corporate church must be about the business of edification to the building up of the Body of Christ? Paul instructed the church at Thessalonica, "Therefore encourage one another, and build up one another, just as you also are doing" (1 Thessalonians 5:11). Jesus has called each individual cell member to become a fisher of men. In a larger sense, the corporate church is charged with the evangelization of this world. Each individual may be encouraged to discover their spiritual gift as a cell

Chapter 8 ☞ *Prepare the Program of God*

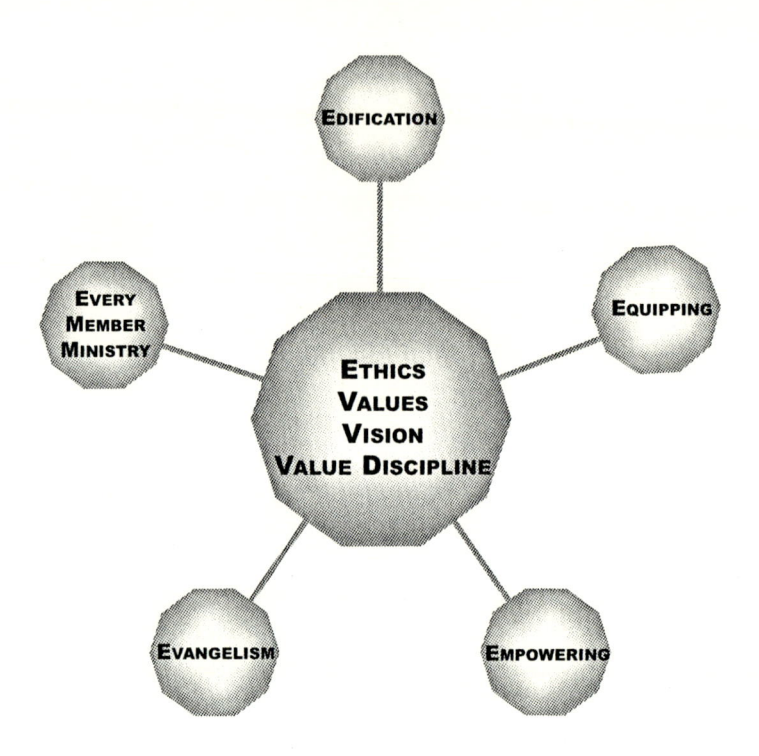

```
                    EDIFICATION

     EVERY                              EQUIPPING
    MEMBER
    MINISTRY       ETHICS
                   VALUES
                   VISION
               VALUE DISCIPLINE

         EVANGELISM         EMPOWERING
```

member, but the employment of their gifts and their release into ministry can only be fully realized on a corporate level at which time "...the whole body, being fitted and held together by what every joint supplies, according to the proper working of each individual part, causes the growth of the body for the building up of itself in love" (Ephesians 4:16). The same can be said of empowering leadership. While the cell can facilitate a degree of equipping, the risen Lord has given to the church apostles, pastors, teachers, evangelists, and prophets for the equipping of the saints for the work of ministry. I believe it fair to say that the Lord expects equipping to be done on a corporate level. Let me hasten to add at this point that corporate level is not to be equivocated with the corporate gathering on Sunday. Just as cell is not a meeting, but is lived out day-by-day, so corporate community is not a meeting, but the daily expression of the life of the local church on mission. This vital point is almost universally missed. Too many pastors and people view corporate community as what happens on Sunday. Let me say again, both the cell and corporate aspect of the church have a meeting time. Both, though, also demand a life lived out throughout the week.

Cell life demands we live daily in community. Corporate life demands we live our lives throughout the week serving the corporate body through the manifestation of our functional spiritual gifts.

Implications

It is only the adoption of the previously discussed ethical base and value system by the leaders and people alike that will allow us to fully address these issues. The demands of this process are impossible apart from the value system the leaders and people have chosen to embrace. The two go hand in glove together. Together they help comprise foundation and edifice, tap root and tree. If the leadership and/or the people still live out of a teleological mindset, then when the going gets rough and times are hard, when results are meager and it looks like cell church will not work, they will give up and turn back. If a core value system has not been articulated and embraced, if the unbiblical worldviews that have infected our thinking have not been exposed to the light and challenged in the minds and hearts of the people, then the time and resources and energy demanded by God to implement His program will not be yielded up. We will not pay the price necessary. I remember a great truth from Bill Beckham. "Where the vision is unclear, the cost is always too high!" If the vision of tomorrow is clouded and unclear, how can we know that the program before us will bring us into His future designs? Why embrace a program and devote your life to something that may not even bring to pass God's future? Without a clearly defined value discipline and articulated value proposition, of what use is it to think about receiving and developing a values-driven operating model from God? The unseen realities already discussed must be in place if we are going to move into the program which God has called us to implement, or failure will be our constant companion. With them in place, we can begin to move forward.

At this point I would like to draw the reader's attention back to the work by Christian Schwarz. Already we have seen in his research the vital importance of the eight quality characteristics. That which follows may be viewed as dealing in detail with what Schwarz has called functional structures. What will be presented will be a keen development of structures promoting ongoing multiplication of the ministry.

However, in our excitement of discovering these functional structures, we must not fail to be aware of the deep abyss of imitation that waits to swallow the unwary explorer. In our enthusiasm the novice and expert alike must not forget to keep separate the purposes and distinctions between a testimony, a model, a principle, and a program. I intend to employ the integrative model developed by Pastor Dion Robert in Cote d'Ivoire in an illustrative manner. For some, it will become too easy to slip into the black of hole of imitating the model or the program developed by Pastor Dion. We Americans, pastors included, are a pragmatic, bottom line people. We want something that works, and works today. One need only examine our advertising industry with its emphasis on instant gratification to see my point.

As we examine the *Program of God* at EPBOM, examining it like a jeweler would examine a precious diamond, continually rotating the gem to observe its multi-faceted beauty, you will be introduced to the testimony of key leaders. Remember that a testimony is simply a personal experience. Allow yourself to be enthused by what you observe to be the power of God operative in their life, but move away from the precipice of demanding to experience what they have experienced. Do not think for a moment, though, that to have their success you must imitate them and do exactly as they have done. Rejoice with their experience, but ask God what He has uniquely in store for you. Their experiences will be presented so that you will be able to identify their reproducible structures. Allow their real life example to motivate you to do something similar, without importing their model.

As you come to see the *Program of God* in the life of *Eglise Protestante Baptiste Oeuvres et Mission Internationale* in Cote d'Ivoire, you will also come to understand that it is how God told Dion to apply universal principles in one situation. You may see the *Program of God* as a kind of pattern, but do not fall down the slippery slope of believing that since it has worked for him, it will certainly be right for your church also. Look behind the testimonies, underneath the model, and beyond the program, until you firmly grasp the universal principles present. Yet, on the other hand, take care lest you relegate universal principles that do not fit your American paradigm to the trash heap of "just another possibility for building the church"! Learn from God how to apply these principles to your individual situation. With this exhortation behind us, let us move on to understand the dynamics undergirding a *Program of God*.

We must know how to listen to God, how to receive from Him, and above all, know Him.

The Lord opened my spirit and my eyes. He communicated His wisdom, which sustains everything living. I started to organize the church according to the model that He showed me, little by little.

It is imperative to work according to the model in view of Christ. A divine work, such as the church of Jesus Christ, is not led with eyes closed!

Dr. Rev. Yaye Dion Robert

PREPARE YE THE WAY OF THE LORD

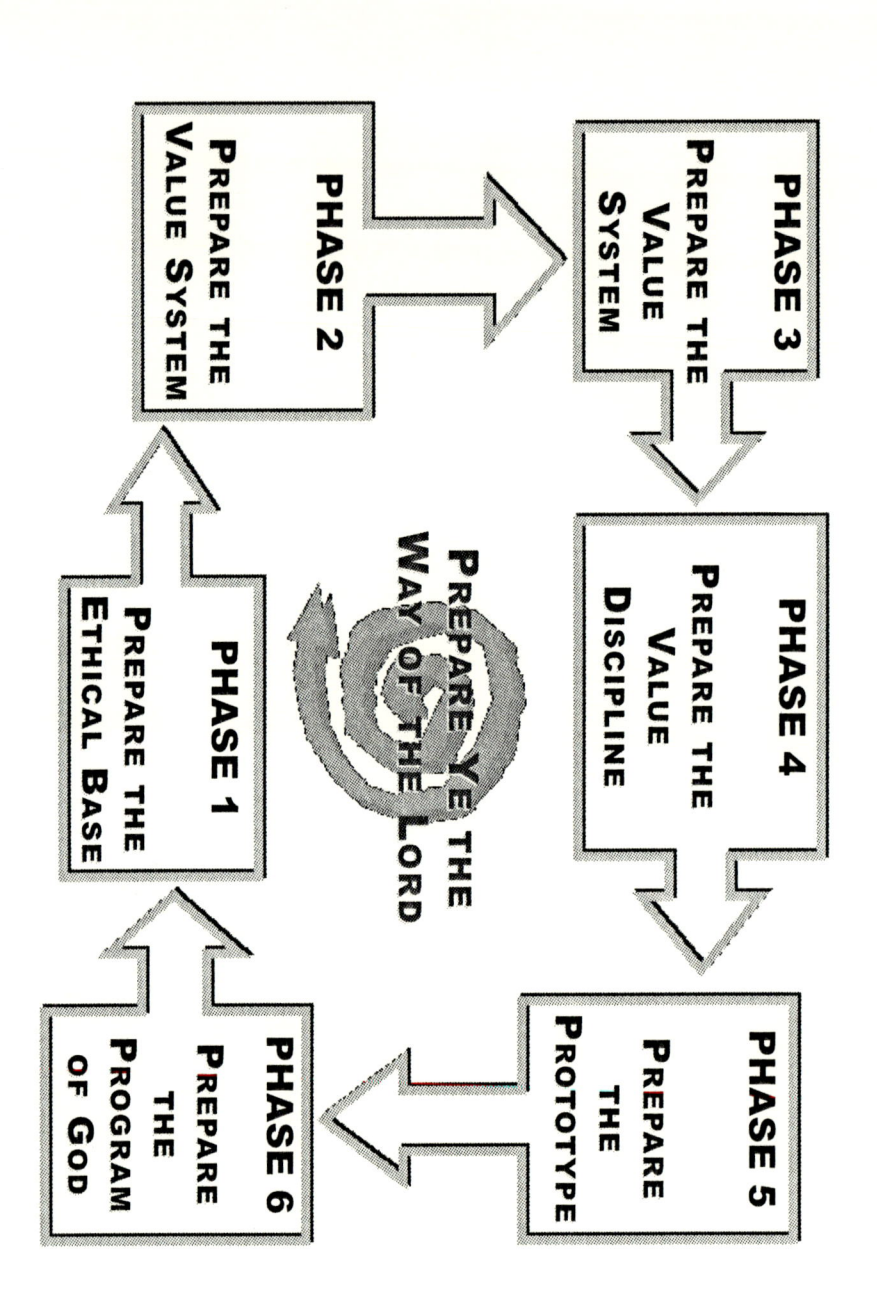

- **PHASE 1** — Prepare the Ethical Base
- **PHASE 2** — Prepare the Value System
- **PHASE 3** — Prepare the Value System
- **PHASE 4** — Prepare the Value Discipline
- **PHASE 5** — Prepare the Prototype
- **PHASE 6** — Prepare the Program of God

9
PREPARE THE PROGRAM OF GOD - EQUIPPING

EQUIPPING

ETHICS
VALUES
VISION
VALUE DISCIPLINE

*A*LL SCRIPTURE IS INSPIRED BY GOD AND PROFITABLE FOR TEACHING, FOR REPROOF, FOR CORRECTION, FOR TRAINING IN RIGHTEOUSNESS; SO THAT THE MAN OF GOD MAY BE ADEQUATE, *EQUIPPED FOR EVERY GOOD WORK.*
2TIM. 3:16-17

Chapter 9 — *Prepare the Program of God - Equipping*

> **Eph. 2:10 For we are His workmanship, created in Christ Jesus for good works, which God prepared beforehand so that we would walk in them.**

A CURRENT GENERATION WITH FEW DISCIPLES

Part of our destiny as Christians is to accomplish the good works which God has prepared from all eternity for us to do. While the will is present, how to perform too often becomes the real problem. We do not know how to do that which we have been called to do. The question, "How will we equip the church to do the works of God?" must be dealt with in a sober way by each church. Any serious response to the question posed must develop a discipleship process that (1) adequately defines discipleship, (2) produces disciples able to imitate both the character and charismatic ministry of Christ, (3) does so in the context of both being and doing, and (4) is completely replicable, if a cell church is to survive and grow. Before looking at the process developed at EPBOM, journey with me as I develop these elements in light of the Scriptures and early church history.

Defining New Testament Discipleship

Making disciples is the goal of all evangelism, the very purpose of the Great Commission. The Great Commission is stated in various ways in all four gospels.

> And Jesus came up and spoke to them, saying, "All authority has been given to Me in heaven and on earth. Go therefore and make disciples of all the nations, baptizing them in the name of the Father and the Son and the Holy Spirit, teaching them to observe all that I commanded you; and lo, I am with you always, even to the end of the age" (Matthew 28:18-20).

> And He said to them, "Go into all the world and preach the gospel to all creation. He who has believed and has been baptized shall be saved; but he who has disbelieved shall be condemned" (Mark 16:15-16).

And He said to them, "Thus it is written, that the Christ would suffer and rise again from the dead the third day, and that repentance for forgiveness of sins would be proclaimed in His name to all the nations, beginning from Jerusalem. You are witnesses of these things" (Luke 24:46-48).

So Jesus said to them again, "Peace be with you; as the Father has sent Me, I also send you." And when He had said this, He breathed on them and said to them, "Receive the Holy Spirit. If you forgive the sins of any, their sins have been forgiven them; if you retain the sins of any, they have been retained" (John 20:21-23).

Due to the very stress the Great Commission places upon its own worldwide extension, it would be incorrect to assume that the Great Commission was limited to only the eleven. While, in all four gospels, those addressed were primarily His eleven disciples, they can be said to represent the incipient church. Thus the Great Commission, while addressed at first to the eleven disciples, extends to the larger group of disciples to come.

The content of the commission is to "make disciples of all nations". Discipleship is entered into as the Church preaches "the gospel to the whole creation" (Mark 16), proclaiming "repentance and forgiveness of sins...to all nations" (Luke 24) in such a way that peoples and nations turn to Christ and become His disciples. While at this point discipleship has been entered into (initiation has been completed), the climax in making disciples is teaching those who have come to faith and been baptized to observe παντα οσα ενετειλαμην, "all things whatsoever" (KJV) that Christ has commanded. In other words, "making disciples" includes teaching believers to observe, keep and obey (therein) all that Christ commanded His original disciples.

Producing Disciples Who are Imitators of Christ

St. Thomas a Kempis wrote the devotional classic, *Imitatio Christi*, as an encouragement for the Christian disciple to replicate or imitate the life of Christ. One need only briefly survey the writings of the Apostolic Fathers to understand that the imitation of Christ has, from the beginning, been a significant aspect of discipleship.

Chapter 9 — *Prepare the Program of God - Equipping*

Let us be imitators also of them, which went about in goatskins and sheepskins, preaching the coming of Christ. We mean Elijah and Elisha and likewise Ezekiel, the prophets, and besides them those men also that obtained a good report. (Clement, 1 Clement 17:1)

With joy in God I welcomed your community, which possesses its dearly beloved name because of a right disposition, enhanced by faith and love through Christ Jesus our Savior. Being imitators of God, you have, once restored to new life in the Blood of God, perfectly accomplished the task so natural to you. (Ignatius, Ephesians 1)

Of no use to me will be the farthest reaches of the universe or the kingdoms of this world. I would rather die and come to Jesus Christ than be king over the entire earth. Him I seek who died for us; Him I love who rose again because of us. The birth pangs are upon me. Forgive me, brethren; do not obstruct my coming to life—do not wish me to die; do not make a gift to the world of one who wants to be God's. Beware of seducing me with matter; suffer me to receive pure light. Once arrived there, I shall be a man. Permit me to be an imitator of my suffering God. If anyone holds Him in his heart, let him understand what I am aspiring to; and then let him sympathize with me, knowing in what distress I am. (Ignatius, Romans 6)

Let us therefore become imitators of His endurance; and if we should suffer for His name's sake, let us glorify Him. For He gave this example to us in His own person, and we believed this. (Polycarp, Epistle 8:2)

For he lingered that he might be delivered up, even as the Lord did, to the end that we too might be imitators of him, not looking only to that which concerneth ourselves, but also to that which concerneth our neighbors. For it is the office of true and steadfast love, not only to desire that oneself be saved, but all the brethren also. (Polycarp, Martyrdom 1:2)

For Him, being the Son of God, we adore, but the martyrs as disciples and imitators of the Lord we cherish as they deserve for their matchless affection towards their own King and Teacher. May it be our lot also to be found partakers and fellow-disciples with them. (Polycarp, Martyrdom 17:3)

And loving Him thou wilt be an imitator of His goodness. And marvel not that a man can be an imitator of God. He can, if God willeth it. (Epistle To Diognetus, 10:4)

The Apostolic Fathers did not originate this understanding of discipleship. The imitation or mimesis theme holds a prominent place in the New Testament writings. This can be observed from the relationship Jesus maintained with the disciples as rabbi and statements He made regarding the continuation of His ministry through them, as well as from the disciples' expectations regarding those who would follow them.

Jesus is frequently described in the Gospels as "rabbi", or "teacher". The followers of Jesus are called "disciples" (μαθητης) over 215 times throughout the Gospels. Ben Sirac (d. ca. 175 BC) cites the goal of a rabbi as the training of his students to such a degree that "When the father [teacher] dies, it is as though he is not dead. For he leaves behind him one like himself" (Ruthven, 16).

Jesus affirmed of Himself this kind of relationship to the disciples (Matthew 23:8-10). In Luke 6:40 He affirmed the traditional rabbinical understanding that "a pupil (μαθητης) is not above his teacher; but everyone, after he has been fully trained, will be like his teacher." "Not above", (ουκ εστιν...υπερ), would suggest that the pupil does not depart from anything the teacher does. Jesus explicitly states this in John 13:34; 17:18,23 and 20:21. He employs the formula, "As I...so you." In John 13:15 Jesus states, "For I gave you an example that you also should do as I did to you." "As" translates the Greek word καθως, a word carrying the strong sense of "exactly as," or, "to the exact same degree and extent." When used as it is in John 20:21, a specific replication of the ministry of Jesus in the lives of His disciples can only be the intention. No detail of the Teacher's life was to either be ignored or left unreplicated by the disciples of Jesus (Ruthven, 7).

Moving from the Gospels to the remaining New Testament record, we find that imitation remains an essential aspect of discipleship. To the

Chapter 9 → *Prepare the Program of God - Equipping*

Corinthians Paul writes, "Imitate me even as [καθως - to the exact same degree and extent] I imitate Christ" (1 Corinthians 11:1). In four additional places he exhorts the churches to imitate him.

> For if you were to have countless tutors in Christ, yet you would not have many fathers, for in Christ Jesus I became your father through the gospel. Therefore I exhort you, be imitators of me. For this reason I have sent to you Timothy, who is my beloved and faithful child in the Lord, and he will remind you of my ways [Semitism that refers to the whole characteristic pattern of life (Wolf, 1: 197)] which are in Christ [Note three generations of imitators: Jesus, Paul, Timothy/Corinthians], just as I teach everywhere in every church (1Corinthians 4:15-17).

> Brethren, join in following my example, and observe those who walk according to the pattern you have in us (Phil. 3:17).

> For you yourselves know how you ought to follow our example, because we did not act in an undisciplined manner among you, nor did we eat anyone's bread without paying for it, but with labor and hardship we kept working night and day so that we would not be a burden to any of you; not because we do not have the right to this, but in order to offer ourselves as a model for you, so that you would follow our example (2Thessalonians 3:7-9).

> The things you have learned and received and heard and seen in me, practice these things, and the God of peace will be with you (Philippians 4:9).

1 Thessalonians and 2 Timothy both further develop this pattern of imitation. 1 Thessalonians takes the pattern to the fourth generation. Paul wrote to the Thessalonians, "You also became imitators of us and of the Lord, having received the word in much tribulation with the joy of the Holy Spirit, so that you became an example [pattern] to all the believers in Macedonia and in Achaia" (1 Thessalonians 1: 5-7). The Thessalonians imitated Paul and then became exemplars themselves. When writing to Timothy (2 Timothy 2:1-2),

Paul expands this pattern to the fifth generation (Ruthven, 8).

Those who become imitators of Paul are themselves to become patterns for others to imitate in exactly the same way. In this way the pattern of Christ is to be transmitted disciple to disciple from generation to generation.

The Content of New Testament Discipleship – Doing and Being

What is the content of New Testament discipleship? If we are to become like our teacher, discipleship must encompass both being and doing. Our becoming like our teacher in inner character will be addressed as we examine the development of a replicable process of discipleship in the concluding section on discipleship. Here we will focus on our doing as our teacher did; not on what our teacher taught, but what our teacher came to do, what He actually spent His time doing, what He told His disciples to do and what they actually did. Our job as disciples will then be to go and do likewise.

John condensed the ministry of Jesus into one succinct sentence. "The Son of God appeared for this purpose, to destroy the works of the devil" (1 John 3:8). Peter likewise summarized the mission of Jesus. "You know of Jesus of Nazareth, how God anointed Him with the Holy Spirit and with power, and how He went about doing good and healing all who were oppressed by the devil, for God was with Him" (Acts 10:38). Jesus Himself outlined His mission in Luke 4:18-19 where He quotes from Isaiah 61. "The Spirit of the Lord is upon me, because He anointed me to preach the gospel to the poor. He has sent me to proclaim release to the captives, and recovery of sight to the blind, to set free those who are oppressed, to proclaim the favorable year of the Lord."

The recorded history of Jesus is one illustration after another of His destroying the works of the devil and releasing the captives. Jesus came preaching the gospel of the Kingdom (Matthew 4:23; 9:35). His public ministry of miracles, healings and exorcisms expressed the present reality of the Kingdom (Matthew 4:23; 9:35; Luke 10:9; 11:20). "As a percentage of the text describing the public ministry of Jesus as recorded in the four gospels, the space devoted to the accounts of miracles amounts to: 44% of Matthew, 65% of Mark, 29% of Luke and 30% of John" (Ruthven, 10).

Turning to the early disciples, we find that Jesus appointed them that they should be with Him, that they should announce the Kingdom (Luke 9:2), and that they should have authority to drive out demons, thereby demonstrating the present reality of the Kingdom (Luke 10:9), even as He did. "And He

Chapter 9 ☛ *Prepare the Program of God - Equipping*

appointed twelve, so that they would be with Him and that He could send them out to preach, and to have authority to cast out the demons" (Mark 3:14-15).

An effective discipleship process must provide for hands on experience in this replication of the charismatic ministry of Jesus and the apostles. Jesus Himself provided ample hands-on ministry experiences for His disciples throughout the course of their training. In both the experience of the feeding of the 4000 (Matthew 15:32-39) and the feeding of the 3000 (Luke 9:12-17), Jesus provides opportunity for the disciples to minister alongside of Him and participate in the miraculous. They have watched the master heal (Luke 8:43-48) and raise the dead (Luke 8:49-56) just prior to Jesus empowering and authorizing them (Luke 9:1-10) to go and preach the kingdom and replicate his works. Jesus holds them to accountability through a time of reporting following their return. Even in times of apparent failure, Jesus turns the failure into a time of further training (Matthew 17:14-21).

Did the disciples become like their teacher? "True, the disciples exhibited the virtues of the traditional notion of Christian discipleship: morality and piety. But Acts devotes no less than 27.2% of its space to miracle stories! This is more space than all of the speeches or sermons of Acts combined, at 22.5%" (Ruthven, 11).

In summary then, what is the New Testament expectation of what the disciple is to do? The New Testament expects the disciple to replicate the ministry of Jesus and the apostles. This demands, then, the development of a replicable discipleship process.

Developing A Replicable Discipleship Process

A basic goal of any discipleship training process should include the giving of information (2 Timothy 3:14-17).

> You, however, continue in the things you have learned and become convinced of, knowing from whom you have learned them, and that from childhood you have known the sacred writings that are able to give you the wisdom that leads to salvation through faith which is in Christ Jesus. All Scripture is inspired by God and profitable for teaching, for reproof, for correction, for training in righteousness; so that the man of God may be adequate, equipped for every good work.

An effective replicable discipleship process must teach both substantively and in detail whatever He commanded. Yet at this level, whatever is selected as worthy for teaching is still being transmitted as cognitive information. More is needed.

The discipleship training process should also encompass revelation. Information must become revealed truth. Paul prayed for the church at Ephesus, "that the God of our Lord Jesus Christ, the Father of glory, may give to you a spirit of wisdom and of revelation in the knowledge of Him. I pray that the eyes of your heart may be enlightened, so that you will know what is the hope of His calling, what are the riches of the glory of His inheritance in the saints, and what is the surpassing greatness of His power toward us who believe" (Ephesians 1:17-19a).

Why must information become revelation? Inward renewal, transformation, comes as a result of revelation. Again, Paul prayed for those at Ephesus "that you be renewed (αναveουσθαι) in the spirit of your mind" (Ephesians 4:23). He urged the church at Rome "by the mercies of God, to present your bodies a living and holy sacrifice, acceptable to God, which is your spiritual service of worship. And do not be conformed to this world, but be transformed (μεταμορφουσθε) by the renewing of your mind, so that you may prove what the will of God is, that which is good and acceptable and perfect" (Romans 12:1-2). Revelation will shape the disciple outwardly and transform him inwardly. The result of transformation will be the formation of Christ in the disciple's life (Galatians 4:19). Only then will the imitation of Christ's character and ethics become a possibility in the life of the disciple.

An effective and replicable discipleship process must be able to move disciples from cognitive understanding to heart-felt transformation. Transformation of the disciple will result in the formation of Christ (what He is to be - character and ethics) in the disciple's life. Until we take seriously the Lord's requirement for making disciples, we will remain a generation lacking genuine disciples and struggling to develop leaders.

Chapter 9 Prepare the Program of God - Equipping

ILLUSTRATION - EPBOM'S MODEL OF EQUIPPING

EPBOM has taken seriously this challenge of disciple making and has developed a model to see this challenge met.

The New Convert

If the church has a clearly articulated vision, then when unbelievers are brought into the Kingdom through evangelization, what must the church do so that this vision of God may be realized in and through these new converts? They obviously must receive teaching and instruction. What, though, must they be taught first and foremost? EPBOM's understanding of the need of a new believer is that they must first specifically be taught obedience and the cross:

> When we bring the people, they must be people that are submitted, submitted to God. If they are not, then the vision will not obtain its goal. God does nothing with people that are not submitted or with people that are indifferent. So you must teach them obedience. You must teach them the cross. Jesus came with the cross to bring humanity to discipline, to come back to God and to submit. So in that case, we teach a practical teaching, the teaching of the cross so that people will obey. That is why teaching is also so important. Because it is through teaching that we open the eyes to the blind so they will see and so they can do the work of God. (Interview)

Here again we observe why the values were graphically displayed as a pie. Teaching, submission, obedience and vision are all interwoven like a tapestry, working together to direct the life of the new convert and see the vision accomplished in their new life. In order to see that vision accomplished, the church must now bring the new believer to the place of crucifixion:

> You must crucify them. They themselves must die and must let God live. The will of God must be free through them to work. So, bring them to obedience. To bring them to obedience is teaching. Teaching is very, very important. Through the practical teaching we bring them to obedience to God. (Interview)

New believers come into the New Kingdom with their old value system. Their former value system must be replaced by a value system reflective of the Kingdom of God. The very first value to be challenged and replaced is obedience. Obedience, recall, is one of the seven core biblical values of the church. That is done through teaching coupled with practical exhortation.

Teaching is accomplished on a number of different levels at EPBOM. Wednesday is a time set aside for corporate instruction. Sunday is then used to follow up the teaching presented on Wednesday. While Wednesday opens the eyes to the will of God, Sunday exhorts into the practical expressions of obedience. Sunday's exhortations instruct the people how to put into practice what they have learned. Their exhortations "dot the i's and cross the t's". If Wednesday is likened to teaching biblical truth, Sunday is comparable to teaching Christian ethics.

Two services are held each Wednesday at the central church in Yopougon. Pastors from the surrounding local churches and annex churches regularly attend one of the two services. These pastors will in turn re-teach the material the next day in their own church. On Sunday they will be free to make their own applications relative to their people and context.

New converts preparing for baptism are assembled for specific teaching each Thursday evening. They come from the surrounding local churches, the annex churches and from the central church. Their instructional material consists of, but is not limited to, the manual by Dion Robert, *So That You're Born Again*. Introductory training in the Christian life is presented in the following chapters: "The Bible", "God", "Jesus Christ", "The Holy Spirit", "The Fall of Man", "Repentance", "Salvation by Grace", "Water Baptism and Holy Communion", "Sanctification", "The Life of Prayer", "The Christian and Worldliness", "The Clothing of a Christian", "Management", "The Christian and His Work", "The Choice, Fiance and Marriage", "Family Life", "Fraternal Communion", "Christian Hope", "The Christian and the Word of God", and "The Church of Jesus Christ".

The duration of this training lasts from three to six months and is taught by the pastor of the local church. As the new convert is systematically trained, he is constantly being impacted cognitively with information. During this period of time, those in the Cell Department follow the new convert's spiritual development. As the information becomes revelation, his inward transformation is observed by his cell members. Based on his changed lifestyle, the cell leader will suggest to the local church Pastor that the new convert is prepared as a can-

Chapter 9 ☞ *Prepare the Program of God - Equipping*

didate for baptism. Following baptism, weekly discipleship training prepares the new convert for eventual release into corporate ministry within one of the many departments based upon their giftings.

At the same time the newly baptized believer is attending weekly corporate discipleship training, he will also be entrusted to the Cell Department to begin his cycle of discipleship.

The Cycle of Discipleship

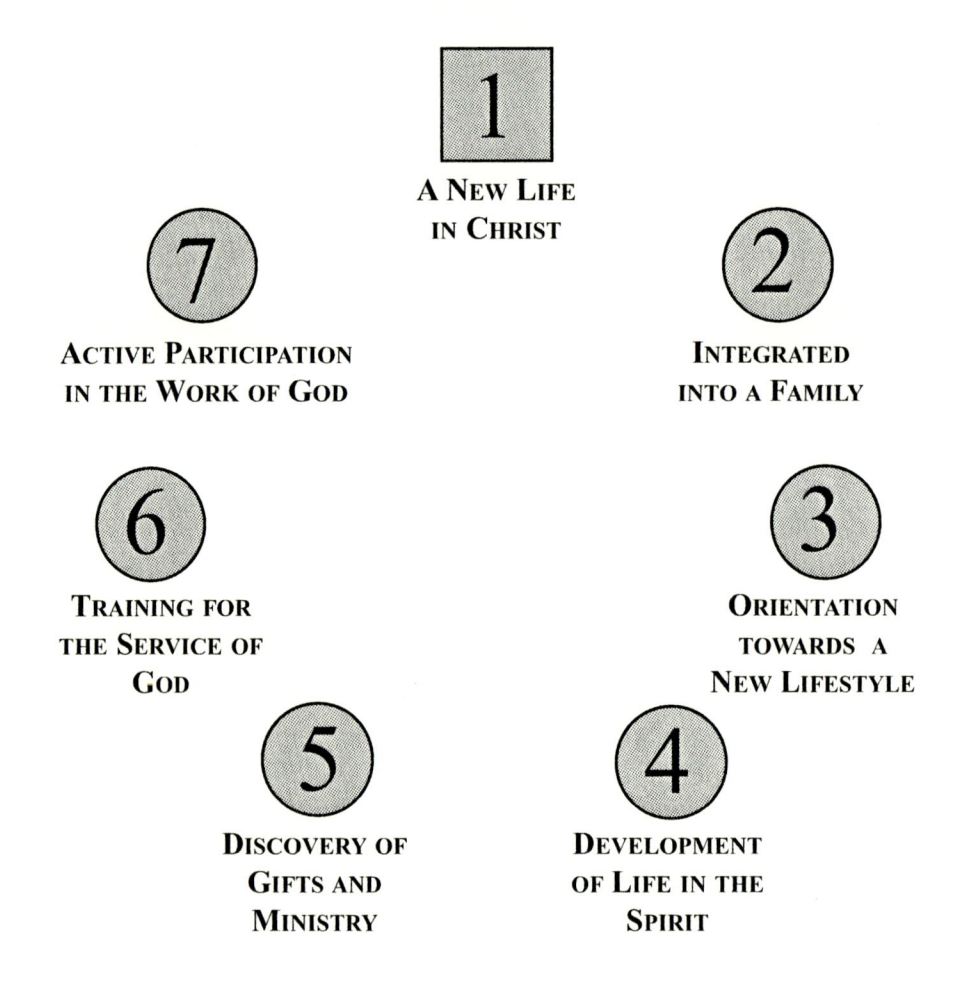

1. A New Life in Christ

2. Integrated into a Family

3. Orientation towards a New Lifestyle

4. Development of Life in the Spirit

5. Discovery of Gifts and Ministry

6. Training for the Service of God

7. Active Participation in the Work of God

If the vision of EPBOM is to really make disciples who will be able to plant cell churches, then a measurable and reproducible system must be created. Discipleship can not be left up to chance. As illustrated in the figure, EPBOM has developed such a systematized cycle for discipleship training.

When a new soul is won to Christ, the one who won him to Christ is the first person responsible for him. Once the new believer has been brought into the church and placed in a cell, he learns to imitate the cell leader. His spiritual father in Christ is the person who led him to the Lord, but his training depends now on the cell leader. The cell leader is obliged to take on the discipleship of the new believer. He may take him from his house to all the programs in the church. During the week, the cell leader will go and visit the new believer. If he discovers a situation of need, the cell leader is the first one to help. He follows the new believer all the way to his baptism, after which he then becomes the cell leader's disciple. Should he later enter into ministry in a department besides the Cell Department, then his continuing training will transfer to another leader in his chosen department.

We see, then, that the initial discipleship training is in the hands of the cell leader. As noted in *The Cycle of Discipleship*, the new disciple will systematically progress through a standardized training cycle of seven stages.

The disciple is first instructed about his new life in Christ. He has a responsibility to maintain what he has obtained from the Lord and to continue to grow. This can only be accomplished as he enters into crucifixion, suffering, death and resurrection. Thus begins his new life in Christ. Next, he experiences what it means to be integrated into a new family. This family represents for him a new environment where he must learn to live his faith. He will learn both his rights as a new family member, and his obligations.

Third, the demand on the new family is to orient him to a new style of living. In this new life he will learn a new style of behavior. As he is brought to understand that he no longer lives for himself (Galatians 2:20; 1 Corinthians 6:19), God's interests will become his own priority. He will come to understand that the priorities of God are evangelization and the care of the souls won. To this end he will now give his time, his goods, his family, and his talents, all the while seeking to maintain a life without reproach before God and man.

Fourth, the new style of living will lead the Christian to the practical manifestation of the life of the Spirit. As he passes through a daily demonstration of the life of the spirit, a walk in obedience and submission, his progress will be evident to all. Notice again the goal, to walk out the dual values of obe-

Chapter 9 ☞ *Prepare the Program of God - Equipping*

dience and submission.

Fifth, as he gives evidence of this new lifestyle, he is given small tasks alongside the cell leader. He needs to be used in the Body of Christ. These small tasks provide opportunities for his potential to be discovered.

Sixth, not only will he be introduced to the different departments and the gifts needed within each one, but he will also have practical exercises that confirm the gifts and the ministries that have already been discovered in him.

Finally, following the discovery of his potential gifts and ministries, he will be released to serve in the appropriate department where he will continue to receive specialized training for further service of God through his gifts. Those serving in ministry continue to gather each Saturday for specialized training within their department. Once again they gather from the surrounding local churches, the annex churches and from the central church. Their instructional materials will be reflective of their various departments. As an example, those released to serve within the Department of Demonology will cover additional training manuals such as those noted previously on page 166. It is at this time that the primary responsibility for his training will be transferred from his cell leader to the department.

As new members are now trained and sent into the different departments, the body of workers of which they are now a member are pulled together in unity and cohesion. Each worker will fulfill his or her ministry, following the function assigned. In this manner each member contributes toward the qualitative and quantitative growth of the body.

Deliverance and Discipleship

The goal at EPBOM is making disciples, not just mass-producing converts. As a consequence, evangelization, deliverance, and discipleship are seen as an integrated whole. They are the principles of the Kingdom. They are in Matthew 28:18ff. Beginning with verse sixteen, Jesus told the eleven disciples to go to the mountain He had designated. But, some of those who worshiped Him doubted. In verse eighteen Jesus approached them and told them that all power was given to Him in heaven and in earth. He told them to go and make all the nations disciples, to baptize them in the name of the Father, the Son and the Holy Spirit. What does this mean?

Going is to announce the gospel. To make disciples you must

bring them to discipline. It is not just announcing. You must also bring them to discipline and make them disciplined. You must take out what is not disciplined in them. The devil that is in them is not disciplined, and never will be disciplined. When he leaves, and it is just man himself that remains, now God can mold him and he can be a good Christian and you can see God through him. That is our objective. (Etienne, Interview)

We often think that the job is complete when a person becomes a Christian. This is not so at EPBOM. Deliverance is a part of the individual's on-going sanctification:

In 1 Thessalonians 5:23 Paul prays that the God of peace would sanctify you entirely and that your spirit, soul and body would be preserved without reproach. Our work is centered on the spirit, because our body depends on our spirit. Our soul depends on our spirit. Do not be distracted. When the spirit of man is freed, his soul is freed. His body is freed. That is the strong point, the basis for the message of deliverance.

Man does not like us to touch his spirit. They say it is their right. That is why you must go with the Word of God. Man enters into contact with the wicked spirits by their spirit. So, we start at the roots. The root of the life of a man is his spirit. It is with his spirit that he enters into contact with God. It is the spirit that receives. If he receives from Satan then it will be things satanic. If he receives from God then it will be good things. That which he receives is what he will be able to act out. If he receives a message, "Be nude, take away your pants," then he communicates it to the soul and he tells it to the body and he'll take off his pants. If God says to him, "Don't lie," it will be communicated to the soul and the body and the mouth now will be mastered. So we center on the spirit.

We read Hebrews 12:14 that we should look for peace with everyone and holiness without which no one will see the Lord, so that none will lack the grace of God and no root of bitterness or rejection will be produced so many will be infected. (Etienne, Interview)

Chapter 9 ☛ Prepare the Program of God - Equipping

Pastoral Training

For those who feel the call of God to enter full time service as a pastor, the church has developed advanced training. Prerequisite to entering advanced training, an individual would have been expected to have totally exercised his gifts in his own department and have become a leader with the power to transmit to others what he has received in view of assuring the continuation of the work.

The one who receives the call and makes the commitment to serve the Lord full time will be enrolled in the Missionary Center for Training (C.M.F.C.) for some years of doctrinal teaching and experience. Before he begins in C.M.F.C., he is placed into an annex church (a church waiting a full time pastor, ranging in size from 50 - 150 people) for one to two years in view of the pre-selection. A regular report of his activities is sent to the Cell, Teaching and Missionary Departments. This allows a record to be kept regarding the nature of his practical work on the field. He is next admitted to the training at C.M.F.C. for two years of detailed instruction. Finally he has three to four additional years of practical work before he is officially ordained. Normally the entire process takes around seven years. This system currently graduates 80 full time pastors per year.

The Effectiveness of EPBOM's System

How effective is EPBOM's equipping system with its cell cycle and system of discipleship, its teaching, and its training? Has the stated objective of the church, "to make in all nations disciples, capable of forming cell churches," been able to be realized? If the equipping/discipleship system is effective, one would expect to see cell churches planted by those who have been products of the system. This is exactly the case.

While there are some missionaries sent out to specifically preach and plant other cell churches, the majority of the 685 cell churches planted worldwide have been planted by disciples. These disciples have been ordinary members who have either moved from one location to another or are businessmen and/or professionals who have planted churches in countries to which they traveled and/or in which they have. One such example is Jonas Kouassi. You were introduced to Jonas and his story earlier. "To make in all the world disciples, capable of forming cell churches to destroy the works of the devil and to re-conquer humanity for Jesus Christ" is more than a mere stated objective at EPBOM. There are countless testimonies of men and women who have been saved, discipled and are planting churches all over Cote d'Ivoire, Africa, and regions beyond. How effective do *you* think their system is?

CHALLENGING THE INEFFECTIVENESS OF OUR OWN SYSTEM

In its present form, how effective is your equipping system? What is the fruit of your labor? Jesus told us to inspect the fruit to see if they are really disciples. In encompassing land and sea to make one disciple, have we in reality made only "converts'?

The fruit of an apple tree is really not simply another apple. The real fruit is another tree. The fruit of a cell is not a cell member, but another cell. The fruit of an evangelist is not a new believer, but another evangelist. The fruit of a cell church is not an ever expanding mass of cells. It is another cell church. For this level of multiplication to occur, equipping must take place. I am not talking about sporadic ad hoc equipping as happens in most of our churches. We must develop a comprehensive reproducible equipping system that will equip members of the Body of Christ for service at every level of ministry. If we do not, who will? Our people are called by God to serve in the Body of Christ. They have a calling. They have a destiny. The Lord of the Church has entrusted us to equip them for their work of service. How are we doing? What will we reply when we are called to account for our responsibility and service. Will He say to us, 'Well done, good and faithful slave. You were faithful with a few things, I will put you in charge of many things; enter into the joy of your master'" (Matthew 25:21)?

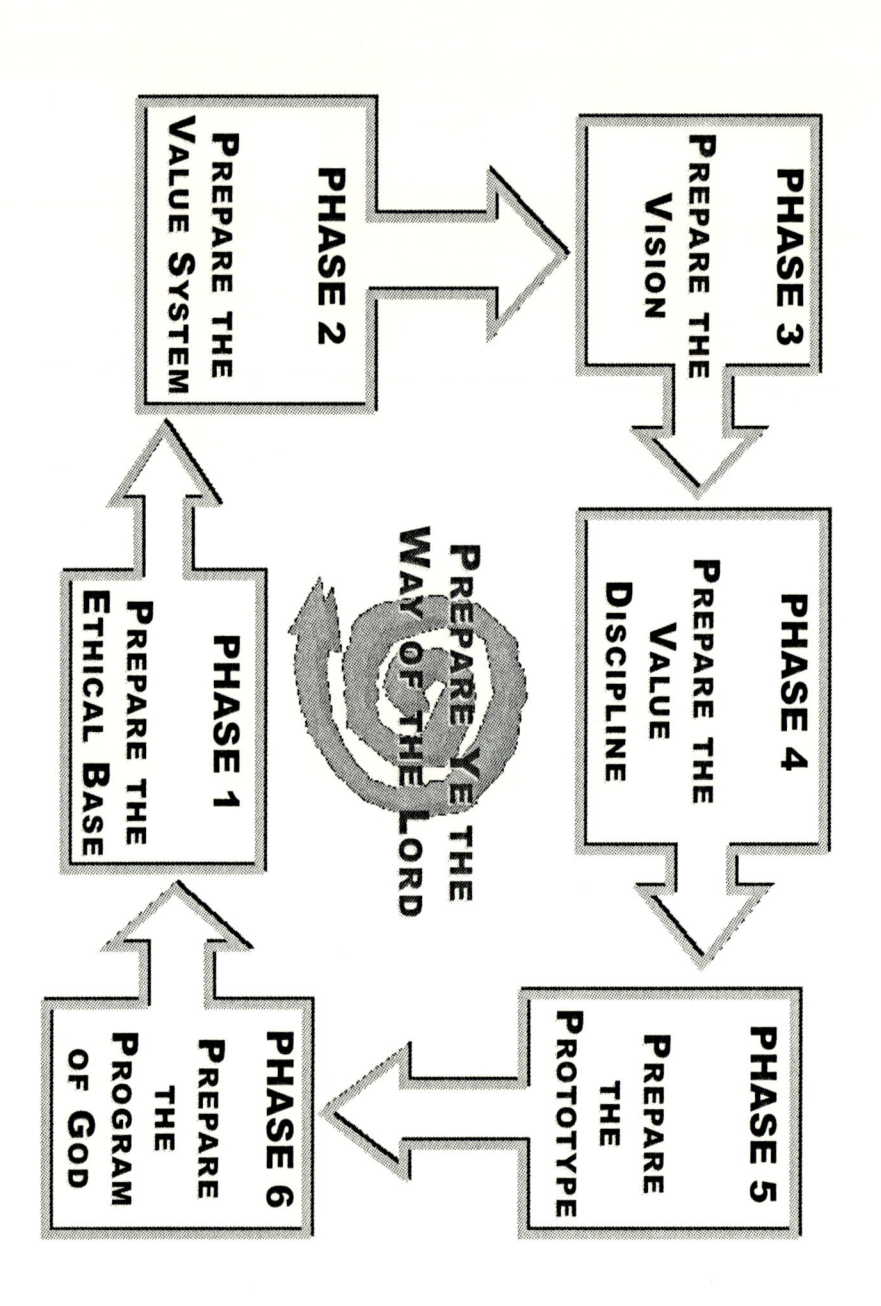

PHASE 1 — Prepare the Ethical Base
PHASE 2 — Prepare the Value System
PHASE 3 — Prepare the Vision
PHASE 4 — Prepare the Value Discipline
PHASE 5 — Prepare the Prototype
PHASE 6 — Prepare the Program of God

Prepare Ye the Way of the Lord

10

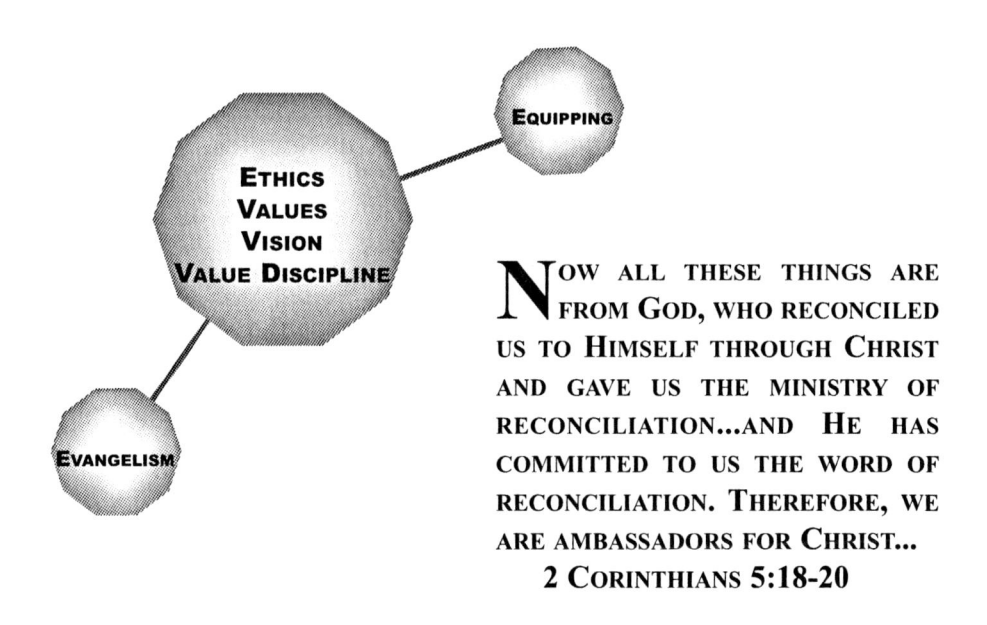

PREPARE THE PROGRAM OF GOD - EVANGELISM

EQUIPPING

**ETHICS
VALUES
VISION
VALUE DISCIPLINE**

EVANGELISM

Now all these things are from God, who reconciled us to Himself through Christ and gave us the ministry of reconciliation...and He has committed to us the word of reconciliation. Therefore, we are ambassadors for Christ...
2 Corinthians 5:18-20

Chapter 10 ☞ *Prepare the Program of God - Evangelism*

EVANGELIZING THIS GENERATION FOR CHRIST

Winning the World for Christ

Vision finds immediate expression in evangelization. "It is from the vision we see that we evangelize. We bring people to Christ. We bring them into the Kingdom" (Robert, Interview). The salvation of souls by evangelization is one of the priorities of the Lord, "Who desires all men to be saved and to come to the knowledge of the truth" (1 Timothy 2:4). Consequently, if we preach the gospel, we have nothing to boast of, for we are under compulsion. "Woe to us if we do not preach the gospel" (1 Corinthians 9:16; Ezekiel 2:3-7, 3:17-21; 2 Timothy 4:5). "The Christian no longer has the right to pass an entire day without sharing the good news of God, with neighbors, friends, colleagues, parents, etc. In refusing to evangelize, we hinder God from reaching souls" (Robert, Discipleship 14). Being God's first priority, evangelization now becomes the church's first priority. It finds expression 1) as the cell members evangelize both individually and through oikos connections, and 2) as the church corporately engages in mass evangelization.

Some Points to Ponder

The cross is NOT the most recognized symbol in the world! A survey revealed that the most recognized symbols in the world are:
1. Olympic rings
2. Golden arches of McDonalds
3. Coca Cola (Foltz, PRMIS 500)

Consider the following statistics:
1. 50.5 million people die every year
2. 31.1 million are non-Christians
3. 12.5 million of those had no contact of any kind with any Christians (Foltz, PRMIS 502)
4. The Current global population is 5.85 billion
   a. Christians   1.7 billion
   b. Muslims   1.2 billion
   c. Hindus   767 Million
   d. Buddhists   357 Million (Foltz, Unfinished 52)

We Serve A Missionary God

God is a missionary God! He has always been concerned about the whole world. (Is. 12, 45:22, 49:6, Ps. 48:10, 66:4, 67, 86:8-10, 96:1-10, Mal.1:11, Ex. 19:5-6, John 3:16 to name a few.) 'The story of God accomplishing His mission is the plot of the entire Bible! The way God accomplishes His mission is to reveal Himself to men by the spoken and Incarnate Word and to enlist them as His co-workers to bring that Word to others. Therefore, God's mission is the very reason that there is a Bible at all." (Hawthorne, Perspectives 1-1)

Though God had existed for all eternity, the Bible narrative begins with God facing a two-fold problem. There had been the rebellion of Lucifer and a third of the angels in heaven, followed by the fall of man. But God was not caught off-guard! He had a strategy: First He would re-conquer His rightful domain and re-establish His rightful reign. God determined to regain victory over the satanic counter-kingdom and in this way to redeem mankind. Second, to reconcile man to Himself through the finished work of the cross of Christ and His resurrection, God purposed through this redemption to reconcile all things to Himself in order to rule over all creation. Simply stated, God's purpose is: To redeem a people from every people and to rule a kingdom over all kingdoms. (Hawthorne, Perspectives 1-1)

God began to deal with mankind as a whole, but then scattered the nations at the Tower of Babel. Why? The nations together were rebelling against God. He would disperse them in order to win them back one at a time. He would reach them person by person, family by family, clan by clan, tribe by tribe, nation by nation. He chose one nation, Israel, to be the chosen vessel to bless all of the other nations. God spoke to Abraham a promise of posterity, land, and blessing.

> And I will make you a great nation, And I will bless you, And make your name great; And so you shall be a blessing; And I will bless those who bless you, And the one who curses you I will curse. And in you all the families of the earth shall be blessed. (Genesis 12:2-3)

> And in your seed all the nations of the earth shall be blessed, because you have obeyed My voice. (Genesis 22:18)

Chapter 10 ☛ *Prepare the Program of God - Evangelism*

The Old Testament contains the story of some of the Gentiles who were blessed as they came to know the God of Israel. Melchizedek, Ruth, Job, Jethro, Rahab, Naaman, and the people of Ninevah were among those whose lives were touched by the voluntary and sometimes involuntary sharing of God's people. This message continued and was embodied as God sent forth His Son to redeem us. Although Jesus focused on Israel, His love even during His early life was still extended to those beyond the Jewish race. Remember His ministry to the Samaritan woman, the Roman Centurion, the Syrophoenician mother & daughter, and the Samaritan leper?

Once redeemed ourselves, we join God in His redemptive work. Jesus said that He as sending us forth just as the Father had sent Him.

> "Peace be with you; as the Father has sent Me, I also send you." (John 20:21)

> And Jesus came up and spoke to them, saying, 'All authority has been given to Me in heaven and on earth. Go therefore and make disciples of all the nations, baptizing them in the name of the Father and the Son and the Holy Spirit, teaching them to observe all that I commanded you; and lo, I am with you always, even to the end of the age. (Matthew 28:18-20)

Even the last words spoken by Jesus on this earth before He was lifted up into heaven were concerning this same mission.

> But you shall receive power when the Holy Spirit has come upon you; and you shall be My witnesses both in Jerusalem, and in all Judea and Samaria, and even to the remotest part of the earth. (Acts 1:8)

Many verses could be quoted from the New Testament, but I believe Paul summarized it best when he called us ambassadors.

> Therefore, we are ambassadors for Christ, as though God were entreating through us; we beg you on behalf of Christ, be reconciled to God. (2 Cor. 5:20)

Thus, God is on a mission and has included each one of us to partner with Him as His mission continues throughout history to our own time. So what is a definition of mission? "God's redemptive activity in establishing His kingdom to the ends of the earth." (Foltz, PRMIS 500) That has always been God's mission and now it has become ours!

A Missionary Theology?

God is a missionary God. He has called us to partner with Himself. Yet, can we really say that Scripture clearly demonstrates what might be called a "missionary theology" that goes beyond the individual work of evangelization? That question must be answered in the affirmative for three reasons.

First, Paul sees the geographical expansion and progress of the church as an essential condition of the church between Christ's ascension and return. Paul views the progress of the Church in the world as a result of the gospel which has been "proclaimed in all creation under heaven" (Colossians 1:23) and which even now is "constantly bearing fruit and increasing" (Colossians 1:6). The very demonstration of this can be seen in the missionary work of Paul himself which drove him from Jerusalem to Illyria, and then onward to Rome and later to Spain (Ro. 15:19).

Second, Paul's mission, vision and theology impel him to involve those that have already experienced Christ's salvation in this missionary work and to awaken the church to this missionary attitude. Intercession for Paul is requested time and again (2 Thessalonians 3:1; Ephesians 6:18; Colossians 4:3). This intercession on the part of the church is seen as a "striving" and laboring together with the apostle in his missionary efforts ("Now I urge you, brethren, by our Lord Jesus Christ and by the love of the Spirit, to strive together with me in your prayers to God for me" Romans 15:30). The church is called by Paul to partner together with him by tangible assistance. In this context Paul repeatedly employs a specific term, προπεμπω, with the meaning of "equipping one for the journey by giving him money, provisions, companions" (3 John 6; Acts 15:3). Vine elaborates on this point:

> PROPEMPO (προπεμπω), translated "accompanied," in Acts 20:38, A.V., lit. means "to send forward;" hence, of assisting a person on a journey either (a) in the sense of fitting him out with the requisites for it, or (b) actually accompanying him for

Chapter 10 ☞ *Prepare the Program of God - Evangelism*

> part of the way. The former seems to be indicated in Romans 15:24 and I Corinthians 16:6, and ver. 11, where the R.V. has "set him forward." So in 2 Corinthians 1:16 and Tit. 3:13, and of John's exhortation to Gaius concerning travelling evangelists, "whom thou wilt do well to set forward on their journey worthily of God," 3 John 6, R.V. While personal accompaniment is not excluded, practical assistance seems to be generally in view, as indicated by Paul's word to Titus to set forward Zenas and Apollos on their journey and to see "that nothing be wanting unto them." In regard to the parting of Paul from the elders of Ephesus at Miletus, personal accompaniment is especially in view, perhaps not without the suggestion of assistance, Acts 20:38, R.V., "they brought him on his way;" accompaniment is also indicated in 21:5; "they all with wives and children brought us on our way, till we were out of the city." In Acts 15:3, both ideas perhaps are suggested. (Vine, 13-14)

The examples cited are not merely an incidental rendering of assistance so the church could express its sympathy for the work. Rather, what is reflected is the church's mode of existence as a missionary church.

Third, a direct stimulus for missionary activity is found in Paul's letter to the Colossian saints (Colossians 4:5-6). Ephesians 6:15 sets forth "preparation of the gospel of peace" as a necessity for the church. That the churches responded is indicated by a number of Scriptures. The Philippian church had an active involvement in the spread of the gospel (Philippians 1:5), as did the church at Thessalonica. They not only followed the pattern of Paul as Paul followed Christ, but they themselves also became a pattern (1 Thessalonians 1:7), an example, "to all the believers in Macedonia and in Achaia." Paul writes of their involvement in the spread of the gospel (1 Thessalonians 1:8) "For the word of the Lord has sounded forth from you, not only in Macedonia and Achaia, but also in every place your faith toward God has gone forth."

The early church embraced the responsibility for both personal localized evangelism as well as far-reaching missionary activity. There was a consciousness that they had been included in the world-encompassing work of God in Jesus Christ. They understood that their personal salvation itself was not the ultimate object of the gospel. As the fullness of Christ (Ephesians 1:23), they were to be the bearers of His glory to the rest of the world (Ephesians 3:1-11).

ILLUSTRATION - EPBOM'S MODEL OF EVANGELISM

EPBOM is passionate about bringing souls to Christ. This is in no small measure due to the passion of Pastor Julien, currently the head of the Department of Mass Evangelization.

Pastor Daingui A. Julien – A Personal Pilgrimage

Pastor Daingui A. Julien was born into a middle class family in a small village in Africa. His early life was extremely rocky as his parents separated while he was still quite young. Although as a child he lived with his mother, during his teen years pastor Julien went to live with his father. Not finding the love he needed in his father's home, he turned to the gangs for purpose, love, and a sense of belonging.

As a gang member he was heavily involved with drugs for six years, until he was twenty. Julien had one guiding principle in life. He never liked to do anything "half way". Whatever he gave himself to, it was to the extreme. His drug habit became so bad that not only his teachers, but even his friends became afraid of him. This led to great isolation and discouragement. Throughout this time, strange as it may seem, he did not give himself to what he called the "debauchery" of his friends. While all his friends were getting girls pregnant, Julien kept himself from away from that sin. Why? His mother had told him she never wanted to hear that he had gotten a woman pregnant. It was a word that struck his spirit and impacted Julien deeply.

Having managed to finish high school in spite of his habit, Julien attended a training school to study, of all things, criminology. Though he graduated with a diploma in the ministry of police technical science, he remained enslaved to his drugs. Throughout it all, though, the Spirit of God was drawing Julien. One day he returned to the village where his mother lived. They fought intensely. In the end, his mother said to him, "May God forgive you." That statement infuriated him. While she was praying, Julien grabbed a heavy piece of wood, fully intending to strike her. But suddenly some unseen power stopped him. In fact, all he could do instead was cry. Two days later as he was watching Billy Graham on television, Julien once more found himself in tears. He resolved in his heart from that day forward to walk with Jesus. Yet sin still reigned over his life and he continued his same lifestyle.

Chapter 10 ☞ *Prepare the Program of God - Evangelism*

In 1981 Julien met one of his old friends who had often spoken to him about the Lord. Julien poured out his heart to his friend, yet still rejected the Lord. He knew his friend was in a Pentecostal church. Even so, he asked his friend to accompany him to the Christian Celeste, a cult, so they could help him change his life. When he and his friend arrived there, one of the leaders looked at Julien and said, "Come back Friday and we will start doing sacrifices." He told Julien there were certain things he must bring to him when he returned. Julien returned that Friday, but God did not permit him to encounter that man. Instead, a miracle of God occurred. Julien met his cousin who had also been speaking to him about the Lord. His cousin took him to his own pastor, Pastor Dion. It was during that fateful meeting that Julien truly gave his life to Jesus. What became of the drugs and the old lifestyle? All of the old life left. The drugs, the violence, the anger, everything left. He experienced what it is like to be in Christ and become a new creature, the old things passing away and all things becoming new.

He immediately began attending the church and before long started sharing with others about Jesus. He grew quickly in the Lord. Later in 1981 the Lord spoke to him to become a minister. He obeyed the voice of God and received all the training necessary to become a pastor. Though a passionate individual, Julien's passion alone was not sufficient to secure his advancement in ministry. He demonstrated proven ministry at each juncture:

> When I started to serve the Lord I had great joy. The fire of God was already acting in my heart. Already the vision of evangelization was present in my spirit. Pastor Dion had seen the zeal that I had. So, prompted by the Holy Spirit, he placed me as an evangelist among the youth. I served from about 1981 to about 1985 there. Starting in 1986 I was established to lead the Department of the Youth. I worked there until 1990. Starting in 1990, around June, I was transferred to the Prison Department where I served as an evangelist. I think I was only five months there. Since October 1990, I have led the Department of Mass Evangelization. (Interview)

EPBOM's Vision for Mass Evangelization – Three-fold Thrust

EPBOM's vision for evangelization does not originate with Pastor Julien, it really is an expression of the vision received by Pastor Dion, the senior pastor. This, by the way, is true of every department at EPBOM. The vision for the Department of Mass Evangelization is based in Acts 26:16ff:

> For this purpose I have appeared to you, to appoint you a minister and a witness not only to the things which you have seen, but also to the things in which I will appear to you; rescuing you from the Jewish people and from the Gentiles, to whom I am sending you, to open their eyes so that they may turn from darkness to light and from the dominion of Satan to God, that they may receive forgiveness of sins and an inheritance among those who have been sanctified by faith in Me.

Evangelization is visualized as a multiple thrust. The first thrust of evangelization is revival of a church that is dead. The second thrust of evangelization is toward pagans who are lost. The third thrust of evangelization is to build an army of evangelists in every local church, in every Missionary Zone, in every Missionary Station, and for every Missionary Division. Each thrust will now be considered in greater detail

Like Peter who at one point is said to have followed Jesus afar off, Christians within the church may also find themselves following Jesus from afar. The first thrust of evangelization is, therefore, revival of a church. Revelation pictures just such a scenario when it presents to us the Lord standing and knocking at the door of the church in Laodicea, seeking entrance. Whenever this occurs and the church loses sight of the Lord, the church herself becomes an evangelization field. Evangelization is then directed towards the people, the chosen people, those that are already a part of the church. Whenever anyone hears His voice and opens the door, he is once again brought into close fellowship with the Lord.

The second thrust of evangelization we read of in Acts 26ff was toward pagans who were lost. The evangelization thrust toward the lost pagan is public evangelization, not personal evangelization. As the department name indicates, it is Mass Evangelization. The department specializes in evangelization to the masses, or public evangelization. We must note at this point an underly-

Chapter 10 ☛ *Prepare the Program of God - Evangelism*

ing assumption of Dion's vision, and therefore this department's vision. Pastor Dion assumes that every member is to be actively involved in one-on-one evangelism in their own personal life and through the cell. It is not the "job" of the Department of Mass Evangelization. In addition, every other department is to evangelize. The Women's Department evangelizes women. The Cell Department evangelizes through the cells. The Hospital Department evangelizes in the hospital. The Children's Department evangelizes children. Even the Public Relations Department evangelizes. At times this evangelization is personal one-on-one evangelization, sometimes door-to-door, at other times on street corners, or even sometimes in busses and taxis. However, the Department of Mass Evangelization is simply the evangelization to the masses, to the crowds, public evangelization.

When we meditate on the ministry of the Apostle Paul as he carried out the vision he received from the Lord, we discover that the Apostle Paul didn't work alone. He shared his vision with others. Where he could not go, the ones he invested in continued the work of the Lord. Like Paul, the third thrust of evangelization is to build an army having workers in every local church, in every Missionary Zone and in every Missionary Station for every Missionary Division.

To accomplish its outward thrust into these three evangelistic arenas, the Department of Mass Evangelization is organized along four specific dimensions: inspection, revival, mass evangelization, and preliminary follow-up. Pastor Julien serves as the department's General Coordinator. He watches over the activity of the department to ensure that everything is done in line with the vision.

Those involved with inspection oversee all the work of the personnel that are in the department. They are in contact with the workers and encourage them through letters, telephone calls, etc. If something is out of order in one of their lives, those charged with inspection know that the worker cannot work effectively for the Lord. Therefore they constantly follow-up in the spiritual, ministerial and social lives of the workers.

Those involved in revival provide for revival in every church. Revival may be done through seminars, conferences of fire, or by campaigns. Seminars are cycles of short thematic systematic training followed by prayer. In this way individuals have time to apply teachings to their life before additional teaching is introduced. Campaigns of revival are short but anointed direct preaching followed by intense prayer. Conferences of fire may continue one, two or even three days, where people remain in the presence of the Lord. They hear the word, pray, and receive prayer, deliverance, healings, etc.

Those involved in mass evangelization organize all the programs of evangelization to the masses. This includes mobile evangelization on the street corners, campaigns and watch nights of prayer and evangelization, as well as crusades. Campaigns of evangelization involve only one church, while the crusades of evangelization bring together many churches. I have made numerous references in this section to churches, plural. The reader needs to remember that EPBOM has over fifty-two local churches in the city of Abidjan alone.

Those members of the Department of Mass Evangelization involved specifically in the area of preliminary follow-up take care of all those who have newly given their lives to Christ. They have established a detailed process for the initial follow-up of every new believer. This is a month long follow-up process which they call, "clinical evangelization." Pastor Julien describes this process in detail:

> When there is a campaign or crusade, we call the people forward and ask, "Do you want to come to Christ?" We register the names of all those who come forward. We do not assume that all who come forward have truly accepted the Lord. Therefore, those who do follow-up have three objectives. The first objective is to evaluate and discern the nature of the decision made. Second, if they have discerned that the person has not accepted Jesus, then they evangelize them. Third, if they have truly accepted the Lord, then they encourage the new convert to continue in the way of the Lord and they set an appointment time to meet with them again. Each of those who respond to the appointment time we further evangelize in what we call "clinical evangelization". Clinical evangelization is head to head, one-on-one. Through the clinical evangelization we maintain contact between the new believer and the evangelist. During this time we come into the new believer's life. We discover their profound problems. Based on what the person tells us, we use the Word of God to give solutions to their problems and to free them from bondages. Once we finish this work, we pray for the person so that they will be able to live the Word that has been given to them.

Chapter 10 ☞ *Prepare the Program of God - Evangelism*

Now, if we see that there are complications, in that case, other ministry departments are brought alongside. If we discover that the person has a problem with wicked spirits and needs deliverance, we take that person to the Department of Demonology. If we discover that the person has a problem in his marriage, then we take him to the Marriage Department. If we discover that the new believer has a social problem, we take him to the Deacons Department or the Social Works Department. If the new believer is a woman and she has a problem that is particularly female related, then we send her to the Women's Department so that a profound work can be done for her there. The worker doing follow-up will set additional meeting times to monitor the progress of the work that is being done.

Normally within one month, though it may vary some case to case, the new believer is placed into a cell. All this ministry is overlapping. There is a saying that when the fire is hot, that is when you go to them. So, while the person has given themselves to the Lord and they are hot, we are doing our work. At the same time we encourage them to go to a newcomers class and to the cell so that an additional work of follow-up can be done by the cell leader. After three or four weeks, the evangelist who is doing follow-up will officially pull back from the new convert so the cell can accomplish its work. By then the person is completely surrounded and they will not slip out, but will continue on in the work of the Lord. (Interview)

Those who come to the services have often been invited guests. The church views this as another occasion for evangelism. At the close of the services, these guests are gathered together with evangelists who set an appointment time during the week to meet with them. If they come to the appointment, they are evangelized and often give themselves to the Lord. If the guest does not respond to the initial meeting time, the evangelists go to their house to have a meeting there and to see why they didn't come. If it is a false address, then the workers by prayer just entrust the person to the Lord. Sometimes by miracles they can find them in the city somewhere. The evangelism is very aggressive in the sense that the workers are not passive, but actively pursuing the person.

They look at the aggressiveness with which the Lord sought and saved the Apostle Paul, and do likewise.

All the work that Pastor Julien spoke about is done with adults, twenty-one years of age and over. What happens to those under twenty-one? The specialized work of each of EPBOM's many departments is replicated in their Youth Department. The Youth Department encompasses ages seven through twenty.

> Everything that is done with the adults is done with the youth. We have a team of workers that work among the youth. Everything we do here, they do there. I was the first evangelist among the youth. That work continues. It is the same exact thing with the youth. The Youth Department of Mass Evangelization also carries out the work of inspection, revival, mass evangelization, and preliminary follow-up. (Interview).

Is the work of the Department of Evangelization effective in both training and winning the lost? In the year 2000, according to internal statistics, EPBOM had about 1500 evangelists throughout her churches. Less than seventy evangelists are in the central church in Yopougon. A minimum of eighty to one hundred unbelievers come to the Lord each month at the central church. Often they see as many as one hundred and fifty come to Christ each month. This means that about seventy workers are regularly involved with evangelizing and following up at least eighty to one hundred converts month after month.

Mass Evangelization – Thorough and Intense

The program of evangelization at EPBOM is thorough and intense. We have seen that it is done at a personal one-on-one level, at a departmental level by each department, to the masses through the Department of General Evangelization, and all aspects of the process are completely replicated under the auspices of the Youth Department. There are yet three additional departments heavily involved in evangelization. According to Pastor Dion, the Department of Hospital Evangelism and the Department of Prison Evangelism join with the Department of Evangelization in more specialized attempts toward evangelization:

The Department of Hospital Evangelism focuses on hospitals, clinics and the sick, bringing the gospel of hope, of comfort and of healing to the sick. Those who work in this ministry area are required to understand the state of the soul and the spirit of the sick so as to be better able to bring them the gospel. The Department of Hospital Evangelism is authorized by the government of Cote d'Ivoire to take care of the sick, and gives proof and demonstrations of power and of faith. As a consequence, hundreds of souls have been saved through the ministry of the Department of Hospital Evangelism.

At the example of the Department of Hospital Evangelism, the Department of Prison Evangelism was formed. It is considered as "the arm of Jesus held out towards the prisoners through His church." It is most important to bring the gospel in a very serious and consecrated manner to the prisoners who are in centers of penitentiary detention. The one who exercises the ministry of prison evangelism must have both wisdom and compassion, because the state of the soul of the prisoner is different than an ordinary man who has freedom. The workers of this Department of Prison Evangelism have made an excellent testimony for Christ. The Lord has used them to bring to Himself hundreds of prisoners who were received by the church. They were trained as workers and disciples, and in following they were integrated into society, who has a tendency to push away those with a prison record. It is written: "I needed clothes and you clothed me, I was sick and you looked after me, I was in prison and you came to visit me" (Matthew 25:36). (Working 50-51)

Evangelization Through the Cell Department

The Cell Department is also evangelistically oriented. Top on the list of the twelve goals and required objectives for an excellent cell system is "individual evangelism by the members" (Robert, Working 57). The cell is considered "a key means of growth" (Robert, Cell Group 5). It is considered a "must" for cell leaders to promote a spirit of evangelization in the life of each of their members. Each member is thought of as a branch that is to bear fruit by preaching the gospel in their surrounding (Robert, Cell Group 19).

> General evangelization aims at all social classes and is the essential vision of the church. However, this vision, established by the Lord, must also use strategies appropriate for the abundant harvest in the different classes. We must spread the nets in all the sectors of our wide 'sea', which is the whole world, to catch different kinds of 'fish' (Robert, Cell Group 15).

Although the entire church is evangelizing in a very broad way, each cell can target those in a very specific location or within a specific people group. In light of this, EPBOM has developed an individualized strategy of cell planting to reach professionals, students, children, men, and women. These strategies are fully developed in Dion's book, *Cell Group Ministry*.

Strategy to Reach Professionals

Within the context of cell ministry, a special section must deal with professionals. EPBOM has been led by the Holy Spirit to create cells led by several trained lay leaders in all circles of their society. They are chosen from the profession to which they belong. Bakers, for instance, work among bakers; members of the medical corps work among their colleagues; members of the military corps and the police work in their own groups, etc. Rather than meeting in homes, the cell group meetings take place in the offices or conference rooms of the particular buildings in which the professionals work. A general meeting gathers all the cell groups once a week in a large lecture room in the business district of the capital of the country or of the region. These meetings enable the believers to invite VIPs, administrative personnel, politicians, businessmen and businesswomen, etc. Many high ranking officials of Cote d'Ivoire who would not have come to a church service or an open-air crusade have been converted because they were invited into an environment that was appropriated for them. Most of the working people in the church were converted through this ministry.

Strategy to Reach Students

As far as evangelization is concerned, EPBOM sees no greater need than in academic circles. They view as one of satan's greatest strategies his

Chapter 10 ☛ *Prepare the Program of God - Evangelism*

strategy to poison the seeds of the gospel by introducing atheistic ideologies into the educational system so that the plants of tomorrow will bear contaminated fruit. In this way he sets himself against the young men and women who will be tomorrow's adults, and also against the students who will one day be the leaders of Cote d'Ivoire's society. Consequently, EPBOM focuses tremendous effort on the evangelization of these vulnerable groups in order to protect their youth and destroy the root of the devil's work. This reality led them, in Abidjan, to raise up and equip hundreds of students committed to missionary work. At the same time, this created the necessity to form student cell groups with the same structure and program of activity as EPBOM's other cell groups. The results have been positive.

Strategy to Reach Children

Apart from the ministry among students and professionals, there is also a children's section that is efficiently handled by the Cell Department. The children's section of the Cell Department is in charge of two different segments of children meeting in groups of 5 to 15: those aged 7 to 12 and those aged 12 to 18 years. Children are taught the ways of the Lord and they participate successfully in the salvation of children through their cell groups, which work in the same way as all the other cell groups. Their activities include large spiritual retreats, seminars, and lectures for children.

Strategy to Reach Men and Women

EPBOM has been led by the Holy Spirit to employ gender based cells throughout the cities and towns. Thus, they have men's cell groups and women's cell groups spread out in male or female zones and sectors. This process has proven efficient on several counts. The separation of men and women has enabled them to better address the problems each particularly face and to provide appropriate spiritual solutions in order to keep the church stable and well balanced. Mixed cell groups, i.e., those in which we find both men and women, are generally located in the parts of the town where the activities of the cell ministry are not intensely developed. Mixed cell groups are expected to work quickly to subdivide into male and female cell groups. The total number of people in a mixed cell group is the same as any other type of cell group: not to exceed 15 people. The period required to "birth" one of these new cell groups depends on the fertility of the ground in individual evangelization, which is the domain of the Cell department. But, generally speaking, about three or four months is enough for most cell groups.

Come and See Evangelism

The employment of the 'come and see' method of evangelism (John 1:39) causes the cells to evangelize very effectively through each of their members. "Let's take the example of a cell composed of 10 members. If each member invites a new member each week, saying "come and see," and if these guests actually come and see the works of God, this cell will reach a total number of 50 members after just one month" (Robert, Cell Group 19).

Deliverance and Evangelization

One the one hand, EPBOM views deliverance as an inseparable element of initial evangelization. On the other hand, deliverance is seen to work hand in glove with and be an inseparable element of soul therapy. Both are true. It is subsumed under evangelization by the department heads in general, and especially by the senior pastor, Dion Robert, and the head of Demonology, Pastor Wouehi Louan Etienne.

The American charismatic mindset often sees deliverance and evangelization only as two distinct activities performed at two separate times in the believer's life. Para-church deliverance ministries proliferate that deal with freeing Christians from demonic bondage. Rarely is deliverance considered to be necessary every time an individual comes to Christ. The theological stance of EPBOM is indeed challenging to our own mindset:

> Deliverance and evangelization are the same thing. Many do not understand this. Every text, in which Jesus spoke of deliverance, he spoke of evangelization. He said, 'The Spirit of the Lord is upon Me. He has anointed me to announce good news to the poor, to heal the broken hearted.' It is deliverance. So, when the Spirit of God comes, it is to evangelize, to heal their hearts. He said to go into all the world and preach the good

> news to all of creation. Those that believe will be saved. Those that do not believe will be condemned. So these are the miracles that will follow those that believe. That is deliverance. We cannot do it without evangelization. We can say, 'Go preach the good news to all creation. Heal the sick, raise the dead and purify the lepers.' That is in Matthew 10, all of this. When we follow it precisely, the evangelization will be clothed with deliverance. (Etienne, Interview)
>
> The Department of Demonology is the ministry of deliverance. The ministry of deliverance is the ministry of follow-up based on evangelization. The ministry of deliverance is the means of persuading a man to give himself to Jesus. Jesus did evangelization and it was during the evangelization that there was deliverance. When you deliver people, they see that, and open their hearts and give themselves to Jesus. But, when it is just evangelization, it is to see and then to leave. When you attach deliverance to evangelization, then it is that you can maintain them. In a way I am an evangelist. My resource is deliverance! (Etienne, Interview).

Pastor Etienne makes an even stronger statement regarding why evangelization and deliverance must go together.

> Evangelization without deliverance is seduction. So deliverance without evangelization is just like children at play. It is just amusing yourself. Whenever you have evangelization without deliverance, you are seducing many people. I seduce them. But now you declare, "I am here to deliver people." But, if you don't do evangelization, then you are just a big deceiver. You are just deceiving yourself. That is to say, you do not know the principle of the Kingdom. (Interview)

A definite link can also be observed at EPBOM between evangelization, deliverance, and the value of humility. Pride desires that men think the best of us. Pride hides the truth. Humility will result in a man's willingness to open up his life and reveal the dark places so the light of God can shine inside:

If you don't do deliverance with evangelization, if he does not let you enter into his intimate life, that is, his private life, what is he going to confess? He can't confess anything. So, he remains to himself. Now, when we announce the gospel to him, he asks, "What must I do to be saved?" In Acts 16 when the apostles sang and prayed and the prison was shaken and they went out, the jailer knew the Word of God, but he fought with the Word of God. There are people in the church that fight with the Word of God. It was the first time he asked, "What must I do to be saved?" that the apostle Paul told him to believe in the Lord Jesus and he would be saved and his family. So, when we announce the gospel at a certain time, the person is going to ask, "How can I be saved? I am among the sinners." We take them to the way of deliverance. He is ready to open his heart. He asked, "What must I do?" Now we enter into the details. No longer can he say, "Why did you enter into my private life? Why are you entering there?" It is he himself that asked you for help. So, it is best to have deliverance at the time of evangelization. But, if you didn't have it then, you must have it later. You cannot do it apart, one from the other. (Etienne, Interview)

Church Planting and World Evangelization

How does EPBOM deal with the issue of church planting and world evangelization? Like the early church, does EPBOM embrace the responsibility for both far-reaching missionary activity as well as localized evangelism?

EPBOM has planted 685 churches worldwide (Faustin, Interview). That averages out to over twenty-seven new churches per year over the course of their twenty-five year history. How has that happened? They have planted a local church in 34% of all African nations (Robert, Interview). Who planted them? They have planted churches in Europe and North America also (Robert, Interview). How has that come about?

The answer is exceedingly simple. It is found in their vision statement: "To make in all the nations disciples, capable of forming cell churches to destroy the works of the devil and to re-conquer humanity for Jesus Christ" (Robert, Interview).

Chapter 10 ☛ Prepare the Program of God - Evangelism

EPBOM has developed a church planting strategy that this author would consider to be unique in the cell church movement. For many years, literature in English regarding cell church planting has been scant to non-existent. The one major exception has been the material published by DOVE Christian Fellowship. Even most of TOUCH Outreach Ministry's material has in the past dealt with church transition, rather than church planting. That changed with the revised edition of *Where Do We Go From Here?*, just recently released. The final chapter is entitled, "How to Plant a Cell Group Church." There is a common denominator running through the material from DOVE, TOUCH Outreach Ministries, TOUCH Global, and even my own organization, Strategic Cell Ministries International. That common denominator is a vision of cell planting that suggests a leadership team possessing certain characteristics must come together to form a leadership cell that will eventually grow and birth a cell church. That church at some future date will send out another leadership team to plant another church. In the meantime, the church will grow and continue to grow as cells are continually birthed.

However, Dion has taken the position that leadership teams do not birth local churches, disciples birth local churches. And any disciple who has been trained in the Program of God can plant and grow a cell! Thus his vision, to go in the entire world and make disciples, disciples who can form cell churches. When did such a strategy develop? It began from the earliest days as Dion trained his initial leaders, and has continued up to the present. Regarding the vision and desire of each cell to eventually develop into a local church, Pastor Dion has this to say:

> The goal of every cell is to become a local church. The 52 local churches we have in Abidjan each began as a cell. Our goal is for each cell to grow quickly and becomes a local church. In the Bible, all the local churches started in houses. The vision God gave the apostles was for those cells to become real churches.
>
> Most cell churches have as their vision simply to have many, many, many cells. Their goal is to be a big cell church with many cells. The cells will multiply, but they will always stay a cell. Our goal is for every cell to plant other cells, and for both the original cell and the daughter cells to each eventually

become a local church. So, instead of being one large church with many, many, many cells, we have many, many churches with many many cells.

That's our vision. We have almost 685 churches presently. Think of it this way. A man has a family. He has children. He doesn't want his children to remain children forever. He wants his children to grow up, mature, and have children of their own. It is not a good thing to simply create a cell group and look to have many, many, many cells. They must become churches. I have children of my own, but I want them all to eventually become mothers and fathers. I don't want to keep them around me as children forever. I don't want a hundred children. I want families. I want to have grandchildren. It is the same in the church. The church is a family. A cell begins in a home. As children are born the cell grows. We continue to teach the children and we prepare the children to become other families. They must also give birth to children. Their children must create other children. Each of the cells, as they become local churches, function according to this vision. (Interview)

The 685 churches Pastor Dion mentions are not all in Cote d'Ivoire. They have been birthed in over one third of the countries on the African continent as well as in Europe and in North America. How did this come about? It is a logical extension of the vision for each cell to become a local church. While at times the church sends out missionaries to begin cells in other countries, the majority of the time international businessmen or ambassadors who have been trained in the church are the ones actually planting the first cells.

Chapter 10 ☛ *Prepare the Program of God - Evangelism*

CHALLENGING THE INEFFECTIVENESS OF OUR OWN SYSTEM

Why is the Body of Christ in America not growing like the Body of Christ around the world? We have all heard the excuses.

"It is the last days. You know the Scriptures teach that in the last days the hearts of men will grow faint and the love of many will grow cold. It is just simply a sign of the times." Yes, we are living in the last days. Yes, the hearts and love of men is growing colder. But, *isn't that true of the rest of the world also*? The days in which we live are the same days our brothers and sisters around the world are living. That answer only begs the question.

"This is a hard field. You haven't ministered any place quite like this place. Our situation is unique. Our culture is unique. We are not like everywhere else!" While ministering in Washington DC I continually was told about the unique travel problems and work pressures of the DC metroplex area. It was funny. I had heard the same argument in Houston, Texas, the fourth largest city in the nation. I moved to St. Petersburg, Russia. I was informed of the very same work and travel conditions hindering evangelism there that I encountered in America. Strange how they felt their situation was also unique. Canada was the same. Poland was the same. "Our situation is unique. The ground is hard here!" Who could possibly be more opposed to the gospel than the established religious structure of Jesus' day? I can just picture Jesus shaking His head, throwing up his hands and declaring, "My culture is too resistant. The hearts of my people are too hard. Their situations are too unique!" Instead, He looked at those around Him and declared to His disciples (Luke 10:2) "The harvest is plentiful, but the laborers are few; therefore beseech the Lord of the harvest to send out laborers into His harvest."

The problem is NOT with the harvest. The problem is with the laborers! EPBOM is passionate about bringing souls to Christ. As a consequence, they not only work in the harvest, but develop each disciple into one more harvester. Jesus was so passionate about bringing back the lost to His Father, that "for the joy set before Him [He] endured the cross, despising the shame, and has sat down at the right hand of the throne of God (Hebrews 12:2)." As in days of old, the Church of the 21st century must prepare the way of the Lord. We must not say, 'There are yet four months, and then comes the harvest'? Behold, I say to you, lift up your eyes and look on the fields, that they are white for harvest" (John 4:35).

Pastor Etienne made two strong statements that shed light on how we in the West seem to operate in the area of evangelism. He said first, "Evangelization without deliverance is seduction." On the heels of that statement he said, "Deliverance without evangelization is like little children waving their arms at play." As you may now understand, evangelization is more than a simple presentation of the gospel. It encompasses all that a man needs to come to the Lord, gain freedom, and remain free. Pastor Etienne believes that man is in need of deliverance at salvation as well as in need of spiritual healing of the soul. This is why he believes that to evangelize a man without ridding him of his demons is to seduce the man into error. That is a disquieting thought. Could he be correct? Are our practices of evangelism in reality seducing man into error? Should we in some way be joining together evangelization and deliverance? Or perhaps, there are just more demons in Africa than in America. Perhaps the Africans are simply more demonized than Americans, and that accounts for why demons seem to manifest when people are saved over there. Ask the Lord what He thinks!

PHASE 2 — Prepare the Value System

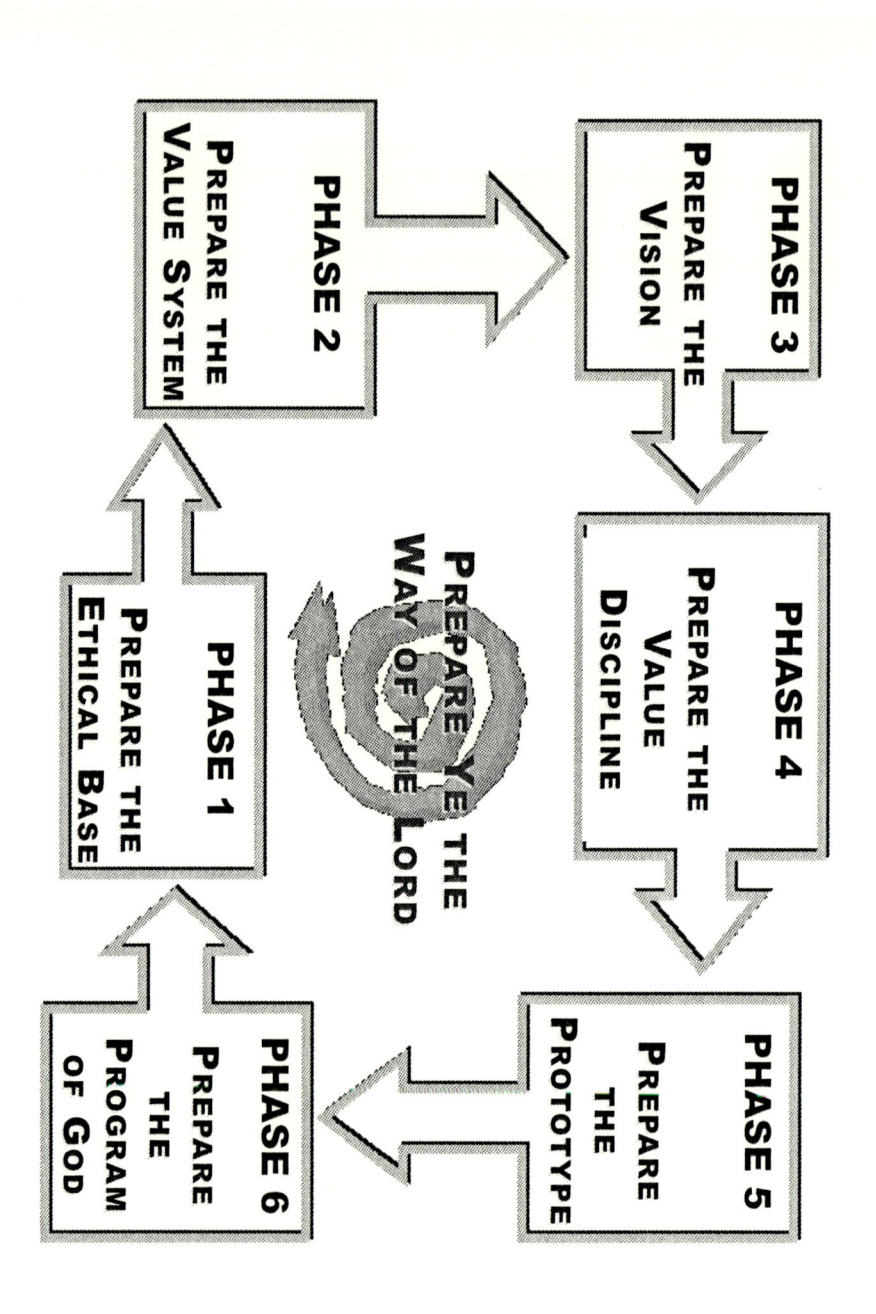

PHASE 3 — Prepare the Vision

PHASE 4 — Prepare the Value Discipline

PHASE 1 — Prepare the Ethical Base

PHASE 6 — Prepare the Program of God

PHASE 5 — Prepare the Prototype

Prepare Ye the Way of the Lord

11
Prepare the Program
of God - Edification

EDIFICATION

EQUIPPING

**ETHICS
VALUES
VISION
VALUE DISCIPLINE**

EVANGELISM

WHAT IS THE OUTCOME THEN, BRETHREN? WHEN YOU ASSEMBLE, EACH ONE HAS A PSALM, HAS A TEACHING, HAS A REVELATION, HAS A TONGUE, HAS AN INTERPRETATION. LET ALL THINGS BE DONE FOR EDIFICATION.
1 CORINTHIANS 14:26

Chapter 11 ☛ *Prepare the Program of God - Edification*

BUILDING UP THE BODY OF CHRIST

It is unthinkable to give birth to a baby, take the newborn home from the hospital to a loving family, and then do nothing further to help the child grow and mature. Luke Benjamin Brickman, my grandson, was born October 16th, 2002. He has received constant and continual follow-up since the moment of his birth. He is constantly watched and cared for. His every need is noticed and attended to. His growth is duly noted. Changes in his behavior are constantly observed. He is fed and changed. His parents are modeling prayer and worship and scripture reading. In short, he is not left to fend for himself.

How unlike the situation in too many of our churches. A new baby is birthed into the Kingdom. Not wanting to intrude upon his private life, Kingdom family members give him his space and leave him on his own. He is now required to fend for himself. He is to learn the art of prayer on his own. He experiences the soiling of this world but is left to wash himself. He is expected to show up for meals and is chided when he misses a feeding. No one is there to help him learn to walk, but many gather around to condemn him for falling. Though in dire need of developing healthy relationships within the family, weekly activities supplant the development of these relationships. He soon crawls, walks, or runs out the church"s revolving back door, only to be missed by a few family members weeks or months later.

Consider this scenario. A new child has joined the family, a son. This time it is not by birth, but by adoption. The child has come from another family who perhaps did not care for him properly, who perhaps did not demonstrate the love he needed, who perhaps birthed him and then left him on his own. All rejoice at the inclusion of this new family member. There is great initial excitement and enthusiasm. Yet, like with the newborn above, the excitement wanes, the enthusiasm subsides, daily regiment takes over, and the once doted over newcomer is now, like the newborn, neglected. In time he decides this is not the right family either, and quietly passes through the revolving back door. In time some will miss him and wonder where he went. Most will never bother.

Are these words too harsh? I know of a church that by its own admission has seen over 50,000 members pass through its door during the course of the decade of the 90's. What a travesty. Yet, how common in America! The Church has a responsibility before God to take care of those birthed into the Kingdom of God. Each church has a responsibility to care for those whom God places as members of a local church family.

Care and follow-up is not an option. The development of a system that will ensure quality care and follow-up is obligatory upon the church. Along with quality care and follow-up, soul therapy, accompanied by the ministry of deliverance, is fundamental to pastoral ministry and the building up of the Body of Christ. God has designed both soul therapy and deliverance as essential elements for the complete ministry program of His church. Soul therapy is what makes the church responsible and stable. It is not sufficient to simply share the gospel and lead an individual to faith in Christ. Evangelization is a process that continues. If it is truly in line with the gospel, evangelization must assure people of complete salvation. The work of soul therapy accompanied by deliverance is done with the person to finalize his level of comprehension and level of decision for Jesus.

After announcing the good news to the poor and proclaiming the year of the Lord's favor, the remainder of Isaiah 61:1-2 has practical implications for soul therapy:

> The Spirit of the Sovereign Lord is on me, because the Lord has anointed me to preach good news to the poor. He has sent me to bind up the brokenhearted, to proclaim freedom for the captives and release from darkness for the prisoners, to proclaim the year of the Lord's favor... (Isaiah 61:1-2a; Luke 4:18-19).

Jesus was sent to bind up the brokenhearted, proclaim freedom for the captives, and proclaim release to the oppressed. In other words, deal with broken hearts that need to be healed, work with those who are captive to demons or other vices, and care for those who are in anguish, depressed, sickly, oppressed by Satan, or who need to be liberated by a word of consolation and given stability. God, who initiates the work of sanctification in His people's lives can be relied upon to complete the work He has begun. A significant process He employs to bring this to pass is the work of soul therapy.

At the sunset of Jesus' life and ministry, He could claim that the devil "has nothing in me" (John 14:30-31). This phraseology reflects the Hebrew עלי אין לו, commonly used in a legal sense to signify that there is no claim possible. There was nothing in the life of Jesus, no area, over which the devil could come and make claim. There were no thought patterns, no strongholds, and no actions that gave place to the enemy in His life.

Chapter 11 ☛ *Prepare the Program of God - Edification*

Paul's closing prayer for the Thessalonians is that they would be "preserved complete, without blame" until the coming of the Lord. He had earlier (4:3,7) emphasized the importance of sanctification and implied that it was the work of the indwelling Holy Spirit (4:8). "Spirit and soul and body" is another way of expressing his desire for their complete (ολοκληρον) sanctification. For the classical ολοκληρος (a synonym of ολοτελης) compare James 1:4, ινα ητε τελειοι και ολοκληροι, "that you may be perfect and complete" and also Acts 3:16 for the ολοκληρια, "perfect health," of the man who had been cured of his congenital lameness. Paul's desire is that every part of the Thessalonians be kept entirely without fault. That his readers be preserved entirely without fault until the Parousia, and be so found at the Parousia, at which time they will then be perfected in holiness. It is God who calls His people to sanctification (1 Peter 1:15). It is God who supplies the grace without which His call cannot be realized (faithful is He who calls you). God who initiates the work of sanctification in His people's lives can also be relied upon to complete the work.

To lead a soul to Christ is one thing, but to train, affirm, look after, and heal that soul is quite another, and is of great importance. Jesus said, "You have not chosen me but I have chosen you and ordained you, that you might go out and bear much fruit, and that your fruit should remain" (John 15:16). It is solely by the ministry of soul therapy that this will be accomplished. God gives us this command: "Know well each one of your sheep, care for your flocks" (Proverbs 27:23). Those who choose to walk with Christ come from different backgrounds (cultural, professional, and social). If the work of soul therapy is not seriously done at their particular levels, these different environments will always influence their nature (i.e. their old nature) and will hinder their spiritual faith.

The work of soul therapy and the goal of the church must be to bring each individual that has been converted to Jesus Christ to complete healing by the Holy Spirit and the Word of God. Soul therapy leads to the strengthening of the sheep. We saw its essence in the stated ministry of Jesus (Luke 4:18-19), a quote from Isaiah 61:1-2a.

Obviously, therefore, soul therapy is never done for one who is still an unbeliever. It is for someone who has accepted Jesus, yet his life is still carnal. When a man is lost he needs the gospel. He needs to be evangelized. In light of 2 Peter 2:22, we might liken trying to perform soul therapy on an unregenerate man to be like washing a pig which, immediately after, will wallow in the same mud and look as if it had never been washed.

ILLUSTRATION - EPBOM'S MODEL OF EDIFICATION

Cradle to Grave Care & Follow-up

Follow-up is a continual process at EPBOM. From the moment a newcomer is registered, throughout his Christian development, he is continually followed-up. It might be viewed as a cradle to grave follow-up.

As noted earlier, when visiting a local church service, the newcomer is introduced and honored at some early stage of the church service. This holds true whether the service is a service of edification, a service of exhortation, a healing service, or the normal Sunday service. Afterwards, they are asked to come forward and together they are taken for an interview with an evangelist. This is unlike the typical evangelical invitation where individuals come forward to receive specific ministry. Here, all newcomers are requested to come forward to be led out en masse to meet with members of the Department of Mass Evangelization who will register them and set up follow-up appointments, generally within the next two to three days. If the newcomer fails to keep the appointment with the evangelist, the evangelist goes to the address provided to seek him out. Those who come forward during an invitation for salvation are again registered in a similar manner and a follow-up appointment is made. Newcomers to cells are followed-up by the cell leader within a few days of their first visit to either present them with salvation or establish them in the cell.

What happens when a newcomer accepts the Lord? We saw earlier how the evangelist would begin three to four weeks of clinical evangelization, meeting with the person regularly and referring him to the appropriate ministry department during this time for additional intensive follow-up in areas of need the evangelist discovered. At the same time, he is assigned to a cell where the cell leader begins the sixteen-week cycle of weekly home visits using the book, *Follow-up of the New Christian at Home.* During this time he is additionally enrolled in a pre-baptismal training class which meets for six months for basic training. If, during these days, areas of strongholds are discerned beyond the ability of the cell leader to handle, they are once again referred for additional ministry to the appropriate ministry department.

The cell leader and interns give individual soul therapy to those having specific problems requiring deeper ministry. All through the week, follow-up visits are organized in the homes of the cell members. Each visit generates a report to the cell leader. This gives him a general idea of the cell's life and will

Chapter 11 ☛ *Prepare the Program of God - Edification*

help him, in turn, prepare a report for his Sector Leader.

How often are visits made? Sometimes the Cell Leaders visit once a week. Sometimes they could go throughout the week. They will take as much time as necessary to take care of the people God has entrusted to them. They believe that regardless of the amount of time the person needs you, you must be there. During those impossible and inconvenient times when people call for help, Cell Leaders go anyway. How important is this follow-up by the cell leader? Boka shares the following true incident:

> There was a man who was going to hang himself. Very early in the morning before going to work his the cell intern thought, "I should go visit him before going to work." It was early in the morning. He discovered that the man was getting ready to hang himself. If a cell intern is really listening to the Word of God, God will tell him what is going on with those around him. The real problem is that we look at the time our work demands and we say, "Oh I'm tired! Oh, what else do I have to do?" We look at those things rather than God. When God has trust in a leader, He will speak to him. God will give him the time to do his work, regardless of the kind of work he has to do. The majority of our leaders have secular jobs. However, when they come home from work, they take the time necessary to visit and take care of their people. (Interview)

Follow-up is not only the responsibility of the cell leader and the interns. If someone brings a friend who accepts the Lord, the one who has brought the newcomer is to view that new believer as his own son. Jesus said that we are no longer born of blood, but we are born of the will of God. This friend must now do everything to help that new believer grow and to make that person a brother. After all, he was the one who brought him into the family of God.

What happens when someone is delivered? The same process is followed. If it occurs at a crusade, the demonologists do their work and release the individual from bondage. After the individual is set free and before he is allowed to leave, he is registered by others from the Department of Demonology. Basic information such as his name, address, strongholds, and demons from which he was delivered are all recorded. The information is correlated and passed on to a cell leader in the appropriate geographical area for immediate follow-up. Follow-up is made to verify the completeness of the deliverance, to enroll the individual in the cell, and to do whatever is necessary to ensure that the new fruit remains and is not lost.

During the evening crusades at CIAMEL 2000, I observed four divisions of demonologists comprised each of 100 four-member teams involved in the deliverance each night of those coming forward. In addition to the 400 demonologists doing deliverance, an additional 100 demonologists were there to register the people who had been set free.

Such a comprehensive system of follow-up ensures that the fruit won for the Kingdom remains. However, simply fruit that remains is not the ultimate goal. The process is not complete until that fruit is trained, discipled, and in turn bears more fruit.

Soul Therapy

EPBOM views the fundamental work of the church and the pastor as consisting of getting close to the sheep with a view towards soul therapy. The first priority of God is to win the lost. The second priority is to take care of those who have been won. In practical terms, taking care of those who have been won entails spending time with the sheep. This means spending time with broken hearts in need of healing. This means taking whatever time is necessary with those who are captive to demons or other vices, in order to deliver them. This means coming alongside of those who are in anguish, depressed, sickly, oppressed by Satan, who need to be liberated by the word of consolation and given spiritual stability. This means engaging in soul therapy.

The ministries of soul therapy and deliverance are under the authority of the Department of Demonology . Pastor Wouehi Louan Etienne oversees that department. Pastor Etienne has quite an unusual history, and is quite an unusual man. Before examining the practice of soul therapy and deliverance, listen to his story and hear his heart beat.

Pastor Wouehi Louan Etienne – Head of the Department of Demonology

Pastor Etienne is Yacobo, from the west of Cote d'Ivoire. According to his papers, he was born in 1959. However, that is not quite correct. Etienne went

Chapter 11 ☛ *Prepare the Program of God - Edification*

to first grade in Cote d'Ivoire. His problems began when he entered fourth or fifth grade. A fight took place between his parents and they tore up his papers. Without papers he could no longer attend school. Even as a young child he wanted to study. He saw his friends go to school, but he was no longer permitted to go. He was heartsick. In addition, because of what had happened, he no longer felt a part of his family. Although it was actually his older brother who tore up the papers, his father for some reason was unwilling at the time to re-do them. Although eventually they later gave Etienne new papers, according to the first papers that were destroyed, Etienne was born in 1956.

With the family situation such as it was, an older man took him to Liberia, where Etienne worked in his bar. The man and his family, of which Etienne was now a part, saw he was a very intelligent child. Etienne was interested in English and so started to speak a little bit. They were amazed that he was speaking English without even going to school.

The man had nine wives. He and his nine wives were continually mocking Etienne. Etienne did all the work in their house. His was, in a sense, truly a "Cinderella" existence, without the prince. It was two years before the man and his wives allowed Etienne to go to school. He studied in Liberia, completing high school and continuing to study technology and mechanical engineering. He received a DRT in mechanical engineering in Liberia. Having acquired his DRT, Etienne decided to return home to his native country, Cote d'Ivoire.

Upon returning, he was shocked to learn that all of his studies in Liberia were rejected. The teaching system between the two countries was totally different. His career evaporated before his very eyes. Faced with the choice of either returning to Liberia or starting over, he decided to stay and start once again from scratch. He had never really liked living in Liberia. He could have stayed there to work, but his heart was in Cote d'Ivoire. He began to read and learn French. He also began to break into Cote d'Ivoire society. Though it took many years, slowly he began to be accepted by those around him.

His parents started going to church in 1975. Because of the problems between Etienne and them he didn't like their church. He thought to himself, "They wronged me. They hurt me. Now, they are going to church? What they are doing is not good."

Etienne entered upon a life of rebellion, drinking alcohol excessively. Because he was hurt, he found his consolation with older women. But God had not forgotten him. He had been preparing Etienne. The Lord brought Etienne to a service at Alogard where he heard the Word and gave his life to Jesus. Jesus also immediately gave strong consolation, comfort, and healing for his wounded heart.

The Lord continued to move over his life. A new struggle, a different struggle began to rise within his heart. While seeking work in the world he did not find joy, only sadness. But, when he participated in the evangelization programs of the church, when the world was behind him and God was doing great things through him, he experienced great joy. During these times of ministry Etienne would not have to lay his hands on people, only speak from a distance, and people would be healed. He had numerous conversations where the pastors over him would say, "God has called you." But Etienne would respond, "No, I do not as yet have work." They would counter, "We don't think work is the will of God for you." When Etienne would go out looking for work, he would always experience problems. On the other hand, when he would go with the pastors he experienced constant joy. It is strange that though we experience joy in the Lord, our hearts too often stray elsewhere toward what can never really satisfy. Etienne was about to experience this truth.

In 1987 Etienne sought work at a development bank. They said he needed to be trained to work with computers. They wanted to send him to France to work and study. First, however, he had to pass their test. Though Etienne had good relations with his leaders, he actually hid from the church. He didn't want the people from the church to know what was happening. They already knew how God was working through him when he was with them. But he wanted to work. He was told that on the 3rd of July, 1987, he was to go and obtain the results of his test. France was but a step away.

On the 2nd of July Etienne was called to go to court. There was a problem. He went, thinking that from there he was going to go and get his test results. He arrived early at the court, only to have to wait a long time. Finally, at 12:30 p.m. they saw him. Seven minutes later they arrested him. They told him, "You are going to prison, because there was a young boy that was burned in your neighborhood and you are guilty." He cried out, "No, I am not guilty. I am a pastor. I am not guilty."

Etienne spent the next two months in prison. It was a time of training. During the previous months of 1987, Etienne had served in pastoral training. Yet, regardless of the training, his heart was divided between spiritual ministry and secular work. It was during those two fateful months in prison that Etienne decided to serve God. He wrote Pastor Dion and said he wanted to be an interpreter. Dion told him it was not yet time, that the work was still small. However,

Chapter 11 ☛ *Prepare the Program of God - Edification*

he assured him that God would put him to work. Etienne was released from prison the 29th of August, 1987.

Of course, after two months in prison his training in France with the bank was no loner possible. However, God sent him to France anyway. He was sent to France by the church to work under one of EPBOM's pastors. In France the two men worked together and put feet to the Department of Demonology. Since that time in 1987, Pastor Etienne has been in the Department of Demonology. At first they only numbered thirty-seven men and women. Now they number in excess of 1,124 people. They work throughout Cote d'Ivoire and wherever else their churches are found.

The Practice of Soul Therapy

Pastor Etienne likens soul therapy to a surgical operation performed in the life of a new believer:

> After he says, "Hey, what can I do to be saved?" that is when we do soul therapy. That is where we do surgery. In surgery, in an operation, that is where it hurts. You like smoking. You like it a lot. You didn't think you could ever separate from it. It is as if we have operated on you. Against your own desires, but because of Jesus, you'll abandon it. "Oh, pastor it is not easy!" "Take courage. Three days. It will work." Little by little he abandons it. He is a thief and he steals. When he steals he then dresses well. In soul therapy we discover that he steals. We tell him, "Stop stealing. God doesn't like it. The thief will not go to heaven." We will read the Bible about what God says about the thief. "If you continue to steal you will not be in agreement with God. If you continue to steal, you will be troubled." He says, "Oh, really. So I need to stop stealing and abandon it." Now Satan at the same time says, "How are you going to dress now?" So, it becomes a fight. Soul therapy is fighting, fighting in the spiritual war. Satan says to steal, but he won't steal. "Steal!" "I won't steal!" It is a fight. That is soul therapy. (Interview)

Soul therapy presupposes a spiritual battle. A sheep fighting against the adversary is desperately seeking and needing support, security and direction from his leaders. "To render the soul of a sheep clean we must come against 3 forces: strongholds, reasoning and arrogance" (Robert, Soul Therapy 46).

In the lives of God's people there are often strongholds that need to be torn down. They may be demonic hereditary ties. They may involve some form of demonization by evil spirits. Through soul therapy these strongholds can be torn down and the man or woman of God freed from bondage and enslavement by the powers of darkness.

Through 2 Corinthians we understand that men through reasoning and speculation create fortresses in their thinking that are not submitted to Christ. There are many people in the church whose lives are not submitted to the gospel, but who live on the basis of reason that is contrary to the word of God. It is necessary to use soul therapy to destroy all forms of reasoning. The intent is to accomplish total submission to the Word of God in place of religious and philosophical practices that lead them astray.

Wherever there is arrogance or a lack of humility, spiritual instability will exist. God resists the proud but gives grace to the humble. Through soul therapy, the child of God can be led to a life of humility under the mighty hand of God.

The practice of soul therapy also presupposes an intimate caring relationship on the part of a pastor with one of his sheep. Soul therapy then becomes the practical application of pastoral love and concern. For that to happen there must be trust between the one applying soul therapy and the one to whom it is applied. As Pastor Etienne illustrates, soul therapy employs the use of testimony, the Bible, and encouragement in the context of a caring, loving relationship:

> You do not do soul therapy just because it needs to be done. You can't say, "Come here! I want to do soul therapy for you." Even if you are going to do soul therapy, you propose yourself as someone who can help the other person spiritually. "I would like to give you some spiritual counsel so you can be strong spiritually, so the devil will be under your feet." He will be encouraged then.
>
> When he comes, you know he is a carnal Christian. As a pastor, I know he is a carnal Christian. So, I start with testimonies. I tell him this is what Jesus did in the life of this per-

Chapter 11 ☛ *Prepare the Program of God - Edification*

son. We read the Scripture and I give practical testimonies. He is touched. "Oh, what He did for that one, He can do for me too?" So he abandons this or that thing. But, if you said, "Why did you do this? Oh, you are always going out, leave this, leave this!" he won't be able to abandon this. But, you see him and ask, "Are you well? Are you well? Are you sleeping? Do you have a subject of prayer to give to me?" He answers, "Yes, I have a subject. No I am not sleeping well. My spirit is troubled." Then we say, "Oh, I want to pray for you." There is no problem. We pray and then I leave and I tell him to come back another day. But when he leaves I am praying for him, "Lord, he is going to come, open his heart." He comes back and I give a testimony and tell him I would like to help him. I think there is something there. I would like to help him set his spirit free. He may be ready right on the spot, or it may be that he would like to go and think about it. All of this is little by little until it is finished.

We do soul therapy with the Bible. We do not do it with our own knowledge. I may do soul therapy with someone and not know his intellectual level. If I just explain my experiences, perhaps he would think, "Oh, that is a small man. He knows nothing." But, I use the Bible and I say, "Read the Bible." I give him the Bible and he reads it and I explain it. "Oh, is that it?" If the person is not proud, then he says, "That is it. Help me." Then we pray together and have prayer for fighting and intercession so that God will do His work. For soul therapy to be effective, the person must embrace obedience. In soul therapy you must know each one of your sheep well. You must give care to your flock. It is the relationship. (Interview)

Pastor Dion is clear on the distinction between merely being acquainted with the sheep and knowing the sheep. Soul therapy will only work if the one applying it knows the one to whom it is being applied and is full of love for them:

> In a church, the pastor must not merely be acquainted with his sheep but must, instead, know them. To know one's sheep

is to know what is in the depth of his being (his hurts, his wounds, his worries, his joys, etc.). If we want to have a mission or a church that is spiritual and has stable sheep, we must work to know each of our sheep in order to take better care of them. (Soul Therapy 24)

Deal with the broken hearts that need to be healed. Work with those who are captive to demons or other vices. Care for those who are in anguish, depressed, sickly, oppressed by Satan, who need to be liberated by the word of consolation and given spiritual stability. The fundamental work of the church or the pastor consists of getting close to the sheep with a view towards soul therapy. (Soul Therapy 25)

You must bring the people to practice love and sharing. For it would be nothing to have community where the people are indifferent one to another. You know that with the goal of evangelization we say, "Come to the Lord. You who are tired and burdened, come." If they come and no one takes care of them, love is not shared, it is finished. You must take care of their problems. It is in this way, through soul therapy, that love is applied. You must love them to set them free. You must love them to work with their problems, which are very deep, and heal the brokenhearted, free them from the powers of darkness and share with them what we have. The life of sharing - sharing their sufferings, that is where soul therapy is necessary. That is where the sharing of life is necessary (Interview).

Soul Therapy and Deliverance – Fruits and Roots

In their ministry of soul therapy and deliverance, those involved make a clear distinction between what might be called "fruits" and "roots", that is, presenting symptoms and underlying causes:

Here within our church, when we first started with the life of the church, the life of the Spirit, there were certain ones of our workers that, when someone with a ring came forward, he just came forward, he hasn't accepted Jesus, they haven't announced the gospel, the worker says, "Hey, this ring, this ring, take it off! It is Satan. It is witchcraft." However, the problem is not in the ring, but in his heart. Maybe he took the ring as a fetish to protect himself from accidents or witches. It is not his finger or his ring that is the problem. It is his heart. If his heart understands, then he himself will take his ring off and get rid of it forever. But if you say, "Take it off, take it off, take it off, take it off! It is not good! Hallelujah! Take it off!", then he will go and take it off, but he will hide it. He didn't take it off in his heart. It is still there. That is our central point. Everywhere God spoke about our holiness, it is our spirit. There is no sanctification without deliverance of the spirit. When the spirit is freed, then we can be totally freed.

In Crusades like CIAMEL, we have first the pastor who preaches the gospel. He is going to do evangelization. He is going to give the foundations of evangelization. Now the people will come forward. We will introduce them to evangelization. From there they entrust them to us. They continue to come to us and we entrust them to a cell. The work that is done there, we also do our work here. So, through our work we have attacked his spirit. We make him understand things by teaching. He comes to church and he hears this. Then, after one month, two months, three months, he says, "Oh, I understand!" Now he remains. (Etienne, Interview)

CHALLENGING THE INEFFECTIVENESS OF OUR OWN SYSTEM

As disciples, imitating as we have seen the life of Christ, there should likewise be no areas in our lives that could be laid claim to by the devil. For a disciple to claim to abide in Christ is to conduct life "in the same manner (καθως)" as Jesus (1 John 2:6). Can a disciple indeed live like this? Our experience would inform our theology that it is not possible. This is the sad state of the American church. However, theology should challenge our experience to change, not vice versa.

It has been my observation that the American church in general has allowed new believers to remain bound by strongholds they developed prior to their conversion. Relatively few cell churches to date have adopted a systematic approach like EPBOM's system of soul therapy to deal with fleshly and demonic strongholds in the life of new believers.

Because the church lacks a system for cleaning up the lives of babes in Christ, new believers are allowed to walk the majority of their Christian life enslaved to habits and sins they should have otherwise been freed from early in their Christian experience. Could it be that many of the conflicts we experience and defeats we suffer in the church is because the devil still has beach heads in the lives of believers from where he launches his insidious attacks?

Three threads continually run through EPBOM's ministry of soul therapy: obedience, submission, and humility. For soul therapy to be effective, the person must embrace obedience. Remember that the goal of soul therapy is to bring the child of God to a life of humility under the mighty hand of God. The intent is to accomplish total submission to the word of God in place of religious and philosophical practices that lead them astray. We have clearly seen again the value system of EPBOM being both the basis for and the manifestation of its ministry, program, and practice. It is impossible to separate "what EPBOM is doing from their underlying values. One cannot merely embrace or adopt or mimic a ministry of soul therapy like EPBOM has developed without a commitment to relationship, obedience, submission, and humility. To do so would be to build a house of cards that would quickly fall.

Yet, in spite of this truth, numbers of pastors and church leaders come to Abidjan every year to observe the church. In particular they find fascinating the deliverance ministry the church is continually involved in. I say continually because deliverance is a normal part of life at EPBOM. I watched as demons manifested during the worship preceding a baptismal service in the church. Demons manifested during an exhortation for the offering during CIAMEL 2000. Demons manifested after the services during times of invitation. In every case, teams of cell leaders physically restrained and then removed the demonized individuals so they could receive ministry by deliverance teams, trained demonologists. While this fascinated and intrigued those from the West, the church simply went on with the Lord's work as those authorized dealt with the demonized. For them it was a common everyday experience.

Not content with simply observing the work of God, many attempt to export EPBOM's deliverance ministry back home. Home is often South Africa, England, the United States, Canada, or sometimes Europe. They look for techniques, principles of warfare, and names of demons. It is not the system itself. Deliverance, as we have seen, does not happen in a vacuum. The evangelists

Chapter 11 ☛ Prepare the Program of God - Edification

and/or cell leaders have first done their work. The intercessors are continually at work. At the large campaigns, hundreds of demonologists may be removing the demons, but scores of demonologists perform record keeping for those delivered before they are allowed to leave. This way immediate follow-up by evangelists or cell leaders can take place within the next 48 hours. Deliverance is not a separate ministry, but works in tandem with the rest of the Program of God as part of an on-going process of edification and sanctification.

Pastor Etienne likens deliverance without evangelization to children at play. How often in this country are men involved in deliverance ministries but there is no provision for follow up or a community in which total healing may be experienced by the one set free? God desires not only to liberate His children, but to keep them free and heal the affected areas. This can only be done as one is a part of small basic Christian communities, cells.

How aggressive the follow-up system at EPBOM must at first appear! How passive we are in our ministry! A large percentage of our visitors too often "fall through the cracks" in our churches. Who among us actively engage each visitor with the gospel before they leave our facilities? We hope they have heard enough in the services and mistakenly believe they will come seeking help when they are ready. How about our new converts, those new babies the Lord entrusts to us? How small a number of those who make professions we actually can find in our churches three months, six months or one year later. They may or may not be placed in a cell. Who will take responsibility for their immediate care and continual follow-up? Yet, we are somehow surprised when the devil woos them back into the world or eats them up for lunch.

We are challenged again by our African brothers to radically embrace the values of obedience, submission, humility, and relationship, and to then develop an integrated ministry in which soul therapy, deliverance, and follow-up will stand as essential elements. To not do so will be to continue to experience retarded growth personally, and in the life of the corporate body of Christ.

Perhaps it would be well for those of us who minister as shepherds on whatever level to review God's rebuke and admonition to His shepherds in Ezekiel 34. I quote in part:

> Those who are sickly you have not strengthened, the diseased you have not healed, the broken you have not bound up, the scattered you have not brought back, nor have you sought for the lost; but with force and with severity you have dominated

them. They were scattered for lack of a shepherd, and they became food for every beast of the field and were scattered. My flock wandered through all the mountains and on every high hill; My flock was scattered over all the surface of the earth, and there was no one to search or seek for them. (Ezekiel 34:4-6)

PHASE 1 — Prepare the Ethical Base

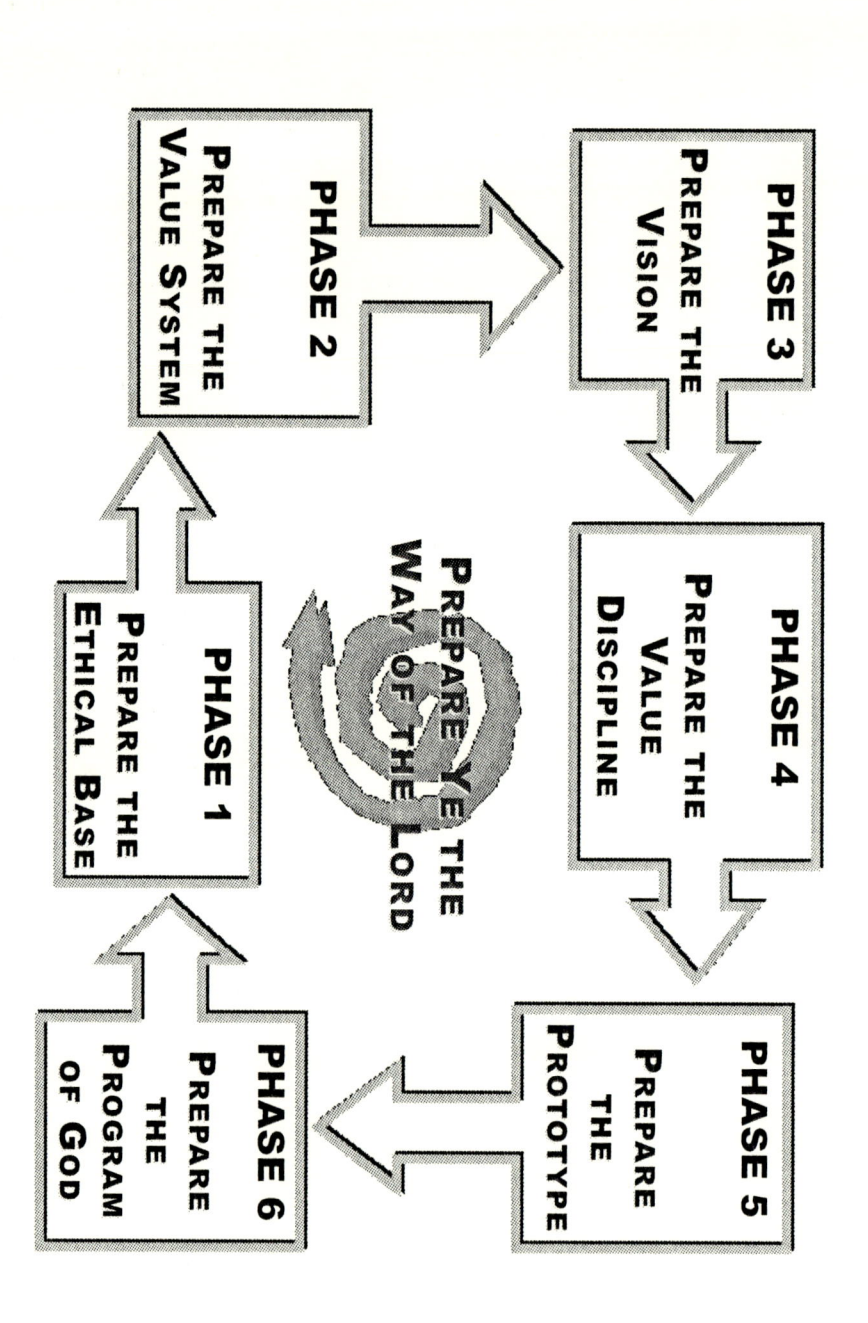

PHASE 2 — Prepare the Value System

PHASE 3 — Prepare the Vision

PHASE 4 — Prepare the Value Discipline

PHASE 5 — Prepare the Prototype

PHASE 6 — Prepare the Program of God

Prepare Ye the Way of the Lord

Preparing the 21st Century Church

12

PREPARE THE PROGRAM
OF GOD - EMPOWERING

And He called the twelve together, and gave them power and authority over all the demons and to heal diseases.
                    LUKE 9:1

291

Chapter 12 ☛ *Prepare the Program of God - Empowering*

EMPOWERING THE BODY OF CHRIST

Empowering Future Leaders

I find that a lack of leadership development is a constant problem I am faced with as a consultant. At whatever level leaders are not being developed, the growth of the cell church is inhibited at that level.

How do we empower leaders? First, we may empower others through our modeling. Our own ministry has been shaped and molded by those who have been our role models. Paul told the Corinthian church to imitate him even as he imitated Christ (1 Corinthians 4:16). Robert Logan has defined being a model in this way: "To model means to do something in such a way that others are: compelled to follow your example (inspiration) and empowered to follow your example (equipping)" (Releasing, 2-6).

Second, we may empower others as we come alongside and help them develop into all that God has called them to be. Those who are already trained, the minority, may be recruited. However, for the most part, those with potential must be identified and moved into the training process. A leadership training process must be established for a church to grow and remain healthy. The system must be reproducible and integrated with the teaching/training process the church develops.

Third, we are empowering others as we equip them for ministry. An apprentice mind-set must be developed. Leaders do not need assistants who will simply function as helpers. Leaders need leaders-in-training who will in time step up to the plate and serve as leaders themselves. An apprentice will experience what it is to lead. They will practice the roles and skills necessary, without having to carry the full weight of responsibility. Apprentice training will touch the head, the heart, and the hands of those trained. In other words, apprentice training must incorporate cognitive information, psycho-motor activities,and aim at transforming life and values. Additionally, the apprentice mind-set will necessitate the development of a coaching system that will ensure that the leader-in-training is properly cared for.

Fourth, leaders can become empowered as we release them into existing ministries. As they demonstrate proven ministry, they can be released as leaders in their own right.

ILLUSTRATION - EPBOM'S MODEL OF EMPOWERING LEADERS

Empowerment Through Modeling - Relational Discipleship

Discipleship is about relationship. Boka explains, "Discipleship is the relationship between the master and the student. If the student understands that he must receive from the master, then he will let himself be taught, oriented and led by the master. The student will work under the direction of the master."

Discipleship is more than the transmission of cognitive information. Discipleship at EPBOM includes the desire to impart to the disciple both character and ability, as well as information. Thus, discipleship is not primarily classroom oriented, but a lifestyle of relationship. Therefore, the goal of the master-disciple relationship at EPBOM is to become like the master in both character and ability. When one begins as a disciple, his character is unlike that of Jesus. In order to change, he must see the master living the character of Christ. Perhaps a situation will arise in which he sees the gentleness of his master. Through this example the master may bring his disciple to a better understanding of gentleness. The disciple learns that he himself lacks that gentle character which he observes in his master. Perhaps it is the first time that the disciple sees the calmness, wisdom and softness of the master in a trying situation. He may learn through inquiry. He may ask, "Why were you able to control yourself in that situation?" He learns that the ability to master oneself is in Christ alone. Maybe the disciple will see the master casting out demons. He asks, "How is this possible?" The master helps him understand that once you accept Christ, you have the power of a child of Christ and in His Name you can cast out demons. Then the disciple will begin to do likewise. Discipleship is seen as a sharing of the life of the master with the disciple.

Everything transmitted is a matter of practical life. When the disciple is faced with a hard situation, he doesn't have to say, "Pastor there is a problem here." He imitates exactly what he has learned. He may often err, but the master is there to correct them, little by little. In this way it allows him to imitate the life of Christ.

In the process of training, the master first works and the disciple watches. Second, the master works and the disciple helps, working alongside. Third, the disciple works and the master both helps and observes. Fourth, the disciple

Chapter 12 ☛ Prepare the Program of God - Empowering

works and the master does not work, but is present to descern further needs. He has had time to copy the master, to see how the master was working. Now the master observes so he can discern any corrections he needs to make in the disciple's work. Finally, the master goes away and the disciple himself becomes a disciple maker.

Empowerment Through Equipping and Release

We have observed earlier how new converts are trained both through the cell and weekly on a corporate level in what is called *Basic Training*. As they draw near to the completion of their cycle of discipleship, they are gathered together from many cells and introduced to the workings of the many departments of the church. Upon completion of their basic discipleship training, they are then released in accordance with their giftings to minister in one, and only one, of these many departments, thereby fulfilling their place in the corporate Body of Christ. Their discipleship training will continue on a weekly basis. The responsibility of their training will be transferred from their cell leader to someone within their chosen department. The content of their training at this point becomes much more specialized also. They are to work within each department manifesting the power of God through their giftings. Toward that end they must be further equipped. The goal at EPBOM is each person in a cell (the family), each person in a corporate ministry (the Body), and every ministry coordinated together and multiplied to "destroy the works of the devil and reconquer humanity for Jesus Christ" (the army).

Development of Leadership Character

The character and lives of the leadership at all levels at EPBOM are critical for the success of the work. They are called upon to demonstrate lives of consecration and faith so that they can lead others into the life of faith. The level of character expected for those serving in the Body, and especially leaders, is easily observable in the normal expectations placed upon those released as soul therapists, demonologists, and cell leaders.

First, what can be said about the lives of those involved in soul therapy? "In order to effectively accomplish this ministry, it is essential that the spirit of the pastor himself be regenerated and his soul healed, because we can only give away that which we have. The pastor must allow his spirit to be purified by the Word of God, and his soul and body must be under the influence of the Holy Spirit. It is as a result of this that the servant of God will, in turn, be capable of doing effective soul therapy" (Robert, Soul Therapy 18). Concerning the state of the soul of those involved in deliverance and soul therapy, Pastor Dion continues:

> If there is disorder in the church, it is very often in the area of marriage. If those making choices in this area refuse to obey scriptural principles on the subject, perhaps it is because the leaders themselves have spurned these principles in order to satisfy their own human desires, instead of leading people to the will of God. Our God is the greatest expert on the matter of soul therapy. We who are His servants must submit ourselves to Him so that this work of inner healing can function through us, because He has promised: "I will sprinkle clean water on you, and you will be clean: I will cleanse you from all your impurities and from all your idols. I will give you a new heart and put a new spirit in you; I will remove from you a heart of stone and give you a heart of flesh. And I will put my Spirit in you and move you to follow my decrees and be careful to keep my laws" (Ezekiel 36:25-27). (Soul Therapy 20)

Second, what character is demanded of the demonologist himself? Pastor Etienne records eleven basic character traits required of those involved in the ministry of deliverance (Demonologue Approuve, 3-12).

- The life should be characterized by repentance from sins formerly practiced (Ephesians 2:1-2).

- A demonologist must walk in honesty before God and man (Proverbs 11:1; Romans 12:17).

- Third, a lifestyle of obedience is indispensable for a demonologist. Disobedience is by its very nature demonic (1 Samuel 15:22-23).

Chapter 12 ☛ *Prepare the Program of God - Empowering*

- Sanctification is to be pursued as it is the will of God for each man, but especially critical for a demonologist (Hebrews 12:14; 1 Thessalonians 4:3).

- The confession, the words spoken, must at all times be proper. They give evidence of that which fills the heart and they defile the man (Matthew 15:18).

- Sixth and seventh, the life of the demonologist must be characterized by compassion (Philippians 2:4-5) and patience (2 Corinthian 1:6).

- The demonologist, to be effective, must be full of faith (Romans 10:17) and have a love for his spiritual brothers and sisters (1 John 4:20) whom he serves.

- Tenth, the demonologist must be regular in the discipline and exercise of fasting (Esther 4 & 5; Isaiah 58:6-14).

- Finally, his life must be characterized by courage (John 16:31-32). The specific details of this lifestyle are spelled out within the training material of the Demonology Department.

Third, the principles of life used at EPBOM to choose a cell leader are the same ones they use for choosing elders and deacons in any normal local church (1 Timothy 3:1-16). The cell leader is considered a shepherd and therefore expected to have certain qualities and abilities as a teacher of God's Word (1Timothy 4:8-16).

At first sight, this might seem by American standards to be a quite high and unattainable standard. It should be kept in mind that 40-60% of those in the cells are either cell leaders or are disciples in process of being trained as leaders (Faustin, Interview). Considering again the vast number of cell groups, a minimum of 14,000 adult cells augmented by an additional 4,000 children cells led by youth/children ages 15-21, and considering that the cells multiply every three to six months, that standard is in reality quite attainable. They appear to be very effective in continually raising up and empowering new leaders.

EPBOM has neither "raised the bar" so that it becomes unattainable by the average church member, nor have they "lowered the bar" so that anyone can easily attain it. What they have done is simply raise the basic level of discipleship throughout the church!

CHALLENGING THE INEFFECTIVENESS OF OUR OWN SYSTEM

The most prevalent cry I hear today from pastors concerns their lack of leaders. Is there really a dearth in the church of those capable of becoming interns and cell leaders and coaches? Their seems to be a more of a lack of those committed to empowerment than of those wanting to be empowered.

Just how committed are we to modeling? Do we burn with the desire to inspire others in their service of the Lord? Do we live in such a way that others are compelled by our life example to follow? The issue is not one of having a charismatic versus a non-charismatic personality. We have a plethora of heroes on the scene today. We have sports heroes. Our heroes from 9/11 are now fireman and policeman and rescue personnel. These are hot market items for kids today. Where are the heroes of the faith that inspire to service, to sacrifice, even to martyrdom? Must we only look back to past generations for inspiration? Must we only look backward to such men and women as Nicholas Von Zinzendorf, or John Wesley, or Praying Hyde, or Amy Carmichal? Where are the heroes in the church? EPBOM has men like Jonas Kouassi, Boka Faustin, and Wouehi Louan Etienne. Just how committed are we to modeling and providing inspiration and life for others?

How committed are we to spending time with a disciple and pouring into that man or woman the life of God? Even the cell leaders at EPBOM take whatever amount of time is necessary during the week to build up and care for those they are mentoring. The exchange of life necessary to empower others does not happen in fifteen, thirty or even sixty minutes a week during a formal time of meeting. It flows during the course of a lifestyle wherein the master and disciple minister together. Where the disciple is able to observe the life of the master. It happens in the course of a relationship lived out in community.

PHASE 2
PREPARE THE VALUE SYSTEM

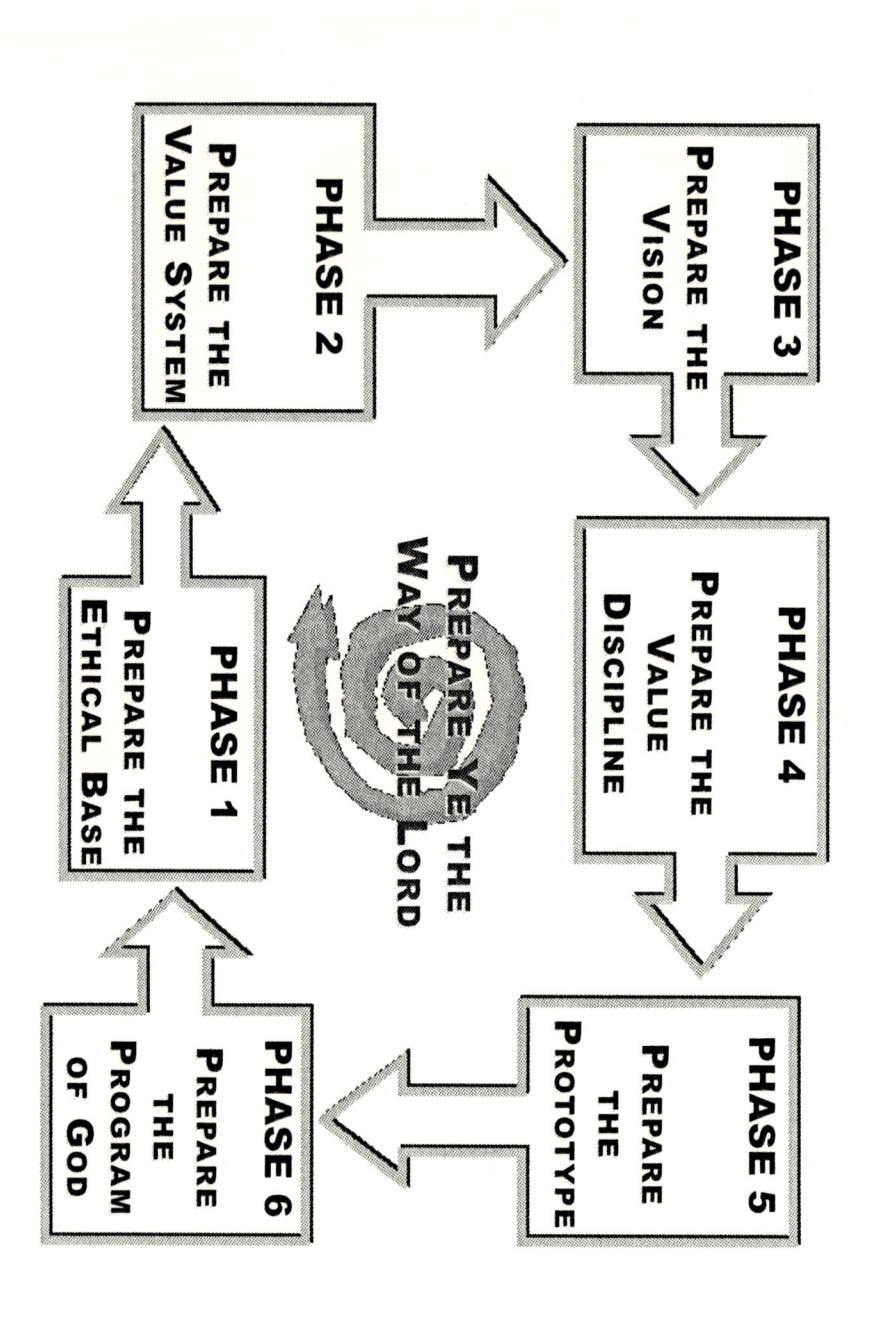

PHASE 3
PREPARE THE VISION

PHASE 4
PREPARE THE VALUE DISCIPLINE

PHASE 1
PREPARE THE ETHICAL BASE

Prepare Ye The Way Of The Lord

PHASE 5
PREPARE THE PROTOTYPE

PHASE 6
PREPARE THE PROGRAM OF GOD

Prepare the Program
of God - Every Member

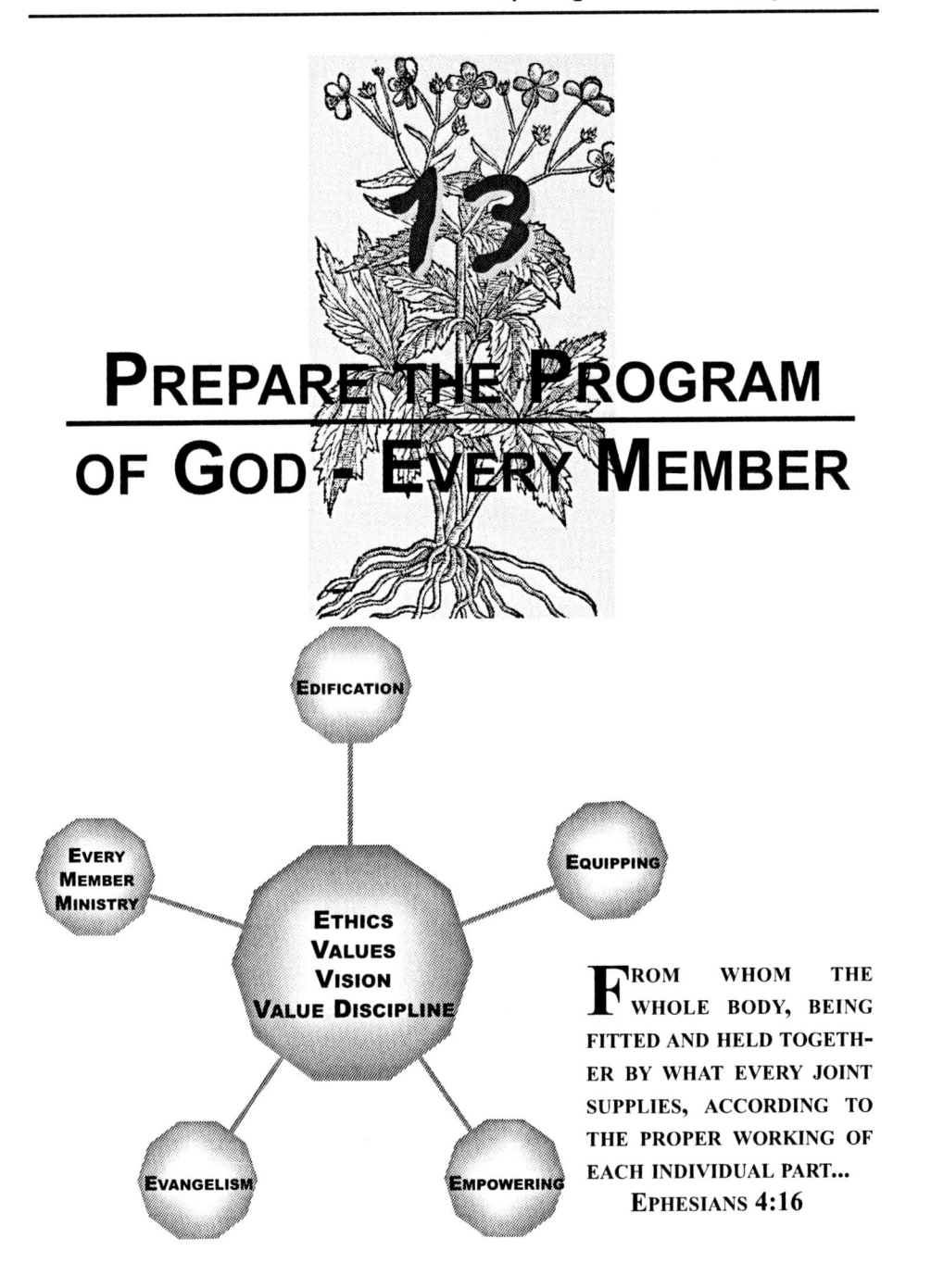

- Edification
- Every Member Ministry
- Equipping
- Ethics / Values / Vision / Value Discipline
- Evangelism
- Empowering

> From whom the whole body, being fitted and held together by what every joint supplies, according to the proper working of each individual part...
> Ephesians 4:16

Chapter 13 ☛ Prepare the Program of God - Every Member Ministry

RELEASING THE BODY OF CHRIST

Organism & Organization - Cell and Corporate Body

The biblical model of the church is that of an organism, not an organization. What is the difference between organization and organism? Why does it make a difference, anyway? Is the difference at all important?

An organization can be thought of as a group of people organized for some end or some work. It has structure and composition. It is characterized by a systematic arrangement of its parts. Organization is to mass what streets are to a growing city. By contrast, an organism is a form of life. It is composed of mutually dependent parts that maintain its various vital processes. Its properties and functions are determined by the character of the whole, as well as of the parts, and by the relationships of the individual parts to the whole. Organizations have great difficulty functioning on the basis of spiritual gifts. Organisms can more easily function according to giftedness.

As an organism, the church which must operate with every part in dependency upon every other part. Every part of the body must operate with humility of mind, aware that that each part will have separate functions as it is graced by the Holy Spirit (I Corinthians 12:12-30 and Romans 12:3-6). It is the leadership that God has given to the body to help perfect the body for service. That leadership must understand how God has so composed the body if they would help perfect and release it into service.

Understanding the difference between organism and organization is critical for understanding the relationship of the cells to the corporate body. The cell must not stand alone. It must be related to the corporate whole. Because the church is an organism rather than an organization, the whole (the corporate church) is greater than the sum of its parts (the totality of the cells). Although the whole does not exist apart from its cells, neither does the whole exist solely or even primarily for the benefit of the cell. The whole is greater than the totality or the sum of its cells. This is often misunderstood by those becoming involved in cell church. Even churches with a good cell system may still function on a corporate level like any traditional church. Too often it is erroneously believed that the corporate exists primarily for the benefit of the cell, that the corporate is there somehow simply to support the work of the cells. Paul noted (1Cor. 15:46) that, "the spiritual is not first, but the natural; then the spiritual."

In this vein, God has provided for us an illustration in our own human bodies of the valid relationship between cell and body in the cell church.

Just as the manifestational gifts of the Spirit are the primary way in which each individual cell is built up and edified, so what may be described as functional gifts (Romans 12:4-6) are expressed for the common building up of the local corporate Body of Christ. In the passage just noted, Paul employs an analogy from the human body to describe how Christ's body should function. The physical body, though one, has many members. Christ's body, though one, is also comprised of many members.

In the natural scheme of things, Paul reminds us that each member of the physical body has a definite function. His word which we translate as function, *praxis* (πραξιν), can be defined as "a deed, the action of which is looked upon as incomplete and in progress". Thus, we can look at the function of the heart, and understand that the heart is set in the body having a specific action to perform, an action which is incomplete and in progress. Aren't we glad that the function of our heart has not been completed and and its progress terminated? We would be dead! In like manner, each member of the body has an activity to perform and keep on performing. Paul states that "all the members do not have the same function" (Romans 12:4). Employing that same analogy, he goes on to state that we who are members of the Body of Christ have "gifts that differ according to the grace given to us" (Romans 12:5). Just as each natural body member is to continue to function, so also each member of the Body of Christ is to function, exercising their giftings. Their giftings express their function within the Body. As this takes place, we find that "...the whole body, being fitted and held together by that which every joint supplies, according to the proper working of each individual part, causes the growth of the body for the building up of itself in love" (Ephesians 4:16). To the degree that any part of the body does not fulfill its function, to that degree the body is paralyzed and dysfunctional. This holds true both in the natural and spiritual realms.

The bottom line is this. The local church, if it is to truly function as a healthy body, must mobilize its members and release them into ministry corresponding to their spiritual giftings. Each member must be mobilized to exercise their gifts according to the grace given them by the Lord. What might this look like in a highly developed cell church? *Eglise Protestante Baptiste Oeuvres et Mission Internationale* provides us with an excellent illustration of a cell church who has balanced both the cell and corporate wing of the church while operating out of a gift-based ministry paradigm! To their model we now turn for inspiration.

Chapter 13 ☞ Prepare the Program of God - Every Member Ministry

ILLUSTRATION - EPBOM'S MODEL OF MOBILIZATION

The Incarnational Manifestation of the Gift of the Spirit

The leadership's understanding of EPBOM is that of an organism composed of mutually dependent parts that maintain its various vital processes. Its properties and functions are determined by the character of the whole, as well as of the parts, and by the relationships of the individual parts to the whole. They understand how God has composed their body.

Unfortunately, the majority of those visiting and observing EPBOM focus on the departmental structure. An American bank officer, having spent time in Abidjan observing EPBOM exclaimed that their model was little different than the bank structure she was already use to. Dion could only shake his head in dismay.

Others have erroneously concluded that the ministries of the other departments support EPBOM's basic cell structure. That thinking places the emphasis on the cells. Other structures are then created to support the cells. This is simply not so. They are mutually interdependent. Though the vast majority of local churches in the United States function more as organizations than as organisms, that simply is not the case with EPBOM. It is incorrect to explain their life using our organizational and structural paradigms. They function out of an organism paradigm, not an organizational paradigm.

They see the departments as incarnations of the manifestations of spiritual gifts. Thus Dion can say that every element of the structure must be the manifestation of a gift. It is the practice of a gift. The gifts of the people are discovered through the cell. The gifts of the people are then expressed through the departments. The structure becomes the means whereby God can express His nature through His gifts. Every member is mobilized and released into a single area of corporate ministry, that is, they express and practice their gifts within the department which is the incarnation of the manifestation of that spiritual gift. There their training continues and their ministry grows. It is organic. It is based upon an organic understanding of the body of Christ and an embracing of a gift-based ministry paradigm.

While historically the church has been guilty of over emphasizing the corporate group almost to the exclusion of the small group, the cell, today, the error of over emphasizing the place and nature of the cell is easily entered into. EPBOM maintains a balanced view of the church as both individual cell and corporate Body. While there can be no Body without cells, the structures of the Body do not exist for the pleasure of the cells. EPBOM has provided us with a clear picture of the interconnectedness and interdependence of cell and body life. We would do well to frequently remember that picture as we develop our own cell churches in America

We would normally look at the manifestation of the gifts of God, the structure of the church, and the mobilization of the people of God as related only peripherally. Yet at EPBOM, they are intimately interwoven and flow from one to the other. They cannot be separated.

Dion is clear in his teaching. Every element of the structure must be the manifestation of a gift. It is the practice of a gift. The gifting is the manifestation of the actions of God through the church. The different elements of the structure, what we call his departments, are actually for Dion the incarnation of the manifestation of a spiritual gift. For example, the Department of Evangelization is a gift. Through evangelization God is manifested to save the lost. The same holds true with the Department of Demonology. The Department of Demonology is a structure that God has given to set free those who are captives. Within the Department of Demonology is the Division of Soul Therapy. They cast out demons, heal the sick, open the eyes of the blind, communicate the year of the Lord's favor, and transmit the life and power of God so that everything the lost have really lost may be regained through Christ.

As we look at a structural overview of EPBOM, remember that the vast majority of the workers in every one of these departments are lay people. Every one without exception is also active in a cell where they have initially been discipled and are continuing to live out their New Testament community life. Having discovered their spiritual gifts, they have then been released to serve in a department corresponding to their gifting. They work effectively because they work through the manifestation of the power of God.

Structural Overview of EPBOM

We might view the creation of a structure to be simply a reflection of a man-made methodology for carrying out a God given vision. However, in the case of Dion, he considers even the instructions detailing the structure to have been given to him by God in a way parallel to how God gave Moses the exact specifications for the building of the Tabernacle. Of this structure he says:

Chapter 13 ☞ *Prepare the Program of God - Every Member Ministry*

All of this must be done in the frame of a structure according to God, not according to my wisdom, but according to God. If I did base it on what God programmed, then God will always be with me. But if it is myself, then God says I am not in it. I am a servant of what God says. I bring the people to what God says. The structure must be based on the structure of God (Interview).

The following departmental descriptions are summarized from Dion's book, *Working According to the Model* (45-60).

- The Local Church Department coordinates all the activities of the local churches in their care, orientation, implantation and strengthening. The Local Church Department follows up on the needs of the local churches and ties them one to another exactly like they were in the New Testament.

- The Teaching Department is charged with maintaining the people in the vision of the work and in the will of God, training workers to guarantee revival, growth and the maturity of the Church. In so doing, they are concerned with the continual inspiration and instruction of future missionaries, and the teaching of the people with a view toward embracing the vision of God.

- The Department of Mass Evangelization brings about an evangelism that is general and individual, targeting evangelism to the masses.

- The Youth Department has recently been renamed from the Children's Department. God, through His Church, wants to take care of the children (ages 7 through 19), the seeds of today and the plants of tomorrow. These grains must be preserved from all attacks and from all corruption. For this to happen, the same work that takes place at the level of adults must take place with the children. In place of the traditional" Sunday School", EPBOM has instituted a complete ministry: Evangelism, Teaching, Deacons, Demonology, Cell, Ushers, Women's Ministry, Music, Financial Administration, etc. All departments of the church are replicated within the Youth Department to function with children/youth. For example, when the youth/children have a crusade, those preaching are part of the Department of Evangelization under the auspices of the Youth Department. The same holds true for the demonologists who will be children. The children will facilitate the worship and the choir will be comprised of children. Those saved will be placed into cells led by children and overseen by children sector leaders. The children's cells (more than 4,000) are accountable to a Pastor within the Youth Department who is over the Children's Cell Department, rather than directly to Pastor Boka.

- The Women's Department is concerned with making women disciples of the Lord to the end that the church would become stable and triumphant over worldliness and spiritual darkness. Leaders from within the Women's Department serve as representatives within all the other departments to ensure that each department ministers to the needs of women. In addition, the Women's Department organizes special functions for the special needs of women.

- The ministry of Jesus in spreading the Kingdom of God rested on the destruction of the works of the devil. Thus EPBOM has created a Department of Demonology. Every local church is to promote the ministry of deliverance through which the freeing power of Christ is manifested. Within the Department of Demonology the Division of Intercession prays day and night. The Division of Soul Therapy takes care of inner healing. The Division of Combat casts out demons and breaks demonic ties.

- In a local church, a ministry devoted to couples and the family is very important. At EPBOM this ministry is

Chapter 13 — *Prepare the Program of God - Every Member Ministry*

accomplished through the Marriage Department. This department is occupied with training, reconciliation, restoration, and the counsel for couples. Couples solidly planted in Christ give birth to a stable local church.

- Activities in the Department of Hospital Evangelization focus on bringing the gospel of hope, comfort and healing to the sick within hospitals and clinics.

- At the example of the Department of Hospital Evangelism, the Department of Prison Evangelization was formed as an arm of Jesus held out through His Church towards the prisoners. It is very important to bring the gospel in a sober, serious and consecrated manner to the prisoners who are in penitentiary detention centers.

- The Department of Traditions and Religions is a ministry designed to help all those who come out of religions or previous sects, providing correct teaching that is based on the Bible and in the knowledge of the true God in Jesus Christ.

- The ministry of the Deacon Department provides many services including but not limited to: discipline within the church, the organization of weddings, celebrations, funerals, care of widows and orphans, fiancées, reception of visitors, housing of guests, and assistance in social cases. The deacons neither displace the pastor nor do they control the pastor. They are truly servants at the service of the pastors.

- The church, in its need of relating to other institutions both public and private, has created the Department of Public Relations. Their ministry on behalf of the church requires that they know and understand public law, civic law and penal law. Admitting that the church needs authorization for public activities, or a letter of allocation for land in view of building a temple or a medical center, it is the Department of Public Relations who is in charge of all these necessary steps. This permits other ministers to occupy themselves with the aspects of the ministry. The efficiency of the Department of Public Relations permits the social development of the church in a way that appears as valuable in the eyes of society. EPBOM has developed a tremendous reputation in Cote d'Ivoire, even at the highest levels of government. CIAMEL 2000 was officially opened by a Cabinet Minister speaking on behalf of the President of the country. That same Minister, along with his entourage and military escort, was unofficially in attendance a number of other times during the week and, as an official representative of the government, spoke once more at the closure.

- God is a God of order. This places an imperative demand upon the church for an Ushers Department. The Ushers Department assures surveillance, maintains order, takes care of the place where the services are held, receives the visitors with a view toward orienting them, gives information, and takes care of security for the services of the church (retreats, crusades, evangelism, conferences etc.).

- God declares that silver and gold belong to Him. Therefore, financial management of a local church requires great care, integrity and wisdom. In some aspects, the management of a local church is no different than the management of an enterprise in secular society. However, those who administer this responsibility as the Department of Financial Administration must add faith to the principles of management and be constantly diligent of the priorities of the Lord in view of their ministry.

- The Department of Patrimony occupies themselves with the management of and inventory of the goods of God in the local church.

- To be efficient and complete, the structure of a local church

Chapter 13 ☞ *Prepare the Program of God - Every Member Ministry*

must include the ministry of secretarial services. Those so involved are part of the Department of Secretarial Services.

- Through the Department of Social Works the church has developed medical works, schools, and agricultural fields to help their members to be balanced socially and spiritually. Through this department, members of the church are trained and then released either back into the secular marketplace or into one of the aforementioned works the church is involved in.

- The Department of Mass Media plays a prominent role in the growth of the church by publishing journals, literature, audio and visual cassettes, and operating the sound system for the special events.

- In the work of God, music occupies a very honorable place. The church must watch over what is praise to God so that it does not take on the same color or the same connotation as the pagans or as the world. This is why it is important to institute a Department of Music ministry consecrated to the music in the church.

- The Cell Department is responsible for training the members of the church as disciples and for doing the work of follow-up through the cells.

The many departments that EPBOM has established do not make the church grow. They are not the life of the church. Neither, however, are they simply irrelevant or lifeless structures. They have been designed to serve a purpose. They help the average member understand why he is living and where he is going. Pastor Dion describes their usefulness in the life of his members:

> God did not create man for uncertainties. Uncertainties bring about questions, and that brings about a void. One who is saved, who is trained, who is consecrated, who is taught, must see where he is going, what he is doing, what is his role, and

what must he do. By the structure we give the rule to each one, the way that each one is occupied. When man is not busy, there is monotony, there is passivity, there is discouragement, there is destruction, and finally his life can become other things. That is why you must have a good structure. The structure must always follow the plan of God, the program of God that the Lord has given. Everyone must attach himself to an element within the structure of the program. He must know why he is living and what is he doing.

So, when he is attached to an element of the program that he is accomplishing, then he goes from victory to victory, from progress to progress and victory is there. God will use him to accomplish His will. The structure must be based upon the program of the Lord. It's not programs that we invent. It must be what is based on the Word of God. The church must be structured in that way. When the church is organized other than the program that the Lord has given, the revival is stopped, because it doesn't come from God, but from man. When it is based upon what the Lord has left as a program, as a structure of His Kingdom, then the revival will continue and the people will become more and more effective. As a result, when the church is attacked we do not feel it so much. We triumph over it! (Interview)

The department structures at EPBOM are highly efficient and functional. Each one promotes the on-going multiplication of the entire ministry at EPBOM, not simply the ministry of its own department. Those who are leaders within the departments do not simply lead. They are busy making disciples and equipping others who can then take their place as leaders, allowing the ministry to grow and expand.

The departmental structure that EPBOM has put into place permits the church to encourage every member to assume a specific responsibility and become a co-laborer in God's work. By so doing, the structures help the average member at EPBOM take the work of God much more seriously. As Dion puts it, "they become more dedicated to the cause of the Lord as they allow the Holy Spirit to manifest Himself powerfully through them by the spiritual gifts and fruit" (Robert, Cell Group 6).

Chapter 13 ☛ *Prepare the Program of God - Every Member Ministry*

Mobilization within the Cell Department

The Development of the Cell System

The development of the cell system came as a response to Dion's vision to win to Christ the neighborhood in which the church was located (evangelization), to strengthen the church (edification), and to make it grow so it could be irreproachable and spotless (maturation).

> "They have accepted Jesus. You have brought them to be broken, to humility, into the will of God. You have taught them. Now, what you need is to teach them a life of consecration. We bring them to a life of consecration. So that their consecration is effective, you must have follow-up and you must have training. And that is where the cells are so important" (Robert, Interview).

The purpose of a cell is not only to win souls to Christ, but also to care for these souls so they can be helped, through teaching and follow up, to grow to the full stature of Christ. The cell ministry thus plays a critical part in the care of a new believer. The main task of the cell ministry is to penetrate, proclaim and preserve. "The ministry of the cell must be well organized and coordinated to answer twelve goals which faces the local church in a living Kingdom of the Lord" (Robert, Working 57). These twelve goals include:

1. Individual evangelism by the members
2. Receiving of souls saved in the assembly
3. The work of taking care and follow-up
4. Encouragement toward a life of sharing
5. Making disciples in view of the work of the ministry
6. Helping the members to avoid passivity and monotony
7. Helping pastors to follow the progress or the weakness of the work in view of dispensing an adequate teaching
8. Facilitate unity in the Church
9. Help pastors detect any shifting in the people
10. Providing opportunities for faithful members to learn to manifest grace and spiritual gifts

11. Strengthening of the families
12. Encouraging mutual assistance of the members in time of trials

EPBOM views the cell as a place for fellowship in holiness, purity, and transparency before one another. It is a place of spiritual healing by the Word of God and His love (Hebrews 10:24-25). The cell is a watch tower where one becomes a watchman over his brothers and sisters to keep them from sinning and to keep the devil from doing them harm. The cell is a place where battle is waged against Satan in order to destroy his works, as did the Lord Jesus (1 John 3:8). The cell system is organized under what has already been termed the Cell Department.

Pastor Boka Faustin – Head of the Cell Department

As mentioned earlier, Pastor Boka Faustin oversees the ministry of the Cell System. He was born into a religious Catholic family. Though he did not know God personally, he knew God existed. As he became older, he practiced fetishism and actively participated in prostitution to such a degree that he became very, very sick. The doctors could do nothing for him. He went to the fetishers and sorcerers, again to no avail. Strange as it seems, a fetisher told him, "It's only prayer that can set you free." That was when he was led to a true church. That church began to pray earnestly for him. He was healed within the week. Although his healing did not immediately culminate in his salvation, it did prepare Boka's heart to receive Jesus.

In 1975, a full two years later he came to the Baptist church led by Pastor Dion Robert. There the gospel was explained to him in a way he could clearly understand. On the day he accepted Christ, he was also delivered from evil spirits within. He was delivered, saved, and entrusted into a cell group who would continue to help him grow spiritually. Through the cell group he came to understand the true nature of discipleship. It was black and white. Either you follow Jesus or you turn away. After being discipled by the church for three or four years, Boka gave himself to become a pastor.

Because of the nature of the work situation in Cote d'Ivoire, leaving his job and becoming a pastor was not an easy task to accomplish. First Boka had to ask his employer to let him go. They didn't want to. In Cote d'Ivoire there is a governmental center for everyone who works. Boka had to go to those in

Chapter 13 ☞ Prepare the Program of God - Every Member Ministry

charge with his request. Only after the Minister gave his agreement was Boka able to leave secular work to serve the Lord. Pastor Dion was then free to also train Boka. As part of his training at the church, Boka was placed in the Department of Cells. At first he was just an adjunct to another pastor. In 1980 the pastor over him was transferred to another church and Boka replaced him leading the Cell Department. He has now served faithfully in that capacity for over 20 years.

The Structure of the Cell Department

In one sense, the Cell Department organizational structure is like many traditional cell churches, employing the Jethro pattern of development. However, unlike the typical traditional cell church structure, the structure at EPBOM is not a 5 x 5 matrix. The 5 x 5 matrix is recognized as the "classic" system for cell churches around the world. Its major users have been David Yonggi Cho in South Korea and Lawrence Khong in Singapore. It is referred to as a "5 x 5 matrix" because of the way it groups multiplying cells together to form Zones and Sub-zones. Accordingly, five cells comprise one Sub-zone. Five Sub-zones comprise one Zone. Five Zones comprise one district, etc. Both the administrative nature of EPBOM's structure and the relational nature of their structure are depicted by the following diagrams:

Administrative Structure
Eglise Protestante Baptiste Oeuvres et Mission Internationale

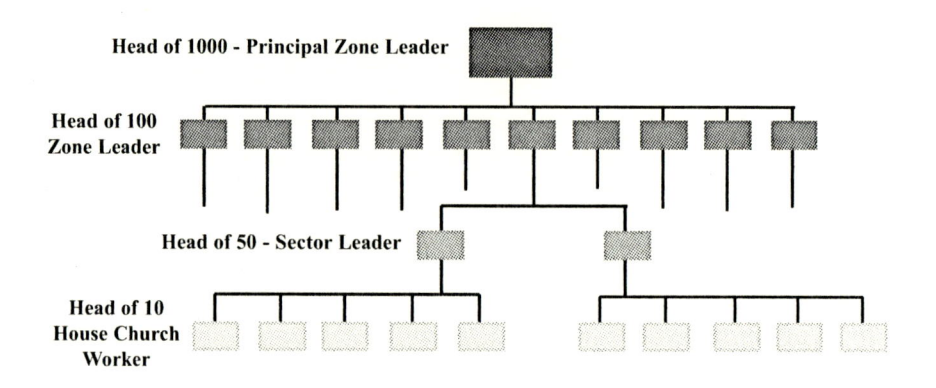

- Head of 1000 - Principal Zone Leader
- Head of 100 Zone Leader
- Head of 50 - Sector Leader
- Head of 10 House Church Worker

Relational Structure
Eglise Protestante Baptiste Oeuvres
et Mission Internationale

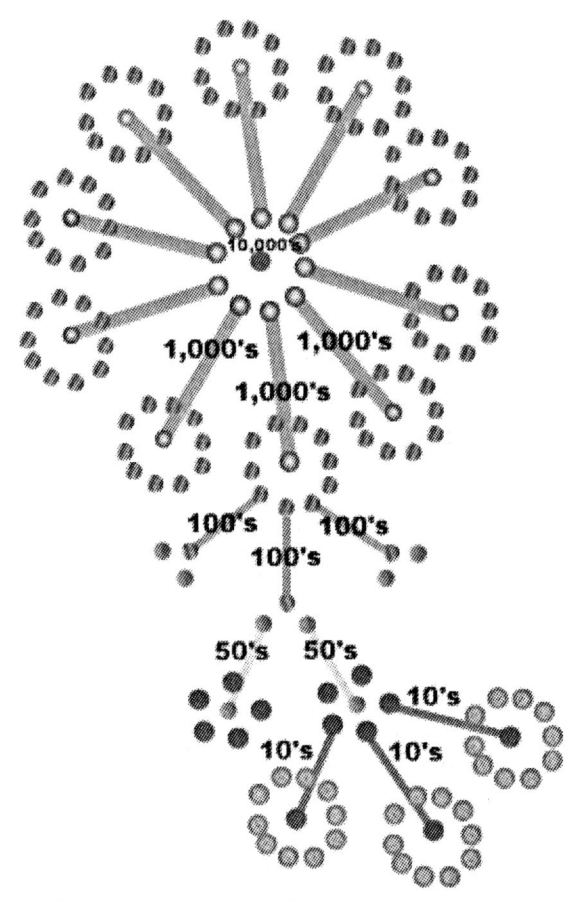

EPBOM has chosen to adhere more strictly to the Jethro structure, so called because it is taken out of the incident in Exodus chapter 18 where Moses' father-in-law, Jethro, was giving him wisdom regarding the manageable breakdown of the children of Israel. He advised a system where you had captains of tens, captains of fifties (responsible for five captains of tens), captains of hundreds (responsible for two groups of fifties), and captains of thousands (those responsible for ten groups of hundreds).

Chapter 13 ☞ Prepare the Program of God - Every Member Ministry

Let's analyze the diagrams together for a moment, in order to discover the relationships at work in EPBOM's cell system.

Zone leaders coordinate the sector leaders' work. Note that the Zone Leader is only responsible for two Sector Leaders, not five as in a 5x5 matrix arrangement. They analyze various problems and find a way to maintain the stability of the cell's work from a general standpoint. They make a report to the general coordinators and help the Sector Leaders care for the cells. The work of the Zone Leader must never be thought of as an administrative duty. The Zone Leader is a shepherd to the Sector Leaders under his care. He views his relationship to the Sector Leader as that of a master to a disciple. The time necessary to care for those under him is the time that he takes. The system at EPBOM is extremely relational!

Sector leaders play a major role in the cell ministry. They visit cells to test the efficiency of the Cell Leaders as well as that of the cell members. They spend time in helping the Cell Leaders to continually keep up the general vision. They receive reports from Cell Leaders, analyze and consolidate them and send the results to their Zone Leaders. Like Zone Leaders, the work of the Sector Leader is highly relational. In many American cell churches structured along a typical 5 x 5 matrix, relational distance exists between the cell members, Cell Leaders and Zone Supervisors. I would suggest that this unfortunate situation has occurred more as a result of the American application of the structure in a non-relational business manner than from the inherent nature of the structure itself. At EPBOM, the employment of a more pure Jethro model has not resulted in relational distance between leaders and people. I would speculate that a partial reason for that is due to the underlying values inculcated in the Cell Leadership, in particular, a lifestyle of sharing and a view of the church as a family, each man his brother's keeper.

The cell leader is also viewed as a shepherd because he is the extension of the pastor. The pastor leads the church, but obviously can't be in all neighborhoods. So, the pastor multiplies himself by smaller shepherds through his Cell Leaders. They do the work of the ministry and bring back the report. They train the new converts and take them to baptisms so they become disciples.

The cell intern is being trained to become the cell leader. He is being trained for the continuation of the work. If he was not being trained, the work would come to a stop. Boka likens this process to Paul entrusting his work to Timothy, who in turn was also to entrust what he had received to other faithful men until the entire world was touched and reached with the gospel.

The success of the cell ministry is dependent on the church that has produced the cells, the local church. It is called the "local church" because all the cells were birthed by it and minister under its jurisdiction. Each of EPBOM's local churches is comprised of a minimum of 150 adults. Annex churches are those cells that have grown and multiplied to between 50 and 150 adults. They will not as yet have a full time pastor assigned to them. The relationship between each cell and its local church is described by Pastor Dion:

> Since the church is the 'mother' that 'gave birth' to all the cells, the local church must provide systematic teaching in order to stimulate the life of the people, maintain the general vision of the work, exhort, correct any deviations, edify and bring the whole body to maturity, stability, growth and the joy of salvation. No cell is independent of the church. "By the grace of God, the success we have known in Cote d'Ivoire is due to this structure, inspired by the wisdom of the Holy Spirit" (Robert, Cell Group 26).

The Cell Department is considered by Pastor Dion to be absolutely vital to the building of the Body of Christ:

> The cell restored in the ministry of the local church plays a role of the first order in the effective edification of the Body of Christ in view of a great victory over sin and the world, over Satan and his demons. It is written: "You know that I have not hesitated to preach anything that would be helpful to you but have taught you publicly and from house to house. I have declared to both Jews and Greeks that they must turn to God in repentance and have faith in our Lord Jesus" Acts 20:20-21. (Robert, Working 58)

From 3 people in 1975, EPBOM has grown to 150,000 members in 2000. Has the Cell Department been a vital factor in this tremendous growth? Absolutely! Dion himself writes:

> The secret of this growth is not only the perfect organization of the different ministries in the church but primarily the Cell

Chapter 13 ☛ *Prepare the Program of God - Every Member Ministry*

ministry, which has been structured since June 10, 1984 and called the Cell Department (H.C.D.). Churches in big cities care for churches in small towns, which in turn care for churches in villages, which also care for churches in encampments. Such a structure inevitably produces tangible growth, thanks to the efficiency of the workers. (Robert, Cell Group 33-34)

Pastor Boka would concur. The proof is in the pudding! As of August 2000, Boka had oversight of more than 14,000 adult cells and more than 4,000 children's cells worldwide. More than 685 local churches have been planted throughout Cote d'Ivoire and beyond. By the third quarter of 2000, Cells had grown into local churches in 16 African nations, as well as in France, Sweden, the United States, Denmark, Great Britain, Italy, and Canada.

CHALLENGING THE INEFFECTIVENESS OF OUR OWN SYSTEM

In the human family, irrespective of position, each family member has familial responsibilities. The more mature the family member, often the greater the responsibility they are delegated. With the exception of the new babies, each family member is to function appropriate to their responsibility, their ability, and their sphere of authority. In short, each member of the family is expected to fulfill their appropriate familial responsibilities toward one another for the good of the family. If the church is indeed the family of God, then each of us can be viewed as fathers, mothers, brothers, sisters, aunts, uncles, grandparents, children, youth, newborns within the family. We each have familial responsibilities that must be embraced and carried out.

In the United States Army, each soldier is trained and assigned appropriate duties. Those who are not AWOL, POW's or in the hospital are to serve and fulfill those assigned duties. If the local church is the army of God, then each member is to be trained and released to fulfill their respective assignments.

We desire each organ and system within our own physical body to function properly. When there is a malfunction, we call such a state *illness*. Our goal is never 50%, or 60%, or even 90% mobilization of our body members. Anything less than 100% we call *paralysis*. If the church is to be thought of as the body of Christ, then each member must function and serve the body in the capacity and position in which God has placed it (Ephesians 4:15-16; 1 Corinthians 12:18 "But now God has placed the members, each one of them, in the body, just as He desired").

However we consider the Church, it should be obvious by now that each member must be mobilized to fulfill the destiny God has mandated for them. It can no longer be left up to 20% of the membership to do 80% of the work. Unlike the typical American church where the 20:80 rule is in effect and the church is paralyzed, EPBOM is for all practical purposes fully mobilized. The only ones not involved in regular corporate ministry are new converts being trained for baptism and those undergoing initial discipleship, i.e., basic training. Because their mobilization is along the lines of their spiritual gifts, each member is able to focus their time, energy and resources like a laser beam in one department.

The employment of a volunteer-based ministry paradigm by a cell church mitigates against member mobilization. It fosters the unbiblical contention that the church is a volunteer organization. If people ever find their gifts and serve out of their giftings, it is in spite of the system. Similar statements could be leveled against a shared-ministry paradigm. Members become frustrated in being forced to serve in capacities for which they are neither gifted nor called, while failing to serve in the very places God would place them in His Body. Yet these two ministry paradigms are the most frequently held by cell churches in America today. The Body of Christ will continue to remain partially paralyzed (isn't paralysis what you call a body which can be only partially mobilized?) until we come to view the church as an organism rather than an organization and adopt structures and a ministry paradigm that cooperate with God's desire to place each one in the Body as it pleases Him, based upon their gifts and calling. It is past time for us to develop a system whereby all of our members are released to work according to their giftings and the grace apportioned to them, to the glory of God.

As we close this chapter, revisit with me a moment the thinking of many pastors today in the U.S. Their underlying contention is that, "Cells will not work in America!" As a consequence, many then decide to develop task groups. How utterly superfluous are task groups in the EPBOM context! The development of task groups is totally anachronistic within the context of church members living in constant community, receiving training for the deployment of their spiritual gifts, being mobilized into a corporate Body whose very structure is considered to be the manifestation of the gift of God and where there exists balance between cell life and corporate life. What can task groups possibly accomplish that cannot be accomplished more effectively and more effi-

Chapter 13 ☞ Prepare the Program of God - Every Member Ministry

ciently on a corporate level through a totally mobilized body of believers? Task groups can add nothing! To have task groups would be a throwback to a bygone era when the church was undeveloped and unable to perform the work of the Kingdom.

I would unequivocally contend that the development of task groups on the scale currently being witnessed today in America and the parading of task groups as somehow being "cells", is by its very nature a sharp rebuke to the American cell church movement and an indication of our own immaturity and failure to bring into balance the large group wing and the small group wing of what Bill Beckham has called the two-winged church. Until we restore that balance, this bird will never be able to soar in the heavens, fulfilling once more the bidding of the Master!

14

PREPARE THE NEXT STEP

T HE MIND OF MAN PLANS HIS WAY,
BUT THE LORD DIRECTS HIS STEPS.

PROV. 16:9

Chapter 14 ☛ *Prepare the Next Step*

Doubtless the reader has wondered and mumbled to himself throughout the course of this book, "Why is it really this difficult? Why does it seem so complex? Is all this really necessary?" The answers are quite simple. Like a butterfly, you are attempting to break free from an inflexible cocoon. You have mistakenly identified multiplicity of parts with complexity and lack of parts with simplicity. What has been set before you is not part of your natural nature. You are colliding head on with the 50:1 principle. Finally, like a salmon, you are swimming upstream. Let's look at each of these answers in greater detail.

A Butterfly Breaking Free

A butterfly is encased in a cocoon. She can no longer be content with a caterpillar existence. Life is encased in death. She must be transformed. Life must break forth, or die. Breaking forth into life is in itself a life and death struggle. The old can no longer contain her. It is only by means of the struggle to break out that the wings of the butterfly are strengthened to permit flight. Help the butterfly by breaking the cocoon for her, and she will fall to the earth and die. Her wings will be unable to sustain her.

Paul writes of our no longer being conformed to this world (Romans 12:1-2). It is our cocoon. It is our encasement of death. We have been transformed. We cannot stay. We must take flight. Yet, sadly, the church today remains encased, incarcerated within a cocoon of culture. The vast majority of American Christians live a segmented lifestyle. The Lord and His Church fills one of those segments of time. Church dictates neither our time nor our schedules, nor our energies. I think of a family that by most standards would be considered mature and fully committed to the Lord. Their life, however, is dictated and controlled by the sports in which their son continuously participates. Then there is the young couple whose time is spent in family commitments, and the young single who is out nearly every evening with friends. They look at the time spent by those in Abidjan and Bogota at the church and in the service of the Lord in ministry and gasp. They just don't have the time! Even as born again, Spirit filled, mature believers, they are encased by the culture of this world. If the church was to ask for that kind of time and energy commitment, it would be called a cult! Why is it so hard? You are a butterfly struggling to break free from the cocoon of cultural bondage and alert other butterflys of the danger of remaining bound.

Philosophy informs us that mankind struggles with answering four basic questions of life. Without purposefully setting about to do so, I believe Dion Robert has successfully answered the four fundamental questions of life for himself, for his leadership team, for his people, and for those he is evangelizing. He has answered them in such a way that those who receive his answers break free from their African culture and immerse themselves in the culture of the Kingdom. My gut instinct tells me that Cesar Castellanos and David Cho have done the same thing. When we attempt such a feat, we are struggling to become free from our American culture and embrace a new Kingdom culture. When we challenge those around us to do likewise, we encounter the butterfly syndrome. Let me pose these four questions.

There is first in man's mind the ontological question, "Who am I?" Man struggles with the question of identity. We consistently seek to answer that question in terms of what we accomplish and what we do, rather that who we are. We define who we are by our tasks. When two men meet for the first time, the first question that is asked once names have been exchanged is, "So, what do you do?" It is as if to say, now that I know your name, I want to know about you, and you are defined and have value based upon what you do. "Who am I?" All identity begins with God. If we are to understand who we are, we must understand who He is. He is the beginning of us all and our total beings cry out to be related back to Him (Psalm 42:1-2). Jesus describes Himself as the Way to knowing God (John 14:6). The Apostle John phrased it this way, "I have written to you, fathers, because you know Him who has been from the beginning" (1 John 2:14). Solving the ontological issue of life begins here. Is this not how God dealt with Moses at the burning bush? First comes a revelation of who God is. Then comes a revelation of who Moses is. Ministry flows from those revelations. The same holds true for the prophet Isaiah (Isaiah 6:1-8). First he receives a revelation of God, then a revelation of Isaiah. Service is gladly entered upon once the question of identity is answered. Isaiah never once asked the Lord, "And Lord, how much time will You require of me?" Pastor Dion has both answered this question and effectively passed on that answer. He has come to understand first who God is, and then who he himself is in relation to God. The result is the same as it was for Moses and Isaiah. The result is a desire to build God's kingdom, not his own kingdom. The result is that he must be "erased" so that only God will be seen in his life. He must die that others might live. Why would anyone embrace death and being "erased" if their very identity were tied to their own existence and accomplishments? Neither is this simply held as a cognitive theological truth. Rather, it is embraced on all levels as

Chapter 14 ☛ *Prepare the Next Step*

a lifestyle. What is truly amazing is that Dion has been able to help thousands of others embrace this answer as well.

The second basic question of life is the epistemological question, "How do I know?" Through what lens do I look at the world? How can I determine whether or not my knowledge is true knowledge? Pilate asked Jesus this question in John 18:38. "What is Truth?" The answers to all of life's questions including how to live rightly before God and man, is to be sought in God's revelation of Himself in His Word and through His Son. Jesus is the Truth. God has communicated this Truth to man through One who is His Son and through the Word of God. How we answer this question will define our moral theory. While the American church has moved in practice, if not in theory, toward a moral lifestyle dictated by a teleological view of life, Dion and EPBOM have decidedly embraced a deontological view of life. What motivates them is not what brings the greatest good to the greatest number. What motivates them is how their actions are directly related to the specific commands that have been issued by God. All things start with God. Identity starts with God. Truth flows from God. He is God. This is what He requires. How very similar to the prophet Micah's word to God's people (Micah 6:8): "He has told you, O man, what is good; and what does the Lord require of you but to do justice, to love kindness, and to walk humbly with your God?" For Dion and EPBOM, "the cross is obedience" is not a catch phrase. They have seen God. They understand who they are in light of who God has revealed Himself to be. They embrace death, the cross. He has made known to them His truth, His ways. He is God; they are not! They obey. They obey His ways because they are true and they are right. "The fear of the LORD is clean, enduring forever; the judgments of the Lord are true; they are righteous altogether" (Psalm 19:9).

Third, we must respond to the axiological question, "What has value to me?" Every person alive possesses what we may call a value set. This value set functions as a traffic signal in our life. It gives us permission to proceed, or it stops us from moving ahead. The place and function of core values was discussed thoroughly in chapters three and four. We each have a "head value set" and a "heart value set," the former expressed by what we say, the latter expressed by what we do. What has value for Dion, the staff and the people of EPBOM? What comprises their head and heart value set? The answer has already been set forth: submission, obedience, humility, consecration, a life of sharing, prayer and fasting, and the supernatural move of the Spirit through spiritual gifts. In their case, the head and heart value sets have been shown to be the same! Why have they embraced these as core values? They believe them to be the most basic biblical values God has revealed as truth. Upon coming into the church, this value set will become the backdrop for all that is taught and all ministry that is done. New believers will be systematically taught this value set and given practical help in embracing it as their lifestyle. Advancement will not be based upon simple knowledge of the Word of God, as is often the case in American churches. Advancement is based upon proven ministry and lifestyle. Leadership requires a certain lifestyle first, and a skill set second. Is this attractive to the lost? Does it impact the lost? Recall the soldier who upon hearing the name of the church, without even examining our papers, flagged our car on past his check point with only the comment, "Pray well!"

The fourth major question of life is the teleological question, "Where am I going to?" What is the purpose, the direction, and the destiny of my life?" Solomon put the importance of this question into perspective in Proverbs 29:18 when he wrote, "Without a vision the people perish." Has Dion answered this question? He begins with a vision from God. The "Program of God" then proceeds to flesh out that vision. What is the purpose of his life? It is to fulfill God's priorities of winning the lost to Christ and taking care of them so they become disciples. What direction does he take to accomplish that vision? He follows the Program of God, not in part, but in whole. Through the departmental structure, every member can assume a specific responsibility and become a co-laborer with God in His work. This brings about a greater dedication on the part of the individual to the cause of the Lord. He both understands and assumes his place in the work of God. While ultimate identity, who we are, is never to be found in what we do, every Christian has a ministry identity. As people are allowed to express their God-given desires and abilities, the service they perform is no longer simply what they may grudgingly do for God, but rather the exercise of their ministry identity. This is the heart of equipping the saints for their work of service. When their identity becomes a part of their service in a healthy way, the way God intended from the beginning, motivated, excited and focused Christians will be the result. Both the leadership and members at EPBOM are motivated, excited, and focused. They understand who the King is, in whose Kingdom they live, and who they are in Christ. They have come to know the source of Truth and have adopted core values of the kingdom. They have been taught their destiny and through their gifts have taken their place of service to further God's Kingdom. They can then stand before their lost world and say, "Come and see the works of God!"

Chapter 14 — Prepare the Next Step

To answer these questions in such a way that those who receive our answers will lay down their agendas, their plans, their careers, their families, yes, and even their very life, is the challenge of breaking free from the cocoon of this world and taking our rightful place and destiny as a butterfly in the Kingdom of our God.

The Issue of Simplicity Versus Complexity

While teaching in Russia, I was challenged by the lack of planning in the church world there. How to plan, the principles of planning, were not generally known. The result was an attitude that was expressed as, "If things go well today, it is the Lord's blessing. If things do not go well, it is the devil's hindrance." Planning the day's activities was just not thought about. While we may find that somewhat incredulous, let me suggest we have a similar kind of simplistic attitude when it comes to simplicity and complexity. It goes something like this. "If there are many steps to take or things to do, the task is difficult. If there are few steps to take or few things to do, the task is simple. The fewer the steps the simpler the task." When applied to the development of cell church it is phrased in this way. "This is too difficult! There is too much to do and too much to remember! Jesus made it very simple [implication being He did less than we are doing]." Is this the truth? Consider the following.

Jesus spent three years preparing the disciples to be the church. He spent the better part of 30,660 hours focused on their spiritual equipping. His life is punctuated by multiple actions designed to teach and reinforce volumes of teaching. He took advantage of thousands of events and teachable moments to train his disciples. He had continuous planned learning experiences and scheduled numerous check up times along the way. His life and their training was anything but haphazard. He was moving according to the Father's plan and schedule. He had to deal with wrong attitudes toward women, gentiles and children. He had to alter their theological thinking about the Kingdom of God. He had to impart to them a brand new value set. Go back and re-study the gospel accounts if you doubt what you just read.

Consider with me the problem encountered by Ezekiel. His reaction is quite like ours. He is brought out in a vision to a valley of dry bones. There are very many bones scattered throughout the valley. God's question is, "Can these bones live?" Ezekiel looked at the multitude of the unconnected bones and I imagine thought to himself, "What a job to piece all these bones back together again!" However, the problem was not with the multiplicity of the pieces, but with the focus of the prophet. For you see, the multitude of disconnected pieces plus God's Spirit plus God's power equals integrated bodies and a great army.

The conclusion is simply this: The multiplicity of the steps (parts) does not equal complexity, and the lack of numerous steps (parts) does not equal simplicity. To the contrary, simplicity equals singleness of focus plus the ability to unify. The steps outlined in this book are neither complex nor out of reach for the average leader. What is needed on our part is singleness of vision coupled with God's Spirit and His power to perform. It is by grace alone. In our weakness His strength is perfected. Can we indeed successfully relay a biblical ethical base in the church? Can we define and articulate our set of core values? Can we receive vision from God? Can we develop a value discipline and create a prototype? Can these bones live? "And I answered, 'O Lord God, You know.'"

This Process is NOT Second Nature

Planting a cell church, transitioning to a cell church paradigm, the changes required to see this happen have not yet become second nature. Few of you would say that the development of a values discipline is *second nature*. Few of you would say that the development of a prototype will seem to be *second nature*.

We have seen earlier that while vision may show us the future and our place in it, and may even give us direction and provide focus for our efforts, vision alone will never get us to that future. We must challenge and motivate others to embrace our God-given vision so they come with us. We must develop an operating model that will move us from vision into practice. We must move into that future with excellence. This, indeed, is a daunting task! Few churches rise to the challenge. Fewer still succeed and actually enter into God's destiny. Ask the world what they think of the church and the response often can be summed up in one word – mediocrity. It is time to change! We must understand how God has made us. We must know who it is He is calling us to reach. Who are the fish? We must know what bait to use! We must employ the right equipment! While living in Jupiter, Florida, I decided one day to fish for snook at the inlet of the Loxahatchee river. Snook fishing is unlike fishing in the slow flowing river far upstream. My bait was wrong, my hooks too small and my line too weak. My equipment was inadequate. The best of intentions that morning profited me nothing. In retrospect I wish I had paid the price to fish correctly. I

Chapter 14 • *Prepare the Next Step*

can only now dream of the snook I never snagged. Would to God we do not spend eternity dreaming of the "fish" we never caught in the river of God, because we were inadequately prepared – an undefined value proposition, an unknown value discipline and an unworkable values-driven operating model!

The message of the movie *Field of Dreams* is clear, "Build it and they will come." So the church builds a cell, believing that people will come and experience...life! What is wrong with this? Unfortunately, too often, New Testament community, the life of Jesus is NOT what they experience! Do you remember the old adage, "Practice makes perfect"? No matter how much you may practice, if you are practicing incorrectly, all you will perfect is your imperfection! If you build incorrectly and multiply your work a hundred fold, you will have only a hundredfold greater headache to bear and a hundredfold greater mess to clean up. And yet, how many of you who have even now reached this point in your reading will still opt for the short cut? Our society, our denominations, our churches, all demand instant success, i.e. instant growth. Prototyping is slow in the beginning. The early results are minimal. The question that needs to be asked is, "What are the long term effects of the decision NOT to prototype?" The short term effects of not prototyping can appear to be highly beneficial. After all, our groups seem to grow by leaps and bounds. What, though, is to be said about the long term effects if we fail to prototype? The consistent result is that the church is fatally bitten by the "cobra effect". Let me relate to you a short story from Christian Schwartz (Implementation, 126) to illustrate this effect.

> A few years ago, one of the southern Indian provinces was hit by a cobra plague. These not so harmless snakes had multiplied until suddenly you could find them everywhere–in the streets, in houses, on the fields, and in the stables. The state authorities stepped in and promised a head fee for each dead cobra. At first, the situation changed according to expectations. The citizen's organized "cobra hunts" and the number of cobras dropped markedly. There was even a new profession that developed–professional cobra hunters could be frequently seen.
>
> Yet after the initial decline of the cobra population, the authorities were shocked to learn that cobras could again be found everywhere. After investigating this phenomenon they found that many snake hunters had become snake breeders,

thus securing their head premiums. The same measure that was suppose to decimate the number of cobras had, in the long run, the opposite effect.

What is the "cobra effect"? Let me spell it out for you, lest there be any remaining question. Frequently, measures which prove to be highly successful in the short run produce exactly the opposite of the desired outcomes in the long run. The application is easy to see. We skip the prototype phase, multiply our cells without taking the time necessary to identify key elements and maintain standards of performance, experience a tremendous initial growth spurt, but our growth plateaus and even seriously declines over the course of time because our cells never quite caught the vision for oikos evangelism, leaders are infrequently raised up, and equipping has become sporadic to non-existent.

The 50:1 Law

Why will it take us so long and so many steps to plant a cell church or transition even a cutting edge church to a cell church paradigm? The answer is the 50:1 law. We will define a *unit* as whatever it takes to perform a task. That unit may be time, resources (money, material, etc.), or even energy. The 50:1 law states that if to perform a task takes one unit, then to correct an error takes 50 units. In other words, it takes 50 times as much energy, resources, or time to correct what we have done incorrectly than to have done it correctly to begin with. The implications for what has gone on before are significant. For two millennium we have compounded error upon error in the church.

The Reformation ignited by Luther in the 16th century made a primary contribution in the area of theological teaching. "In almost all questions Luther dealt with, personal values replaced the objectivist categories [of the Roman Catholic Church]. He understood that faith is not the obedient assent to doctrine, but rather an encounter with Christ, who is present in his word and his Spirit" (Paradigm Shift, 86). Think of the enormous energy, time and resources spent in simply correcting basic errors in biblical thinking!

The Pietistic Reformation in the 17th century has been called "the most significant religious renewal movement in Protestantism since the reformation" (Paradigm Shift, 88). It was a reform of spiritual life, emphasizing the devotion of the heart, a new relationship to the Bible, regeneration, assurance of salvation, evangelism and sanctification. "It was not concerned with a new theology but with the practical application of what the Reformers had formulated theologically" (Paradigm Shift, 90). Once again, consider the immensity of the energy, resources and time that went into correcting what should never have needed correction in the first place.

In a sense, the cell church is part of a third reformation. We are creating structures which will be suitable vessels so that what the first two reformations demanded can be actually put into practice. We are still correcting theology, calling people back to devotion of heart, and attempting to create a structure in which they can live it out. How much time and effort will it take? The 50:1 law provides us with an unwelcome answer. More than we thought!

A Salmon Swimming Upstream

You are swimming upstream every time you press in and challenge a specific teleological view of life, calling for it to be replaced with a deontological ethic, or whenever you point out that your denominational literature is really teaching its readers to live teleologically instead of deontologically. You are not going with the flow when you challenge God's people to overcome the effects on their thinking of the post-modern world view, or the pragmatic economic worldview. Whenever you challenge the lifestyle of the average church member to change and reflect a new view of God, of man, or of history, you are swimming like a salmon. You know you are heading in the right direction, but you are fighting for every step you take.

Is it vital to define and articulate our core values? Will the cell church movement in America make significant progress and gain maturity before it does? I sincerely doubt it. But, as soon as you engage in the process of values development, you begin to swim against the flow. The majority of pastors and churches have not yet defined and articulated their set of core values. Consequently, church members do not pull together like a team of horses. Energy is dissipated as each pulls in their own direction. It is difficult to make decisions because we are pulled in multiple directions by conflicting values. We often chance risk at the lowest level that everyone is willing to assume. When we do attempt to solve problems and resolve conflicts in the church, we find it nearly impossible because we are operating out of differing sets of core values. Even the priorities of the church remain blurred. This being the situation, is it any wonder that every attempt to build a cohesive unified cell church faces constant attack from those possessing conflicting values? As a result of undefined and unarticulated core values, our churches and leadership teams too often are schizophrenic. Changing values is akin to shooting the rapids, while swimming upstream! Take a lesson from the salmon, though. It is possible. Press on!

Without a vision the people are unrestrained and perish. Where the vision is unclear, the cost is always too high. When will the church begin to *act* like a family? Will it perhaps be when she regains a vision of God as Father and herself as His family? When will the church take seriously the spiritual war she seems to be losing in America? When she regains her vision of Jesus as the Lord of Hosts and the church as His army! When will she cease living as a paralytic? When her vision embraces her destiny as the Body of Christ! Without clear vision before her, the church will never provide relevant answers to the basic questions of life with which she is faced; how can she edify, equip, empower and release every member of Christ's body into ministry, while at the same time evangelizing this world with the good news of Jesus Christ? The salmon "sees" the end, and keeps on going. Sometimes the direction the vision leads is the least trodden path, as it were. But the salmon must be faithful to the vision, whether others press onward with it or not. The vision has gripped the salmon's life. It must reach its destination and fulfill its destiny.

A Final Call to Prepare

A number of years ago, Dr. Ralph Neighbour, Jr. wrote the now classic book, *Where Do We Go From Here*. The question is still apropos for today. Where *do* we go from here? The Program of God must be prepared! We must equip the people of God for service in the household of God. We must empower them to rise up as leaders. We must release every member to take their place in His Body and fulfill their destiny in God, that for which Christ has apprehended them. We must edify the Body of Christ and evangelize the world for His sake. The Program of God must be prepared, but we must not neglect the roots as we focus our concentration on the fruits.

As I write, I can look out my study window and see the devastation left by the worst ice storm in Kansas City history. They estimate that over 500,000 trees were uprooted or to some lesser degree damaged. Driving down the street, one is overwhelmed by the trees and branches lying along the berm, tons upon tons, waiting patiently to be chewed up and spit into the back of a large dump truck, then to be carried off to regions unknown for disposal. In one of my member's back yard lies what at one time was a fifty foot high tree. Now, on its side,

Chapter 14 — *Prepare the Next Step*

it is only a fifty foot long tree, its root system unable to save it from the destructive winds and pressure of ice. When the winds of God blow, it matters little how high the tree has grown. What matters is how deep the roots have gone down.

While in Abidjan for three weeks, I watched as godly men came from many parts of Africa, Europe, and America. Judging by their words and actions, what impressed them about EPBOM was its Department of Demonology, with its tremendous programs of deliverance and soul therapy and intercession–the branches of the tree. This, however, is not uncommon. Have you noticed how many "How to" books fill the bookshelves of Christian bookstores? Are we not guilty of attending conference after conference, reading book after book, and listening to tape after tape, all in the vain hope of finding just the right "key" or discovering the magic "formula" for success? Do we not unconsciously hope that if we employ the right structures, then growth and success is assured? If that is not true, then why do we busy ourselves so much with that which is above ground, the visible ministries of the church, while neglecting the root system that facilitates its growth and guarantees its longevity?

Where *do* we go from here? The existing forms of the cell church must not be accepted as sacrosanct, but must be radically questioned in terms of their meaning and their effect. As a reformation movement, the cell church movement must effect the theology, spirituality and structures of the 21st century church. This can only be accomplished as we look both to the underground realities, the roots, and the above ground realities, the program of God. This can only happen as we then make the changes necessary to become a church prepared to meet her Bridegroom.

This book has been a call to prepare, a call to prepare that which has been sadly neglected. The night is coming when no man will be able to work (John 9:4). When the Bridegroom returns will not be the time to run and prepare the lanterns (Matthew 25:1-10). When the winds of God blow against the wall is not the time to plaster over what has been whitewashed (Ezekiel 13:10-14). A voice is still calling in the wilderness, "Prepare the way of the Lord."

Is. 40:3-8

A voice is calling in the wilderness,
"Prepare the way of the LORD;
Make smooth in the desert a highway for our God.

Let every valley be lifted up,
And every mountain and hill be made low;
And let the rough ground become a plain,
And the rugged terrain a broad valley;

Then the glory of the LORD will be revealed,
And all flesh will see it together;
For the mouth of the LORD has spoken."

A voice says, "Call out."
Then he answered, "What shall I call out?"
All flesh is grass, and all its loveliness is like the flower of the field.

The grass withers, the flower fades,
When the breath of the LORD blows upon it;
Surely the people are grass.

The grass withers, the flower fades,
But the word of our God stands forever.

WORKS CITED

Beach, Waldo, and H. Richard Niebuhr. Christian Ethics. New York: Ronald Press, 1955.

Birch, Bruce C., and Larry L. Rasmussen. Bible and Ethics in the Christian Life. Minneapolis: Augsburg, 1976.

Childs, Brevard S. Biblical Theology in Crises. Philadelphia: Westminster, 1970.

Clement of Alexandria. "The First Epistle of Clement to the Corinthians." Accordance Bible Software. CD-ROM. Oaktree Software, Inc. 1999.

Curran, Charles E. "Dialogue with the Scriptures: The Role and Function of the Scriptures in Moral Theology." Catholic Moral Theology in Dialogue. Notre Dame: University of Notre Dame Press, 1976.

"Epistle To Diognetus." Accordance Bible Software. CD-ROM. Oaktree Software, Inc., 1999.

Etienne, Wouehi Louan. Personal interview. 10 August 2000.

---. Theme: Le Demonologue Approuve. Abidjan, Cote d'Ivoire: O.M.C.I. Publications, 2000.

Faustin, Boka B. Follow-Up of the New Christian at Home Abidjan, Cote d'Ivoire: O.M.C.I. Publications, 1993.

---. Our Objectives. Abidjan, Cote d'Ivoire: O.M.C.I. Publications, 1993.

---. Personal interview. 8-10 August 2000.

Goetzmann, J. "House." The New International Dictionary of New Testament Theology. Ed. Colin Brown. 3 vols. Grand Rapids: Zondervan, 1982.

Greene, William Brenton, Jr. "The Ethics of the Old Testament." Princeton Theological Review 27 (1929): 157.

Gustafson, James M. "The Place of Scripture in Christian Ethics: A Methodological Study." Interpretation 24 (1970): 439-47.

Henry, Carl F. H. Christian Personal Ethics. Grand Rapids: Eerdmans, 1957.

Ignatius. "Saint Ignatius to the Ephesians." Accordance Bible Software. CD-ROM. Oaktree Software, Inc. 1999.

Ignatius. "Saint Ignatius to the Romans." Accordance Bible Software. CD-ROM. Oaktree Software, Inc. 1999.

Jacobo, Marvin. Training Manual: A High School Ministry of Small Groups. Modesto: First Baptist Church, 1996.

Julien, Daingui A. Personal interview. 10 August 2000.

Kaiser, Walter C., Jr. Toward Old Testament Ethics. Grand Rapids: Zondervan, 1983.

Kasemann, E. "Ministry and Community in the New Testament." Essays on New Testament Themes. Santa Rosa: Polebridge Press, 1994.

Kouassi, Jonas. Personal interview. 21 August 2000.

Ladd, George Eldon. The Presence of the Future. Grand Rapids: Eerdmans, 1974.

Lincoln, Andrew T. The Word Biblical Commentary. 52 vols. Dallas: Word, 1990.

Long, Edward LeRoy, Jr. "The Use of the Bible in Christian Ethics." Interpretation 19 (1965): 149-62.

Malphurs, Aubrey. Values-Driven Leadership. Grand Rapids: Baker, 1996.

Maston, T. B. Biblical Ethics. Cleveland: World Publishing Co., 1967.

Merrill, E. "Derek." New International Dictionary of Old Testament Theology and Exegesis. Ed. Willem VanGemeren. 5 vols. Grand Rapids: Zondervan Publishing House, 1996.

Michaelis, W. "Hodos." Theological Dictionary of the New Testament [Abridged]. Ed. Gerhard Kittel. Trans. Geoffrey W. Bromiley. Grand Rapids: Eerdmans, 1986.

Mitton, C. Leslie. "Ephesians." The New Century Bible Commentary. Grand Rapids: Eerdmans, 1973.

Newbigin, Leslie. The Household of God: Lectures on the Nature of the Church. New York: Friendship, 1954.

Paul, Kpre Amoa. Personal interview. 10 August 2000.

Polycarp. "The Epistle of Polycarp." Accordance Bible Software. CD-ROM. Oaktree Software, Inc. 1999.

Polycarp. "The Martyrdom of Polycarp." Accordance Bible Software. CD-ROM. Oaktree Software, Inc., 1999.

Richardson, Alan. A Dictionary of Christian Theology. Philadelphia: Westminster, 1969.

Ridderbos, Herman. Paul: An Outline of His Theology. Grand Rapids: Eeedmans, 1975.

Robert, Yaye Dion. Cell Group Ministry. Abidjan, Cote d'Ivoire: O.M.C.I. Publications, 2000.

---. Discipleship! Abidjan, Cote d'Ivoire: O.M.C.I. Publications, 2000.

---. Now That You're Born Again! Abidjan, Cote d'Ivoire: O.M.C.I. Publications, 2000.

---. Personal interview. 9-11 August 2000.

---. Soul Therapy. Abidjan, Cote d'Ivoire: O.M.C.I. Publications, 1996.

---. "Tearing Down the State of Weakness." Cell Church Spring 1997: 5.

---. Working According to the Model. Abidjan, Cote d'Ivoire: O.M.C.I. Publications, 2000.

Robertson, Archibald Thomas. Word Pictures in the New Testament. 6 vols. Grand Rapids: Baker, 1930.

Ruthven, Jon. Jesus as Rabbi: A Mimesis Christology. 1997. 1 April. 1998 <http://home.regent.edu/ruthven/disciple.htm>

Schaller, Lyle E. Getting Things Done. Nashville: Abingdon Press, 1986.

Schwarz, Christian A. Natural Church Development. Carol Stream: ChurchSmart Resources, 1996.

---. NCD Implementation Guide. Carol Stream: ChurchSmart Resources, 1996.

Seraphin, Zorodou. Personal interview. 9 August 2000.
Sleeper, C. Freedman. "Ethics as a Context for Biblical Interpretation." Interpretation 22 (1968): 443-60.

Vine, W. E. "Accompany." The Expanded Vine's Expository Dictionary of New Testament Words. Ed. John R. Kohlenberger III. Minneapolis: Bethany House, 1984.

Warren, Rick. The Purpose Driven Church. Grand Rapids: Zondervan, 1995.

Chapter 12 ☞ *Works Cited*

Williams, J. Rodman. Renewal Theology: the Church, the Kingdom and last Things. Grand Rapids: Zondervan, 1992.

Wolf, H. "Derek." Theological Wordbook of the Old Testament. Ed. R. Laird Harris. 2 vols. Chicago: Moody Press, 1980.

Printed in the United States
1336700001B/103-114